Stephen Crane (November 1, 1871 – June 5, 1900) was an American poet, novelist, and short story writer. Prolific throughout his short life, he wrote notable works in the Realist tradition as well as early examples of American Naturalism and Impressionism. He is recognized by modern critics as one of the most innovative writers of his generation. The ninth surviving child of Methodist parents, Crane began writing at the age of four and had published several articles by the age of 16. Having little interest in university studies though he was active in a fraternity, he left Syracuse University in 1891 to work as a reporter and writer. Crane's first novel was the 1893 Bowery tale Maggie: A Girl of the Streets, generally considered by critics to be the first work of American literary Naturalism. He won international acclaim in 1895 for his Civil War novel The Red Badge of Courage, which he wrote without having any battle experience. (Source: Wikipedia)

Literary works:
Maggie: A Girl of the Streets (1893)
The Red Badge of Courage (1895)
The Black Riders and Other Lines (1895)
George's Mother (1896)
The Third Violet (1897)
The Open Boat and Other Tales of Adventure (1898)
War is Kind (1899)
Active Service (1899)
The Monster and Other Stories (1899)
Wounds in the Rain (1900)
Great Battles of the World
The O'Ruddy (1903)
The Monster. London
Last Words. London
Whilomville Stories

PRINCE CLASSICS

WAR IS KIND, WHILOMVILLE STORIES & THE THIRD VIOLET

STEPHEN CRANE

PRINCE CLASSICS

First Printing: 2020

ISBN 978-1-6627-2230-1 (Paperback)

ISBN 978-1-6627-2231-8 (Hardcover)

Published by Prince Classics

www.princeclassics.com

Contents

WAR IS KIND,
WHILOMVILLE
STORIES
&
THE THIRD VIOLET

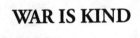

WAR IS KIND

WAR IS KIND

Do not weep, maiden, for war is kind.

Because your lover threw wild hands toward the sky

And the affrighted steed ran on alone,

Do not weep.

War is kind.

      Hoarse, booming drums of the

           regiment,

      Little souls who thirst for fight,

      These men were born to drill and die.

      The unexplained glory files above

           them,

      Great is the battle-god, great, and his

           kingdom—;

      A field where a thousand corpses lie.

Do not weep, babe, for war is kind.

Because your father tumbled in the yellow

      trenches,

Raged at his breast, gulped and died,

Do not weep.

War is kind.

Swift blazing flag of the regiment,

Eagle with crest of red and gold,

These men were born to drill and die.

Point for them the virtue of the slaughter,

Make plain to them the excellence of killing

And a field where a thousand corpses

lie.

Mother whose heart hung humble as a button

On the bright splendid shroud of your son,

Do not weep.

War is kind.

What says the sea, little shell?

"What says the sea?

"Long has our brother been silent to us,

"Kept his message for the ships,

"Awkward ships, stupid ships."

"The sea bids you mourn, O Pines,

"Sing low in the moonlight.

"He sends tale of the land of doom,

"Of place where endless falls

"A rain of women's tears,

"And men in grey robes—

"Men in grey robes—

"Chant the unknown pain."

"What says the sea, little shell?

"What says the sea?

"Long has our brother been silent to us,

"Kept is message for the ships,

"Puny ships, silly ships."

"The sea bids you teach, O Pines,

"Sing low in the moonlight;

"Teach the gold of patience,

"Cry gospel of gentle hands,

"Cry a brotherhood of hearts.

"The sea bids you teach, O Pines."

"And where is the reward, little shell?

"What says the sea?

"Long has our brother been silent to us,

"Kept his message for the ships,

"Puny ships, silly ships."

"No word says the sea, O Pines,

"No word says the sea.

"Long will your brother be silent to you,

"Keep his message for the ships,

"O puny ships, silly pines."

To the maiden

The sea was blue meadow,

Alive with little froth-people

Singing.

To the sailor, wrecked,

The sea was dead grey walls

Superlative in vacancy,

Upon which nevertheless at fateful time

Was written

The grim hatred of nature.

A little ink more or less!

It surely can't matter?

Even the sky and the opulent sea,

The plains and the hills, aloof,

Hear the uproar of all these books.

But it is only a little ink more or less.

What?

You define me God with these trinkets?

Can my misery meal on an ordered walking

Of surpliced numskulls?

And a fanfare of lights?

Or even upon the measured pulpitings

Of the familiar false and true?

Is this God?

Where, then is hell?

Show me some bastard mushrooms

Sprung from a pollution of blood.

It is better.

Where is God?

"Have you ever made a just man?"

"Oh, I have made three," answered

    God,

"But two of them are dead,

"And the third—

"Listen! Listen!

"And you will hear the thud of his defeat."

I explain the silvered passing of a ship

    at night,

The sweep of each sad lost wave,

The dwindling boom of the steel thing's striving,

The little cry of a man to a man,

A shadow falling across the greyer night,

And the sinking of the small star;

Then the waste, the far waste of waters,

And the soft lashing of black waves

For long and in loneliness.

Remember, thou, O ship of love,

Thou leavest a far waste of waters,

And the soft lashing of black waves

For long and in loneliness.

"I have heard the sunset song of the

birches,

"A white melody in the silence,

"I have seen a quarrel of the pines.

"At nightfall

"The little grasses have rushed by me

"With the wind men.

"These things have I lived," quoth the

maniac,

"Possessing only eyes and ears.

"But you—

"You don green spectacles before you look at roses."

Fast rode the knight

With spurs, hot and reeking,

Ever waving an eager sword,

"To save my lady!"

Fast rode the knight,

And leaped from saddle to war.

Men of steel flickered and gleamed

Like riot of silver lights,

And the gold of the knight's good banner

Still waved on a castle wall.

.   .   .   .

A horse,

Blowing, staggering, bloody thing,

Forgotten at foot of castle wall.

A horse

Dead at foot of castle wall.

Forth went the candid man

And spoke freely to the wind—

When he looked about him he was in a far

      strange country.

Forth went the candid man

And spoke freely to the stars—

Yellow light tore sight from his eye.

"My good fool," said a learned bystander,

"Your operations are mad."

"You are too candid," cried the candid man.

And when his stick left the head of the

      learned bystander

It was two sticks.

You tell me this is God?

I tell you this is a printed list,

A burning candle and an ass.

On the desert

A silence from the moon's deepest

      valley.

Fire rays fall athwart the robes

Of hooded men, squat and dumb.

Before them, a woman

Moves to the blowing of shrill whistles

And distant thunder of drums,

While mystic things, sinuous, dull with

      terrible color,

Sleepily fondle her body

Or move at her will, swishing stealthily over

      the sand.

The snakes whisper softly;

The whispering, whispering snakes,

Dreaming and swaying and staring,

But always whispering, softly whispering.

The wind streams from the lone reaches

Of Arabia, solemn with night,

And the wild fire makes shimmer of blood

Over the robes of the hooded men

Squat and dumb.

Bands of moving bronze, emerald, yellow,

Circle the throat and arms of her,

And over the sands serpents move warily

Slow, menacing and submissive,

Swinging to the whistles and drums,

The whispering, whispering snakes,

Dreaming and swaying and staring,

But always whispering, softly whispering.

The dignity of the accursed;

The glory of slavery, despair, death,

Is in the dance of the whispering snakes.

A newspaper is a collection of half-injustices

Which, bawled by boys from mile to mile,

Spreads its curious opinion

To a million merciful and sneering men,

While families cuddle the joys of the fireside

When spurred by tale of dire lone agony.

A newspaper is a court

Where every one is kindly and unfairly tried

By a squalor of honest men.

A newspaper is a market

Where wisdom sells its freedom

And melons are crowned by the crowd.

A newspaper is a game

Where his error scores the player victory

While another's skill wins death.

A newspaper is a symbol;

It is fetless life's chronical,

A collection of loud tales

Concentrating eternal stupidities,

That in remote ages lived unhaltered,

Roaming through a fenceless world.

The wayfarer,

Perceiving the pathway to truth,

Was struck with astonishment.

It was thickly grown with weeds.

"Ha," he said,

"I see that none has passed here

"In a long time."

Later he saw that each weed

Was a singular knife.

"Well," he mumbled at last,

"Doubtless there are other roads."

A slant of sun on dull brown walls,

A forgotten sky of bashful blue.

Toward God a mighty hymn,

A song of collisions and cries,

Rumbling wheels, hoof-beats, bells,

Welcomes, farewells, love-calls, final moans,

Voices of joy, idiocy, warning, despair,

The unknown appeals of brutes,

The chanting of flowers,

The screams of cut trees,

The senseless babble of hens and wise men—

A cluttered incoherency that says at the

stars;

"O God, save us!"

Once a man clambering to the housetops

Appealed to the heavens.

With a strong voice he called to the deaf

   spheres;

A warrior's shout he raised to the suns.

Lo, at last, there was a dot on the clouds,

And—at last and at last—

—God—the sky was filled with armies.

There was a man with tongue of wood

Who essayed to sing,

And in truth it was lamentable.

But there was one who heard

The clip-clapper of this tongue of wood

And knew what the man

Wished to sing,

And with that the singer was content.

The successful man has thrust himself

Through the water of the years,

Reeking wet with mistakes,—

Bloody mistakes;

Slimed with victories over the lesser,

A figure thankful on the shore of money.

Then, with the bones of fools

He buys silken banners

Limned with his triumphant face;

With the skins of wise men

He buys the trivial bows of all.

Flesh painted with marrow

Contributes a coverlet,

A coverlet for his contented slumber.

In guiltless ignorance, in ignorant guilt,

He delivered his secrets to the riven multitude.

    "Thus I defended: Thus I wrought."

Complacent, smiling,

He stands heavily on the dead.

Erect on a pillar of skulls

He declaims his trampling of babes;

Smirking, fat, dripping,

He makes speech in guiltless ignorance,

Innocence.

In the night

Grey heavy clouds muffled the valleys,

And the peaks looked toward God alone.

"O Master that movest the wind with a

finger,

"Humble, idle, futile peaks are we.

"Grant that we may run swiftly across

the world

"To huddle in worship at Thy feet."

In the morning

A noise of men at work came the clear blue miles,

And the little black cities were apparent.

"O Master that knowest the meaning of raindrops,

"Humble, idle, futile peaks are we.

"Give voice to us, we pray, O Lord,

"That we may sing Thy goodness to the sun."

In the evening

The far valleys were sprinkled with tiny lights.

"O Master,

"Thou that knowest the value of kings and birds,

"Thou hast made us humble, idle, futile peaks.

"Thous only needest eternal patience;

"We bow to Thy wisdom, O Lord—

"Humble, idle, futile peaks."

In the night

Grey heavy clouds muffles the valleys,

And the peaks looked toward God alone.

The chatter of a death-demon from a tree-top.

Blood—blood and torn grass—

Had marked the rise of his agony—

This lone hunter.

The grey-green woods impassive

Had watched the threshing of his limbs.

A canoe with flashing paddle,

A girl with soft searching eyes,

A call: "John!"

.   .   .   .

Come, arise, hunter!

Can you not hear?

The chatter of a death-demon from a tree-top.

The impact of a dollar upon the heart

Smiles warm red light,

Sweeping from the hearth rosily upon the

    white table,

With the hanging cool velvet shadows

Moving softly upon the door.

The impact of a million dollars

Is a crash of flunkys,

And yawning emblems of Persia

Cheeked against oak, France and a sabre,

The outcry of old beauty

Whored by pimping merchants

To submission before wine and chatter.

Silly rich peasants stamp the carpets of men,

Dead men who dreamed fragrance and light

Into their woof, their lives;

The rug of an honest bear

Under the feet of a cryptic slave

Who speaks always of baubles,

Forgetting state, multitude, work, and state,

Champing and mouthing of hats,

Making ratful squeak of hats,

Hats.

A man said to the universe:

"Sir, I exist!"

"However," replied the universe,

"The fact has not created in me

"A sense of obligation."

When the prophet, a complacent fat

     man,

Arrived at the mountain-top,

He cried: "Woe to my knowledge!

"I intended to see good white lands

"And bad black lands,

"But the scene is grey."

There was a land where lived no

     violets.

A traveller at once demanded: "Why?"

The people told him:

"Once the violets of this place spoke thus:

"'Until some woman freely give her lover

"'To another woman

"'We will fight in bloody scuffle.'"

Sadly the people added:

"There are no violets here."

There was one I met upon the road

Who looked at me with kind eyes.

He said: "Show me of your wares."

And I did,

Holding forth one,

He said: "It is a sin."

Then I held forth another.

He said: "It is a sin."

Then I held forth another.

He said: "It is a sin."

And so to the end.

Always He said: "It is a sin."

At last, I cried out:

"But I have non other."

He looked at me

With kinder eyes.

"Poor soul," he said.

Aye, workman, make me a dream,

A dream for my love.

Cunningly weave sunlight,

Breezes, and flowers.

Let it be of the cloth of meadows.

And—good workman—

And let there be a man walking thereon.

Each small gleam was a voice,

A lantern voice—

In little songs of carmine, violet, green, gold.

A chorus of colors came over the water;

The wondrous leaf-shadow no longer wavered,

No pines crooned on the hills,

The blue night was elsewhere a silence,

When the chorus of colors came over the

    water,

Little songs of carmine, violet, green, gold.

Small glowing pebbles

Thrown on the dark plane of evening

Sing good ballads of God

And eternity, with soul's rest.

Little priests, little holy fathers,

None can doubt the truth of hour hymning.

When the marvellous chorus comes over the
     water,

Songs of carmine, violet, green, gold.

The trees in the garden rained flowers.

Children ran there joyously.

They gathered the flowers

Each to himself.

Now there were some

Who gathered great heaps—

Having opportunity and skill—

Until, behold, only chance blossoms

Remained for the feeble.

Then a little spindling tutor

Ran importantly to the father, crying:

"Pray, come hither!

"See this unjust thing in your garden!"

But when the father had surveyed,

He admonished the tutor:

"Not so, small sage!

"This thing is just.

"For, look you,

"Are not they who possess the flowers

"Stronger, bolder, shrewder

"Than they who have none?

"Why should the strong—

"The beautiful strong—

"Why should they not have the flowers?

Upon reflection, the tutor bowed to the

    ground.

"My lord," he said,

"The stars are displaced

"By this towering wisdom."

INTRIGUE

Thou art my love,

And thou art the peace of sundown

When the blue shadows soothe,

And the grasses and the leaves sleep

To the song of the little brooks,

Woe is me.

Thou art my love,

And thou art a strorm

That breaks black in the sky,

And, sweeping headlong,

Drenches and cowers each tree,

And at the panting end

There is no sound

Save the melancholy cry of a single owl—

Woe is me!

Thou are my love,

And thou art a tinsel thing,

And I in my play

Broke thee easily,

And from the little fragments

Arose my long sorrow—

Woe is me.

Thou art my love,

And thou art a wary violet,

Drooping from sun-caresses,

Answering mine carelessly—

Woe is me.

Thou art my love,

And thou art the ashes of other men's love,

And I bury my face in these ashes,

And I love them—

Woe is me.

Thou art my love,

And thou art the beard

On another man's face—

Woe is me.

Thou art my love,

And thou art a temple,

And in this temple is an altar,

And on this altar is my heart—

Woe is me.

Thou art my love,

And thou art a wretch.

Let these sacred love-lies choke thee,

From I am come to where I know your lies

    as truth

And you truth as lies—

Woe is me.

Thou art my love,

And thou art a priestess,

And in they hand is a bloody dagger,

And my doom comes to me surely—

Woe is me.

Thou art my love,

And thou art a skull with ruby eyes,

And I love thee—

Woe is me.

Thou art my love,

And I doubt thee.

And if peace came with thy murder

Then would I murder—

Woe is me.

Thou art my love,

And thou art death,

Aye, thou art death

Black and yet black,

But I love thee,

I love thee—

Woe, welcome woe, to me.

Love, forgive me if I wish you grief,

For in your grief

You huddle to my breast,

And for it

Would I pay the price of your grief.

You walk among men

And all men do not surrender,

And thus I understand

That love reaches his hand

In mercy to me.

He had your picture in his room,

A scurvy traitor picture,

And he smiled

—Merely a fat complacence of men who

    know fine women—

And thus I divided with him

A part of my love.

Fool, not to know that thy little shoe

Can make men weep!

—Some men weep.

I weep and I gnash,

And I love the little shoe,

The little, little shoe.

God give me medals,

God give me loud honors,

That I may strut before you, sweetheart,

And be worthy of—

The love I bear you.

Now let me crunch you

With full weight of affrighted love.

I doubted you

—I doubted you—

And in this short doubting

My love grew like a genie

For my further undoing.

Beware of my friends,

Be not in speech too civil,

For in all courtesy

My weak heart sees spectres,

Mists of desire

Arising from the lips of my chosen;

Be not civil.

The flower I gave thee once

Was incident to a stride,

A detail of a gesture,

But search those pale petals

And see engraven thereon

A record of my intention.

Ah, God, the way your little finger moved,

As you thrust a bare arm backward

And made play with your hair

And a comb, a silly gilt comb

—Ah, God—that I should suffer
Because of the way a little finger moved.

Once I saw thee idly rocking
—Idly rocking—
And chattering girlishly to other girls,
Bell-voiced, happy,
Careless with the stout heart of unscarred
      womanhood,
And life to thee was all light melody.
I thought of the great storms of love as I
      knew it,
Torn, miserable, and ashamed of my open
      sorrow,
I thought of the thunders that lived in my
      head,
And I wish to be an ogre,
And hale and haul my beloved to a castle,
And make her mourn with my mourning.

Tell me why, behind thee,
I see always the shadow of another lover?
Is it real,

Or is this the thrice damned memory of a

   better happiness?

Plague on him if he be dead,

Plague on him if he be alive—

A swinish numskull

To intrude his shade

Always between me and my peace!

And yet I have seen thee happy with me.

I am no fool

To poll stupidly into iron.

I have heard your quick breaths

And seen your arms writhe toward me;

At those times

—God help us—

I was impelled to be a grand knight,

And swagger and snap my fingers,

And explain my mind finely.

Oh, lost sweetheart,

I would that I had not been a grand knight.

I said: "Sweetheart."

Thou said'st: "Sweetheart."

And we preserved an admirable mimicry

Without heeding the drip of the blood
From my heart.

I heard thee laugh,
And in this merriment
I defined the measure of my pain;
I knew that I was alone,
Alone with love,
Poor shivering love,
And he, little sprite,
Came to watch with me,
And at midnight,
We were like two creatures by a dead camp-
      fire.

I wonder if sometimes in the dusk,
When the brave lights that gild thy
      evenings
Have not yet been touched with flame,
I wonder if sometimes in the dusk
Thou rememberest a time,
A time when thou loved me
And our love was to thee thy all?

Is the memory rubbish now?

An old gown

Worn in an age of other fashions?

Woe is me, oh, lost one,

For that love is now to me

A supernal dream,

White, white, white with many suns.

Love met me at noonday,

—Reckless imp,

To leave his shaded nights

And brave the glare,—

And I saw him then plainly

For a bungler,

A stupid, simpering, eyeless bungler,

Breaking the hearts of brave people

As the snivelling idiot-boy cracks his bowl,

And I cursed him,

Cursed him to and fro, back and forth,

Into all the silly mazes of his mind,

But in the end

He laughed and pointed to my breast,

Where a heart still beat for thee, beloved.

I have seen thy face aflame

For love of me,

Thy fair arms go mad,

Thy lips tremble and mutter and rave.

And—surely—

This should leave a man content?

Thou lovest not me now,

But thou didst love me,

And in loving me once

Thou gavest me an eternal privilege,

For I can think of thee.

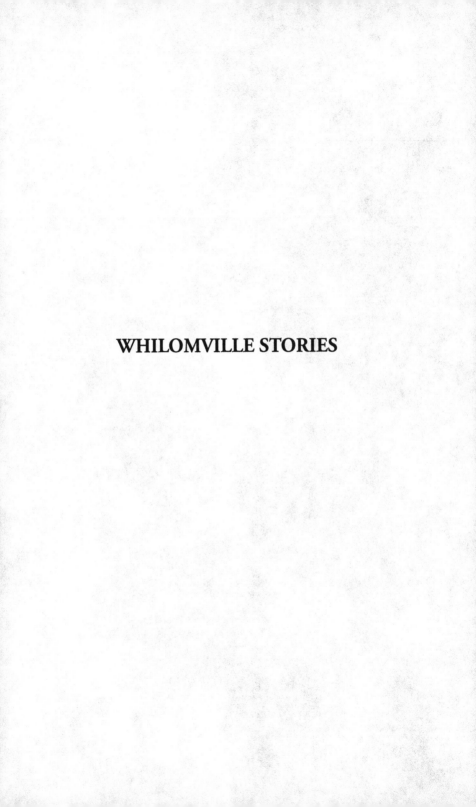

WHILOMVILLE STORIES

I. THE ANGEL CHILD

I

ALTHOUGH Whilomville was in no sense a summer resort, the advent of the warm season meant much to it, for then came visitors from the city—people of considerable confidence—alighting upon their country cousins. Moreover, many citizens who could afford to do so escaped at this time to the sea-side. The town, with the commercial life quite taken out of it, drawled and drowsed through long months, during which nothing was worse than the white dust which arose behind every vehicle at blinding noon, and nothing was finer than the cool sheen of the hose sprays over the cropped lawns under the many maples in the twilight.

One summer the Trescotts had a visitation. Mrs. Trescott owned a cousin who was a painter of high degree. I had almost said that he was of national reputation, but, come to think of it, it is better to say that almost everybody in the United States who knew about art and its travail knew about him. He had picked out a wife, and naturally, looking at him, one wondered how he had done it. She was quick, beautiful, imperious, while he was quiet, slow, and misty. She was a veritable queen of health, while he, apparently, was of a most brittle constitution. When he played tennis, particularly, he looked every minute as if he were going to break.

They lived in New York, in awesome apartments wherein Japan and Persia, and indeed all the world, confounded the observer. At the end was a cathedral-like studio. They had one child. Perhaps it would be better to say that they had one CHILD. It was a girl. When she came to Whilomville with her parents, it was patent that she had an inexhaustible store of white frocks, and that her voice was high and commanding. These things the town knew quickly. Other things it was doomed to discover by a process.

Her effect upon the children of the Trescott neighborhood was singular.

They at first feared, then admired, then embraced. In two days she was a Begum. All day long her voice could be heard directing, drilling, and compelling those free-born children; and to say that they felt oppression would be wrong, for they really fought for records of loyal obedience.

All went well until one day was her birthday.

On the morning of this day she walked out into the Trescott garden and said to her father, confidently, "Papa, give me some money, because this is my birthday."

He looked dreamily up from his easel. "Your birthday?" he murmured. Her envisioned father was never energetic enough to be irritable unless some one broke through into that place where he lived with the desires of his life. But neither wife nor child ever heeded or even understood the temperamental values, and so some part of him had grown hardened to their inroads. "Money?" he said. "Here." He handed her a five-dollar bill. It was that he did not at all understand the nature of a five-dollar bill. He was deaf to it. He had it; he gave it; that was all.

She sallied forth to a waiting people—Jimmie Trescott, Dan Earl, Ella Earl, the Margate twins, the three Phelps children, and others. "I've got some pennies now," she cried, waving the bill, "and I am going to buy some candy." They were deeply stirred by this announcement. Most children are penniless three hundred days in the year, and to another possessing five pennies they pay deference. To little Cora waving a bright green note these children paid heathenish homage. In some disorder they thronged after her to a small shop on Bridge Street hill. First of all came ice-cream. Seated in the comic little back parlor, they clamored shrilly over plates of various flavors, and the shopkeeper marvelled that cream could vanish so quickly down throats that seemed wide open, always, for the making of excited screams.

These children represented the families of most excellent people. They were all born in whatever purple there was to be had in the vicinity of Whilomville. The Margate twins, for example, were out-and-out prize-winners. With their long golden curls and their countenances of similar vacuity, they shone upon the front bench of all Sunday-school functions, hand in hand, while their uplifted mother felt about her the envy of a hundred other parents, and less heavenly children scoffed from near the door.

Then there was little Dan Earl, probably the nicest boy in the world, gentle, fine-grained, obedient to the point where he obeyed anybody. Jimmie Trescott himself was, indeed, the only child who was at all versed in villany, but in these particular days he was on his very good behavior. As a matter of fact, he was in love. The beauty of his regal little cousin had stolen his manly heart.

Yes, they were all most excellent children, but, loosened upon this candy-shop with five dollars, they resembled, in a tiny way, drunken revelling soldiers within the walls of a stormed city. Upon the heels of ice-cream and cake came chocolate mice, butter-scotch, "everlastings," chocolate cigars, taffy-on-a-stick, taffy-on-a-slate-pencil, and many semi-transparent devices resembling lions, tigers, elephants, horses, cats, dogs, cows, sheep, tables, chairs, engines (both railway and for the fighting of fire), soldiers, fine ladies, odd-looking men, clocks, watches, revolvers, rabbits, and bedsteads. A cent was the price of a single wonder.

Some of the children, going quite daft, soon had thought to make fight over the spoils, but their queen ruled with an iron grip. Her first inspiration was to satisfy her own fancies, but as soon as that was done she mingled prodigality with a fine justice, dividing, balancing, bestowing, and sometimes taking away from somebody even that which he had.

It was an orgy. In thirty-five minutes those respectable children looked as if they had been dragged at the tail of a chariot. The sacred Margate twins, blinking and grunting, wished to take seat upon the floor, and even the most durable Jimmie Trescott found occasion to lean against the counter, wearing at the time a solemn and abstracted air, as if he expected something to happen to him shortly.

Of course their belief had been in an unlimited capacity, but they found there was an end. The shopkeeper handed the queen her change.

"Two seventy-three from five leaves two twenty-seven, Miss Cora," he said, looking upon her with admiration.

She turned swiftly to her clan. "O-oh!" she cried, in amazement. "Look how much I have left!" They gazed at the coins in her palm. They knew then that it was not their capacities which were endless; it was the five dollars.

The queen led the way to the street. "We must think up some way of spending more money," she said, frowning. They stood in silence, awaiting her further speech.

Suddenly she clapped her hands and screamed with delight. "Come on!" she cried. "I know what let's do." Now behold, she had discovered the red and white pole in front of the shop of one William Neeltje, a barber by trade.

It becomes necessary to say a few words concerning Neeltje. He was new to the town. He had come and opened a dusty little shop on dusty Bridge Street hill, and although the neighborhood knew from the courier winds that his diet was mainly cabbage, they were satisfied with that meagre data. Of course Riefsnyder came to investigate him for the local Barbers' Union, but he found in him only sweetness and light, with a willingness to charge any price at all for a shave or a haircut. In fact, the advent of Neeltje would have made barely a ripple upon the placid bosom of Whilomville if it were not that his name was Neeltje.

At first the people looked at his sign-board out of the eye corner, and wondered lazily why any one should bear the name of Neeltje; but as time went on, men spoke to other men, saying, "How do you pronounce the name of that barber up there on Bridge Street hill?" And then, before any could prevent it, the best minds of the town were splintering their lances against William Neeltje's sign-board. If a man had a mental superior, he guided him seductively to this name, and watched with glee his wrecking. The clergy of the town even entered the lists. There was one among them who had taken a collegiate prize in Syriac, as well as in several less opaque languages, and the other clergymen—at one of their weekly meetings—sought to betray him into this ambush. He pronounced the name correctly, but that mattered little, since none of them knew whether he did or did not; and so they took triumph according to their ignorance. Under these arduous circumstances it was certain that the town should look for a nickname, and at this time the nickname was in process of formation. So William Neeltje lived on with his secret, smiling foolishly towards the world.

"Come on," cried little Cora. "Let's all get our hair cut. That's what let's do. Let's all get our hair cut! Come on! Come on! Come on!" The others were carried off their feet by the fury of this assault. To get their hair cut! What joy! Little did they know if this were fun; they only knew that their small leader said it was fun. Chocolate-stained but confident, the band marched into William Neeltje's barber shop.

"We wish to get our hair cut," said little Cora, haughtily.

Neeltje, in his shirt-sleeves, stood looking at them with his half-idiot smile.

"Hurry, now!" commanded the queen. A dray-horse toiled step by step, step by step, up Bridge Street hill; a far woman's voice arose; there could be heard the ceaseless hammers of shingling carpenters; all was summer peace. "Come on, now. Who's goin' first? Come on, Ella; you go first. Gettin' our hair cut! Oh what fun!"

Little Ella Earl would not, however, be first in the chair. She was drawn towards it by a singular fascination, but at the same time she was afraid of it, and so she hung back, saying: "No! You go first! No! You go first!" The question was precipitated by the twins and one of the Phelps children. They made simultaneous rush for the chair, and screamed and kicked, each pair preventing the third child. The queen entered this mêlée, and decided in favor of the Phelps boy. He ascended the chair. Thereat an awed silence fell upon the band. And always William Neeltje smiled fatuously.

He tucked a cloth in the neck of the Phelps boy, and taking scissors, began to cut his hair. The group of children came closer and closer. Even the queen was deeply moved. "Does it hurt any?" she asked, in a wee voice.

"Naw," said the Phelps boy, with dignity. "Anyhow, I've had m' hair cut afore."

When he appeared to them looking very soldierly with his cropped little head, there was a tumult over the chair. The Margate twins howled; Jimmie Trescott was kicking them on the shins. It was a fight.

But the twins could not prevail, being the smallest of all the children. The queen herself took the chair, and ordered Neeltje as if he were a lady's-maid. To the floor there fell proud ringlets, blazing even there in their humiliation with a full fine bronze light. Then Jimmie Trescott, then Ella Earl (two long ash-colored plaits), then a Phelps girl, then another Phelps girl; and so on from head to head. The ceremony received unexpected check when the turn came to Dan Earl. This lad, usually docile to any rein, had suddenly grown mulishly obstinate. No, he would not, he would not. He himself did not seem to know why he refused to have his hair cut, but, despite the shrill derision of the company, he remained obdurate. Anyhow, the twins, long held in check, and now feverishly eager, were already struggling for the chair.

And so to the floor at last came the golden Margate curls, the heart treasure and glory of a mother, three aunts, and some feminine cousins.

All having been finished, the children, highly elate, thronged out into the street. They crowed and cackled with pride and joy, anon turning to scorn the cowardly Dan Earl.

Ella Earl was an exception. She had been pensive for some time, and now the shorn little maiden began vaguely to weep. In the door of his shop William Neeltje stood watching them, upon his face a grin of almost inhuman idiocy.

II

It now becomes the duty of the unfortunate writer to exhibit these children to their fond parents. "Come on, Jimmie," cried little Cora, "let's go show mamma." And they hurried off, these happy children, to show mamma.

The Trescotts and their guests were assembled indolently awaiting the luncheon-bell. Jimmie and the angel child burst in upon them. "Oh, mamma," shrieked little Cora, "see how fine I am! I've had my hair cut! Isn't it splendid? And Jimmie too!"

The wretched mother took one sight, emitted one yell, and fell into a chair. Mrs. Trescott dropped a large lady's journal and made a nerveless mechanical clutch at it. The painter gripped the arms of his chair and leaned forward, staring until his eyes were like two little clock faces. Dr. Trescott did not move or speak.

To the children the next moments were chaotic. There was a loudly wailing mother, and a pale-faced, aghast mother; a stammering father, and a grim and terrible father. The angel child did not understand anything of it save the voice of calamity, and in a moment all her little imperialism went to the winds. She ran sobbing to her mother. "Oh, mamma! mamma! mamma!"

The desolate Jimmie heard out of this inexplicable situation a voice which he knew well, a sort of colonel's voice, and he obeyed like any good soldier. "Jimmie!"

He stepped three paces to the front. "Yes, sir."

"How did this—how did this happen?" said Trescott.

Now Jimmie could have explained how had happened anything which had happened, but he did not know what had happened, so he said, "I—I—nothin'."

"And, oh, look at her frock!" said Mrs. Trescott, brokenly.

The words turned the mind of the mother of the angel child. She looked up, her eyes blazing. "Frock!" she repeated. "Frock! What do I care for her frock? Frock!" she choked out again from the depths of her bitterness. Then she arose suddenly, and whirled tragically upon her husband. "Look!" she declaimed. "All—her lovely—hair—all her lovely hair—gone—gone!" The painter was apparently in a fit; his jaw was set, his eyes were glazed, his body was stiff and straight. "All gone—all—her lovely hair—all gone—my poor little darlin'—my—poor—little—darlin'!" And the angel child added her heart-broken voice to her mother's wail as they fled into each other's arms.

In the mean time Trescott was patiently unravelling some skeins of Jimmie's tangled intellect. "And then you went to this barber's on the hill.

Yes. And where did you get the money? Yes. I see. And who besides you and Cora had their hair cut? The Margate twi—Oh, lord!"

Over at the Margate place old Eldridge Margate, the grandfather of the twins, was in the back garden picking pease and smoking ruminatively to himself. Suddenly he heard from the house great noises. Doors slammed, women rushed up-stairs and down-stairs calling to each other in voices of agony. And then full and mellow upon the still air arose the roar of the twins in pain.

Old Eldridge stepped out of the pea-patch and moved towards the house, puzzled, staring, not yet having decided that it was his duty to rush forward. Then around the corner of the house shot his daughter Mollie, her face pale with horror.

"What's the matter?" he cried.

"Oh, father," she gasped, "the children! They—"

Then around the corner of the house came the twins, howling at the top of their power, their faces flowing with tears. They were still hand in hand, the ruling passion being strong even in this suffering. At sight of them old Eldridge took his pipe hastily out of his mouth. "Good God!" he said.

And now what befell one William Neeltje, a barber by trade? And what was said by angry parents of the mother of such an angel child? And what was the fate of the angel child herself?

There was surely a tempest. With the exception of the Margate twins, the boys could well be eliminated from the affair. Of course it didn't matter if their hair was cut. Also the two little Phelps girls had had very short hair, anyhow, and their parents were not too greatly incensed. In the case of Ella Earl, it was mainly the pathos of the little girl's own grieving; but her mother played a most generous part, and called upon Mrs. Trescott, and condoled with the mother of the angel child over their equivalent losses. But the Margate contingent! They simply screeched.

Trescott, composed and cool-blooded, was in the middle of a giddy whirl. He was not going to allow the mobbing of his wife's cousins, nor was he going to pretend that the spoliation of the Margate twins was a virtuous and beautiful act. He was elected, gratuitously, to the position of a buffer.

But, curiously enough, the one who achieved the bulk of the misery was old Eldridge Margate, who had been picking pease at the time. The feminine Margates stormed his position as individuals, in pairs, in teams, and *en masse*. In two days they may have aged him seven years. He must destroy the utter Neeltje. He must midnightly massacre the angel child and her mother. He must dip his arms in blood to the elbows.

Trescott took the first opportunity to express to him his concern over the affair, but when the subject of the disaster was mentioned, old Eldridge, to the doctor's great surprise, actually chuckled long and deeply. "Oh, well, look-a-here," he said. "I never was so much in love with them there damn curls. The curls was purty—yes—but then I'd a darn sight rather see boys look more like boys than like two little wax figgers. An', ye know, the little cusses like it themselves. *They* never took no stock in all this washin' an' combin' an' fixin' an' goin' to church an' paradin' an' showin' off. They stood it because they were told to. That's all. Of course this here Neel-te-gee, er whatever his name is, is a plumb dumb ijit, but I don't see what's to be done, now that the kids is full well cropped. I might go and burn his shop over his head, but that wouldn't bring no hair back onto the kids. They're even kicking on sashes now, and that's all right, 'cause what fer does a boy want a sash?"

Whereupon Trescott perceived that the old man wore his brains above his shoulders, and Trescott departed from him rejoicing greatly that it was only women who could not know that there was finality to most disasters, and that when a thing was fully done, no amount of door-slammings, rushing up-stairs and down-stairs, calls, lamentations, tears, could bring back a single hair to the heads of twins.

But the rains came and the winds blew in the most biblical way when a certain fact came to light in the Trescott household. Little Cora, corroborated by Jimmie, innocently remarked that five dollars had been given her by her father on her birthday, and with this money the evil had been wrought. Trescott had known it, but he—thoughtful man—had said nothing. For her part, the mother of the angel child had up to that moment never reflected that the consummation of the wickedness must have cost a small sum of money. But now it was all clear to her. He was the guilty one—he! "My angel child!"

The scene which ensued was inspiriting. A few days later, loungers at the railway station saw a lady leading a shorn and still undaunted lamb. Attached to them was a husband and father, who was plainly bewildered, but still more plainly vexed, as if he would be saying: "Damn 'em! Why can't they leave me alone?"

II. LYNX-HUNTING

JIMMIE lounged about the dining-room and watched his mother with large, serious eyes. Suddenly he said, "Ma—now—can I borrow pa's gun?"

She was overcome with the feminine horror which is able to mistake preliminary words for the full accomplishment of the dread thing. "Why, Jimmie!" she cried. "Of al-l wonders! Your father's gun! No indeed you can't!"

He was fairly well crushed, but he managed to mutter, sullenly, "Well, Willie Dalzel, he's got a gun." In reality his heart had previously been beating with such tumult—he had himself been so impressed with the daring and sin of his request—that he was glad that all was over now, and his mother could do very little further harm to his sensibilities. He had been influenced into the venture by the larger boys.

"Huh!" the Dalzel urchin had said; "your father's got a gun, hasn't he? Well, why don't you bring that?"

Puffing himself, Jimmie had replied, "Well, I can, if I want to." It was a black lie, but really the Dalzel boy was too outrageous with his eternal bill-posting about the gun which a beaming uncle had intrusted to him. Its possession made him superior in manfulness to most boys in the neighborhood—or at least they enviously conceded him such position—but he was so overbearing, and stuffed the fact of his treasure so relentlessly down their throats, that on this occasion the miserable Jimmie had lied as naturally as most animals swim.

Willie Dalzel had not been checkmated, for he had instantly retorted, "Why don't you get it, then?"

"Well, I can, if I want to."

"Well, get it, then!"

"Well, I can, if I want to."

Thereupon Jimmie had paced away with great airs of surety as far as the door of his home, where his manner changed to one of tremulous misgiving as it came upon him to address his mother in the dining-room. There had happened that which had happened.

When Jimmie returned to his two distinguished companions he was blown out with a singular pomposity. He spoke these noble words: "Oh, well, I guess I don't want to take the gun out to-day."

They had been watching him with gleaming ferret eyes, and they detected his falsity at once. They challenged him with shouted gibes, but it was not in the rules for the conduct of boys that one should admit anything whatsoever, and so Jimmie, backed into an ethical corner, lied as stupidly, as desperately, as hopelessly as ever lone savage fights when surrounded at last in his jungle.

Such accusations were never known to come to any point, for the reason that the number and kind of denials always equalled or exceeded the number of accusations, and no boy was ever brought really to book for these misdeeds.

In the end they went off together, Willie Dalzel with his gun being a trifle in advance and discoursing upon his various works. They passed along a maple-lined avenue, a highway common to boys bound for that free land of hills and woods in which they lived in some part their romance of the moment, whether it was of Indians, miners, smugglers, soldiers, or outlaws. The paths were their paths, and much was known to them of the secrets of the dark green hemlock thickets, the wastes of sweet-fern and huckleberry, the cliffs of gaunt bluestone with the sumach burning red at their feet. Each boy had, I am sure, a conviction that some day the wilderness was to give forth to him a marvellous secret. They felt that the hills and the forest knew much, and they heard a voice of it in the silence. It was vague, thrilling, fearful, and altogether fabulous. The grown folk seemed to regard these wastes merely as so much distance between one place and another place, or as a rabbit-cover, or as a district to be judged according to the value of the timber; but to the boys it spoke some great inspiring word, which they knew even as those who pace the shore know the enigmatic speech of the surf. In the mean time they lived there, in season, lives of ringing adventure—by dint of imagination.

The boys left the avenue, skirted hastily through some private grounds, climbed a fence, and entered the thickets. It happened that at school the previous day Willie Dalzel had been forced to read and acquire in some part a solemn description of a lynx. The meagre information thrust upon him had caused him grimaces of suffering, but now he said, suddenly, "I'm goin' to shoot a lynx."

The other boys admired this statement, but they were silent for a time. Finally Jimmie said, meekly, "What's a lynx?" He had endured his ignorance as long as he was able.

The Dalzel boy mocked him. "Why, don't you know what a lynx is? A lynx? Why, a lynx is a animal somethin' like a cat, an' it's got great big green eyes, and it sits on the limb of a tree an' jus' glares at you. It's a pretty bad animal, I tell you. Why, when I—"

"Huh!" said the third boy. "Where'd you ever see a lynx?"

"Oh, I've seen 'em—plenty of 'em. I bet you'd be scared if you seen one once."

Jimmie and the other boy each demanded, "How do you know I would?"

They penetrated deeper into the wood. They climbed a rocky zigzag path which led them at times where with their hands they could almost touch the tops of giant pines. The gray cliffs sprang sheer towards the sky. Willie Dalzel babbled about his impossible lynx, and they stalked the mountain-side like chamois-hunters, although no noise of bird or beast broke the stillness of the hills. Below them Whilomville was spread out somewhat like the cheap green and black lithograph of the time—"A Bird's-eye View of Whilomville, N. Y."

In the end the boys reached the top of the mountain and scouted off among wild and desolate ridges. They were burning with the desire to slay large animals. They thought continually of elephants, lions, tigers, crocodiles. They discoursed upon their immaculate conduct in case such monsters confronted them, and they all lied carefully about their courage.

The breeze was heavy with the smell of sweet-fern. The pines and hemlocks sighed as they waved their branches. In the hollows the leaves of the laurels were lacquered where the sunlight found them. No matter the weather, it would be impossible to long continue an expedition of this kind without a fire, and presently they built one, snapping down for fuel the brittle under-branches of the pines. About this fire they were willed to conduct a sort of play, the Dalzel boy taking the part of a bandit chief, and the other boys being his trusty lieutenants. They stalked to and fro, long-strided, stern yet devil-may-care, three terrible little figures.

Jimmie had an uncle who made game of him whenever he caught him in this kind of play, and often this uncle quoted derisively the following classic: "Once aboard the lugger, Bill, and the girl is mine. Now to burn the château and destroy all evidence of our crime. But, hark'e, Bill, no wiolence." Wheeling abruptly, he addressed these dramatic words to his comrades. They were impressed; they decided at once to be smugglers, and in the most ribald fashion they talked about carrying off young women.

At last they continued their march through the woods. The smuggling *motif* was now grafted fantastically upon the original lynx idea, which Willie Dalzel refused to abandon at any price.

Once they came upon an innocent bird who happened to be looking another way at the time. After a great deal of manœvering and big words, Willie Dalzel reared his fowling-piece and blew this poor thing into a mere rag of wet feathers, of which he was proud.

Afterwards the other big boy had a turn at another bird. Then it was plainly Jimmie's chance. The two others had, of course, some thought of cheating him out of this chance, but of a truth he was timid to explode such a thunderous weapon, and as soon as they detected this fear they simply overbore him, and made it clearly understood that if he refused to shoot he would lose his caste, his scalp-lock, his girdle, his honor.

They had reached the old death-colored snake-fence which marked the limits of the upper pasture of the Fleming farm. Under some hickory-trees the path ran parallel to the fence. Behold! a small priestly chipmonk came to a rail, and folding his hands on his abdomen, addressed them in his own tongue. It was Jimmie's shot. Adjured by the others, he took the gun. His face was stiff with apprehension. The Dalzel boy was giving forth fine words. "Go ahead. Aw, don't be afraid. It's nothin' to do. Why, I've done it a million times. Don't shut both your eyes, now. Jus' keep one open and shut the other one. He'll get away if you don't watch out. Now you're all right. Why don't you let'er go? Go ahead."

Jimmie, with his legs braced apart, was in the centre of the path. His back was greatly bent, owing to the mechanics of supporting the heavy gun. His companions were screeching in the rear. There was a wait.

Then he pulled trigger. To him there was a frightful roar, his cheek and his shoulder took a stunning blow, his face felt a hot flush of fire, and opening his two eyes, he found that he was still alive. He was not too dazed to instantly adopt a becoming egotism. It had been the first shot of his life.

But directly after the well-mannered celebration of this victory a certain cow, which had been grazing in the line of fire, was seen to break wildly across the pasture, bellowing and bucking. The three smugglers and lynx-hunters looked at each other out of blanched faces. Jimmie had hit the cow. The first evidence of his comprehension of this fact was in the celerity with which he returned the discharged gun to Willie Dalzel.

They turned to flee. The land was black, as if it had been overshadowed suddenly with thick storm-clouds, and even as they fled in their horror a gigantic Swedish farm-hand came from the heavens and fell upon them, shrieking in eerie triumph. In a twinkle they were clouted prostrate. The Swede was elate and ferocious in a foreign and fulsome way. He continued to beat them and yell.

From the ground they raised their dismal appeal. "Oh, please, mister, we didn't do it! He did it! I didn't do it! We didn't do it! We didn't mean to do it! Oh, please, mister!"

In these moments of childish terror little lads go half-blind, and it is possible that few moments of their after-life made them suffer as they did when the Swede flung them over the fence and marched them towards the farm-house. They begged like cowards on the scaffold, and each one was for himself. "Oh, please let me go, mister! I didn't do it, mister! He did it! Oh, p-l-ease let me go, mister!"

The boyish view belongs to boys alone, and if this tall and knotted laborer was needlessly without charity, none of the three lads questioned it. Usually when they were punished they decided that they deserved it, and the more they were punished the more they were convinced that they were criminals of a most subterranean type. As to the hitting of the cow being a pure accident, and therefore not of necessity a criminal matter, such reading never entered their heads. When things happened and they were caught, they commonly paid dire consequences, and they were accustomed to measure the probabilities of woe utterly by the damage done, and not in any way by the culpability. The shooting of the cow was plainly heinous, and undoubtedly their dungeons would be knee-deep in water.

"He did it, mister!" This was a general outcry. Jimmie used it as often as did the others. As for them, it is certain that they had no direct thought of betraying their comrade for their own salvation. They thought themselves guilty because they were caught; when boys were not caught they might possibly be innocent. But captured boys were guilty. When they cried out that Jimmie was the culprit, it was principally a simple expression of terror.

Old Henry Fleming, the owner of the farm, strode across the pasture towards them. He had in his hand a most cruel whip. This whip he flourished. At his approach the boys suffered the agonies of the fire regions. And yet anybody with half an eye could see that the whip in his hand was a mere accident, and that he was a kind old man—when he cared.

When he had come near he spoke crisply. "What you boys ben doin' to my cow?" The tone had deep threat in it. They all answered by saying that none of them had shot the cow. Their denials were tearful and clamorous, and they crawled knee by knee. The vision of it was like three martyrs being dragged towards the stake. Old Fleming stood there, grim, tight-lipped. After a time he said, "Which boy done it?"

There was some confusion, and then Jimmie spake. "I done it, mister."

Fleming looked at him. Then he asked, "Well, what did you shoot 'er fer?"

Jimmie thought, hesitated, decided, faltered, and then formulated this: "I thought she was a lynx."

Old Fleming and his Swede at once lay down in the grass and laughed themselves helpless.

III. THE LOVER AND THE TELLTALE

WHEN the angel child returned with her parents to New York, the fond heart of Jimmie Trescott felt its bruise greatly. For two days he simply moped, becoming a stranger to all former joys. When his old comrades yelled invitation, as they swept off on some interesting quest, he replied with mournful gestures of disillusion.

He thought often of writing to her, but of course the shame of it made him pause. Write a letter to a girl? The mere enormity of the idea caused him shudders. Persons of his quality never wrote letters to girls. Such was the occupation of mollycoddles and snivellers. He knew that if his acquaintances and friends found in him evidences of such weakness and general milkiness, they would fling themselves upon him like so many wolves, and bait him beyond the borders of sanity.

However, one day at school, in that time of the morning session when children of his age were allowed fifteen minutes of play in the school-grounds, he did not as usual rush forth ferociously to his games. Commonly he was of the worst hoodlums, preying upon his weaker brethren with all the cruel disregard of a grown man. On this particular morning he stayed in the school-room, and with his tongue stuck from the corner of his mouth, and his head twisting in a painful way, he wrote to little Cora, pouring out to her all the poetry of his hungry soul, as follows: "My dear Cora I love thee with all my hart oh come bac again, bac, bac gain for I love thee best of all oh come bac again When the spring come again we'l fly and we'l fly like a brid."

As for the last word, he knew under normal circumstances perfectly well how to spell "bird," but in this case he had transposed two of the letters through excitement, supreme agitation.

Nor had this letter been composed without fear and furtive glancing. There was always a number of children who, for the time, cared more for the quiet of the school-room than for the tempest of the play-ground, and there was always that dismal company who were being forcibly deprived of their recess—who were being "kept in." More than one curious eye was turned upon the desperate and lawless Jimmie Trescott suddenly taken to ways of peace, and as he felt these eyes he flushed guiltily, with felonious glances from side to side.

It happened that a certain vigilant little girl had a seat directly across the aisle from Jimmie's seat, and she had remained in the room during the intermission, because of her interest in some absurd domestic details concerning her desk. Parenthetically it might be stated that she was in the habit of imagining this desk to be a house, and at this time, with an important little frown, indicative of a proper matron, she was engaged in dramatizing her ideas of a household.

But this small Rose Goldege happened to be of a family which numbered few males. It was, in fact, one of those curious middle-class families that hold much of their ground, retain most of their position, after all their visible means of support have been dropped in the grave. It contained now only a collection of women who existed submissively, defiantly, securely, mysteriously, in a pretentious and often exasperating virtue. It was often too triumphantly clear that they were free of bad habits. However, bad habits is a term here used in a commoner meaning, because it is certainly true that the principal and indeed solitary joy which entered their lonely lives was the joy of talking wickedly and busily about their neighbors. It was all done without dream of its being of the vulgarity of the alleys. Indeed it was simply a constitutional but not incredible chastity and honesty expressing itself in its ordinary superior way of the whirling circles of life, and the vehemence of the criticism was not lessened by a further infusion of an acid of worldly defeat, worldly suffering, and worldly hopelessness.

Out of this family circle had sprung the typical little girl who discovered Jimmie Trescott agonizingly writing a letter to his sweetheart. Of course all the children were the most abandoned gossips, but she was peculiarly adapted to the purpose of making Jimmie miserable over this particular point. It was her life to sit of evenings about the stove and hearken to her mother and a lot of spinsters talk of many things. During these evenings she was never licensed to utter an opinion either one way or the other way. She was then simply a very little girl sitting open-eyed in the gloom, and listening to many things which she often interpreted wrongly. They on their part kept up a kind of a smug-faced pretence of concealing from her information in detail of the widespread crime, which pretence may have been more elaborately dangerous than no pretence at all. Thus all her home-teaching fitted her to recognize at once in Jimmie Trescott's manner that he was concealing something that would properly interest the world. She set up a scream. "Oh! Oh! Oh! Jimmie Trescott's writing to his girl! Oh! Oh!"

Jimmie cast a miserable glance upon her—a glance in which hatred mingled with despair. Through the open window he could hear the boisterous cries of his friends—his hoodlum friends—who would no more understand the utter poetry of his position than they would understand an ancient tribal sign-language. His face was set in a truer expression of horror than any of the romances describe upon the features of a man flung into a moat, a man shot in the breast with an arrow, a man cleft in the neck with a battle-axe. He was suppedaneous of the fullest power of childish pain. His one course was to rush upon her and attempt, by an impossible means of strangulation, to keep her important news from the public.

The teacher, a thoughtful young woman at her desk upon the platform, saw a little scuffle which informed her that two of her scholars were larking. She called out sharply. The command penetrated to the middle of an early world struggle. In Jimmie's age there was no particular scruple in the minds of the male sex against laying warrior hands upon their weaker sisters. But, of course, this voice from the throne hindered Jimmie in what might have been a berserk attack.

Even the little girl was retarded by the voice, but, without being unlawful, she managed soon to shy through the door and out upon the play-ground, yelling, "Oh, Jimmie Trescott's been writing to his girl!"

The unhappy Jimmie was following as closely as he was allowed by his knowledge of the decencies to be preserved under the eye of the teacher.

Jimmie himself was mainly responsible for the scene which ensued on the play-ground. It is possible that the little girl might have run, shrieking his infamy, without exciting more than a general but unmilitant interest. These barbarians were excited only by the actual appearance of human woe; in that event they cheered and danced. Jimmie made the strategic mistake of pursuing little Rose, and thus exposed his thin skin to the whole school. He had in his cowering mind a vision of a hundred children turning from their play under the maple-trees and speeding towards him over the gravel with sudden wild taunts. Upon him drove a yelping demoniac mob, to which his words were futile. He saw in this mob boys that he dimly knew, and his deadly enemies, and his retainers, and his most intimate friends. The virulence of his deadly enemy was no greater than the virulence of his intimate friend. From the outskirts the little informer could be heard still screaming the news, like a toy parrot with clock-work inside of it. It broke up all sorts of games, not so much because of the mere fact of the letter-writing, as because the children knew that some sufferer was at the last point, and, like little blood-fanged wolves, they thronged to the scene of his destruction. They galloped about him shrilly chanting insults. He turned from one to another, only to meet with howls. He was baited.

Then, in one instant, he changed all this with a blow. Bang! The most pitiless of the boys near him received a punch, fairly and skilfully, which made him bellow out like a walrus, and then Jimmie laid desperately into the whole world, striking out frenziedly in all directions. Boys who could handily whip him, and knew it, backed away from this onslaught. Here was intention—serious intention. They themselves were not in frenzy, and their cooler judgment respected Jimmie's efforts when he ran amuck. They saw that it really was none of their affair. In the mean time the wretched little girl who had caused the bloody riot was away, by the fence, weeping because boys were fighting.

Jimmie several times hit the wrong boy—that is to say, he several times hit a wrong boy hard enough to arouse also in him a spirit of strife. Jimmie wore a little shirt-waist. It was passing now rapidly into oblivion. He was sobbing, and there was one blood stain upon his cheek. The school-ground sounded like a pinetree when a hundred crows roost in it at night.

Then upon the situation there pealed a brazen bell. It was a bell that these children obeyed, even as older nations obey the formal law which is printed in calf-skin. It smote them into some sort of inaction; even Jimmie was influenced by its potency, although, as a finale, he kicked out lustily into the legs of an intimate friend who had been one of the foremost in the torture.

When they came to form into line for the march into the school-room it was curious that Jimmie had many admirers. It was not his prowess; it was the soul he had infused into his gymnastics; and he, still panting, looked about him with a stern and challenging glare.

And yet when the long tramping line had entered the school-room his status had again changed. The other children then began to regard him as a boy in disrepair, and boys in disrepair were always accosted ominously from the throne. Jimmie's march towards his seat was a feat. It was composed partly of a most slinking attempt to dodge the perception of the teacher and partly of pure braggadocio erected for the benefit of his observant fellow-men.

The teacher looked carefully down at him. "Jimmie Trescott," she said.

"Yes'm," he answered, with businesslike briskness, which really spelled out falsity in all its letters.

"Come up to the desk."

He rose amid the awe of the entire school-room. When he arrived she said,

"Jimmie, you've been fighting."

"Yes'm," he answered. This was not so much an admission of the fact as it was a concessional answer to anything she might say.

"Who have you been fighting?" she asked.

"I dunno', 'm."

Whereupon the empress blazed out in wrath. "You don't know who you've been fighting?"

Jimmie looked at her gloomily. "No, 'm."

She seemed about to disintegrate to mere flaming fagots of anger. "You don't know who you've been fighting?" she demanded, blazing. "Well, you stay in after school until you find out."

As he returned to his place all the children knew by his vanquished air that sorrow had fallen upon the house of Trescott. When he took his seat he saw gloating upon him the satanic black eyes of the little Goldege girl.

IV. "SHOWIN' OFF"

JIMMIE TRESCOTT'S new velocipede had the largest front wheel of any velocipede in Whilomville. When it first arrived from New York he wished to sacrifice school, food, and sleep to it. Evidently he wished to become a sort of a perpetual velocipede-rider. But the powers of the family laid a number of judicious embargoes upon him, and he was prevented from becoming a fanatic. Of course this caused him to retain a fondness for the three-wheeled thing much longer than if he had been allowed to debauch himself for a span of days. But in the end it was an immaterial machine to him. For long periods he left it idle in the stable.

One day he loitered from school towards home by a very circuitous route. He was accompanied by only one of his retainers. The object of this détour was the wooing of a little girl in a red hood. He had been in love with her for some three weeks. His desk was near her desk in school, but he had never spoken to her. He had been afraid to take such a radical step. It was not customary to speak to girls. Even boys who had school-going sisters seldom addressed them during that part of a day which was devoted to education.

The reasons for this conduct were very plain. First, the more robust boys considered talking with girls an unmanly occupation; second, the greater part of the boys were afraid; third, they had no idea of what to say, because they esteemed the proper sentences should be supernaturally incisive and eloquent. In consequence, a small contingent of blue-eyed weaklings were the sole intimates of the frail sex, and for it they were boisterously and disdainfully called "girl-boys."

But this situation did not prevent serious and ardent wooing. For instance, Jimmie and the little girl who wore the red hood must have exchanged glances at least two hundred times in every school-hour, and this exchange of glances accomplished everything. In them the two children renewed their curious inarticulate vows.

Jimmie had developed a devotion to school which was the admiration of his father and mother. In the mornings he was so impatient to have it made known to him that no misfortune had befallen his romance during the night that he was actually detected at times feverishly listening for the "first bell." Dr. Trescott was exceedingly complacent of the change, and as for Mrs. Trescott, she had ecstatic visions of a white-haired Jimmie leading the nations in knowledge, comprehending all from bugs to comets. It was merely the doing of the little girl in the red hood.

When Jimmie made up his mind to follow his sweetheart home from school, the project seemed such an arbitrary and shameless innovation that he hastily lied to himself about it. No, he was not following Abbie. He was merely making his way homeward through the new and rather longer route of Bryant Street and Oakland Park. It had nothing at all to do with a girl. It was a mere eccentric notion.

"Come on," said Jimmie, gruffly, to his retainer. "Let's go home this way."

"What fer?" demanded the retainer.

"Oh, b'cause."

"Huh?"

"Oh, it's more fun—goin' this way."

The retainer was bored and loath, but that mattered very little. He did not know how to disobey his chief. Together they followed the trail of red-hooded Abbie and another small girl. These latter at once understood the object of the chase, and looking back giggling, they pretended to quicken their pace. But they were always looking back. Jimmie now began his courtship in earnest. The first thing to do was to prove his strength in battle. This was transacted by means of the retainer. He took that devoted boy and flung him heavily to the ground, meanwhile mouthing a preposterous ferocity.

The retainer accepted this behavior with a sort of bland resignation. After his overthrow he raised himself, coolly brushed some dust and dead leaves from his clothes, and then seemed to forget the incident.

"I can jump farther'n you can," said Jimmie, in a loud voice.

"I know it," responded the retainer, simply.

But this would not do. There must be a contest.

"Come on," shouted Jimmie, imperiously. "Let's see you jump."

The retainer selected a footing on the curb, balanced and calculated a moment, and jumped without enthusiasm. Jimmie's leap of course was longer.

"There!" he cried, blowing out his lips. "I beat you, didn't I? Easy. I beat you." He made a great hubbub, as if the affair was unprecedented.

"Yes," admitted the other, emotionless.

Later, Jimmie forced his retainer to run a race with him, held more jumping matches, flung him twice to earth, and generally behaved as if a retainer was indestructible. If the retainer had been in the plot, it is conceivable that he would have endured this treatment with mere whispered, half-laughing protests. But he was not in the plot at all, and so he became enigmatic. One cannot often sound the profound well in which lie the meanings of boyhood.

Following the two little girls, Jimmie eventually passed into that suburb of Whilomville which is called Oakland Park. At his heels came a badly battered retainer. Oakland Park was a somewhat strange country to the boys. They were dubious of the manners and customs, and of course they would have to meet the local chieftains, who might look askance upon this invasion.

Jimmie's girl departed into her home with a last backward glance that almost blinded the thrilling boy. On this pretext and that pretext, he kept his retainer in play before the house. He had hopes that she would emerge as soon as she had deposited her school-bag.

A boy came along the walk. Jimmie knew him at school. He was Tommie Semple, one of the weaklings who made friends with the fair sex. "Hello, Tom," said Jimmie. "You live round here?"

"Yeh," said Tom, with composed pride. At school he was afraid of Jimmie, but he did not evince any of this fear as he strolled well inside his own frontiers. Jimmie and his retainer had not expected this boy to display the manners of a minor chief, and they contemplated him attentively. There was a silence. Finally Jimmie said:

"I can put you down." He moved forward briskly. "Can't I?" he demanded.

The challenged boy backed away. "I know you can," he declared, frankly and promptly.

The little girl in the red hood had come out with a hoop. She looked at Jimmie with an air of insolent surprise in the fact that he still existed, and began to trundle her hoop off towards some other little girls who were shrilly playing near a nurse-maid and a perambulator.

Jimmie adroitly shifted his position until he too was playing near the perambulator, pretentiously making mince-meat out of his retainer and Tommie Semple.

Of course little Abbie had defined the meaning of Jimmie's appearance in Oakland Park. Despite this nonchalance and grand air of accident, nothing could have been more plain. Whereupon she of course became insufferably vain in manner, and whenever Jimmie came near her she tossed her head and turned away her face, and daintily swished her skirts as if he were contagion itself. But Jimmie was happy. His soul was satisfied with the mere presence of the beloved object so long as he could feel that she furtively gazed upon him from time to time and noted his extraordinary prowess, which he was proving upon the persons of his retainer and Tommie Semple. And he was making an impression. There could be no doubt of it. He had many times caught her eye fixed admiringly upon him as he mauled the retainer. Indeed, all the little girls gave attention to his deeds, and he was the hero of the hour.

Presently a boy on a velocipede was seen to be tooling down towards them. "Who's this comin'?" said Jimmie, bluntly, to the Semple boy.

"That's Horace Glenn," said Tommie, "an' he's got a new velocipede, an' he can ride it like anything."

"Can you lick him?" asked Jimmie.

"I don't—I never fought with 'im," answered the other. He bravely tried to appear as a man of respectable achievement, but with Horace coming towards them the risk was too great. However, he added, *"Maybe* I could."

The advent of Horace on his new velocipede created a sensation which he haughtily accepted as a familiar thing. Only Jimmie and his retainer remained silent and impassive. Horace eyed the two invaders.

"Hello, Jimmie!"

"Hello, Horace!"

After the typical silence Jimmie said, pompously, "I got a velocipede."

"Have you?" asked Horace, anxiously. He did not wish anybody in the world but himself to possess a velocipede.

"Yes," sang Jimmie. "An' it's a bigger one than that, too! A good deal bigger! An' it's a better one, too!"

"Huh!" retorted Horace, sceptically.

"'Ain't I, Clarence? 'Ain't I? 'Ain't I got one bigger'n that?"

The retainer answered with alacrity:

"Yes, he has! A good deal bigger! An' it's a dindy, too!"

This corroboration rather disconcerted Horace, but he continued to scoff at any statement that Jimmie also owned a velocipede. As for the contention that this supposed velocipede could be larger than his own, he simply wouldn't hear of it.

Jimmie had been a very gallant figure before the coming of Horace, but the new velocipede had relegated him to a squalid secondary position. So he affected to look with contempt upon it. Voluminously he bragged of the velocipede in the stable at home. He painted its virtues and beauty in loud and extravagant words, flaming words. And the retainer stood by, glibly endorsing everything.

The little company heeded him, and he passed on vociferously from extravagance to utter impossibility. Horace was very sick of it. His defence was reduced to a mere mechanical grumbling: "Don't believe you got one 'tall. Don't believe you got one 'tall."

Jimmie turned upon him suddenly. "How fast can you go? How fast can you go?" he demanded. "Let's see. I bet you can't go fast."

Horace lifted his spirits and answered with proper defiance. "Can't I?" he mocked. "Can't I?"

"No, you can't," said Jimmie. "You can't go fast."

Horace cried: "Well, you see me now! I'll show you! I'll show you if I can't go fast!" Taking a firm seat on his vermilion machine, he pedalled furiously up the walk, turned, and pedalled back again. "There, now!" he shouted, triumphantly. "Ain't that fast? There, now!" There was a low murmur of appreciation from the little girls. Jimmie saw with pain that even his divinity was smiling upon his rival. "There! Ain't that fast? Ain't that fast?" He strove to pin Jimmie down to an admission. He was exuberant with victory.

Notwithstanding a feeling of discomfiture, Jimmie did not lose a moment of time. "Why," he yelled, "that ain't goin' fast 'tall! That ain't goin' fast 'tall! Why, I can go almost *twice* as fast as that! Almost twice as fast! Can't I, Clarence?"

The royal retainer nodded solemnly at the wide-eyed group. "Course you can!"

"Why," spouted Jimmie, "you just ought to see me ride once! You just ought to see me! Why, I can go like the wind! Can't I, Clarence? And I can ride far, too—oh, awful far! Can't I, Clarence? Why, I wouldn't have that one! 'Tain't any good! You just ought to see mine once!"

The overwhelmed Horace attempted to reconstruct his battered glories. "I can ride right over the curb-stone—at some of the crossin's," he announced, brightly.

Jimmie's derision was a splendid sight. "'*Right over the curb-stone!*' Why, that wouldn't be *nothin'* for me to do! I've rode mine down Bridge Street hill. Yessir! 'Ain't I, Clarence? Why, it ain't nothin' to ride over a curb-stone—not for *me*! Is it, Clarence?"

"Down Bridge Street hill? You never!" said Horace, hopelessly.

"Well, didn't I, Clarence? Didn't I, now?"

The faithful retainer again nodded solemnly at the assemblage.

At last Horace, having fallen as low as was possible, began to display a spirit for climbing up again. "Oh, you can do wonders!" he said, laughing. "You can do wonders! I s'pose you could ride down that bank there?" he asked, with art. He had indicated a grassy terrace some six feet in height which bounded one side of the walk. At the bottom was a small ravine in which the reckless had flung ashes and tins. "I s'pose you could ride down that bank?"

All eyes now turned upon Jimmie to detect a sign of his weakening, but he instantly and sublimely arose to the occasion. "That bank?" he asked, scornfully. "Why, I've ridden down banks like that many a time. 'Ain't I, Clarence?"

This was too much for the company. A sound like the wind in the leaves arose; it was the song of incredulity and ridicule. "O—o—o—o—o!" And on the outskirts a little girl suddenly shrieked out, "Story-teller!"

Horace had certainly won a skirmish. He was gleeful. "Oh, you can do wonders!" he gurgled. "You can do wonders!" The neighborhood's superficial hostility to foreigners arose like magic under the influence of his sudden success, and Horace had the delight of seeing Jimmie persecuted in that manner known only to children and insects.

Jimmie called angrily to the boy on the velocipede, "If you'll lend me yours, I'll show you whether I can or not."

Horace turned his superior nose in the air. "Oh no! I don't ever lend it." Then he thought of a blow which would make Jimmie's humiliation complete. "Besides," he said, airily, "'tain't really anything hard to do. I could do it—easy—if I wanted to."

But his supposed adherents, instead of receiving this boast with cheers, looked upon him in a sudden blank silence. Jimmie and his retainer pounced like cats upon their advantage.

"Oh," they yelled, "you *could*, eh? Well, let's see you do it, then! Let's see you do it! Let's see you do it! Now!" In a moment the crew of little spectators were gibing at Horace.

The blow that would make Jimmie's humiliation complete! Instead, it had boomeranged Horace into the mud. He kept up a sullen muttering:

"'Tain't really anything! I could if I wanted to!"

"Dare you to!" screeched Jimmie and his partisans. "Dare you to! Dare you to! Dare you to!"

There were two things to be done—to make gallant effort or to retreat. Somewhat to their amazement, the children at last found Horace moving through their clamor to the edge of the bank. Sitting on the velocipede, he looked at the ravine, and then, with gloomy pride, at the other children. A hush came upon them, for it was seen that he was intending to make some kind of an ante-mortem statement.

"I—" he began. Then he vanished from the edge of the walk. The start had been unintentional—an accident.

The stupefied Jimmie saw the calamity through a haze. His first clear vision was when Horace, with a face as red as a red flag, arose bawling from his tangled velocipede. He and his retainer exchanged a glance of horror and fled the neighborhood. They did not look back until they had reached the top of the hill near the lake. They could see Horace walking slowly under the maples towards his home, pushing his shattered velocipede before him. His chin was thrown high, and the breeze bore them the sound of his howls.

V. MAKING AN ORATOR

IN the school at Whilomville it was the habit, when children had progressed to a certain class, to have them devote Friday afternoon to what was called elocution. This was in the piteously ignorant belief that orators were thus made. By process of school law, unfortunate boys and girls were dragged up to address their fellow-scholars in the literature of the mid-century. Probably the children who were most capable of expressing themselves, the children who were most sensitive to the power of speech, suffered the most wrong. Little blockheads who could learn eight lines of conventional poetry, and could get up and spin it rapidly at their classmates, did not undergo a single pang. The plan operated mainly to agonize many children permanently against arising to speak their thought to fellow-creatures.

Jimmie Trescott had an idea that by exhibition of undue ignorance he could escape from being promoted into the first class room which exacted such penalty from its inmates. He preferred to dwell in a less classic shade rather than venture into a domain where he was obliged to perform a certain duty which struck him as being worse than death. However, willy-nilly, he was somehow sent ahead into the place of torture.

Every Friday at least ten of the little children had to mount the stage beside the teacher's desk and babble something which none of them understood. This was to make them orators. If it had been ordered that they should croak like frogs, it would have advanced most of them just as far towards oratory.

Alphabetically Jimmie Trescott was near the end of the list of victims, but his time was none the less inevitable. "Tanner, Timmens, Trass, Trescott—" He saw his downfall approaching.

He was passive to the teacher while she drove into his mind the incomprehensible lines of "The Charge of the Light Brigade":

Half a league, half a league,

Half a league onward—

He had no conception of a league. If in the ordinary course of life somebody had told him that he was half a league from home, he might have been frightened that half a league was fifty miles; but he struggled manfully with the valley of death and a mystic six hundred, who were performing something there which was very fine, he had been told. He learned all the verses.

But as his own Friday afternoon approached he was moved to make known to his family that a dreadful disease was upon him, and was likely at any time to prevent him from going to his beloved school.

On the great Friday when the children of his initials were to speak their pieces Dr. Trescott was away from home, and the mother of the boy was alarmed beyond measure at Jimmie's curious illness, which caused him to lie on the rug in front of the fire and groan cavernously.

She bathed his feet in hot mustard water until they were lobster-red. She also placed a mustard plaster on his chest.

He announced that these remedies did him no good at all—no good at all. With an air of martyrdom he endured a perfect downpour of motherly attention all that day. Thus the first Friday was passed in safety.

With singular patience he sat before the fire in the dining-room and looked at picture-books, only complaining of pain when he suspected his mother of thinking that he was getting better.

The next day being Saturday and a holiday, he was miraculously delivered from the arms of disease, and went forth to play, a blatantly healthy boy.

He had no further attack until Thursday night of the next week, when he announced that he felt very, very poorly. The mother was already chronically alarmed over the condition of her son, but Dr. Trescott asked him questions which denoted some incredulity. On the third Friday Jimmie was dropped at the door of the school from the doctor's buggy. The other children, notably those who had already passed over the mountain of distress, looked at him with glee, seeing in him another lamb brought to butchery. Seated at his desk in the school-room, Jimmie sometimes remembered with dreadful distinctness every line of "The Charge of the Light Brigade," and at other times his mind was utterly empty of it. Geography, arithmetic, and spelling—usually great tasks—quite rolled off him. His mind was dwelling with terror upon the time when his name should be called and he was obliged to go up to the platform, turn, bow, and recite his message to his fellow-men.

Desperate expedients for delay came to him. If he could have engaged the services of a real pain, he would have been glad. But steadily, inexorably, the minutes marched on towards his great crisis, and all his plans for escape blended into a mere panic fear.

The maples outside were defeating the weakening rays of the afternoon sun, and in the shadowed school-room had come a stillness, in which, nevertheless, one could feel the complacence of the little pupils who had already passed through the flames. They were calmly prepared to recognize as a spectacle the torture of others.

Little Johnnie Tanner opened the ceremony. He stamped heavily up to the platform, and bowed in such a manner that he almost fell down. He blurted out that it would ill befit him to sit silent while the name of his fair Ireland was being reproached, and he appealed to the gallant soldier before him if every British battle-field was not sown with the bones of sons of the Emerald Isle. He was also heard to say that he had listened with deepening surprise and scorn to the insinuation of the honorable member from North Glenmorganshire that the loyalty of the Irish regiments in her Majesty's service could be questioned. To what purpose, then, he asked, had the blood of Irishmen flowed on a hundred fields? To what purpose had Irishmen gone to their death with bravery and devotion in every part of the world where the victorious flag of England had been carried? If the honorable member for North Glenmorganshire insisted upon construing a mere pothouse row between soldiers in Dublin into a grand treachery to the colors and to her Majesty's uniform, then it was time for Ireland to think bitterly of her dead sons, whose graves now marked every step of England's progress, and yet who could have their honors stripped from them so easily by the honorable member for North Glenmorganshire. Furthermore, the honorable member for North Glenmorganshire—

It is needless to say that little Johnnie Tanner's language made it exceedingly hot for the honorable member for North Glenmorganshire. But Johnnie was not angry. He was only in haste. He finished the honorable member for North Glenmorganshire in what might be called a gallop.

Susie Timmens then went to the platform, and with a face as pale as death whisperingly reiterated that she would be Queen of the May. The child represented there a perfect picture of unnecessary suffering. Her small lips were quite blue, and her eyes, opened wide, stared with a look of horror at nothing.

The phlegmatic Trass boy, with his moon face only expressing peasant parentage, calmly spoke some undeniably true words concerning destiny.

In his seat Jimmie Trescott was going half blind with fear of his approaching doom. He wished that the Trass boy would talk forever about destiny. If the school-house had taken fire he thought that he would have felt simply relief. Anything was better. Death amid the flames was preferable to a recital of "The Charge of the Light Brigade."

But the Trass boy finished his remarks about destiny in a very short time. Jimmie heard the teacher call his name, and he felt the whole world look at him. He did not know how he made his way to the stage. Parts of him seemed to be of lead, and at the same time parts of him seemed to be light as air, detached. His face had gone as pale as had been the face of Susie Timmens. He was simply a child in torment; that is all there is to be said specifically about it; and to intelligent people the exhibition would have been not more edifying than a dog-fight.

He bowed precariously, choked, made an inarticulate sound, and then he suddenly said,

"Half a leg—"

"*League*," said the teacher, coolly.

"Half a leg—"

"*League*," said the teacher.

"*League*," repeated Jimmie, wildly.

"Half a league, half a league, half a league onward."

He paused here and looked wretchedly at the teacher.

"Half a league," he muttered—"half a league—"

He seemed likely to keep continuing this phrase indefinitely, so after a time the teacher said, "Well, go on."

"Half a league," responded Jimmie.

The teacher had the opened book before her, and she read from it:

"'All in the valley of Death
  Rode the—'

Go on," she concluded.

Jimmie said,

"All in the valley of Death

Rode the—the—the—"

He cast a glance of supreme appeal upon the teacher, and breathlessly whispered, "Rode the what?"

The young woman flushed with indignation to the roots of her hair.

"Rode the six hundred,"

she snapped at him.

The class was arustle with delight at this cruel display. They were no better than a Roman populace in Nero's time.

Jimmie started off again:

"Half a leg—league, half a league, half a league onward.

All in the valley of death rode the six hundred.

Forward—forward—forward—"

"The Light Brigade," suggested the teacher, sharply.

"The Light Brigade," said Jimmie. He was about to die of the ignoble pain of his position.

As for Tennyson's lines, they had all gone grandly out of his mind, leaving it a whited wall.

The teacher's indignation was still rampant. She looked at the miserable wretch before her with an angry stare.

"You stay in after school and learn that all over again," she commanded. "And be prepared to speak it next Friday. I am astonished at you, Jimmie. Go to your seat."

If she had suddenly and magically made a spirit of him and left him free to soar high above all the travail of our earthly lives she could not have overjoyed him more. He fled back to his seat without hearing the low-toned gibes of his schoolmates. He gave no thought to the terrors of the next Friday. The evils of the day had been sufficient, and to a childish mind a week is a great space of time.

With the delightful inconsistency of his age he sat in blissful calm, and watched the sufferings of an unfortunate boy named Zimmerman, who was the next victim of education. Jimmie, of course, did not know that on this day there had been laid for him the foundation of a finished incapacity for public speaking which would be his until he died.

VI. SHAME

DON'T come in here botherin' me," said the cook, intolerantly. "What with your mother bein' away on a visit, an' your father comin' home soon to lunch, I have enough on my mind—and that without bein' bothered with *you*. The kitchen is no place for little boys, anyhow. Run away, and don't be interferin' with my work." She frowned and made a grand pretence of being deep in herculean labors; but Jimmie did not run away.

"Now—they're goin' to have a picnic," he said, half audibly.

"What?"

"Now—they're goin' to have a picnic."

"Who's goin' to have a picnic?" demanded the cook, loudly. Her accent could have led one to suppose that if the projectors did not turn out to be the proper parties, she immediately would forbid this picnic.

Jimmie looked at her with more hopefulness. After twenty minutes of futile skirmishing, he had at least succeeded in introducing the subject. To her question he answered, eagerly:

"Oh, everybody! Lots and lots of boys and girls. Everybody."

"Who's everybody?"

According to custom, Jimmie began to singsong through his nose in a quite indescribable fashion an enumeration of the prospective picnickers: "Willie Dalzel an' Dan Earl an' Ella Earl an' Wolcott Margate an' Reeves Margate an' Walter Phelps an' Homer Phelps an' Minnie Phelps an'—oh—lots more girls an'—everybody. An' their mothers an' big sisters too." Then he announced a new bit of information: "They're goin' to have a picnic."

"Well, let them," said the cook, blandly.

Jimmie fidgeted for a time in silence. At last he murmured, "I—now—I thought maybe you'd let me go."

The cook turned from her work with an air of irritation and amazement that Jimmie should still be in the kitchen. "Who's stoppin' you?" she asked, sharply. "I ain't stoppin' you, am I?"

"No," admitted Jimmie, in a low voice.

"Well, why don't you go, then? Nobody's stoppin' you."

"But," said Jimmie, "I—you—now—each fellow has got to take somethin' to eat with 'm."

"Oh ho!" cried the cook, triumphantly. "So that's it, is it? So that's what you've been shyin' round here fer, eh? Well, you may as well take yourself off without more words. What with your mother bein' away on a visit, an' your father comin' home soon to his lunch, I have enough on my mind—an' that without being bothered with *you!*"

Jimmie made no reply, but moved in grief towards the door. The cook continued: "Some people in this house seem to think there's 'bout a thousand cooks in this kitchen. Where I used to work b'fore, there was some reason in 'em. I ain't a horse. A picnic!"

Jimmie said nothing, but he loitered.

"Seems as if I had enough to do, without havin' you come round talkin' about picnics. Nobody ever seems to think of the work I have to do. Nobody ever seems to think of it. Then they come and talk to me about picnics! What do I care about picnics?"

Jimmie loitered.

"Where I used to work b'fore, there was some reason in 'em. I never heard tell of no picnics right on top of your mother bein' away on a visit an' your father comin' home soon to his lunch. It's all foolishness."

Little Jimmie leaned his head flat against the wall and began to weep. She stared at him scornfully. "Cryin', eh? Cryin'? What are you cryin' fer?"

"N-n-nothin'," sobbed Jimmie.

There was a silence, save for Jimmie's convulsive breathing. At length the cook said: "Stop that blubberin', now. Stop it! This kitchen ain't no place fer it. Stop it!... Very well! If you don't stop, I won't give you nothin' to go to the picnic with—there!"

For the moment he could not end his tears. "You never said," he sputtered—"you never said you'd give me anything."

"An' why would I?" she cried, angrily. "Why would I—with you in here a-cryin' an' a-blubberin' an' a-bleatin' round? Enough to drive a woman crazy! I don't see how you could expect me to! The idea!"

Suddenly Jimmie announced: "I've stopped cryin'. I ain't goin' to cry no more 'tall."

"Well, then," grumbled the cook—"well, then, stop it. I've got enough on my mind." It chanced that she was making for luncheon some salmon croquettes. A tin still half full of pinky prepared fish was beside her on the table. Still grumbling, she seized a loaf of bread and, wielding a knife, she cut from this loaf four slices, each of which was as big as a six-shilling novel. She profligately spread them with butter, and jabbing the point of her knife into the salmon-tin, she brought up bits of salmon, which she flung and flattened upon the bread. Then she crashed the pieces of bread together in pairs, much as one would clash cymbals. There was no doubt in her own mind but that she had created two sandwiches.

"There," she cried. "That'll do you all right. Lemme see. What 'll I put 'em in? There—I've got it." She thrust the sandwiches into a small pail and jammed on the lid. Jimmie was ready for the picnic. "Oh, thank you, Mary!" he cried, joyfully, and in a moment he was off, running swiftly.

The picnickers had started nearly half an hour earlier, owing to his inability to quickly attack and subdue the cook, but he knew that the rendezvous was in the grove of tall, pillarlike hemlocks and pines that grew on a rocky knoll at the lake shore. His heart was very light as he sped, swinging his pail. But a few minutes previously his soul had been gloomed in despair; now he was happy. He was going to the picnic, where privilege of participation was to be bought by the contents of the little tin pail.

When he arrived in the outskirts of the grove he heard a merry clamor, and when he reached the top of the knoll he looked down the slope upon a scene which almost made his little breast burst with joy. They actually had two camp-fires! Two camp-fires! At one of them Mrs. Earl was making something—chocolate, no doubt—and at the other a young lady in white duck and a sailor hat was dropping eggs into boiling water. Other grown-up people had spread a white cloth and were laying upon it things from baskets. In the deep cool shadow of the trees the children scurried, laughing. Jimmie hastened forward to join his friends.

Homer Phelps caught first sight of him. "Ho!" he shouted; "here comes Jimmie Trescott! Come on, Jimmie; you be on our side!" The children had divided themselves into two bands for some purpose of play. The others of Homer Phelps's party loudly endorsed his plan. "Yes, Jimmie, you be on our side." Then arose the usual dispute. "Well, we got the weakest side."

"'Tain't any weaker'n ours."

Homer Phelps suddenly started, and looking hard, said, "What you got in the pail, Jim?"

Jimmie answered, somewhat uneasily, "Got m' lunch in it."

Instantly that brat of a Minnie Phelps simply tore down the sky with her shrieks of derision. "Got his *lunch* in it! In a *pail!*" She ran screaming to her mother. "Oh, mamma! Oh, mamma! Jimmie Trescott's got his picnic in a pail!"

Now there was nothing in the nature of this fact to particularly move the others—notably the boys, who were not competent to care if he had brought his luncheon in a coal-bin; but such is the instinct of childish society that they all immediately moved away from him. In a moment he had been made a social leper. All old intimacies were flung into the lake, so to speak. They dared not compromise themselves. At safe distances the boys shouted, scornfully: "Huh! Got his picnic in a pail!" Never again during that picnic did the little girls speak of him as Jimmie Trescott. His name now was Him.

His mind was dark with pain as he stood, the hangdog, kicking the gravel, and muttering as defiantly as he was able, "Well, I can have it in a pail if I want to." This statement of freedom was of no importance, and he knew it, but it was the only idea in his head.

He had been baited at school for being detected in writing a letter to little Cora, the angel child, and he had known how to defend himself, but this situation was in no way similar. This was a social affair, with grown people on all sides. It would be sweet to catch the Margate twins, for instance, and hammer them into a state of bleating respect for his pail; but that was a matter for the jungles of childhood, where grown folk seldom penetrated. He could only glower.

The amiable voice of Mrs. Earl suddenly called: "Come, children! Everything's ready!" They scampered away, glancing back for one last gloat at Jimmie standing there with his pail.

He did not know what to do. He knew that the grown folk expected him at the spread, but if he approached he would be greeted by a shameful chorus from the children—more especially from some of those damnable little girls. Still, luxuries beyond all dreaming were heaped on that cloth. One could not forget them. Perhaps if he crept up modestly, and was very gentle and very nice to the little girls, they would allow him peace. Of course it had been dreadful to come with a pail to such a grand picnic, but they might forgive him.

Oh no, they would not! He knew them better. And then suddenly he remembered with what delightful expectations he had raced to this grove, and self-pity overwhelmed him, and he thought he wanted to die and make every one feel sorry.

The young lady in white duck and a sailor hat looked at him, and then spoke to her sister, Mrs. Earl. "Who's that hovering in the distance, Emily?"

Mrs. Earl peered. "Why, it's Jimmie Trescott! Jimmie, come to the picnic! Why don't you come to the picnic, Jimmie?" He began to sidle towards the cloth.

But at Mrs. Earl's call there was another outburst from many of the children. "He's got his picnic in a pail! In a *pail*! Got it in a pail!"

Minnie Phelps was a shrill fiend. "Oh, mamma, he's got it in that pail! See! Isn't it funny? Isn't it dreadful funny?"

"What ghastly prigs children are, Emily!" said the young lady. "They are spoiling that boy's whole day, breaking his heart, the little cats! I think I'll go over and talk to him."

"Maybe you had better not," answered Mrs. Earl, dubiously. "Somehow these things arrange themselves. If you interfere, you are likely to prolong everything."

"Well, I'll try, at least," said the young lady.

At the second outburst against him Jimmie had crouched down by a tree, half hiding behind it, half pretending that he was not hiding behind it. He turned his sad gaze towards the lake. The bit of water seen through the shadows seemed perpendicular, a slate-colored wall. He heard a noise near him, and turning, he perceived the young lady looking down at him. In her hand she held plates. "May I sit near you?" she asked, coolly.

Jimmie could hardly believe his ears. After disposing herself and the plates upon the pine needles, she made brief explanation. "They're rather crowded, you see, over there. I don't like to be crowded at a picnic, so I thought I'd come here. I hope you don't mind."

Jimmie made haste to find his tongue. "Oh, I don't mind! I *like* to have you here." The ingenuous emphasis made it appear that the fact of his liking to have her there was in the nature of a law-dispelling phenomenon, but she did not smile.

"How large is that lake?" she asked.

Jimmie, falling into the snare, at once began to talk in the manner of a proprietor of the lake. "Oh, it's almost twenty miles long, an' in one place it's almost four miles wide! an' it's *deep* too—awful deep—an' it's got real steamboats on it, an'—oh—lots of other boats, an'—an'—an'—"

"Do you go out on it sometimes?"

"Oh, lots of times! My father's got a boat," he said, eying her to note the effect of his words.

She was correctly pleased and struck with wonder. "Oh, has he?" she cried, as if she never before had heard of a man owning a boat.

Jimmie continued: "Yes, an' it's a grea' big boat, too, with sails, real sails; an' sometimes he takes me out in her, too; an' once he took me fishin', an' we had sandwiches, plenty of 'em, an' my father he drank beer right out of the bottle—*right out of the bottle!*"

The young lady was properly overwhelmed by this amazing intelligence. Jimmie saw the impression he had created, and he enthusiastically resumed his narrative: "An' after, he let me throw the bottles in the water, and I throwed 'em 'way, 'way, 'way out. An' they sank, an'—never comed up," he concluded, dramatically.

His face was glorified; he had forgotten all about the pail; he was absorbed in this communion with a beautiful lady who was so interested in what he had to say.

She indicated one of the plates, and said, indifferently: "Perhaps you would like some of those sandwiches. I made them. Do you like olives? And there's a deviled egg. I made that also."

"Did you really?" said Jimmie, politely. His face gloomed for a moment because the pail was recalled to his mind, but he timidly possessed himself of a sandwich.

"Hope you are not going to scorn my deviled egg," said his goddess. "I am very proud of it." He did not; he scorned little that was on the plate.

Their gentle intimacy was ineffable to the boy. He thought he had a friend, a beautiful lady, who liked him more than she did anybody at the picnic, to say the least. This was proved by the fact that she had flung aside the luxuries of the spread cloth to sit with him, the exile. Thus early did he fall a victim to woman's wiles.

"Where do you live?" he asked, suddenly.

"Oh, a long way from here! In New York."

His next question was put very bluntly. "Are you married?"

"Oh no!" she answered, gravely.

Jimmie was silent for a time, during which he glanced shyly and furtively up at her face. It was evident that he was somewhat embarrassed. Finally he said, "When I grow up to be a man—"

"Oh, that is some time yet!" said the beautiful lady.

"But when I *do*, I—I should like to marry you."

"Well, I will remember it," she answered; "but don't talk of it now, because it's such a long time; and—I wouldn't wish you to consider yourself bound." She smiled at him.

He began to brag. "When I grow up to be a man, I'm goin' to have lots an' lots of money, an' I'm goin' to have a grea' big house, an' a horse an' a shot-gun, an' lots an' lots of books 'bout elephants an' tigers, an' lots an' lots of ice-cream an' pie an'—caramels." As before, she was impressed; he could see it. "An' I'm goin' to have lots an' lots of children—'bout three hundred, I guess—an' there won't none of 'em be girls. They'll all be boys—like me."

"Oh, my!" she said.

His garment of shame was gone from him. The pail was dead and well buried. It seemed to him that months elapsed as he dwelt in happiness near the beautiful lady and trumpeted his vanity.

At last there was a shout. "Come on! we're going home." The picnickers trooped out of the grove. The children wished to resume their jeering, for Jimmie still gripped his pail, but they were restrained by the circumstances. He was walking at the side of the beautiful lady.

During this journey he abandoned many of his habits. For instance, he never travelled without skipping gracefully from crack to crack between the stones, or without pretending that he was a train of cars, or without some mumming device of childhood. But now he behaved with dignity. He made no more noise than a little mouse. He escorted the beautiful lady to the gate of the Earl home, where he awkwardly, solemnly, and wistfully shook hands in good-by. He watched her go up the walk; the door clanged.

On his way home he dreamed. One of these dreams was fascinating. Supposing the beautiful lady was his teacher in school! Oh, my! wouldn't he be a good boy, sitting like a statuette all day long, and knowing every lesson to perfection, and—everything. And then supposing that a boy should sass her. Jimmie painted himself waylaying that boy on the homeward road, and the fate of the boy was a thing to make strong men cover their eyes with their hands. And she would like him more and more—more and more. And he— he would be a little god.

But as he was entering his father's grounds an appalling recollection came to him. He was returning with the bread-and-butter and the salmon untouched in the pail! He could imagine the cook, nine feet tall, waving her fist. "An' so that's what I took trouble for, is it? So's you could bring it back? So's you could bring it back?" He skulked towards the house like a marauding bushranger. When he neared the kitchen door he made a desperate rush past it, aiming to gain the stables and there secrete his guilt. He was nearing them, when a thunderous voice hailed him from the rear:

"Jimmie Trescott, where you goin' with that pail?"

It was the cook. He made no reply, but plunged into the shelter of the stables. He whirled the lid from the pail and dashed its contents beneath a heap of blankets. Then he stood panting, his eyes on the door. The cook did not pursue, but she was bawling:

"Jimmie Trescott, what you doin' with that pail?"

He came forth, swinging it. "Nothin'," he said, in virtuous protest.

"I know better," she said, sharply, as she relieved him of his curse.

In the morning Jimmie was playing near the stable, when he heard a shout from Peter Washington, who attended Dr. Trescott's horse:

"Jim! Oh, Jim!"

"What?"

"Come yah."

Jimmie went reluctantly to the door of the stable, and Peter Washington asked:

"Wut's dish yere fish an' brade doin' unner dese yer blankups?"

"I don't know. I didn't have nothin' to do with it," answered Jimmie, indignantly.

"Don' tell *me!*" cried Peter Washington, as he flung it all away—"don' tell *me!* When I fin' fish an' brade unner dese yer blankups, I don' go an' think dese yer ho'ses er yer pop's put 'em. I *know.* An' if I caitch enny more dish yer fish an' brade in dish yer stable, I'*ll* tell yer pop."

VII. THE CARRIAGE-LAMPS

IT was the fault of a small nickel-plated revolver, a most incompetent weapon, which, wherever one aimed, would fling the bullet as the devil willed, and no man, when about to use it, could tell exactly what was in store for the surrounding country. This treasure had been acquired by Jimmie Trescott after arduous bargaining with another small boy. Jimmie wended homeward, patting his hip pocket at every three paces.

Peter Washington, working in the carriage-house, looked out upon him with a shrewd eye. "Oh, Jim," he called, "wut you got in yer hind pocket?"

"Nothin'," said Jimmie, feeling carefully under his jacket to make sure that the revolver wouldn't fall out.

Peter chuckled. "S'more foolishness, I raikon. You gwine be hung one day, Jim, you keep up all dish yer nonsense."

Jimmie made no reply, but went into the back garden, where he hid the revolver in a box under a lilac-bush. Then he returned to the vicinity of Peter, and began to cruise to and fro in the offing, showing all the signals of one wishing to open treaty. "Pete," he said, "how much does a box of cartridges cost?"

Peter raised himself violently, holding in one hand a piece of harness, and in the other an old rag. "Ca'tridgers! *Ca'tridgers!* Lan'sake! wut the kid want with ca'tridgers? Knew it! Knew it! Come home er-holdin' on to his hind pocket like he got money in it. An' now he want ca'tridgers."

Jimmie, after viewing with dismay the excitement caused by his question, began to move warily out of the reach of a possible hostile movement.

"Ca'tridgers!" continued Peter, in scorn and horror. "Kid like you! No bigger'n er minute! Look yah, Jim, you done been swappin' round, an' you done got hol' of er pistol!" The charge was dramatic.

The wind was almost knocked out of Jimmie by this display of Peter's terrible miraculous power, and as he backed away his feeble denials were more convincing than a confession.

"I'll tell yer pop!" cried Peter, in virtuous grandeur. "I'll tell yer pop!"

In the distance Jimmie stood appalled. He knew not what to do. The dread adult wisdom of Peter Washington had laid bare the sin, and disgrace stared at Jimmie.

There was a whirl of wheels, and a high, lean trotting-mare spun Doctor Trescott's buggy towards Peter, who ran forward busily. As the doctor climbed out, Peter, holding the mare's head, began his denunciation:

"Docteh, I gwine tell on Jim. He come home er-holdin' on to his hind pocket, an' proud like he won a tuhkey-raffle, an' I sure know what he been up to, an' I done challenge him, an' he nev' say he didn't."

"Why, what do you mean?" said the doctor. "What's this, Jimmie?"

The boy came forward, glaring wrathfully at Peter. In fact, he suddenly was so filled with rage at Peter that he forgot all precautions. "It's about a pistol," he said, bluntly. "I've got a pistol. I swapped for it."

"I done tol' 'im his pop wouldn' stand no fiah-awms, an' him a kid like he is. I done tol' 'im. Lan' sake! he strut like he was a soldier! Come in yere proud, an' er-holdin' on to his hind pocket. He think he was Jesse James, I raikon. But I done tol' 'im his pop stan' no sech foolishness. First thing—*blam*—he shoot his haid off. No, seh, he too tinety t' come in yere er-struttin' like he jest bought Main Street. I tol' 'im. I done tol' 'im—shawp. I don' wanter be loafin' round dis yer stable if Jim he gwine go shootin' round an' shootin' round—*blim—blam—blim—blam*! No, seh. I retiahs. I retiahs. It's all right if er grown man got er gun, but ain't no kids come foolishin' round *me* with fiah-awms. No, seh. I retiahs."

"Oh, be quiet, Peter!" said the doctor. "Where is this thing, Jimmie?"

The boy went sulkily to the box under the lilac-bush and returned with the revolver. "Here 'tis," he said, with a glare over his shoulder at Peter. The doctor looked at the silly weapon in critical contempt.

"It's not much of a thing, Jimmie, but I don't think you are quite old enough for it yet. I'll keep it for you in one of the drawers of my desk."

Peter Washington burst out proudly: "I done tol' 'im th' docteh wouldn' stan' no traffickin' round yere with fiah-awms. I done tol' 'im."

Jimmie and his father went together into the house, and as Peter unharnessed the mare he continued his comments on the boy and the revolver. He was not cast down by the absence of hearers. In fact, he usually talked better when there was no one to listen save the horses. But now his observations bore small resemblance to his earlier and public statements. Admiration and the keen family pride of a Southern negro who has been long in one place were now in his tone.

"That boy! He's er devil! When he get to be er man—wow! He'll jes take an' make things whirl round yere. Raikon we'll all take er back seat when he come erlong er-raisin' Cain."

He had unharnessed the mare, and with his back bent was pushing the buggy into the carriage-house.

"Er pistol! An' him no bigger than er minute!"

A small stone whizzed past Peter's head and clattered on the stable. He hastily dropped all occupation and struck a curious attitude. His right knee was almost up to his chin, and his arms were wreathed protectingly about his head. He had not looked in the direction from which the stone had come, but he had begun immediately to yell:

"You Jim! Quit! Quit, I tell yer, Jim! Watch out! You gwine break somethin', Jim!"

"Yah!" taunted the boy, as with the speed and ease of a light-cavalryman he manœuvred in the distance. "Yah! Told on me, did you! Told on me, hey! There! How do you like that?" The missiles resounded against the stable.

"Watch out, Jim! You gwine break something, Jim, I tell yer! Quit yer foolishness, Jim! Ow! Watch out, boy! I—"

There was a crash. With diabolic ingenuity, one of Jimmie's pebbles had entered the carriage-house and had landed among a row of carriage-lamps on a shelf, creating havoc which was apparently beyond all reason of physical law. It seemed to Jimmie that the racket of falling glass could have been heard in an adjacent county.

Peter was a prophet who after persecution was suffered to recall everything to the mind of the persecutor. "*There!* Knew it! Knew it! *Now* I raikon you'll quit. Hi! jes look ut dese yer lamps! Fer lan' sake! Oh, now yer pop jes break ev'ry bone in yer body!"

In the doorway of the kitchen the cook appeared with a startled face. Jimmie's father and mother came suddenly out on the front veranda. "What was that noise?" called the the doctor.

Peter went forward to explain. "Jim he was er-heavin' rocks at me, docteh, an' erlong come one rock an' go *blam* inter all th' lamps an' jes skitter 'em t' bits. I declayah—"

Jimmie, half blinded with emotion, was nevertheless aware of a lightning glance from his father, a glance which cowed and frightened him to the ends of his toes. He heard the steady but deadly tones of his father in a fury: "Go into the house and wait until I come."

Bowed in anguish, the boy moved across the lawn and up the steps. His mother was standing on the veranda still gazing towards the stable. He loitered in the faint hope that she might take some small pity on his state. But she could have heeded him no less if he had been invisible. He entered the house.

When the doctor returned from his investigation of the harm done by Jimmie's hand, Mrs. Trescott looked at him anxiously, for she knew that he was concealing some volcanic impulses. "Well?" she asked.

"It isn't the lamps," he said at first. He seated himself on the rail. "I don't know what we are going to do with that boy. It isn't so much the lamps as it is the other thing. He was throwing stones at Peter because Peter told me about the revolver. What are we going to do with him?"

"I'm sure I don't know," replied the mother. "We've tried almost everything. Of course much of it is pure animal spirits. Jimmie is not naturally vicious—"

"Oh, I know," interrupted the doctor, impatiently. "Do you suppose, when the stones were singing about Peter's ears, he cared whether they were flung by a boy who was naturally vicious or a boy who was not? The question might interest him afterward, but at the time he was mainly occupied in dodging these effects of pure animal spirits."

"Don't be too hard on the boy, Ned. There's lots of time yet. He's so young yet, and—I believe he gets most of his naughtiness from that wretched Dalzel boy. That Dalzel boy—well, he's simply awful!" Then, with true motherly instinct to shift blame from her own boy's shoulders, she proceeded to sketch the character of the Dalzel boy in lines that would have made that talented young vagabond stare. It was not admittedly her feeling that the doctor's attention should be diverted from the main issue and his indignation divided among the camps, but presently the doctor felt himself burn with wrath for the Dalzel boy.

"Why don't you keep Jimmie away from him?" he demanded. "Jimmie has no business consorting with abandoned little predestined jail-birds like him. If I catch him on the place I'll box his ears."

"It is simply impossible, unless we kept Jimmie shut up all the time," said Mrs. Trescott. "I can't watch him every minute of the day, and the moment my back is turned, he's off."

"I should think those Dalzel people would hire somebody to bring up their child for them," said the doctor. "They don't seem to know how to do it themselves."

Presently you would have thought from the talk that one Willie Dalzel had been throwing stones at Peter Washington because Peter Washington had told Doctor Trescott that Willie Dalzel had come into possession of a revolver.

In the mean time Jimmie had gone into the house to await the coming of his father. He was in a rebellious mood. He had not intended to destroy the carriage-lamps. He had been merely hurling stones at a creature whose perfidy deserved such action, and the hitting of the lamps had been merely another move of the great conspirator Fate to force one Jimmie Trescott into dark and troublous ways. The boy was beginning to find the world a bitter place. He couldn't win appreciation for a single virtue; he could only achieve quick, rigorous punishment for his misdemeanors. Everything was an enemy. Now there were those silly old lamps—what were they doing up on that shelf, anyhow? It would have been just as easy for them at the time to have been in some other place. But no; there they had been, like the crowd that is passing under the wall when the mason for the first time in twenty years lets fall a brick. Furthermore, the flight of that stone had been perfectly unreasonable. It had been a sort of freak in physical law. Jimmie understood that he might have thrown stones from the same fatal spot for an hour without hurting a single lamp. He was a victim—that was it. Fate had conspired with the detail of his environment to simply hound him into a grave or into a cell.

But who would understand? Who would understand? And here the boy turned his mental glance in every direction, and found nothing but what was to him the black of cruel ignorance. Very well; some day they would—

From somewhere out in the street he heard a peculiar whistle of two notes. It was the common signal of the boys in the neighborhood, and judging from the direction of the sound, it was apparently intended to summon him. He moved immediately to one of the windows of the sitting-room. It opened upon a part of the grounds remote from the stables and cut off from the veranda by a wing. He perceived Willie Dalzel loitering in the street. Jimmie whistled the signal after having pushed up the window-sash some inches. He saw the Dalzel boy turn and regard him, and then call several other boys. They stood in a group and gestured. These gestures plainly said: "Come out. We've got something on hand." Jimmie sadly shook his head.

But they did not go away. They held a long consultation. Presently Jimmie saw the intrepid Dalzel boy climb the fence and begin to creep among the shrubbery, in elaborate imitation of an Indian scout. In time he arrived under Jimmie's window, and raised his face to whisper: "Come on out! We're going on a bear-hunt."

A bear-hunt! Of course Jimmie knew that it would not be a real bear-hunt, but would be a sort of carouse of pretension and big talking and preposterous lying and valor, wherein each boy would strive to have himself called Kit Carson by the others. He was profoundly affected. However, the parental word was upon him, and he could not move. "No," he answered, "I can't. I've got to stay in."

"Are you a prisoner?" demanded the Dalzel boy, eagerly.

"No-o—yes—I s'pose I am."

The other lad became much excited, but he did not lose his wariness. "Don't you want to be rescued?"

"Why—no—I dun'no'," replied Jimmie, dubiously.

Willie Dalzel was indignant. "Why, of course you want to be rescued! We'll rescue you. I'll go and get my men." And thinking this a good sentence, he repeated, pompously, "I'll go and get my men." He began to crawl away, but when he was distant some ten paces he turned to say: "Keep up a stout heart. Remember that you have friends who will be faithful unto death. The time is not now far off when you will again view the blessed sunlight."

The poetry of these remarks filled Jimmie with ecstasy, and he watched eagerly for the coming of the friends who would be faithful unto death. They delayed some time, for the reason that Willie Dalzel was making a speech.

"Now, men," he said, "our comrade is a prisoner in yon—in yond—in that there fortress. We must to the rescue. Who volunteers to go with me?" He fixed them with a stern eye.

There was a silence, and then one of the smaller boys remarked,

"If Doc Trescott ketches us trackin' over his lawn—"

Willie Dalzel pounced upon the speaker and took him by the throat. The two presented a sort of a burlesque of the wood-cut on the cover of a dime novel which Willie had just been reading—*The Red Captain: A Tale of the Pirates of the Spanish Main.*

"You are a coward!" said Willie, through his clinched teeth.

"No, I ain't, Willie," piped the other, as best he could.

"I say you are," cried the great chieftain, indignantly. "Don't tell me I'm a liar." He relinquished his hold upon the coward and resumed his speech. "You know me, men. Many of you have been my followers for long years. You saw me slay Six-handed Dick with my own hand. You know I never falter. Our comrade is a prisoner in the cruel hands of our enemies. Aw, Pete Washington? He dassent. My pa says if Pete ever troubles me he'll brain 'im. Come on! To the rescue! Who will go with me to the rescue? Aw, come on! What are you afraid of?"

It was another instance of the power of eloquence upon the human mind. There was only one boy who was not thrilled by this oration, and he was a boy whose favorite reading had been of the road-agents and gun-fighters of the great West, and he thought the whole thing should be conducted in the Deadwood Dick manner. This talk of a "comrade" was silly; "pard" was the proper word. He resolved that he would make a show of being a pirate, and keep secret the fact that he really was Hold-up Harry, the Terror of the Sierras.

But the others were knit close in piratical bonds. One by one they climbed the fence at a point hidden from the house by tall shrubs. With many a low-breathed caution they went upon their perilous adventure.

Jimmie was grown tired of waiting for his friends who would be faithful unto death. Finally he decided that he would rescue himself. It would be a gross breach of rule, but he couldn't sit there all the rest of the day waiting for his faithful-unto-death friends. The window was only five feet from the ground. He softly raised the sash and threw one leg over the sill. But at the same time he perceived his friends snaking among the bushes. He withdrew his leg and waited, seeing that he was now to be rescued in an orthodox way. The brave pirates came nearer and nearer.

Jimmie heard a noise of a closing door, and turning, he saw his father in the room looking at him and the open window in angry surprise. Boys never faint, but Jimmie probably came as near to it as may the average boy.

"What's all this?" asked the doctor, staring. Involuntarily Jimmie glanced over his shoulder through the window. His father saw the creeping figures. "What are those boys doing?" he said, sharply, and he knit his brows.

"Nothin'."

"Nothing! Don't tell me that. Are they coming here to the window?"

"Y-e-s, sir."

"What for?"

"To—to see me."

"What about?"

"About—about nothin'."

"What about?"

Jimmie knew that he could conceal nothing.

He said, "They're comin' to—to—to rescue me." He began to whimper.

The doctor sat down heavily.

"What? To rescue you?" he gasped.

"Y-yes, sir."

The doctor's eyes began to twinkle. "Very well," he said presently. "I will sit here and observe this rescue. And on no account do you warn them that I am here. Understand?"

Of course Jimmie understood. He had been mad to warn his friends, but his father's mere presence had frightened him from doing it. He stood trembling at the window, while the doctor stretched in an easy-chair near at hand. They waited. The doctor could tell by his son's increasing agitation that the great moment was near. Suddenly he heard Willie Dalzel's voice hiss out a word: "S-s-silence!" Then the same voice addressed Jimmie at the window: "Good cheer, my comrade. The time is now at hand. I have come. Never did the Red Captain turn his back on a friend. One minute more and you will be free. Once aboard my gallant craft and you can bid defiance to your haughty enemies. Why don't you hurry up? What are you standin' there lookin' like a cow for?"

"I—er—now—you—" stammered Jimmie.

Here Hold-up Harry, the Terror of the Sierras, evidently concluded that Willie Dalzel had had enough of the premier part, so he said:

"Brace up, pard. Don't ye turn white-livered now, fer ye know that Hold-up Harry, the Terrar of the Sarahs, ain't the man ter—"

"Oh, stop it!" said Willie Dalzel. "He won't understand that, you know. He's a pirate. Now, Jimmie, come on. Be of light heart, my comrade. Soon you—"

"I 'low arter all this here long time in jail ye thought ye had no friends mebbe, but I tell ye Hold-up Harry, the Terrar of the Sarahs—"

"A boat is waitin'—"

"I have ready a trusty horse—"

Willie Dalzel could endure his rival no longer.

"Look here, Henry, you're spoilin' the whole thing. We're all pirates, don't you see, and you're a pirate too."

"I ain't a pirate. I'm Hold-up Harry, the Terrar of the Sarahs."

"You ain't, I say," said Willie, in despair. "You're spoilin' everything, you are. All right, now. You wait. I'll fix you for this, see if I don't! Oh, come on, Jimmie. A boat awaits us at the foot of the rocks. In one short hour you'll be free forever from your ex—exewable enemies, and their vile plots. Hasten, for the dawn approaches."

The suffering Jimmie looked at his father, and was surprised at what he saw. The doctor was doubled up like a man with the colic. He was breathing heavily. The boy turned again to his friends. "I—now—look here," he began, stumbling among the words. "You—I—I don't think I'll be rescued to-day."

The pirates were scandalized. "What?" they whispered, angrily. "Ain't you goin' to be rescued? Well, all right for you, Jimmie Trescott. That's a nice way to act, that is!" Their upturned eyes glowered at Jimmie.

Suddenly Doctor Trescott appeared at the window with Jimmie. "Oh, go home, boys!" he gasped, but they did not hear him. Upon the instant they had whirled and scampered away like deer. The first lad to reach the fence was the Red Captain, but Hold-up Harry, the Terror of the Sierras, was so close that there was little to choose between them.

Doctor Trescott lowered the window, and then spoke to his son in his usual quiet way. "Jimmie, I wish you would go and tell Peter to have the buggy ready at seven o'clock."

"Yes, sir," said Jimmie, and he swaggered

out to the stables. "Pete, father wants the buggy ready at seven o'clock."

Peter paid no heed to this order, but with the tender sympathy of a true friend he inquired, "Hu't?"

"Hurt? Did what hurt?"

"Yer trouncin'."

"Trouncin'!" said Jimmie, contemptuously. "I didn't get any trouncin'."

"No?" said Peter. He gave Jimmie a quick shrewd glance, and saw that he was telling the truth. He began to mutter and mumble over his work. "Ump! Ump! Dese yer white folks act like they think er boy's made er glass. No trouncin'! Ump!" He was consumed with curiosity to learn why Jimmie had not felt a heavy parental hand, but he did not care to lower his dignity by asking questions about it. At last, however, he reached the limits of his endurance, and in a voice pretentiously careless he asked, "Didn' yer pop take on like mad er-bout dese yer cay'ge-lamps?"

"Carriage-lamps?" inquired Jimmie.

"Ump."

"No, he didn't say anything about carriage-lamps—not that I remember. Maybe he did, though. Lemme see.... No, he never mentioned 'em."

VIII. THE KNIFE

I

SI BRYANT'S place was on the shore of the lake, and his garden-patch, shielded from the north by a bold little promontory and a higher ridge inland, was accounted the most successful and surprising in all Whilomville township. One afternoon Si was working in the garden-patch, when Doctor Trescott's man, Peter Washington, came trudging slowly along the road, observing nature. He scanned the white man's fine agricultural results. "Take your eye off them there mellons, you rascal," said Si, placidly.

The negro's face widened in a grin of delight. "Well, Mist' Bryant, I raikon I ain't on'y make m'se'f covertous er-lookin' at dem yere mellums, sure 'nough. Dey suhtainly is grand."

"That's all right," responded Si, with affected bitterness of spirit. "That's all right. Just don't you admire 'em too much, that's all." Peter chuckled and chuckled. "Ma Lode! Mist' Bryant, y-y-you don' think I'm gwine come prowlin' in dish yer gawden?"

"No, I know you hain't," said Si, with solemnity. "B'cause, if you did, I'd shoot you so full of holes you couldn't tell yourself from a sponge."

"Um—no, seh! No, seh! I don' raikon you'll get chance at Pete, Mist' Bryant. No, seh. I'll take an' run 'long an' rob er bank 'fore I'll come foolishin' 'round *your* gawden, Mist' Bryant."

Bryant, gnarled and strong as an old tree, leaned on his hoe, and laughed a Yankee laugh. His mouth remained tightly closed, but the sinister lines which ran from the sides of his nose to the meetings of his lips developed to form a comic oval, and he emitted a series of grunts, while his eyes gleamed merrily and his shoulders shook. Pete, on the contrary, threw back his head and guffawed thunderously. The effete joke in regard to an American negro's fondness for watermelons was still an admirable pleasantry to them, and this was not the first time they had engaged in badinage over it. In fact, this venerable survival had formed between them a friendship of casual roadside quality.

Afterwards Peter went on up the road. He continued to chuckle until he was far away. He was going to pay a visit to old Alek Williams, a negro who lived with a large family in a hut clinging to the side of a mountain. The scattered colony of negroes which hovered near Whilomville was of interesting origin, being the result of some contrabands who had drifted as far north as Whilomville during the great civil war. The descendants of these adventurers were mainly conspicuous for their bewildering number, and the facility which they possessed for adding even to this number. Speaking, for example, of the Jacksons—one couldn't hurl a stone into the hills about Whilomville without having it land on the roof of a hut full of Jacksons. The town reaped little in labor from these curious suburbs. There were a few men who came in regularly to work in gardens, to drive teams, to care for horses, and there were a few women who came in to cook or to wash. These latter had usually drunken husbands. In the main the colony loafed in high spirits, and the industrious minority gained no direct honor from their fellows, unless they spent their earnings on raiment, in which case they were naturally treated with distinction. On the whole, the hardships of these people were the wind, the rain, the snow, and any other physical difficulties which they could cultivate. About twice a year the lady philanthropists of Whilomville went up against them, and came away poorer in goods but rich in complacence. After one of these attacks the colony would preserve a comic air of rectitude for two days, and then relapse again to the genial irresponsibility of a crew of monkeys.

Peter Washington was one of the industrious class who occupied a position of distinction, for he surely spent his money on personal decoration. On occasion he could dress better than the Mayor of Whilomville himself, or at least in more colors, which was the main thing to the minds of his admirers. His ideal had been the late gallant Henry Johnson, whose conquests in Watermelon Alley, as well as in the hill shanties, had proved him the equal if not the superior of any Pullman-car porter in the country. Perhaps Peter had too much Virginia laziness and humor in him to be a wholly adequate successor to the fastidious Henry Johnson, but, at any rate, he admired his memory so attentively as to be openly termed a dude by envious people.

On this afternoon he was going to call on old Alek Williams because Alek's eldest girl was just turned seventeen, and, to Peter's mind, was a triumph of beauty. He was not wearing his best clothes, because on his last visit Alek's half-breed hound Susie had taken occasion to forcefully extract a quite large and valuable part of the visitor's trousers. When Peter arrived at the end of the rocky field which contained old Alek's shanty he stooped and provided himself with several large stones, weighing them carefully in his hand, and finally continuing his journey with three stones of about eight ounces each. When he was near the house, three gaunt hounds, Rover and Carlo and Susie, came sweeping down upon him. His impression was that they were going to climb him as if he were a tree, but at the critical moment they swerved and went growling and snapping around him, their heads low, their eyes malignant. The afternoon caller waited until Susie presented her side to him, then he heaved one of his eight-ounce rocks. When it landed, her hollow ribs gave forth a drumlike sound, and she was knocked sprawling, her legs in the air. The other hounds at once fled in horror, and she followed as soon as she was able, yelping at the top of her lungs. The afternoon caller resumed his march.

At the wild expressions of Susie's anguish old Alek had flung open the door and come hastily into the sunshine. "Yah, you Suse, come erlong outa dat now. What fer you—Oh, how do, how do, Mist' Wash'ton—how do?"

"How do, Mist' Willums? I done foun' it necessa'y fer ter damnearkill dish yer dawg a yourn, Mist' Willums."

"Come in, come in, Mist' Wash'ton. Dawg no 'count, Mist' Wash'ton." Then he turned to address the unfortunate animal. "Hu't, did it? Hu't? 'Pears like you gwine dun some saince by time somebody brek yer back. 'Pears like I gwine club yer inter er frazzle 'fore you fin' out some saince. Gw'on 'way f'm yah!"

As the old man and his guest entered the shanty a body of black children spread out in crescent-shape formation and observed Peter with awe. Fat old Mrs. Williams greeted him turbulently, while the eldest girl, Mollie, lurked in a corner and giggled with finished imbecility, gazing at the visitor with eyes that were shy and bold by turns. She seemed at times absurdly over-confident, at times foolishly afraid; but her giggle consistently endured. It was a giggle on which an irascible but right-minded judge would have ordered her forthwith to be buried alive.

Amid a great deal of hospitable gabbling, Peter was conducted to the best chair out of the three that the house contained. Enthroned therein, he made himself charming in talk to the old people, who beamed upon him joyously. As for Mollie, he affected to be unaware of her existence. This may have been a method for entrapping the sentimental interest of that young gazelle, or it may be that the giggle had worked upon him.

He was absolutely fascinating to the old people. They could talk like rotary snow-ploughs, and he gave them every chance, while his face was illumined with appreciation. They pressed him to stay for supper, and he consented, after a glance at the pot on the stove which was too furtive to be noted.

During the meal old Alek recounted the high state of Judge Oglethorpe's kitchen-garden, which Alek said was due to his unremitting industry and fine intelligence. Alek was a gardener, whenever impending starvation forced him to cease temporarily from being a lily of the field.

"Mist' Bryant he suhtainly got er grand gawden," observed Peter.

"Dat so, dat so, Mist' Wash'ton," assented Alek. "He got fine gawden."

"Seems like I nev' *did* see sech mellums, big as er bar'l, layin' dere. I don't raikon an'body in dish yer county kin hol' it with Mist' Bryant when comes ter mellums."

"Dat so, Mist' Wash'ton."

They did not talk of watermelons until their heads held nothing else, as the phrase goes. But they talked of watermelons until, when Peter started for home that night over a lonely road, they held a certain dominant position in his mind. Alek had come with him as far as the fence, in order to protect him from a possible attack by the mongrels. There they had cheerfully parted, two honest men.

The night was dark, and heavy with moisture. Peter found it uncomfortable to walk rapidly. He merely loitered on the road. When opposite Si Bryant's place he paused and looked over the fence into the garden. He imagined he could see the form of a huge melon lying in dim stateliness not ten yards away. He looked at the Bryant house. Two windows, down-stairs, were lighted. The Bryants kept no dog, old Si's favorite child having once been bitten by a dog, and having since died, within that year, of pneumonia.

Peering over the fence, Peter fancied that if any low-minded night-prowler should happen to note the melon, he would not find it difficult to possess himself of it. This person would merely wait until the lights were out in the house, and the people presumably asleep. Then he would climb the fence, reach the melon in a few strides, sever the stem with his ready knife, and in a trice be back in the road with his prize. There need be no noise, and, after all, the house was some distance.

Selecting a smooth bit of turf, Peter took a seat by the road-side. From time to time he glanced at the lighted window.

II

When Peter and Alek had said good-bye, the old man turned back in the rocky field and shaped a slow course towards that high dim light which marked the little window of his shanty. It would be incorrect to say that Alek could think of nothing but watermelons. But it was true that Si Bryant's watermelon-patch occupied a certain conspicuous position in his thoughts.

He sighed; he almost wished that he was again a conscienceless pickaninny, instead of being one of the most ornate, solemn, and look-at-me-sinner deacons that ever graced the handle of a collection-basket. At this time it made him quite sad to reflect upon his granite integrity. A weaker man might perhaps bow his moral head to the temptation, but for him such a fall was impossible. He was a prince of the church, and if he had been nine princes of the church he could not have been more proud. In fact, religion was to the old man a sort of personal dignity. And he was on Sundays so obtrusively good that you could see his sanctity through a door. He forced it on you until you would have felt its influence even in a forecastle.

It was clear in his mind that he must put watermelon thoughts from him, and after a moment he told himself, with much ostentation, that he had done so. But it was cooler under the sky than in the shanty, and as he was not sleepy, he decided to take a stroll down to Si Bryant's place and look at the melons from a pinnacle of spotless innocence. Reaching the road, he paused to listen. It would not do to let Peter hear him, because that graceless rapscallion would probably misunderstand him. But, assuring himself that Peter was well on his way, he set out, walking briskly until he was within four hundred yards of Bryant's place. Here he went to the side of the road, and walked thereafter on the damp, yielding turf. He made no sound.

He did not go on to that point in the main road which was directly opposite the water-melon-patch. He did not wish to have his ascetic contemplation disturbed by some chance wayfarer. He turned off along a short lane which led to Si Bryant's barn. Here he reached a place where he could see, over the fence, the faint shapes of the melons.

Alek was affected. The house was some distance away, there was no dog, and doubtless the Bryants would soon extinguish their lights and go to bed. Then some poor lost lamb of sin might come and scale the fence, reach a melon in a moment, sever the stem with his ready knife, and in a trice be back in the road with his prize. And this poor lost lamb of sin might even be a bishop, but no one would ever know it. Alek singled out with his eye a very large melon, and thought that the lamb would prove his judgment if he took that one.

He found a soft place in the grass, and arranged himself comfortably. He watched the lights in the windows.

III

It seemed to Peter Washington that the Bryants absolutely consulted their own wishes in regard to the time for retiring; but at last he saw the lighted windows fade briskly from left to right, and after a moment a window on the second floor blazed out against the darkness. Si was going to bed. In five minutes this window abruptly vanished, and all the world was night.

Peter spent the ensuing quarter-hour in no mental debate. His mind was fixed. He was here, and the melon was there. He would have it. But an idea of being caught appalled him. He thought of his position. He was the beau of his community, honored right and left. He pictured the consternation of his friends and the cheers of his enemies if the hands of the redoubtable Si Bryant should grip him in his shame.

He arose, and going to the fence, listened. No sound broke the stillness, save the rhythmical incessant clicking of myriad insects, and the guttural chanting of the frogs in the reeds at the lake-side. Moved by sudden decision, he climbed the fence and crept silently and swiftly down upon the melon. His open knife was in his hand. There was the melon, cool, fair to see, as pompous in its fatness as the cook in a monastery.

Peter put out a hand to steady it while he cut the stem. But at the instant he was aware that a black form had dropped over the fence lining the lane in front of him and was coming stealthily towards him. In a palsy of terror he dropped flat upon the ground, not having strength enough to run away. The next moment he was looking into the amazed and agonized face of old Alek Williams.

There was a moment of loaded silence, and then Peter was overcome by a mad inspiration. He suddenly dropped his knife and leaped upon Alek. "I got che!" he hissed. "I got che! I got che!" The old man sank down as limp as rags. "I got che! I got che! Steal Mist' Bryant's mellums, hey?"

Alek, in a low voice, began to beg. "Oh, Mist' Peter Wash'ton, don' fer ter be too ha'd on er ole man! I nev' come yere fer ter steal 'em. 'Deed

I didn't, Mist' Wash'ton! I come yere jes fer ter *feel* 'em. Oh, please, Mist' Wash'ton—"

"Come erlong outa yere, you ol' rip," said Peter, "an' don' trumple on dese yer baids. I gwine put you wah you won' ketch col'."

Without difficulty he tumbled the whining Alek over the fence to the roadway, and followed him with sheriff-like expedition! He took him by the scruff. "Come erlong, deacon. I raikon I gwine put you wah you kin pray, deacon. Come erlong, deacon."

The emphasis and reiteration of his layman's title in the church produced a deadly effect upon Alek. He felt to his marrow the heinous crime into which this treacherous night had betrayed him. As Peter marched his prisoner up the road towards the mouth of the lane, he continued his remarks: "Come erlong, deacon. Nev' see er man so anxious like erbout er mellum-paitch, deacon. Seem like you jes must see'em er-growin' an' *feel* 'em, deacon. Mist' Bryant he'll be s'prised, deacon, findin' out you come fer ter *feel* his mellums. Come erlong, deacon. Mist' Bryant he expectin' some ole rip like you come soon."

They had almost reached the lane when Alek's cur Susie, who had followed her master, approached in the silence which attends dangerous dogs; and seeing indications of what she took to be war, she appended herself swiftly but firmly to the calf of Peter's left leg. The mêlée was short, but spirited. Alek had no wish to have his dog complicate his already serious misfortunes, and went manfully to the defence of his captor. He procured a large stone, and by beating this with both hands down upon the resounding skull of the animal, he induced her to quit her grip. Breathing heavily, Peter dropped into the long grass at the road-side. He said nothing.

"Mist' Wash'ton," said Alek at last, in a quavering voice, "I raikon I gwine wait yere see what you gwine do ter me."

Whereupon Peter passed into a spasmodic state, in which he rolled to and fro and shook.

"Mist' Wash'ton, I hope dish yer dog 'ain't gone an' give you fitses?"

Peter sat up suddenly. "No, she 'ain't," he answered; "but she gin me er big skeer; an' fer yer 'sistance with er cobblestone, Mist' Willums, I tell you what I gwine do—I tell you what I gwine do." He waited an impressive moment. "I gwine 'lease you!"

Old Alek trembled like a little bush in a wind. "Mist' Wash'ton?"

Quoth Peter, deliberately, "I gwine 'lease you."

The old man was filled with a desire to negotiate this statement at once, but he felt the necessity of carrying off the event without an appearance of haste. "Yes, seh; thank 'e, seh; thank 'e, Mist' Wash'ton. I raikon I ramble home pressenly." He waited an interval, and then dubiously said, "Good-evenin', Mist' Wash'ton."

"Good-evenin', deacon. Don' come foolin' roun' *feelin'* no mellums, and I say troof. Good-evenin', deacon."

Alek took off his hat and made three profound bows. "Thank 'e, seh. Thank 'e, seh. Thank 'e, seh."

Peter underwent another severe spasm, but the old man walked off towards his home with a humble and contrite heart.

IV

The next morning Alek proceeded from his shanty under the complete but customary illusion that he was going to work. He trudged manfully along until he reached the vicinity of Si Bryant's place. Then, by stages, he relapsed into a slink. He was passing the garden-patch under full steam, when, at some distance ahead of him, he saw Si Bryant leaning casually on the garden fence.

"Good-mornin', Alek."

"Good-mawnin', Mist' Bryant," answered Alek, with a new deference. He was marching on, when he was halted by a word—"Alek!"

He stopped. "Yes, seh."

"I found a knife this mornin' in th' road," drawled Si, "an' I thought maybe it was yourn."

Improved in mind by this divergence from the direct line of attack, Alek stepped up easily to look at the knife. "No, seh," he said, scanning it as it lay in Si's palm, while the cold steel-blue eyes of the white man looked down into his stomach, "'tain't no knife er mine." But he knew the knife. He knew it as if it had been his mother. And at the same moment a spark flashed through his head and made wise his understanding. He knew everything. "'Tain't much of er knife, Mist' Bryant," he said, deprecatingly.

"'Tain't much of a knife, I know that," cried Si, in sudden heat, "but I found it this mornin' in my watermelon-patch—hear?"

"Watahmellum-paitch?" yelled Alek, not astounded.

"Yes, in my watermelon-patch," sneered Si, "an' I think you know something about it, too!"

"Me?" cried Alek. "Me?"

"Yes—you!" said Si, with icy ferocity. "Yes—you!" He had become convinced that Alek was not in any way guilty, but he was certain that the old man knew the owner of the knife, and so he pressed him at first on criminal lines. "Alek, you might as well own up now. You've been meddlin' with my watermelons!"

"Me?" cried Alek again. "Yah's *ma* knife. I done cah'e it foh yeahs."

Bryant changed his ways. "Look here, Alek," he said, confidentially: "I know you and you know me, and there ain't no use in any more skirmishin'. *I* know that *you* know whose knife that is. Now whose is it?"

This challenge was so formidable in character that Alek temporarily quailed and began to stammer. "Er—now—Mist' Bryant—you—you—frien' er mine—"

"I know I'm a friend of yours, but," said Bryant, inexorably, "who owns this knife?"

Alek gathered unto himself some remnants of dignity and spoke with reproach: "Mist' Bryant, dish yer knife ain' mine."

"No," said Bryant, "it ain't. But you know who it belongs to, an' I want you to tell me—quick."

"Well, Mist' Bryant," answered Alek, scratching his wool, "I won't say 's I *do* know who b'longs ter dish yer knife, an' I won't say 's I *don't.*"

Bryant again laughed his Yankee laugh, but this time there was little humor in it. It was dangerous.

Alek, seeing that he had gotten himself into hot water by the fine diplomacy of his last sentence, immediately began to flounder and totally submerge himself. "No, Mist' Bryant," he repeated, "I won't say 's I *do* know who b'longs ter dish yer knife, an' I won't say 's I *don't.*" And he began to parrot this fatal sentence again and again. It seemed wound about his tongue. He could not rid himself of it. Its very power to make trouble for him seemed to originate the mysterious Afric reason for its repetition.

"Is he a very close friend of yourn?" said Bryant, softly.

"F-frien'?" stuttered Alek. He appeared to weigh this question with much care. "Well, seems like he *was* er frien', an' then agin, it seems like he—"

"It seems like he *wasn't.*" asked Bryant.

"Yes, seh, jest so, jest so," cried Alek. "Sometimes it seems like he wasn't. Then agin—" He stopped for profound meditation.

The patience of the white man seemed inexhaustible. At length his low and oily voice broke the stillness. "Oh, well, of course if he's a friend of yourn, Alek! You know I wouldn't want to make no trouble for a friend of yourn."

"Yes, seh," cried the negro at once. "He's er frien' er mine. He is dat."

"Well, then, it seems as if about the only thing to do is for you to tell me his name so's I can send him his knife, and that's all there is to it."

Alek took off his hat, and in perplexity ran his hand over his wool. He studied the ground. But several times he raised his eyes to take a sly peep at the imperturbable visage of the white man. "Y—y—yes, Mist' Bryant. ...I raikon dat's erbout all what kin be done. I gwine tell you who b'longs ter dish yer knife."

"Of course," said the smooth Bryant, "it ain't a very nice thing to have to do, but—"

"No, seh," cried Alek, brightly; "I'm gwine tell you, Mist' Bryant. I gwine tell you erbout dat knife. Mist' Bryant," he asked, solemnly, "does you know who b'longs ter dat knife?"

"No, I—"

"Well, I gwine tell. I gwine tell who, Mr Bryant—" The old man drew himself to a stately pose and held forth his arm. "I gwine tell who, Mist' Bryant, *dish yer knife b'longs ter Sam Jackson!*"

Bryant *was* startled into indignation. "Who in hell is Sam Jackson?" he growled.

"He's a nigger," said Alek, impressively, "and he wuks in er lumber-yawd up yere in Hoswego."

IX. THE STOVE

I

THEY'LL bring her," said Mrs. Trescott, dubiously. Her cousin, the painter, the bewildered father of the angel child, had written to say that if they were asked, he and his wife would come to the Trescotts for the Christmas holidays. But he had not officially stated that the angel child would form part of the expedition. "But of course they'll bring her," said Mrs. Trescott to her husband.

The doctor assented. "Yes, they'll have to bring her. They wouldn't dare leave New York at her mercy."

"Well," sighed Mrs. Trescott, after a pause, "the neighbors will be pleased. When they see her they'll immediately lock up their children for safety."

"Anyhow," said Trescott, "the devastation of the Margate twins was complete. She can't do that particular thing again. I shall be interested to note what form her energy will take this time."

"Oh yes! that's it!" cried the wife. "You'll be interested. You've hit it exactly. You'll be interested to note what form her energy will take this time. And then, when the real crisis comes, you'll put on your hat and walk out of the house and leave me to straighten things out. This is not a scientific question; this is a practical matter."

"Well, as a practical man, I advocate chaining her out in the stable," answered the doctor.

When Jimmie Trescott was told that his old flame was again to appear, he remained calm. In fact, time had so mended his youthful heart that it was a regular apple of oblivion and peace. Her image in his thought was as the track of a bird on deep snow—it was an impression, but it did not concern the depths. However, he did what befitted his state. He went out and bragged in the street: "My cousin is comin' next week f'om New York." ..."My cousin is comin' to-morrow f'om New York."

"Girl or boy?" said the populace, bluntly; but, when enlightened, they speedily cried, "Oh, we remember *her!*" They were charmed, for they thought of her as an outlaw, and they surmised that she could lead them into a very ecstasy of sin. They thought of her as a brave bandit, because they had been whipped for various pranks into which she had led them. When Jimmie made his declaration, they fell into a state of pleased and shuddering expectancy.

Mrs. Trescott pronounced her point of view: "The child is a nice child, if only Caroline had some sense. But she hasn't. And Willis is like a wax figure. I don't see what can be done, unless—unless you simply go to Willis and put the whole thing right at him." Then, for purposes of indication, she improvised a speech: "Look here, Willis, you've got a little daughter, haven't you? But, confound it, man, she is not the only girl child ever brought into the sunlight. There are a lot of children. Children are an ordinary phenomenon. In China they drown girl babies. If you wish to submit to this frightful impostor and tyrant, that is all very well, but why in the name of humanity do you make us submit to it?"

Doctor Trescott laughed. "I wouldn't dare say it to him."

"Anyhow," said Mrs. Trescott, determinedly, "that is what you *should* say to him."

"It wouldn't do the slightest good. It would only make him very angry, and I would lay myself perfectly open to a suggestion that I had better attend to my own affairs with more rigor."

"Well, I suppose you are right," Mrs. Trescott again said.

"Why don't you speak to Caroline?" asked the doctor, humorously.

"Speak to Caroline! Why, I wouldn't for the *world!* She'd fly through the roof. She'd snap my head off! Speak to Caroline! You must be mad!"

One afternoon the doctor went to await his visitors on the platform of the railway station. He was thoughtfully smiling. For some quaint reason he was convinced that he was to be treated to a quick manifestation of little Cora's peculiar and interesting powers. And yet, when the train paused at the station, there appeared to him only a pretty little girl in a fur-lined hood, and with her nose reddening from the sudden cold, and—attended respectfully by her parents. He smiled again, reflecting that he had comically exaggerated the dangers of dear little Cora. It amused his philosophy to note that he had really been perturbed.

As the big sleigh sped homeward there was a sudden shrill outcry from the angel child: "Oh, mamma! mamma! They've forgotten my stove!"

"Hush, dear; hush!" said the mother. "It's all right."

"Oh, but, mamma, they've forgotten my stove!"

The doctor thrust his chin suddenly out of his top-coat collar. "Stove?" he said. "Stove? What stove?"

"Oh, just a toy of the child's," explained the mother. "She's grown so fond of it, she loves it so, that if we didn't take it everywhere with her she'd suffer dreadfully. So we always bring it."

"Oh!" said the doctor. He pictured a little tin trinket. But when the stove was really unmasked, it turned out to be an affair of cast iron, as big as a portmanteau, and, as the stage people say, practicable. There was some trouble that evening when came the hour of children's bedtime. Little Cora burst into a wild declaration that she could not retire for the night unless the stove was carried up-stairs and placed, at her bedside. While the mother was trying to dissuade the child, the Trescott's held their peace and gazed with awe. The incident closed when the lamb-eyed father gathered the stove in his arms and preceded the angel child to her chamber.

In the morning, Trescott was standing with his back to the dining room fire, awaiting breakfast, when he heard a noise of descending guests. Presently the door opened, and the party entered in regular order. First came the angel child, then the cooing mother, and last the great painter with his arm full of the stove. He deposited it gently in a corner, and sighed. Trescott wore a wide grin.

"What are you carting that thing all over the house for?" he said, brutally. "Why don't you put it some place where she can play with it, and leave it there?"

The mother rebuked him with a look. "Well, if it gives her pleasure, Ned?" she expostulated, softly. "If it makes the child happy to have the stove with her, why shouldn't she have it?"

"Just so," said the doctor, with calmness.

Jimmie's idea was the roaring fireplace in the cabin of the lone mountaineer. At first he was not able to admire a girl's stove built on well-known domestic lines. He eyed it and thought it was very pretty, but it did not move him immediately. But a certain respect grew to an interest, and he became the angel child's accomplice. And even if he had not

had an interest grow upon him, he was certain to have been implicated sooner or later, because of the imperious way of little Cora, who made a serf of him in a few swift sentences. Together they carried the stove out into the desolate garden and squatted it in the snow. Jimmie's snug little muscles had been pitted against the sheer nervous vigor of this little golden-haired girl, and he had not won great honors. When the mind blazed inside the small body, the angel child was pure force. She began to speak: "Now, Jim, get some paper. Get some wood-little sticks at first. Now we want a match. You got a match? Well, go get a match. Get some more wood. Hurry up, now! No. *No!* I'll light it my own self. You get some more wood. There! Isn't that splendid? You get a whole lot of wood an' pile it up here by the stove. An' now what'll we cook? We must have somethin' to cook, you know, else it ain't like the real."

"Potatoes," said Jimmie, at once.

The day was clear, cold, bright. An icy wind sped from over the waters of the lake. A grown person would hardly have been abroad save on compulsion of a kind, and yet, when they were called to luncheon, the two little simpletons protested with great cries.

II

The ladies of Whilomville were somewhat given to the pagan habit of tea parties. When a tea party was to befall a certain house one could read it in the manner of the prospective hostess, who for some previous days would go about twitching this and twisting that, and dusting here and polishing there; the ordinary habits of the household began then to disagree with her, and her unfortunate husband and children fled to the lengths of their tethers. Then there was a hush. Then there was a tea party. On the fatal afternoon a small picked company of latent enemies would meet. There would be a fanfare of affectionate greetings, during which everybody would measure to an inch the importance of what everybody else was wearing. Those who wore old dresses would wish then that they had not come; and those who saw that, in the company, they were well clad, would be pleased or exalted, or filled with the joys of cruelty. Then they had tea, which was a habit and a delight with none of them, their usual beverage being coffee with milk.

Usually the party jerked horribly in the beginning, while the hostess strove and pulled and pushed to make its progress smooth. Then suddenly it would be off like the wind, eight, fifteen, or twenty-five tongues clattering, with a noise like a cotton-mill combined with the noise of a few penny whistles. Then the hostess had nothing to do but to look glad, and see that everybody had enough tea and cake. When the door was closed behind the last guest, the hostess would usually drop into a chair and say: "Thank Heaven! They're gone!" There would be no malice in this expression. It simply would be that, womanlike, she had flung herself headlong at the accomplishment of a pleasure which she could not even define, and at the end she felt only weariness.

The value and beauty, or oddity, of the tea-cups was another element which entered largely into the spirit of these terrible enterprises. The quality of the tea was an element which did not enter at all. Uniformly it was rather bad. But the cups! Some of the more ambitious people aspired to have cups each of a different pattern, possessing, in fact, the sole similarity that with their odd curves and dips of form they each resembled anything but a teacup. Others of the more ambitious aspired to a quite severe and godly "set," which, when viewed, appalled one with its austere and rigid family resemblances, and made one desire to ask the hostess if the teapot was not the father of all the little cups, and at the same time protesting gallantly that such a young and charming cream-jug surely could not be their mother.

But of course the serious part is that these collections so differed in style and the obvious amount paid for them that nobody could be happy. The poorer ones envied; the richer ones feared; the poorer ones continually striving to overtake the leaders; the leaders always with their heads turned back to hear overtaking footsteps. And none of these things here written did they know. Instead of seeing that they were very stupid, they thought they were very fine. And they gave and took heart-bruises—fierce, deep heart-bruises—under the clear impression that of such kind of rubbish was the kingdom of nice people. The characteristics of outsiders of course emerged in shreds from these tea parties, and it is doubtful if the characteristics of insiders escaped entirely. In fact, these tea parties were in the large way the result of a conspiracy of certain unenlightened people to make life still more uncomfortable.

Mrs. Trescott was in the circle of tea-fighters largely through a sort of artificial necessity—a necessity, in short, which she had herself created in a spirit of femininity.

When the painter and his family came for the holidays, Mrs. Trescott had for some time been feeling that it was her turn to give a tea party, and she was resolved upon it now that she was reinforced by the beautiful wife of the painter, whose charms would make all the other women feel badly. And Mrs. Trescott further resolved that the affair should be notable in more than one way. The painter's wife suggested that, as an innovation, they give the people good tea; but Mrs. Trescott shook her head; she was quite sure they would not like it.

It was an impressive gathering. A few came to see if they could not find out the faults of the painter's wife, and these, added to those who would have attended even without that attractive prospect, swelled the company to a number quite large for Whilomville. There were the usual preliminary jolts, and then suddenly the tea party was in full swing, and looked like an unprecedented success.

Mrs. Trescott exchanged a glance with the painter's wife. They felt proud and superior. This tea party was almost perfection.

III

Jimmie and the angel child, after being oppressed by innumerable admonitions to behave correctly during the afternoon, succeeded in reaching the garden, where the stove awaited them. They were enjoying themselves grandly, when snow began to fall so heavily that it gradually dampened their ardor as well as extinguished the fire in the stove. They stood ruefully until the angel child devised the plan of carrying the stove into the stable, and there, safe from the storm, to continue the festivities. But they were met at the door of the stable by Peter Washington.

"What you 'bout, Jim?"

"Now—it's snowin' so hard, we thought we'd take the stove into the stable."

"An' have er fiah in it? No, seh! G'w'on 'way f'm heh!—g'w'on! Don' 'low no sech foolishin' round yer. No, seh!"

"Well, we ain't goin' to hurt your old stable, are we?" asked Jimmie, ironically.

"Dat you ain't, Jim! Not so long's I keep my two eyes right plumb squaah pinted at ol' Jim. No, seh!" Peter began to chuckle in derision.

The two vagabonds stood before him while he informed them of their iniquities as well as their absurdities, and further made clear his own masterly grasp of the spirit of their devices. Nothing affects children so much as rhetoric. It may not involve any definite presentation of common-sense, but if it is picturesque they surrender decently to its influence. Peter was by all means a rhetorician, and it was not long before the two children had dismally succumbed to him. They went away.

Depositing the stove in the snow, they straightened to look at each other. It did not enter either head to relinquish the idea of continuing the game. But the situation seemed invulnerable.

The angel child went on a scouting tour. Presently she returned, flying. "I know! Let's have it in the cellar! In the cellar! Oh, it'll be lovely!"

The outer door of the cellar was open, and they proceeded down some steps with their treasure. There was plenty of light; the cellar was high-walled, warm, and dry. They named it an ideal place. Two huge cylindrical furnaces were humming away, one at either end. Overhead the beams detonated with the different emotions which agitated the tea party.

Jimmie worked like a stoker, and soon there was a fine bright fire in the stove. The fuel was of small brittle sticks which did not make a great deal of smoke.

"Now what'll we cook?" cried little Cora. "What'll we cook, Jim? We must have something to cook, you know."

"Potatoes?" said Jimmie.

But the angel child made a scornful gesture. "No. I've cooked 'bout a million potatoes, I guess. Potatoes aren't nice any more."

Jimmie's mind was all said and done when the question of potatoes had been passed, and he looked weakly at his companion.

"Haven't you got any turnips in your house?" she inquired, contemptuously. "In my house we have *turnips.*"

"Oh, turnips!" exclaimed Jimmie, immensely relieved to find that the honor of his family was safe. "Turnips? Oh, bushels an' bushels an' bushels! Out in the shed."

"Well, go an' get a whole lot," commanded the angel child. "Go an' get a whole lot. Grea' big ones. *We* always have grea' big ones."

Jimmie went to the shed and kicked gently at a company of turnips which the frost had amalgamated. He made three journeys to and from the cellar, carrying always the very largest types from his father's store. Four of them filled the oven of little Cora's stove. This fact did not please her, so they placed three rows of turnips on the hot top. Then the angel child, profoundly moved by an inspiration, suddenly cried out,

"Oh, Jimmie, let's play we're keepin' a hotel, an' have got to cook for 'bout a thousand people, an' those two furnaces will be the ovens, an' I'll be the chief cook—"

"No; I want to be chief cook some of the time," interrupted Jimmie.

"No; I'll be chief cook my own self. You must be my 'sistant. Now I'll prepare 'em—see? An' then you put 'em in the ovens. Get the shovel. We'll play that's the pan. I'll fix 'em, an' then you put 'em in the oven. Hold it still now."

Jim held the coal-shovel while little Cora, with a frown of importance, arranged turnips in rows upon it. She patted each one daintily, and then backed away to view it, with her head critically sideways.

"There!" she shouted at last. "That'll do, I guess. Put 'em in the oven."

Jimmie marched with his shovelful of turnips to one of the furnaces. The door was already open, and he slid the shovel in upon the red coals.

"Come on," cried little Cora. "I've got another batch nearly ready."

"But what am I goin' to do with these?" asked Jimmie. "There ain't only one shovel."

"Leave 'm in there," retorted the girl, passionately. "Leave 'm in there, an' then play you're comin' with another pan. 'Tain't right to stand there an' *hold* the pan, you goose."

So Jimmie expelled all his turnips from his shovel out upon the furnace fire, and returned obediently for another batch.

"These are puddings," yelled the angel child, gleefully. "Dozens an' dozens of puddings for the thousand people at our grea' big hotel."

IV

At the first alarm the painter had fled to the doctor's office, where he hid his face behind a book and pretended that he did not hear the noise of feminine revelling. When the doctor came from a round of calls, he too retreated upon the office, and the men consoled each other as well as they were able. Once Mrs. Trescott dashed in to say delightedly that her tea party was not only the success of the season, but it was probably the very nicest tea party that had ever been held in Whilomville. After vainly beseeching them to return with her, she dashed away again, her face bright with happiness.

The doctor and the painter remained for a long time in silence, Trescott tapping reflectively upon the window-pane. Finally he turned to the painter, and sniffing, said: "What is that, Willis? Don't you smell something?"

The painter also sniffed. "Why, yes! It's like—it's like turnips."

"Turnips? No; it can't be.

"Well, it's very much like it."

The puzzled doctor opened the door into the hall, and at first it appeared that he was going to give back two paces. A result of frizzling turnips, which was almost as tangible as mist, had blown in upon his face and made him gasp. "Good God! Willis, what can this be?" he cried.

"Whee!" said the painter. "It's awful, isn't it?"

The doctor made his way hurriedly to his wife, but before he could speak with her he had to endure the business of greeting a score of women. Then he whispered, "Out in the hall there's an awful—"

But at that moment it came to them on the wings of a sudden draught. The solemn odor of burning turnips rolled in like a sea-fog, and fell upon that dainty, perfumed tea party. It was almost a personality; if some unbidden and extremely odious guest had entered the room, the effect would have been much the same. The sprightly talk stopped with a jolt, and people looked at each other. Then a few brave and considerate persons made the usual attempt to talk away as if nothing had happened. They all looked at their hostess, who wore an air of stupefaction.

The odor of burning turnips grew and grew. To Trescott it seemed to make a noise. He thought he could hear the dull roar of this outrage. Under some circumstances he might have been able to take the situation from a point of view of comedy, but the agony of his wife was too acute, and, for him, too visible. She was saying: "Yes, we saw the play the last time we were in New York. I liked it very much. That scene in the second act—the gloomy church, you know, and all that—and the organ playing—and then when the four singing little girls came in—" But Trescott comprehended that she did not know if she was talking of a play or a parachute.

He had not been in the room twenty seconds before his brow suddenly flushed with an angry inspiration. He left the room hastily, leaving behind him an incoherent phrase of apology, and charged upon his office, where he found the painter somnolent.

"Willis!" he cried, sternly, "come with me. It's that damn kid of yours!"

The painter was immediately agitated. He always seemed to feel more than any one else in the world the peculiar ability of his child to create resounding excitement, but he seemed always to exhibit his feelings very late. He arose hastily, and hurried after Trescott to the top of the inside cellar stairway. Trescott motioned him to pause, and for an instant they listened.

"Hurry up, Jim," cried the busy little Cora. "Here's another whole batch of lovely puddings. Hurry up now, an' put 'em in the oven."

Trescott looked at the painter; the painter groaned. Then they appeared violently in the middle of the great kitchen of the hotel with a thousand people in it. "Jimmie, go up-stairs!" said Trescott, and then he turned to watch the painter deal with the angel child.

With some imitation of wrath, the painter stalked to his daughter's side and grasped her by the arm.

131

"Oh, papa! papa!" she screamed. "You're pinching me! You're pinching me! You're pinching me, papa!"

At first the painter had seemed resolved to keep his grip, but suddenly he let go her arm in a panic. "I've hurt her," he said, turning to Trescott.

Trescott had swiftly done much towards the obliteration of the hotel kitchen, but he looked up now and spoke, after a short period of reflection. "You've hurt her, have you? Well, hurt her again. Spank her!" he cried, enthusiastically. "Spank her, confound you, man! She needs it. Here's your chance. Spank her, and spank her good. Spank her!"

The painter naturally wavered over this incendiary proposition, but at last, in one supreme burst of daring, he shut his eyes and again grabbed his precious offspring.

The spanking was lamentably the work of a perfect bungler. It couldn't have hurt at all; but the angel child raised to heaven a loud, clear soprano howl that expressed the last word in even mediæval anguish. Soon the painter was aghast. "Stop it, darling! I didn't mean—I didn't mean to—to hurt you so much, you know." He danced nervously. Trescott sat on a box, and devilishly smiled.

But the pasture call of suffering motherhood came down to them, and a moment later a splendid apparition appeared on the cellar stairs. She understood the scene at a glance. "Willis! What have you been doing?"

Trescott sat on his box, the painter guiltily moved from foot to foot, and the angel child advanced to her mother with arms outstretched, making a piteous wail of amazed and pained pride that would have moved Peter the Great. Regardless of her frock, the panting mother knelt on the stone floor and took her child to her bosom, and looked, then, bitterly, scornfully, at the cowering father and husband.

The painter, for his part, at once looked reproachfully at Trescott, as if to say: "There! You see?"

Trescott arose and extended his hands in a quiet but magnificent gesture of despair and weariness. He seemed about to say something classic, and, quite instinctively, they waited. The stillness was deep, and the wait was longer than a moment. "Well," he said, "we can't live in the cellar. Let's go up-stairs."

X. THE TRIAL, EXECUTION, AND BURIAL OF HOMER PHELPS

FROM time to time an enwearied pine bough let fall to the earth its load of melting snow, and the branch swung back glistening in the faint wintry sunlight. Down the gulch a brook clattered amid its ice with the sound of a perpetual breaking of glass. All the forest looked drenched and forlorn.

The sky-line was a ragged enclosure of gray cliffs and hemlocks and pines. If one had been miraculously set down in this gulch one could have imagined easily that the nearest human habitation was hundreds of miles away, if it were not for an old half-discernible wood-road that led towards the brook.

"Halt! Who's there?"

This low and gruff cry suddenly dispelled the stillness which lay upon the lonely gulch, but the hush which followed it seemed even more profound. The hush endured for some seconds, and then the voice of the challenger was again raised, this time with a distinctly querulous note in it.

"Halt! Who's there? Why don't you answer when I holler? Don't you know you're likely to get shot?"

A second voice answered, "Oh, you knew who I was easy enough."

"That don't make no diff'rence." One of the Margate twins stepped from a thicket and confronted Homer Phelps on the old wood-road. The majestic scowl of official wrath was upon the brow of Reeves Margate, a long stick was held in the hollow of his arm as one would hold a rifle, and he strode grimly to the other boy. "That don't make no diff'rence. You've got to answer when I holler, anyhow. Willie says so."

At the mention of the dread chieftain's name the Phelps boy daunted a trifle, but he still sulkily murmured, "Well, you knew it was me."

He started on his way through the snow, but the twin sturdily blocked the path. "You can't pass less'n you give the countersign."

"Huh?" said the Phelps boy. "Countersign?"

"Yes—countersign," sneered the twin, strong in his sense of virtue.

But the Phelps boy became very angry. "Can't I, hey? Can't I, hey? I'll show you whether I can or not! I'll show you, Reeves Margate!"

There was a short scuffle, and then arose the anguished clamor of the sentry: "Hey, fellers! Here's a man tryin' to run a-past the guard. Hey, fellers! Hey!"

There was a great noise in the adjacent underbrush. The voice of Willie could be heard exhorting his followers to charge swiftly and bravely. Then they appeared—Willie Dalzel, Jimmie Trescott, the other Margate twin, and Dan Earl. The chieftain's face was dark with wrath. "What's the matter? Can't you play it right? 'Ain't you got any sense?" he asked the Phelps boy.

The sentry was yelling out his grievance. "Now—he came along an' I hollered at 'im, an' he didn't pay no 'tention, an' when I ast 'im for the countersign, he wouldn't say nothin'. That ain't no way."

"Can't you play it right?" asked the chief again, with gloomy scorn.

"He knew it was me easy enough," said the Phelps boy.

"That 'ain't got nothin' to do with it," cried the chief, furiously. "That 'ain't got nothin' to do with it. If you're goin' to play, you've got to play it right. It ain't no fun if you go spoilin' the whole thing this way. Can't you play it right?"

"I forgot the countersign," lied the culprit, weakly.

Whereupon the remainder of the band yelled out, with one triumphant voice: "War to the knife! War to the knife! I remember it, Willie. Don't I, Willie?"

The leader was puzzled. Evidently he was trying to develop in his mind a plan for dealing correctly with this unusual incident. He felt, no doubt, that he must proceed according to the books, but unfortunately the books did not cover the point precisely. However, he finally said to Homer Phelps, "You are under arrest." Then with a stentorian voice he shouted, "Seize him!"

His loyal followers looked startled for a brief moment, but directly they began to move upon the Phelps boy. The latter clearly did not intend to be seized. He backed away, expostulating wildly. He even seemed somewhat frightened. "No, no; don't you touch me, I tell you; don't you dare touch me."

The others did not seem anxious to engage. They moved slowly, watching the desperate light in his eyes. The chieftain stood with folded arms, his face growing darker and darker with impatience. At length he burst out: "Oh, seize him, I tell you! Why don't you seize him? Grab him by the leg, Dannie! Hurry up, all of you! Seize him, I keep a-say-in'!"

Thus adjured, the Margate twins and Dan Earl made another pained effort, while Jimmie Trescott manœuvred to cut off a retreat. But, to tell the truth, there was a boyish law which held them back from laying hands of violence upon little Phelps under these conditions. Perhaps it was because they were only playing, whereas he was now undeniably serious. At any rate, they looked very sick of their occupation.

"Don't you dare!" snarled the Phelps boy, facing first one and then the other; he was almost in tears—"don't you dare touch me!"

The chieftain was now hopping with exasperation. "Oh, seize him, can't you? You're no good at all!" Then he loosed his wrath upon the Phelps boy: "Stand still, Homer, can't you? You've got to be seized, you know. That ain't the way. It ain't any fun if you keep a-dodgin' that way. Stand still, can't you! You've got to be seized."

"I don't want to be seized," retorted the Phelps boy, obstinate and bitter.

"But you've *got* to be seized!" yelled the maddened chief. "Don't you see? That's the way to play it."

The Phelps boy answered, promptly, "But I don't want to play that way."

"But that's the *right* way to play it. Don't you see? You've got to play it the right way. You've got to be seized, an' then we'll hold a trial on you, an'— an' all sorts of things."

But this prospect held no illusions for the Phelps boy. He continued doggedly to repeat, "I don't want to play that way!"

Of course in the end the chief stooped to beg and beseech this unreasonable lad. "Oh, come on, Homer! Don't be so mean. You're a-spoilin' everything. We won't hurt you any. Not the tiniest bit. It's all just playin'. What's the matter with you?"

The different tone of the leader made an immediate impression upon the other. He showed some signs of the beginning of weakness. "Well," he asked, "what you goin' to do?"

"Why, first we're goin' to put you in a dungeon, or tie you to a stake, or something like that—just pertend, you know," added the chief, hurriedly, "an' then we'll hold a trial, awful solemn, but there won't be anything what'll hurt you. Not a thing."

And so the game was readjusted. The Phelps boy was marched off between Dan Earl and a Margate twin. The party proceeded to their camp, which was hidden some hundred feet back in the thickets. There was a miserable little hut with a pine-bark roof, which so frankly and constantly leaked that existence in the open air was always preferable. At present it was noisily dripping melted snow into the black mouldy interior. In front of this hut a feeble fire was flickering through its unhappy career. Underfoot, the watery snow was of the color of lead.

The party having arrived at the camp, the chief leaned against a tree, and balancing on one foot, drew off a rubber boot. From this boot he emptied about a quart of snow. He squeezed his stocking, which had a hole from which protruded a lobster-red toe. He resumed his boot. "Bring up the prisoner," said he. They did it. "Guilty or not guilty?" he asked.

"Huh?" said the Phelps boy.

"Guilty or not guilty?" demanded the chief,

peremptorily. "Guilty or not guilty? Don't you understand?"

Homer Phelps looked profoundly puzzled. "Guilty or not guilty?" he asked, slowly and weakly.

The chief made a swift gesture, and turned in despair to the others. "Oh, he don't do it right! He does it all wrong!" He again faced the prisoner with an air of making a last attempt, "Now look-a-here, Homer, when I say, 'Guilty or not guilty?' you want to up an' say, 'Not Guilty.' Don't you see?"

"Not guilty," said Homer, at once.

"No, no, no. Wait till I ask you. Now wait." He called out, pompously, "Pards, if this prisoner before us is guilty, what shall be his fate?"

All those well-trained little infants with one voice sung out, "*Death!*"

"Prisoner," continued the chief, "are you guilty or not guilty?"

"But look-a-here," argued Homer, "you said it wouldn't be nothin' that would hurt. I—"

"Thunder an' lightnin'!" roared the wretched chief. "Keep your mouth shut, can't ye? What in the mischief—"

But there was an interruption from Jimmie Trescott, who shouldered a twin aside and stepped to the front. "Here," he said, very contemptuously, "let me be the prisoner. I'll show 'im how to do it."

"All right, Jim," cried the chief, delighted; "you be the prisoner, then. Now all you fellers with guns stand there in a row! Get out of the way, Homer!" He cleared his throat, and addressed Jimmie. "Prisoner, are you guilty or not guilty?"

"Not guilty," answered Jimmie, firmly. Standing there before his judge— unarmed, slim, quiet, modest—he was ideal.

The chief beamed upon him, and looked aside to cast a triumphant and withering glance upon Homer Phelps. He said: "There! That's the way to do it."

The twins and Dan Earl also much admired Jimmie.

"That's all right so far, anyhow," said the satisfied chief. "An' now we'll— now we'll—we'll perceed with the execution."

"That ain't right," said the new prisoner, suddenly. "That ain't the next thing. You've got to have a trial first. You've got to fetch up a lot of people first who'll say I done it."

"That's so," said the chief. "I didn't think. Here, Reeves, you be first witness. Did the prisoner do it?"

The twin gulped for a moment in his anxiety to make the proper reply. He was at the point where the roads forked. Finally he hazarded, "Yes."

"There," said the chief, "that's one of 'em. Now, Dan, you be a witness. Did he do it?"

Dan Earl, having before him the twin's example, did not hesitate. "Yes," he said.

"Well, then, pards, what shall be his fate?"

Again came the ringing answer, "*Death!*"

With Jimmie in the principal rôle, this drama, hidden deep in the hemlock thicket neared a kind of perfection. "You must blind-fold me," cried the condemned lad, briskly, "an' then I'll go off an' stand, an' you must all get in a row an' shoot me."

The chief gave this plan his urbane countenance, and the twins and Dan Earl were greatly pleased. They blindfolded Jimmie under his careful directions. He waded a few paces into snow, and then turned and stood with quiet dignity, awaiting his fate. The chief marshalled the twins and Dan Earl in line with their sticks. He gave the necessary commands: "Load! Ready! Aim! Fire!" At the last command the firing party all together yelled, "Bang!"

Jimmie threw his hands high, tottered in agony for a moment, and then crashed full length into the snow—into, one would think, a serious case of pneumonia. It was beautiful.

He arose almost immediately and came back to them, wondrously pleased with himself. They acclaimed him joyously.

The chief was particularly grateful. He was always trying to bring off these little romantic affairs, and it seemed, after all, that the only boy who could ever really help him was Jimmie Trescott. "There," he said to the others, "that's the way it ought to be done."

They were touched to the heart by the whole thing, and they looked at Jimmie with big, smiling eyes. Jimmie, blown out like a balloon-fish with pride of his performance, swaggered to the fire and took seat on some wet hemlock boughs. "Fetch some more wood, one of you kids," he murmured, negligently. One of the twins came fortunately upon a small cedar-tree the lower branches of which were dead and dry. An armful of these branches flung upon the sick fire soon made a high, ruddy, warm blaze, which was like an illumination in honor of Jimmie's success.

The boys sprawled about the fire and talked the regular language of the game. "Waal, pards," remarked the chief, "it's many a night we've had together here in the Rockies among the b'ars an' the Indyuns, hey?"

"Yes, pard," replied Jimmie Trescott, "I reckon you're right. Our wild, free life is—there ain't nothin' to compare with our wild, free life."

Whereupon the two lads arose and magnificently shook hands, while the others watched them in an ecstasy. "I'll allus stick by ye, pard," said Jimmie, earnestly. "When yer in trouble, don't forget that Lightnin' Lou is at yer back."

"Thanky, pard," quoth Willie Dalzel, deeply affected. "I'll not forget it, pard. An' don't you forget, either, that Dead-shot Demon, the leader of the Red Raiders, never forgits a friend."

But Homer Phelps was having none of this great fun. Since his disgraceful refusal to be seized and executed he had been hovering unheeded on the outskirts of the band. He seemed very sorry; he cast a wistful eye at the romantic scene. He knew too well that if he went near at that particular time he would be certain to encounter a pitiless snubbing. So he vacillated modestly in the background.

At last the moment came when he dared venture near enough to the fire to gain some warmth, for he was now bitterly suffering with the cold. He sidled close to Willie Dalzel. No one heeded him. Eventually he looked at his chief, and with a bright face said,

"Now—if I was seized now to be executed, I could do it as well as Jimmie Trescott, I could."

The chief gave a crow of scorn, in which he was followed by the other boys. "Ho!" he cried, "why didn't you do it, then? Why didn't you do it?" Homer Phelps felt upon him many pairs of disdainful eyes. He wagged his shoulders in misery.

"You're dead," said the chief, frankly. "That's what you are. We executed you, we did."

"When?" demanded the Phelps boy, with some spirit.

"Just a little while ago. Didn't we, fellers? Hey, fellers, didn't we?"

The trained chorus cried: "Yes, of course we did. You're dead, Homer. You can't play any more. You're dead."

"That wasn't me. It was Jimmie Trescott," he said, in a low and bitter voice, his eyes on the ground. He would have given the world if he could have retracted his mad refusals of the early part of the drama.

"No," said the chief, "it was you. We're playin' it was you, an' it *was* you. You're dead, you are." And seeing the cruel effect of his words, he did not refrain from administering some advice: "The next time, don't be such a chuckle-head."

Presently the camp imagined that it was attacked by Indians, and the boys dodged behind trees with their stick-rifles, shouting out, "Bang!" and encouraging each other to resist until the last. In the mean time the dead lad hovered near the fire, looking moodily at the gay and exciting scene. After the fight the gallant defenders returned one by one to the fire, where they grandly clasped hands, calling each other "old pard," and boasting of their deeds.

Parenthetically, one of the twins had an unfortunate inspiration. "I killed the Indy-un chief, fellers. Did you see me kill the Indy-un chief?"

But Willie Dalzel, his own chief, turned upon him wrathfully: "*You* didn't kill no chief. *I* killed 'im with me own hand."

"Oh!" said the twin, apologetically, at once. "It must have been some other Indy-un."

"Who's wounded?" cried Willie Dalzel. "Ain't anybody wounded?" The party professed themselves well and sound. The roving and inventive eye of the chief chanced upon Homer Phelps. "Ho! Here's a dead man! Come on, fellers, here's a dead man! We've got to bury him, you know." And at his bidding they pounced upon the dead Phelps lad. The unhappy boy saw clearly his road to rehabilitation, but mind and body revolted at the idea of burial, even as they had revolted at the thought of execution. "No!" he said, stubbornly. "No! I don't want to be buried! I don't want to be buried!"

"You've *got* to be buried!" yelled the chief, passionately. "'Tain't goin' to hurt ye, is it? Think you're made of glass? Come on, fellers, get the grave ready!"

They scattered hemlock boughs upon the snow in the form of a rectangle, and piled other boughs near at hand. The victim surveyed these preparations with a glassy eye. When all was ready, the chief turned determinedly to him: "Come on now, Homer. We've got to carry you to the grave. Get him by the legs, Jim!"

Little Phelps had now passed into that state which may be described as a curious and temporary childish fatalism. He still objected, but it was only feeble muttering, as if he did not know what he spoke. In some confusion

they carried him to the rectangle of hemlock boughs and dropped him. Then they piled other boughs upon him until he was not to be seen. The chief stepped forward to make a short address, but before proceeding with it he thought it expedient, from certain indications, to speak to the grave itself. "Lie still, can't ye? Lie still until I get through." There was a faint movement of the boughs, and then a perfect silence.

The chief took off his hat. Those who watched him could see that his face was harrowed with emotion. "Pards," he began, brokenly—"pards, we've got one more debt to pay them murderin' red-skins. Bowie-knife Joe was a brave man an' a good pard, but—he's gone now—gone." He paused for a moment, overcome, and the stillness was only broken by the deep manly grief of Jimmie Trescott.

XI. THE FIGHT

I

THE child life of the neighborhood was sometimes moved in its deeps at the sight of wagon-loads of furniture arriving in front of some house which, with closed blinds and barred doors, had been for a time a mystery, or even a fear. The boys often expressed this fear by stamping bravely and noisily on the porch of the house, and then suddenly darting away with screams of nervous laughter, as if they expected to be pursued by something uncanny. There was a group who held that the cellar of a vacant house was certainly the abode of robbers, smugglers, assassins, mysterious masked men in council about the dim rays of a candle, and possessing skulls, emblematic bloody daggers, and owls. Then, near the first of April, would come along a wagon-load of furniture, and children would assemble on the walk by the gate and make serious examination of everything that passed into the house, and taking no thought whatever of masked men.

One day it was announced in the neighborhood that a family was actually moving into the Hannigan house, next door to Dr. Trescott's. Jimmie was one of the first to be informed, and by the time some of his friends came dashing up he was versed in much.

"Any boys?" they demanded, eagerly.

"Yes," answered Jimmie, proudly. "One's a little feller, and one's most as big as me. I saw 'em, I did."

"Where are they?" asked Willie Dalzel, as if under the circumstances he could not take Jimmie's word, but must have the evidence of his senses.

"Oh, they're in there," said Jimmie, carelessly. It was evident he owned these new boys.

Willie Dalzel resented Jimmie's proprietary way.

"Ho!" he cried, scornfully. "Why don't they come out, then? Why don't they come out?"

"How d' I know?" said Jimmie.

"Well," retorted Willie Dalzel, "you seemed to know so thundering much about 'em."

At the moment a boy came strolling down the gravel walk which led from the front door to the gate. He was about the height and age of Jimmie Trescott, but he was thick through the chest and had fat legs. His face was round and rosy and plump, but his hair was curly black, and his brows were naturally darkling, so that he resembled both a pudding and a young bull.

He approached slowly the group of older inhabitants, and they had grown profoundly silent. They looked him over; he looked them over. They might have been savages observing the first white man, or white men observing the first savage. The silence held steady.

As he neared the gate the strange boy wandered off to the left in a definite way, which proved his instinct to make a circular voyage when in doubt. The motionless group stared at him. In time this unsmiling scrutiny worked upon him somewhat, and he leaned against the fence and fastidiously examined one shoe.

In the end Willie Dalzel authoritatively broke the stillness. "What's your name?" said he, gruffly.

"Johnnie Hedge 'tis," answered the new boy. Then came another great silence while Whilomville pondered this intelligence.

Again came the voice of authority—"Where'd you live b'fore?"

"Jersey City."

These two sentences completed the first section of the formal code. The second section concerned itself with the establishment of the new-comer's exact position in the neighborhood.

"I kin lick you," announced Willie Dalzel, and awaited the answer.

144

The Hedge boy had stared at Willie Dalzel, but he stared at him again. After a pause he said, "I know you kin."

"Well," demanded Willie, "kin *he* lick you?" And he indicated Jimmie Trescott with a sweep which announced plainly that Jimmie was the next in prowess.

Whereupon the new boy looked at Jimmie respectfully but carefully, and at length said, "I dun'no'."

This was the signal for an outburst of shrill screaming, and everybody pushed Jimmie forward. He knew what he had to say, and, as befitted the occasion, he said it fiercely: "Kin you lick me?"

The new boy also understood what he had to say, and, despite his unhappy and lonely state, he said it bravely: "Yes."

"Well," retorted Jimmie, bluntly, "come out and do it, then! Jest come out and do it!" And these words were greeted with cheers. These little rascals yelled that there should be a fight at once. They were in bliss over the prospect. "Go on, Jim! Make 'im come out. He said he could lick you. Aw-aw-aw! He said he could lick you!" There probably never was a fight among this class in Whilomville which was not the result of the goading and guying of two proud lads by a populace of urchins who simply wished to see a show.

Willie Dalzel was very busy. He turned first to the one and then to the other. "You said you could lick him. Well, why don't you come out and do it, then? You said you could lick him, didn't you?"

"Yes," answered the new boy, dogged and dubious.

Willie tried to drag Jimmie by the arm. "Aw, go on, Jimmie! You ain't afraid, are you?"

"No," said Jimmie.

The two victims opened wide eyes at each other. The fence separated them, and so it was impossible for them to immediately engage; but they seemed to understand that they were ultimately to be sacrificed to the

145

ferocious aspirations of the other boys, and each scanned the other to learn something of his spirit. They were not angry at all. They were merely two little gladiators who were being clamorously told to hurt each other. Each displayed hesitation and doubt without displaying fear. They did not exactly understand what were their feelings, and they moodily kicked the ground and made low and sullen answers to Willie Dalzel, who worked like a circus-manager.

"Aw, go on, Jim! What's the matter with you? You ain't afraid, are you? Well, then, say something." This sentiment received more cheering from the abandoned little wretches who wished to be entertained, and in this cheering there could be heard notes of derision of Jimmie Trescott. The latter had a position to sustain; he was well known; he often bragged of his willingness and ability to thrash other boys; well, then, here was a boy of his size who said that he could not thrash him. What was he going to do about it? The crowd made these arguments very clear, and repeated them again and again.

Finally Jimmie, driven to aggression, walked close to the fence and said to the new boy, "The first time I catch you out of your own yard I'll lam the head off'n you!" This was received with wild plaudits by the Whilomville urchins.

But the new boy stepped back from the fence. He was awed by Jimmie's formidable mien. But he managed to get out a semi-defiant sentence. "Maybe you will, and maybe you won't," said he.

However, his short retreat was taken as a practical victory for Jimmie, and the boys hooted him bitterly. He remained inside the fence, swinging one foot and scowling, while Jimmie was escorted off down the street amid acclamations. The new boy turned and walked back towards the house, his face gloomy, lined deep with discouragement, as if he felt that the new environment's antagonism and palpable cruelty were sure to prove too much for him.

II

The mother of Johnnie Hedge was a widow, and the chief theory of her life was that her boy should be in school on the greatest possible number of days. He himself had no sympathy with this ambition, but she detected the truth of his diseases with an unerring eye, and he was required to be really ill before he could win the right to disregard the first bell, morning and noon. The chicken-pox and the mumps had given him vacations—vacations of misery, wherein he nearly died between pain and nursing. But bad colds in the head did nothing for him, and he was not able to invent a satisfactory hacking cough. His mother was not consistently a tartar. In most things he swayed her to his will. He was allowed to have more jam, pickles, and pie than most boys; she respected his profound loathing of Sunday-school; on summer evenings he could remain out-of-doors until 8.30; but in this matter of school she was inexorable. This single point in her character was of steel.

The Hedges arrived in Whilomville on a Saturday, and on the following Monday Johnnie wended his way to school with a note to the principal and his Jersey City school-books. He knew perfectly well that he would be told to buy new and different books, but in those days mothers always had an idea that old books would "do," and they invariably sent boys off to a new school with books which would not meet the selected and unchangeable views of the new administration. The old books never would "do." Then the boys brought them home to annoyed mothers and asked for ninety cents or sixty cents or eighty-five cents or some number of cents for another outfit. In the garret of every house holding a large family there was a collection of effete school-books, with mother rebellious because James could not inherit his books from Paul, who should properly be Peter's heir, while Peter should be a beneficiary under Henry's will.

But the matter of the books was not the measure of Johnnie Hedge's unhappiness. This whole business of changing schools was a complete torture. Alone he had to go among a new people, a new tribe, and he apprehended his serious time. There were only two fates for him. One meant victory. One meant a kind of serfdom in which he would subscribe to every word of some superior boy and support his every word. It was not anything like an English system of fagging, because boys invariably drifted into the figurative service of other boys whom they devotedly admired, and if they were obliged to subscribe to everything, it is true that they would have done so freely in any case. One means to suggest that Johnnie Hedge had to find his place. Willie Dalzel was a type of the little chieftain, and Willie was a master, but he was not a bully in a special physical sense. He did not drag little boys by the ears until they cried, nor make them tearfully fetch and carry for him. They fetched and carried, but it was because of their worship of his prowess and genius. And so all through the strata of boy life were chieftains and subchieftains and assistant subchieftains. There was no question of little Hedge being towed about by the nose; it was, as one has said, that he had to find his place in a new school. And this in itself was a problem which awed his boyish heart. He was a stranger cast away upon the moon. None knew him, understood him, felt for him. He would be surrounded for this initiative time by a horde of jackal creatures who might turn out in the end to be little boys like himself, but this last point his philosophy could not understand in its fulness.

He came to a white meeting-house sort of a place, in the squat tower of which a great bell was clanging impressively. He passed through an iron gate into a play-ground worn bare as the bed of a mountain brook by the endless runnings and scufflings of little children. There was still a half-hour before the final clangor in the squat tower, but the play-ground held a number of frolicsome imps. A loitering boy espied Johnnie Hedge, and he howled: "Oh! oh! Here's a new feller! Here's a new feller!" He advanced upon the strange arrival. "What's your name?" he demanded, belligerently, like a particularly offensive custom-house officer.

"Johnnie Hedge," responded the new-comer, shyly.

This name struck the other boy as being very comic. All new names strike boys as being comic. He laughed noisily.

"Oh, fellers, he says his name is Johnnie Hedge! Haw! haw! haw!"

The new boy felt that his name was the most disgraceful thing which had ever been attached to a human being.

"Johnnie Hedge! Haw! haw! What room you in?" said the other lad.

"I dun'no'," said Johnnie. In the mean time a small flock of interested vultures had gathered about him. The main thing was his absolute strangeness. He even would have welcomed the sight of his tormentors of Saturday; he had seen them before at least. These creatures were only so many incomprehensible problems. He diffidently began to make his way towards the main door of the school, and the other boys followed him. They demanded information.

"Are you through subtraction yet? We study jogerfre—did you, ever? You live here now? You goin' to school here now?"

To many questions he made answer as well as the clamor would permit, and at length he reached the main door and went quaking unto his new kings. As befitted them, the rabble stopped at the door. A teacher strolling along a corridor found a small boy holding in his hand a note. The boy palpably did not know what to do with the note, but the teacher knew, and took it. Thereafter this little boy was in harness.

A splendid lady in gorgeous robes gave him a seat at a double desk, at the end of which sat a hoodlum with grimy finger-nails, who eyed the inauguration with an extreme and personal curiosity. The other desks were gradually occupied by children, who first were told of the new boy, and then turned upon him a speculative and somewhat derisive eye. The school opened; little classes went forward to a position in front of the teacher's platform and tried to explain that they knew something. The new boy was not requisitioned a great deal; he was allowed to lie dormant until he became used to the scenes and until the teacher found, approximately, his mental position. In the mean time he suffered a shower of stares and whispers and giggles, as if he were a man-ape, whereas he was precisely like other children. From time to time he made funny and pathetic little overtures to other boys, but these overtures could not yet be received; he was not known; he was a foreigner. The village school was like a nation. It was tight. Its amiability or friendship must be won in certain ways.

At recess he hovered in the school-room around the weak lights of society and around the teacher, in the hope that somebody might be good to him, but none considered him save as some sort of a specimen. The teacher of course had a secondary interest in the fact that he was an additional one to a class of sixty-three.

At twelve o'clock, when the ordered files of boys and girls marched towards the door, he exhibited—to no eye—the tremblings of a coward in a charge. He exaggerated the lawlessness of the play-ground and the street.

But the reality was hard enough. A shout greeted him:

"Oh, here's the new feller! Here's the new feller!"

Small and utterly obscure boys teased him. He had a hard time of it to get to the gate. There never was any actual hurt, but everything was competent to smite the lad with shame. It was a curious, groundless shame, but nevertheless it was shame. He was a new-comer, and he definitely felt the disgrace of the fact. In the street he was seen and recognized by some lads who had formed part of the group of Saturday. They shouted:

"Oh, Jimmie! Jimmie! Here he is! Here's that new feller!"

Jimmie Trescott was going virtuously towards his luncheon when he heard these cries behind him. He pretended not to hear, and in this deception he was assisted by the fact that he was engaged at the time in a furious argument with a friend over the relative merits of two "Uncle Tom's Cabin" companies. It appeared that one company had only two bloodhounds, while the other had ten. On the other hand, the first company had two Topsys and two Uncle Toms, while the second had only one Topsy and one Uncle Tom.

But the shouting little boys were hard after him. Finally they were even pulling at his arms.

"Jimmie—"

"What?" he demanded, turning with a snarl. "What d'you want? Leggo my arm!"

"Here he is! Here's the new feller! Here's the new feller! Now!"

"I don't care if he is," said Jimmie, with grand impatience. He tilted his chin. "I don't care if he is."

150

Then they reviled him. "Thought you was goin' to lick him first time you caught him! Yah! You're a 'fraid-cat!" They began to sing "'Fraid-cat! 'Fraidcat! 'Fraid-cat!" He expostulated hotly, turning from one to the other, but they would not listen. In the mean time the Hedge boy slunk on his way, looking with deep anxiety upon this attempt to send Jimmie against him. But Jimmie would have none of the plan.

III

When the children met again on the play-ground, Jimmie was openly challenged with cowardice. He had made a big threat in the hearing of comrades, and when invited by them to take advantage of an opportunity, he had refused. They had been fairly sure of their amusement, and they were indignant. Jimmie was finally driven to declare that as soon as school was out for the day, he would thrash the Hedge boy.

When finally the children came rushing out of the iron gate, filled with the delights of freedom, a hundred boys surrounded Jimmie in high spirits, for he had said that he was determined. They waited for the lone lad from Jersey City. When he appeared, Jimmie wasted no time. He walked straight to him and said, "Did you say you kin lick me?"

Johnnie Hedge was cowed, shrinking, affrighted, and the roars of a hundred boys thundered in his ears, but again he knew what he had to say. "Yes," he gasped, in anguish.

"Then," said Jimmie, resolutely, "you've got to fight." There was a joyous clamor by the mob. The beleaguered lad looked this way and that way for succor, as Willie Dalzel and other officious youngsters policed an irregular circle in the crowd. He saw Jimmie facing him; there was no help for it; he dropped his books—the old books which would not "do."

Now it was the fashion among tiny Whilomville belligerents to fight much in the manner of little bear cubs. Two boys would rush upon each other, immediately grapple, and—the best boy having probably succeeded in getting the coveted "under hold"—there would presently be a crash to the earth of the inferior boy, and he would probably be mopped around in the dust, or the mud, or the snow, or whatever the material happened to be, until the engagement was over. Whatever havoc was dealt out to him was ordinarily the result of his wild endeavors to throw off his opponent and arise. Both infants wept during the fight, as a common thing, and if they wept very hard, the fight was a harder fight. The result was never very bloody, but the complete dishevelment of both victor and vanquished was extraordinary. As for the spectacle, it more resembled a collision of boys in a fog than it did the manly art of hammering another human being into speechless inability.

The fight began when Jimmie made a mad, bear-cub rush at the new boy, amid savage cries of encouragement. Willie Dalzel, for instance, almost howled his head off. Very timid boys on the outskirts of the throng felt their hearts leap to their throats. It was a time when certain natures were impressed that only man is vile.

But it appeared that bear-cub rushing was no part of the instruction received by boys in Jersey City. Boys in Jersey City were apparently schooled curiously. Upon the onslaught of Jimmie, the stranger had gone wild with rage—boylike. Some spark had touched his fighting-blood, and in a moment he was a cornered, desperate, fire-eyed little man. He began to swing his arms, to revolve them so swiftly that one might have considered him a small, working model of an extra-fine patented windmill which was caught in a gale. For a moment this defence surprised Jimmie more than it damaged him, but two moments later a small, knotty fist caught him squarely in the eye, and with a shriek he went down in defeat. He lay on the ground so stunned that he could not even cry; but if he had been able to cry, he would have cried over his prestige—or something—not over his eye.

There was a dreadful tumult. The boys cast glances of amazement and terror upon the victor, and thronged upon the beaten Jimmie Trescott. It was a moment of excitement so intense that one cannot say what happened. Never before had Whilomville seen such a thing—not the little tots. They were aghast, dumfounded, and they glanced often over their shoulders at the new boy, who stood alone, his clinched fists at his side, his face crimson, his lips still working with the fury of battle.

But there was another surprise for Whilomville. It might have been seen that the little victor was silently debating against an impulse.

But the impulse won, for the lone lad from Jersey City suddenly wheeled, sprang like a demon, and struck another boy.

A curtain should be drawn before this deed. A knowledge of it is really too much for the heart to bear. The other boy was Willie Dalzel. The lone lad from Jersey City had smitten him full sore.

There is little to say of it. It must have been that a feeling worked gradually to the top of the little stranger's wrath that Jimmie Trescott had been a mere tool, that the front and centre of his persecutors had been Willie Dalzel, and being rendered temporarily lawless by his fighting-blood, he raised his hand and smote for revenge.

Willie Dalzel had been in the middle of a vandal's cry, which screeched out over the voices of everybody. The new boy's fist cut it in half, so to say. And then arose the howl of an amazed and terrorized walrus.

One wishes to draw a second curtain. Without discussion or inquiry or brief retort, Willie Dalzel ran away. He ran like a hare straight for home, this redoubtable chieftain. Following him at a heavy and slow pace ran the impassioned new boy. The scene was long remembered.

Willie Dalzel was no coward; he had been panic-stricken into running away from a new thing. He ran as a man might run from the sudden appearance of a vampire or a ghoul or a gorilla. This was no time for academics—he ran.

Jimmie slowly gathered himself and came to his feet. "Where's Willie?" said he, first of all. The crowd sniggered. "Where's Willie?" said Jimmie again.

"Why, he licked him *too*!" answered a boy suddenly.

"He did?" said Jimmie. He sat weakly down on the roadway. "He did?" After allowing a moment for the fact to sink into him, he looked up at the crowd with his one good eye and his one bunged eye, and smiled cheerfully

XII. THE CITY URCHIN AND THE CHASTE VILLAGERS

AFTER the brief encounters between the Hedge boy and Jimmie Trescott and the Hedge boy and Willie Dalzel, the neighborhood which contained the homes of the boys was, as far as child life is concerned, in a state resembling anarchy. This was owing to the signal overthrow and shameful retreat of the boy who had for several years led a certain little clan by the nose. The adherence of the little community did not go necessarily to the boy who could whip all the others, but it certainly could not go to a boy who had run away in a manner that made his shame patent to the whole world. Willie Dalzel found himself in a painful position. This tiny tribe which had followed him with such unwavering faith was now largely engaged in whistling and catcalling and hooting. He chased a number of them into the sanctity of their own yards, but from these coigns they continued to ridicule him.

But it must not be supposed that the fickle tribe went over in a body to the new light. They did nothing of the sort. They occupied themselves with avenging all which they had endured—gladly enough, too—for many months. As for the Hedge boy, he maintained a curious timid reserve, minding his own business with extreme care, and going to school with that deadly punctuality of which his mother was the genius. Jimmie Trescott suffered no adverse criticism from his fellows. He was entitled to be beaten by a boy who had made Willie Dalzel bellow like a bull-calf and run away. Indeed, he received some honors. He had confronted a very superior boy and received a bang in the eye which for a time was the wonder of the children, and he had not bellowed like a bull-calf. As a matter of fact, he was often invited to tell how it had felt, and this he did with some pride, claiming arrogantly that he had been superior to any particular pain.

Early in the episode he and the Hedge boy had patched up a treaty. Living next door to each other, they could not fail to have each other often in sight. One afternoon they wandered together in the strange indefinite diplomacy of boyhood. As they drew close the new boy suddenly said, "Napple?"

"Yes," said Jimmie, and the new boy bestowed upon him an apple. It was one of those green-coated winter-apples which lie for many months in safe and dry places, and can at any time be brought forth for the persecution of the unwary and inexperienced. An older age would have fled from this apple, but to the unguided youth of Jimmie Trescott it was a thing to be possessed and cherished. Wherefore this apple was the emblem of something more than a truce, despite the fact that it tasted like wet Indian meal; and Jimmie looked at the Hedge boy out of one good eye and one bunged eye. The long-drawn animosities of men have no place in the life of a boy. The boy's mind is flexible; he readjusts his position with an ease which is derived from the fact—simply—that he is not yet a man.

But there were other and more important matters. Johnnie Hedge's exploits had brought him into such prominence among the school-boys that it was necessary to settle a number of points once and for all. There was the usual number of boys in the school who were popularly known to be champions in their various classes. Among these Johnnie Hedge now had to thread his way, every boy taking it upon himself to feel anxious that Johnnie's exact position should be soon established. His fame as a fighter had gone forth to the world, but there were other boys who had fame as fighters, and the world was extremely anxious to know where to place the new-comer. Various heroes were urged to attempt this classification. Usually it was not accounted a matter of supreme importance, but in this boy life it was essential.

In all cases the heroes were backward enough. It was their followings who agitated the question. And so Johnnie Hedge was more or less beset.

He maintained his bashfulness. He backed away from altercation. It was plain that to bring matters to a point he must be forced into a quarrel. It was also plain that the proper person for the business was some boy who could whip Willie Dalzel, and these formidable warriors were distinctly averse to undertaking the new contract. It is a kind of a law in boy life that a quiet, decent, peace-loving lad is able to thrash a wide-mouthed talker. And so it had transpired that by a peculiar system of elimination most of the real chiefs were quiet, decent, peace-loving boys, and they had no desire to engage in a fight with a boy on the sole grounds that it was not known who could whip. Johnnie Hedge attended his affairs, they attended their affairs, and around them waged this discussion of relative merit. Jimmie Trescott took a prominent part in these arguments. He contended that Johnnie Hedge could thrash any boy in the world. He was certain of it, and to any one who opposed him he said, "You just get one of those smashes in the eye, and then you'll see." In the mean time there was a grand and impressive silence in the direction of Willie Dalzel. He had gathered remnants of his clan, but the main parts of his sovereignty were scattered to the winds. He was an enemy.

Owing to the circumspect behavior of the new boy, the commotions on the school grounds came to nothing. He was often asked, "Kin you lick him?" And he invariably replied, "I dun'no'." This idea of waging battle with the entire world appalled him.

A war for complete supremacy of the tribe which had been headed by Willie Dalzel was fought out in the country of the tribe. It came to pass that a certain half-dime blood-and-thunder pamphlet had a great vogue in the tribe at this particular time. This story relates the experience of a lad who began his career as cabin-boy on a pirate ship. Throughout the first fifteen chapters he was rope's-ended from one end of the ship to the other end, and very often he was felled to the deck by a heavy fist. He lived through enough hardships to have killed a battalion of Turkish soldiers, but in the end he rose upon them. Yes, he rose upon them. Hordes of pirates fell before his intrepid arm, and in the last chapters of the book he is seen jauntily careering on his own hook as one of the most gallous pirate captains that ever sailed the seas.

Naturally, when this tale was thoroughly understood by the tribe, they had to dramatize it, although it was a dramatization that would gain no royalties for the author. Now it was plain that the urchin who was cast for the cabin-boy's part would lead a life throughout the first fifteen chapters which would attract few actors. Willie Dalzel developed a scheme by which some small lad would play cabin-boy during this period of misfortune and abuse, and then, when the cabin-boy came to the part where he slew all his enemies and reached his zenith, that he, Willie Dalzel, should take the part.

This fugitive and disconnected rendering of a great play opened in

Jimmie Trescott's back garden. The path between the two lines of gooseberry-bushes was elected unanimously to be the ship. Then Willie Dalzel insisted that Homer Phelps should be the cabin-boy. Homer tried the position for a time, and then elected that he would resign in favor of some other victim. There was no other applicant to succeed him, whereupon it became necessary to press some boy. Jimmie Trescott was a great actor, as is well known, but he steadfastly refused to engage for the part. Ultimately they seized upon little Dan Earl, whose disposition was so milky and docile that he would do whatever anybody asked of him. But Dan Earl made the one firm revolt of his life after trying existence as cabin-boy for some ten minutes. Willie Dalzel was in despair. Then he suddenly sighted the little brother of Johnnie Hedge, who had come into the garden, and in a poor-little-stranger sort of fashion was looking wistfully at the play. When he was invited to become the cabin-boy he accepted joyfully, thinking that it was his initiation into the tribe. Then they proceeded to give him the rope's end and to punch him with a realism which was not altogether painless. Directly he began to cry out. They exhorted him not to cry out, not to mind it, but still they continued to hurt him.

There was a commotion among the gooseberry-bushes, two branches were swept aside, and Johnnie Hedge walked down upon them. Every boy stopped in his tracks. Johnnie was boiling with rage.

"Who hurt him?" he said, ferociously. "Did *you?*" He had looked at Willie Dalzel.

Willie Dalzel began to mumble: "We was on'y playin'. Wasn't nothin' fer him to cry fer."

The new boy had at his command some big phrases, and he used them. "I am goin' to whip you within an inch of your life. I am goin' to tan the hide off'n you." And immediately there was a mixture—an infusion of two boys which looked as if it had been done by a chemist. The other children stood back, stricken with horror. But out of this whirl they presently perceived the figure of Willie Dalzel seated upon the chest of the Hedge boy.

"Got enough?" asked Willie, hoarsely.

"No," choked out the Hedge boy. Then there was another flapping and floundering, and finally another calm.

"Got enough?" asked Willie.

"No," said the Hedge boy. A sort of war-cloud again puzzled the sight of the observers. Both combatants were breathless, bloodless in their faces, and very weak.

"Got enough?" said Willie.

"No," said the Hedge boy. The carnage was again renewed. All the spectators were silent but Johnnie Hedge's little brother, who shrilly exhorted him to continue the struggle. But it was not plain that the Hedge boy needed any encouragement, for he was crying bitterly, and it has been explained that when a boy cried it was a bad time to hope for peace. He had managed to wriggle over upon his hands and knees. But Willie Dalzel was tenaciously gripping him from the back, and it seemed that his strength would spend itself in futility. The bear cub seemed to have the advantage of the working model of the windmill. They heaved, uttered strange words, wept, and the sun looked down upon them with steady, unwinking eye.

Peter Washington came out of the stable and observed this tragedy of the back garden. He stood transfixed for a moment, and then ran towards it, shouting: "Hi! What's all dish yere? Hi! Stopper dat, stopper dat, you two! For lan' sake, what's all dish yere?" He grabbed the struggling boys and pulled them apart. He was stormy and fine in his indignation. "For lan' sake! You two kids act like you gwine mad dogs. Stopper dat!" The whitened, tearful, soiled combatants, their clothing all awry, glared fiercely at each other as Peter stood between them, lecturing. They made several futile attempts to circumvent him and again come to battle. As he fended them off with his open hands he delivered his reproaches at Jimmie. "I's s'prised at you! I suhtainly is!"

"Why?" said Jimmie. "I 'ain't done nothin'. What have I done?"

"Y-y-you done 'courage dese yere kids ter scrap," said Peter, virtuously.

"Me?" cried Jimmie. "I 'ain't had nothin' to do with it."

"I raikon you 'ain't," retorted Peter, with heavy sarcasm. "I raikon you been er-prayin', 'ain't you?" Turning to Willie Dalzel, he said, "You jest take an' run erlong outer dish yere or I'll jest nachually take an' damnearkill you." Willie Dalzel went. To the new boy Peter said: "You look like you had some saince, but I raikon you don't know no more'n er rabbit. You jest take an' trot erlong off home, an' don' lemme caitch you round yere er-fightin' or I'll break yer back." The Hedge boy moved away with dignity, followed by his little brother. The latter, when he had placed a sufficient distance between himself and Peter, played his fingers at his nose and called out:

"Nig-ger-r-r! Nig-ger-r-r!"

Peter Washington's resentment poured out upon Jimmie.

"'Pears like you never would understan' you ain't reg'lar common trash. You take an' 'sociate with an'body what done come erlong."

"Aw, go on," retorted Jimmie, profanely. "Go soak your head, Pete."

The remaining boys retired to the street, whereupon they perceived Willie Dalzel in the distance. He ran to them.

"I licked him!" he shouted, exultantly. "I licked him! Didn't I, now?"

From the Whilomville point of view he was entitled to a favorable answer. They made it. "Yes," they said, "you did."

"I run in," cried Willie, "an' I grabbed 'im, an' afore he knew what it was I throwed 'im. An' then it was easy." He puffed out his chest and smiled like an English recruiting-sergeant. "An' now," said he, suddenly facing Jimmie Trescott, "whose side were you on?"

The question was direct and startling. Jimmie gave back two paces. "He licked you once," he explained, haltingly.

"He never saw the day when he could lick one side of me. I could lick him with my left hand tied behind me. Why, I could lick him when I was asleep." Willie Dalzel was magnificent.

A gate clicked, and Johnnie Hedge was seen to be strolling towards them.

"You said," he remarked, coldly, "you licked me, didn't you?"

Willie Dalzel stood his ground. "Yes," he said, stoutly.

"Well, you're a liar," said the Hedge boy.

"You're another," retorted Willie.

"No, I ain't, either, but you're a liar."

"You're another," retorted Willie.

"Don't you dare tell me I'm a liar, or I'll smack your mouth for you," said the Hedge boy.

"Well, I did, didn't I?" barked Willie. "An' whatche goin' to do about it?"

"I'm goin' to lam you," said the Hedge boy.

He approached to attack warily, and the other boys held their breaths. Willie Dalzel winced back a pace. "Hol' on a minute," he cried, raising his palm. "I'm not—"

But the comic windmill was again in motion, and between gasps from his exertions Johnnie Hedge remarked, "I'll show—you—whether—you kin—lick me—or not."

The first blows did not reach home on Willie, for he backed away with expedition, keeping up his futile cry, "Hol' on a minute." Soon enough a swinging fist landed on his cheek. It did not knock him down, but it hurt him a little and frightened him a great deal. He suddenly opened his mouth to an amazing and startling extent, tilted back his head, and howled, while his eyes, glittering with tears, were fixed upon this scowling butcher of a Johnnie Hedge. The latter was making slow and vicious circles, evidently intending to renew the massacre.

But the spectators really had been desolated and shocked by the terrible thing which had happened to Willie Dalzel. They now cried out: "No, no; don't hit 'im any more! Don't hit 'im any more!"

Jimmie Trescott, in a panic of bravery, yelled, "We'll all jump on you if you do."

160

The Hedge boy paused, at bay. He breathed angrily, and flashed his glance from lad to lad.

They still protested: "No, no; don't hit 'im any more. Don't hit 'im no more."

"I'll hammer him until he can't stand up," said Johnnie, observing that they all feared him. "I'll fix him so he won't know hisself, an' if any of you kids bother with me—"

Suddenly he ceased, he trembled, he collapsed. The hand of one approaching from behind had laid hold upon his ear, and it was the hand of one whom he knew.

The other lads heard a loud, iron-filing voice say, "Caught ye at it again, ye brat, ye." They saw a dreadful woman with gray hair, with a sharp red nose, with bare arms, with spectacles of such magnifying quality that her eyes shone through them like two fierce white moons. She was Johnnie Hedge's mother. Still holding Johnnie by the ear, she swung out swiftly and dexterously, and succeeded in boxing the ears of two boys before the crowd regained its presence of mind and stampeded. Yes, the war for supremacy was over, and the question was never again disputed. The supreme power was Mrs. Hedge.

XIII. A LITTLE PILGRIMAGE

ONE November it became clear to childish minds in certain parts of Whilomville that the Sunday-school of the Presbyterian church would not have for the children the usual tree on Christmas eve. The funds free for that ancient festival would be used for the relief of suffering among the victims of the Charleston earthquake.

The plan had been born in the generous head of the superintendent of the Sunday-school, and during one session he had made a strong plea that the children should forego the vain pleasures of a tree and, in glorious application of the Golden Rule, refuse a local use of the fund, and will that it be sent where dire pain might be alleviated. At the end of a tearfully eloquent speech the question was put fairly to a vote, and the children in a burst of virtuous abandon carried the question for Charleston. Many of the teachers had been careful to preserve a finely neutral attitude, but even if they had cautioned the children against being too impetuous they could not have checked the wild impulses.

But this was a long time before Christmas.

Very early, boys held important speech together. "Huh! you ain't goin' to have no Christmas tree at the Presbyterian Sunday-school."

Sullenly the victim answered, "No, we ain't."

"Huh!" scoffed the other denomination, "we are goin' to have the all-firedest biggest tree that you ever saw in the world."

The little Presbyterians were greatly downcast.

It happened that Jimmie Trescott had regularly attended the Presbyterian Sunday-school. The Trescotts were consistently undenominational, but they had sent their lad on Sundays to one of the places where they thought he would receive benefits. However, on one day in December, Jimmie appeared before his father and made a strong spiritual appeal to be forthwith attached to the Sunday-school of the Big Progressive church. Doctor Trescott mused this question considerably. "Well, Jim," he said, "why do you conclude that the Big Progressive Sunday-school is better for you than the Presbyterian Sunday-school?"

"Now—it's nicer," answered Jimmie, looking at his father with an anxious eye.

"How do you mean?"

"Why—now—some of the boys what go to the Presbyterian place, they ain't very nice," explained the flagrant Jimmie.

Trescott mused the question considerably once more. In the end he said: "Well, you may change if you wish, this one time, but you must not be changing to and fro. You decide now, and then you must abide by your decision."

"Yessir," said Jimmie, brightly. "Big Progressive."

"All right," said the father. "But remember what I've told you."

On the following Sunday morning Jimmie presented himself at the door of the basement of the Big Progressive church. He was conspicuously washed, notably raimented, prominently polished. And, incidentally, he was very uncomfortable because of all these virtues.

A number of acquaintances greeted him contemptuously. "Hello, Jimmie! What you doin' here? Thought you was a Presbyterian?"

Jimmie cast down his eyes and made no reply. He was too cowed by the change. However, Homer Phelps, who was a regular patron of the Big Progressive Sunday-school, suddenly appeared and said, "Hello, Jim!" Jimmie seized upon him. Homer Phelps was amenable to Trescott laws, tribal if you like, but iron-bound, almost compulsory.

"Hello, Homer!" said Jimmie, and his manner was so good that Homer felt a great thrill in being able to show his superior a new condition of life.

"You 'ain't never come here afore, have you?" he demanded, with a new arrogance.

"No, I 'ain't," said Jimmie. Then they stared at each other and manœuvred.

"You don't know my teacher," said Homer.

"No, I don't know her" admitted Jimmie, but in a way which contended, modestly, that he knew countless other Sunday-school teachers.

"Better join our class," said Homer, sagely. "She wears spectacles; don't see very well. Sometimes we do almost what we like."

"All right," said Jimmie, glad to place himself in the hands of his friends. In due time they entered the Sunday-school room, where a man with benevolent whiskers stood on a platform and said, "We will now sing No. 33—'Pull for the Shore, Sailor, Pull for the Shore.'" And as the obedient throng burst into melody the man on the platform indicated the time with a fat, white, and graceful hand. He was an ideal Sunday-school superintendent—one who had never felt hunger or thirst or the wound of the challenge of dishonor; a man, indeed, with beautiful flat hands who waved them in greasy victorious beneficence over a crowd of children.

Jimmie, walking carefully on his toes, followed Homer Phelps. He felt that the kingly superintendent might cry out and blast him to ashes before he could reach a chair. It was a desperate journey. But at last he heard Homer muttering to a young lady, who looked at him through glasses which greatly magnified her eyes. "A new boy," she said, in an oily and deeply religious voice.

"Yes'm," said Jimmie, trembling. The five other boys of the class scanned him keenly and derided his condition.

"We will proceed to the lesson," said the young lady. Then she cried sternly, like a sergeant, "The seventh chapter of Jeremiah!"

There was a swift fluttering of leaflets. Then the name of Jeremiah, a wise man, towered over the feelings of these boys. Homer Phelps was doomed to read the fourth verse. He took a deep breath, he puffed out his lips, he gathered his strength for a great effort. His beginning was childishly explosive. He hurriedly said:

"Trust ye not in lying words, saying The temple of the Lord, the temple of the Lord, the temple of the Lord, are these."

"Now," said the teacher, "Johnnie Scanlan, tell us what these words mean." The Scanlan boy shamefacedly muttered that he did not know. The teacher's countenance saddened. Her heart was in her work; she wanted to make a success of this Sunday-school class. "Perhaps Homer Phelps can tell us," she remarked.

Homer gulped; he looked at Jimmie. Through the great room hummed a steady hum. A little circle, very near, was being told about Daniel in the lion's den. They were deeply moved. At the moment they liked Sunday-school.

"Why—now—it means," said Homer, with a grand pomposity born of a sense of hopeless ignorance—"it means—why it means that they were in the wrong place."

"No," said the teacher, profoundly; "it means that we should be good, very good indeed. That is what it means. It means that we should love the Lord and be good. Love the Lord and be good. That is what it means."

The little boys suddenly had a sense of black wickedness as their teacher looked austerely upon them. They gazed at her with the wide-open eyes of simplicity. They were stirred again. This thing of being good—this great business of life—apparently it was always successful. They knew from the fairy tales. But it was difficult, wasn't it? It was said to be the most heart-breaking task to be generous, wasn't it? One had to pay the price of one's eyes in order to be pacific, didn't one? As for patience, it was tortured martyrdom to be patient, wasn't it? Sin was simple, wasn't it? But virtue was so difficult that it could only be practised by heavenly beings, wasn't it?

And the angels, the Sunday-school superintendent, and the teacher swam in the high visions of the little boys as beings so good that if a boy scratched his shin in the same room he was a profane and sentenced devil.

"And," said the teacher, "'The temple of the Lord'—what does that mean? I'll ask the new boy. What does that mean?"

"I dun'no'," said Jimmie, blankly.

But here the professional bright boy of the class suddenly awoke to his obligations. "Teacher," he cried, "it means church, same as this."

"Exactly," said the teacher, deeply satisfied with this reply. "You know your lesson well, Clarence. I am much pleased."

The other boys, instead of being envious, looked with admiration upon Clarence, while he adopted an air of being habituated to perform such feats every day of his life. Still, he was not much of a boy. He had the virtue of being able to walk on very high stilts, but when the season of stilts had passed he possessed no rank save this Sunday-school rank, this clever-little-Clarence business of knowing the Bible and the lesson better than the other boys. The other boys, sometimes looking at him meditatively, did not actually decide to thrash him as soon as he cleared the portals of the church, but they certainly decided to molest him in such ways as would re-establish their self-respect. Back of the superintendent's chair hung a lithograph of the martyrdom of St. Stephen.

Jimmie, feeling stiff and encased in his best clothes, waited for the ordeal to end. A bell pealed: the fat hand of the superintendent had tapped a bell. Slowly the rustling and murmuring dwindled to silence. The benevolent man faced the school. "I have to announce," he began, waving his body from side to side in the conventional bows of his kind, "that—" Bang went the bell. "Give me your attention, please, children. I have to announce that the Board has decided that this year there will be no Christmas tree, but the—"

Instantly the room buzzed with the subdued clamor of the children. Jimmie was speechless. He stood morosely during the singing of the closing hymn. He passed out into the street with the others, pushing no more than was required.

Speedily the whole idea left him. If he remembered Sunday-school at all, it was to remember that he did not like it.

THE THIRD VIOLET

CHAPTER I.

The engine bellowed its way up the slanting, winding valley. Grey crags, and trees with roots fastened cleverly to the steeps looked down at the struggles of the black monster.

When the train finally released its passengers they burst forth with the enthusiasm of escaping convicts. A great bustle ensued on the platform of the little mountain station. The idlers and philosophers from the village were present to examine the consignment of people from the city. These latter, loaded with bundles and children, thronged at the stage drivers. The stage drivers thronged at the people from the city.

Hawker, with his clothes case, his paint-box, his easel, climbed awkwardly down the steps of the car. The easel swung uncontrolled and knocked against the head of a little boy who was disembarking backward with fine caution. "Hello, little man," said Hawker, "did it hurt?" The child regarded him in silence and with sudden interest, as if Hawker had called his attention to a phenomenon. The young painter was politely waiting until the little boy should conclude his examination, but a voice behind him cried, "Roger, go on down!" A nursemaid was conducting a little girl where she would probably be struck by the other end of the easel. The boy resumed his cautious descent.

The stage drivers made such great noise as a collection that as individuals their identities were lost. With a highly important air, as a man proud of being so busy, the baggageman of the train was thundering trunks at the other employees on the platform. Hawker, prowling through the crowd, heard a voice near his shoulder say, "Do you know where is the stage for Hemlock Inn?" Hawker turned and found a young woman regarding him. A wave of astonishment whirled into his hair, and he turned his eyes quickly for fear that she would think that he had looked at her. He said, "Yes, certainly, I think I can find it." At the same time he was crying to himself: "Wouldn't I like to paint her, though! What a glance—oh, murder! The—the—the distance in her eyes!"

He went fiercely from one driver to another. That obdurate stage for Hemlock Inn must appear at once. Finally he perceived a man who grinned expectantly at him. "Oh," said Hawker, "you drive the stage for Hemlock Inn?" The man admitted it. Hawker said, "Here is the stage." The young woman smiled.

The driver inserted Hawker and his luggage far into the end of the vehicle. He sat there, crooked forward so that his eyes should see the first coming of the girl into the frame of light at the other end of the stage. Presently she appeared there. She was bringing the little boy, the little girl, the nursemaid, and another young woman, who was at once to be known as the mother of the two children. The girl indicated the stage with a small gesture of triumph. When they were all seated uncomfortably in the huge covered vehicle the little boy gave Hawker a glance of recognition. "It hurted then, but it's all right now," he informed him cheerfully.

"Did it?" replied Hawker. "I'm sorry."

"Oh, I didn't mind it much," continued the little boy, swinging his long, red-leather leggings bravely to and fro. "I don't cry when I'm hurt, anyhow." He cast a meaning look at his tiny sister, whose soft lips set defensively.

The driver climbed into his seat, and after a scrutiny of the group in the gloom of the stage he chirped to his horses. They began a slow and thoughtful trotting. Dust streamed out behind the vehicle. In front, the green hills were still and serene in the evening air. A beam of gold struck them aslant, and on the sky was lemon and pink information of the sun's sinking. The driver knew many people along the road, and from time to time he conversed with them in yells.

The two children were opposite Hawker. They sat very correctly mucilaged to their seats, but their large eyes were always upon Hawker, calmly valuing him.

"Do you think it nice to be in the country? I do," said the boy.

"I like it very well," answered Hawker.

"I shall go fishing, and hunting, and everything. Maybe I shall shoot a bears."

"I hope you may."

"Did you ever shoot a bears?"

"No."

"Well, I didn't, too, but maybe I will. Mister Hollanden, he said he'd look around for one. Where I live——"

"Roger," interrupted the mother from her seat at Hawker's side, "perhaps every one is not interested in your conversation." The boy seemed embarrassed at this interruption, for he leaned back in silence with an apologetic look at Hawker. Presently the stage began to climb the hills, and the two children were obliged to take grip upon the cushions for fear of being precipitated upon the nursemaid.

Fate had arranged it so that Hawker could not observe the girl with the—the—the distance in her eyes without leaning forward and discovering to her his interest. Secretly and impiously he wriggled in his seat, and as the bumping stage swung its passengers this way and that way, he obtained fleeting glances of a cheek, an arm, or a shoulder.

The driver's conversation tone to his passengers was also a yell. "Train was an hour late t'night," he said, addressing the interior. "It'll be nine o'clock before we git t' th' inn, an' it'll be perty dark travellin'."

Hawker waited decently, but at last he said, "Will it?"

"Yes. No moon." He turned to face Hawker, and roared, "You're ol' Jim Hawker's son, hain't yeh?"

"Yes."

"I thort I'd seen yeh b'fore. Live in the city now, don't yeh?"

"Yes."

"Want t' git off at th' cross-road?"

173

"Yes."

"Come up fer a little stay doorin' th' summer?"

"Yes."

"On'y charge yeh a quarter if yeh git off at cross-road. Useter charge 'em fifty cents, but I ses t' th' ol' man. 'Tain't no use. Goldern 'em, they'll walk ruther'n put up fifty cents.' Yep. On'y a quarter."

In the shadows Hawker's expression seemed assassinlike. He glanced furtively down the stage. She was apparently deep in talk with the mother of the children.

CHAPTER II.

When Hawker pushed at the old gate, it hesitated because of a broken hinge. A dog barked with loud ferocity and came headlong over the grass.

"Hello, Stanley, old man!" cried Hawker. The ardour for battle was instantly smitten from the dog, and his barking swallowed in a gurgle of delight. He was a large orange and white setter, and he partly expressed his emotion by twisting his body into a fantastic curve and then dancing over the ground with his head and his tail very near to each other. He gave vent to little sobs in a wild attempt to vocally describe his gladness. "Well, 'e was a dreat dod," said Hawker, and the setter, overwhelmed, contorted himself wonderfully.

There were lights in the kitchen, and at the first barking of the dog the door had been thrown open. Hawker saw his two sisters shading their eyes and peering down the yellow stream. Presently they shouted, "Here he is!" They flung themselves out and upon him. "Why, Will! why, Will!" they panted.

"We're awful glad to see you!" In a whirlwind of ejaculation and unanswerable interrogation they grappled the clothes case, the paint-box, the easel, and dragged him toward the house.

He saw his old mother seated in a rocking-chair by the table. She had laid aside her paper and was adjusting her glasses as she scanned the darkness. "Hello, mother!" cried Hawker, as he entered. His eyes were bright. The old mother reached her arms to his neck. She murmured soft and half-articulate words. Meanwhile the dog writhed from one to another. He raised his muzzle high to express his delight. He was always fully convinced that he was taking a principal part in this ceremony of welcome and that everybody was heeding him.

"Have you had your supper?" asked the old mother as soon as she recovered herself. The girls clamoured sentences at him. "Pa's out in the barn,

Will. What made you so late? He said maybe he'd go up to the cross-roads to see if he could see the stage. Maybe he's gone. What made you so late? And, oh, we got a new buggy!"

The old mother repeated anxiously, "Have you had your supper?"

"No," said Hawker, "but——"

The three women sprang to their feet. "Well, we'll git you something right away." They bustled about the kitchen and dove from time to time into the cellar. They called to each other in happy voices.

Steps sounded on the line of stones that led from the door toward the barn, and a shout came from the darkness. "Well, William, home again, hey?" Hawker's grey father came stamping genially into the room. "I thought maybe you got lost. I was comin' to hunt you," he said, grinning, as they stood with gripped hands. "What made you so late?"

While Hawker confronted the supper the family sat about and contemplated him with shining eyes. His sisters noted his tie and propounded some questions concerning it. His mother watched to make sure that he should consume a notable quantity of the preserved cherries. "He used to be so fond of 'em when he was little," she said.

"Oh, Will," cried the younger sister, "do you remember Lil' Johnson? Yeh? She's married. Married las' June."

"Is the boy's room all ready, mother?" asked the father.

"We fixed it this mornin'," she said.

"And do you remember Jeff Decker?" shouted the elder sister. "Well, he's dead. Yep. Drowned, pickerel fishin'—poor feller!"

"Well, how are you gitting along, William?" asked the father. "Sell many pictures?"

"An occasional one."

"Saw your illustrations in the May number of Perkinson's." The old man paused for a moment, and then added, quite weakly, "Pretty good."

176

"How's everything about the place?"

"Oh, just about the same—'bout the same. The colt run away with me last week, but didn't break nothin', though. I was scared, because I had out the new buggy—we got a new buggy—but it didn't break nothin'. I'm goin' to sell the oxen in the fall; I don't want to winter 'em. And then in the spring I'll get a good hoss team. I rented th' back five-acre to John Westfall. I had more'n I could handle with only one hired hand. Times is pickin' up a little, but not much—not much."

"And we got a new school-teacher," said one of the girls.

"Will, you never noticed my new rocker," said the old mother, pointing. "I set it right where I thought you'd see it, and you never took no notice. Ain't it nice? Father bought it at Monticello for my birthday. I thought you'd notice it first thing."

When Hawker had retired for the night, he raised a sash and sat by the window smoking. The odour of the woods and the fields came sweetly to his nostrils. The crickets chanted their hymn of the night. On the black brow of the mountain he could see two long rows of twinkling dots which marked the position of Hemlock Inn.

CHAPTER III.

Hawker had a writing friend named Hollanden. In New York Hollanden had announced his resolution to spend the summer at Hemlock Inn. "I don't like to see the world progressing," he had said; "I shall go to Sullivan County for a time."

In the morning Hawker took his painting equipment, and after manœuvring in the fields until he had proved to himself that he had no desire to go toward the inn, he went toward it. The time was only nine o'clock, and he knew that he could not hope to see Hollanden before eleven, as it was only through rumour that Hollanden was aware that there was a sunrise and an early morning.

Hawker encamped in front of some fields of vivid yellow stubble on which trees made olive shadows, and which was overhung by a china-blue sky and sundry little white clouds. He fiddled away perfunctorily at it. A spectator would have believed, probably, that he was sketching the pines on the hill where shone the red porches of Hemlock Inn.

Finally, a white-flannel young man walked into the landscape. Hawker waved a brush. "Hi, Hollie, get out of the colour-scheme!"

At this cry the white-flannel young man looked down at his feet apprehensively. Finally he came forward grinning. "Why, hello, Hawker, old boy! Glad to find you here." He perched on a boulder and began to study Hawker's canvas and the vivid yellow stubble with the olive shadows. He wheeled his eyes from one to the other. "Say, Hawker," he said suddenly, "why don't you marry Miss Fanhall?"

Hawker had a brush in his mouth, but he took it quickly out, and said, "Marry Miss Fanhall? Who the devil is Miss Fanhall?"

Hollanden clasped both hands about his knee and looked thoughtfully away. "Oh, she's a girl."

"She is?" said Hawker.

"Yes. She came to the inn last night with her sister-in-law and a small tribe of young Fanhalls. There's six of them, I think."

"Two," said Hawker, "a boy and a girl."

"How do you—oh, you must have come up with them. Of course. Why, then you saw her."

"Was that her?" asked Hawker listlessly.

"Was that her?" cried Hollanden, with indignation. "Was that her?"

"Oh!" said Hawker.

Hollanden mused again. "She's got lots of money," he said. "Loads of it. And I think she would be fool enough to have sympathy for you in your work. They are a tremendously wealthy crowd, although they treat it simply. It would be a good thing for you. I believe—yes, I am sure she could be fool enough to have sympathy for you in your work. And now, if you weren't such a hopeless chump——"

"Oh, shut up, Hollie," said the painter.

For a time Hollanden did as he was bid, but at last he talked again. "Can't think why they came up here. Must be her sister-in-law's health. Something like that. She——"

"Great heavens," said Hawker, "you speak of nothing else!"

"Well, you saw her, didn't you?" demanded Hollanden. "What can you expect, then, from a man of my sense? You—you old stick—you——"

"It was quite dark," protested the painter.

"Quite dark," repeated Hollanden, in a wrathful voice. "What if it was?"

"Well, that is bound to make a difference in a man's opinion, you know."

"No, it isn't. It was light down at the railroad station, anyhow. If you had any sand—thunder, but I did get up early this morning! Say, do you play tennis?"

"After a fashion," said Hawker. "Why?"

"Oh, nothing," replied Hollanden sadly. "Only they are wearing me out at the game. I had to get up and play before breakfast this morning with the Worcester girls, and there is a lot more mad players who will be down on me before long. It's a terrible thing to be a tennis player."

"Why, you used to put yourself out so little for people," remarked Hawker.

"Yes, but up there"—Hollanden jerked his thumb in the direction of the inn—"they think I'm so amiable."

"Well, I'll come up and help you out."

"Do," Hollanden laughed; "you and Miss Fanhall can team it against the littlest Worcester girl and me." He regarded the landscape and meditated. Hawker struggled for a grip on the thought of the stubble.

"That colour of hair and eyes always knocks me kerplunk," observed Hollanden softly.

Hawker looked up irascibly. "What colour hair and eyes?" he demanded. "I believe you're crazy."

"What colour hair and eyes?" repeated Hollanden, with a savage gesture. "You've got no more appreciation than a post."

"They are good enough for me," muttered Hawker, turning again to his work. He scowled first at the canvas and then at the stubble. "Seems to me you had best take care of yourself, instead of planning for me," he said.

"Me!" cried Hollanden. "Me! Take care of myself! My boy, I've got a past of sorrow and gloom. I——"

"You're nothing but a kid," said Hawker, glaring at the other man.

"Oh, of course," said Hollanden, wagging his head with midnight wisdom. "Oh, of course."

"Well, Hollie," said Hawker, with sudden affability, "I didn't mean to be unpleasant, but then you are rather ridiculous, you know, sitting up there and howling about the colour of hair and eyes."

"I'm not ridiculous."

"Yes, you are, you know, Hollie."

The writer waved his hand despairingly. "And you rode in the train with her, and in the stage."

"I didn't see her in the train," said Hawker.

"Oh, then you saw her in the stage. Ha-ha, you old thief! I sat up here, and you sat down there and lied." He jumped from his perch and belaboured Hawker's shoulders.

"Stop that!" said the painter.

"Oh, you old thief, you lied to me! You lied—— Hold on—bless my life, here she comes now!"

CHAPTER IV.

One day Hollanden said: "There are forty-two people at Hemlock Inn, I think. Fifteen are middle-aged ladies of the most aggressive respectability. They have come here for no discernible purpose save to get where they can see people and be displeased at them. They sit in a large group on that porch and take measurements of character as importantly as if they constituted the jury of heaven. When I arrived at Hemlock Inn I at once cast my eye searchingly about me. Perceiving this assemblage, I cried, 'There they are!' Barely waiting to change my clothes, I made for this formidable body and endeavoured to conciliate it. Almost every day I sit down among them and lie like a machine. Privately I believe they should be hanged, but publicly I glisten with admiration. Do you know, there is one of 'em who I know has not moved from the inn in eight days, and this morning I said to her, 'These long walks in the clear mountain air are doing you a world of good.' And I keep continually saying, 'Your frankness is so charming!' Because of the great law of universal balance, I know that this illustrious corps will believe good of themselves with exactly the same readiness that they will believe ill of others. So I ply them with it. In consequence, the worst they ever say of me is, 'Isn't that Mr. Hollanden a peculiar man?' And you know, my boy, that's not so bad for a literary person." After some thought he added: "Good people, too. Good wives, good mothers, and everything of that kind, you know. But conservative, very conservative. Hate anything radical. Can not endure it. Were that way themselves once, you know. They hit the mark, too, sometimes. Such general volleyings can't fail to hit everything. May the devil fly away with them!"

Hawker regarded the group nervously, and at last propounded a great question: "Say, I wonder where they all are recruited? When you come to think that almost every summer hotel——"

"Certainly," said Hollanden, "almost every summer hotel. I've studied the question, and have nearly established the fact that almost every summer hotel is furnished with a full corps of——"

"To be sure," said Hawker; "and if you search for them in the winter, you can find barely a sign of them, until you examine the boarding houses, and then you observe——"

"Certainly," said Hollanden, "of course. By the way," he added, "you haven't got any obviously loose screws in your character, have you?"

"No," said Hawker, after consideration, "only general poverty—that's all."

"Of course, of course," said Hollanden. "But that's bad. They'll get on to you, sure. Particularly since you come up here to see Miss Fanhall so much."

Hawker glinted his eyes at his friend. "You've got a deuced open way of speaking," he observed.

"Deuced open, is it?" cried Hollanden. "It isn't near so open as your devotion to Miss Fanhall, which is as plain as a red petticoat hung on a hedge."

Hawker's face gloomed, and he said, "Well, it might be plain to you, you infernal cat, but that doesn't prove that all those old hens can see it."

"I tell you that if they look twice at you they can't fail to see it. And it's bad, too. Very bad. What's the matter with you? Haven't you ever been in love before?"

"None of your business," replied Hawker.

Hollanden thought upon this point for a time. "Well," he admitted finally, "that's true in a general way, but I hate to see you managing your affairs so stupidly."

Rage flamed into Hawker's face, and he cried passionately, "I tell you it is none of your business!" He suddenly confronted the other man.

Hollanden surveyed this outburst with a critical eye, and then slapped his knee with emphasis. "You certainly have got it—a million times worse than I thought. Why, you—you—you're heels over head."

"What if I am?" said Hawker, with a gesture of defiance and despair.

Hollanden saw a dramatic situation in the distance, and with a bright smile he studied it. "Say," he exclaimed, "suppose she should not go to the picnic to-morrow? She said this morning she did not know if she could go. Somebody was expected from New York, I think. Wouldn't it break you up, though! Eh?"

"You're so dev'lish clever!" said Hawker, with sullen irony.

Hollanden was still regarding the distant dramatic situation. "And rivals, too! The woods must be crowded with them. A girl like that, you know. And then all that money! Say, your rivals must number enough to make a brigade of militia. Imagine them swarming around! But then it doesn't matter so much," he went on cheerfully; "you've got a good play there. You must appreciate them to her—you understand?—appreciate them kindly, like a man in a watch-tower. You must laugh at them only about once a week, and then very tolerantly—you understand?—and kindly, and—and appreciatively."

"You're a colossal ass, Hollie!" said Hawker. "You——"

"Yes, yes, I know," replied the other peacefully; "a colossal ass. Of course." After looking into the distance again, he murmured: "I'm worried about that picnic. I wish I knew she was going. By heavens, as a matter of fact, she must be made to go!"

"What have you got to do with it?" cried the painter, in another sudden outburst.

"There! there!" said Hollanden, waving his hand. "You fool! Only a spectator, I assure you."

Hawker seemed overcome then with a deep dislike of himself. "Oh, well, you know, Hollie, this sort of thing——" He broke off and gazed at the trees. "This sort of thing—— It——"

"How?" asked Hollanden.

"Confound you for a meddling, gabbling idiot!" cried Hawker suddenly.

Hollanden replied, "What did you do with that violet she dropped at the side of the tennis court yesterday?"

184

CHAPTER V.

Mrs. Fanhall, with the two children, the Worcester girls, and Hollanden, clambered down the rocky path. Miss Fanhall and Hawker had remained on top of the ledge. Hollanden showed much zeal in conducting his contingent to the foot of the falls. Through the trees they could see the cataract, a great shimmering white thing, booming and thundering until all the leaves gently shuddered.

"I wonder where Miss Fanhall and Mr. Hawker have gone?" said the younger Miss Worcester. "I wonder where they've gone?"

"Millicent," said Hollander, looking at her fondly, "you always had such great thought for others."

"Well, I wonder where they've gone?"

At the foot of the falls, where the mist arose in silver clouds and the green water swept into the pool, Miss Worcester, the elder, seated on the moss, exclaimed, "Oh, Mr. Hollanden, what makes all literary men so peculiar?"

"And all that just because I said that I could have made better digestive organs than Providence, if it is true that he made mine," replied Hollanden, with reproach. "Here, Roger," he cried, as he dragged the child away from the brink, "don't fall in there, or you won't be the full-back at Yale in 1907, as you have planned. I'm sure I don't know how to answer you, Miss Worcester. I've inquired of innumerable literary men, and none of 'em know. I may say I have chased that problem for years. I might give you my personal history, and see if that would throw any light on the subject." He looked about him with chin high until his glance had noted the two vague figures at the top of the cliff. "I might give you my personal history——"

Mrs. Fanhall looked at him curiously, and the elder Worcester girl cried, "Oh, do!"

After another scanning of the figures at the top of the cliff, Hollanden established himself in an oratorical pose on a great weather-beaten stone. "Well—you must understand—I started my career—my career, you understand—with a determination to be a prophet, and, although I have ended in being an acrobat, a trained bear of the magazines, and a juggler of comic paragraphs, there was once carved upon my lips a smile which made many people detest me, for it hung before them like a banshee whenever they tried to be satisfied with themselves. I was informed from time to time that I was making no great holes in the universal plan, and I came to know that one person in every two thousand of the people I saw had heard of me, and that four out of five of these had forgotten it. And then one in every two of those who remembered that they had heard of me regarded the fact that I wrote as a great impertinence. I admitted these things, and in defence merely built a maxim that stated that each wise man in this world is concealed amid some twenty thousand fools. If you have eyes for mathematics, this conclusion should interest you. Meanwhile I created a gigantic dignity, and when men saw this dignity and heard that I was a literary man they respected me. I concluded that the simple campaign of existence for me was to delude the populace, or as much of it as would look at me. I did. I do. And now I can make myself quite happy concocting sneers about it. Others may do as they please, but as for me," he concluded ferociously, "I shall never disclose to anybody that an acrobat, a trained bear of the magazines, a juggler of comic paragraphs, is not a priceless pearl of art and philosophy."

"I don't believe a word of it is true," said Miss Worcester.

"What do you expect of autobiography?" demanded Hollanden, with asperity.

"Well, anyhow, Hollie," exclaimed the younger sister, "you didn't explain a thing about how literary men came to be so peculiar, and that's what you started out to do, you know."

"Well," said Hollanden crossly, "you must never expect a man to do what he starts to do, Millicent. And besides," he went on, with the gleam of a sudden idea in his eyes, "literary men are not peculiar, anyhow."

The elder Worcester girl looked angrily at him. "Indeed? Not you, of course, but the others."

"They are all asses," said Hollanden genially.

The elder Worcester girl reflected. "I believe you try to make us think and then just tangle us up purposely!"

The younger Worcester girl reflected. "You are an absurd old thing, you know, Hollie!"

Hollanden climbed offendedly from the great weather-beaten stone. "Well, I shall go and see that the men have not spilled the luncheon while breaking their necks over these rocks. Would you like to have it spread here, Mrs. Fanhall? Never mind consulting the girls. I assure you I shall spend a great deal of energy and temper in bullying them into doing just as they please. Why, when I was in Brussels——"

"Oh, come now, Hollie, you never were in Brussels, you know," said the younger Worcester girl.

"What of that, Millicent?" demanded Hollanden. "This is autobiography."

"Well, I don't care, Hollie. You tell such whoppers."

With a gesture of despair he again started away; whereupon the Worcester girls shouted in chorus, "Oh, I say, Hollie, come back! Don't be angry. We didn't mean to tease you, Hollie—really, we didn't!"

"Well, if you didn't," said Hollanden, "why did you——"

The elder Worcester girl was gazing fixedly at the top of the cliff. "Oh, there they are! I wonder why they don't come down?"

CHAPTER VI.

Stanley, the setter, walked to the edge of the precipice and, looking over at the falls, wagged his tail in friendly greeting. He was braced warily, so that if this howling white animal should reach up a hand for him he could flee in time.

The girl stared dreamily at the red-stained crags that projected from the pines of the hill across the stream. Hawker lazily aimed bits of moss at the oblivious dog and missed him.

"It must be fine to have something to think of beyond just living," said the girl to the crags.

"I suppose you mean art?" said Hawker.

"Yes, of course. It must be finer, at any rate, than the ordinary thing."

He mused for a time. "Yes. It is—it must be," he said. "But then—I'd rather just lie here."

The girl seemed aggrieved. "Oh, no, you wouldn't. You couldn't stop. It's dreadful to talk like that, isn't it? I always thought that painters were——"

"Of course. They should be. Maybe they are. I don't know. Sometimes I am. But not to-day."

"Well, I should think you ought to be so much more contented than just ordinary people. Now, I——"

"You!" he cried—"you are not 'just ordinary people.'"

"Well, but when I try to recall what I have thought about in my life, I can't remember, you know. That's what I mean."

"You shouldn't talk that way," he told her.

"But why do you insist that life should be so highly absorbing for me?"

"You have everything you wish for," he answered, in a voice of deep gloom.

"Certainly not. I am a woman."

"But——"

"A woman, to have everything she wishes for, would have to be Providence. There are some things that are not in the world."

"Well, what are they?" he asked of her.

"That's just it," she said, nodding her head, "no one knows. That's what makes the trouble."

"Well, you are very unreasonable."

"What?"

"You are very unreasonable. If I were you—an heiress——"

The girl flushed and turned upon him angrily.

"Well!" he glowered back at her. "You are, you know. You can't deny it."

She looked at the red-stained crags. At last she said, "You seemed really contemptuous."

"Well, I assure you that I do not feel contemptuous. On the contrary, I am filled with admiration. Thank Heaven, I am a man of the world. Whenever I meet heiresses I always have the deepest admiration." As he said this he wore a brave hang-dog expression. The girl surveyed him coldly from his chin to his eyebrows. "You have a handsome audacity, too."

He lay back in the long grass and contemplated the clouds.

"You should have been a Chinese soldier of fortune," she said.

He threw another little clod at Stanley and struck him on the head.

"You are the most scientifically unbearable person in the world," she said.

Stanley came back to see his master and to assure himself that the clump on the head was not intended as a sign of serious displeasure. Hawker took the dog's long ears and tried to tie them into a knot.

"And I don't see why you so delight in making people detest you," she continued.

Having failed to make a knot of the dog's ears, Hawker leaned back and surveyed his failure admiringly. "Well, I don't," he said.

"You do."

"No, I don't."

"Yes, you do. You just say the most terrible things as if you positively enjoyed saying them."

"Well, what did I say, now? What did I say?"

"Why, you said that you always had the most extraordinary admiration for heiresses whenever you met them."

"Well, what's wrong with that sentiment?" he said. "You can't find fault with that!"

"It is utterly detestable."

"Not at all," he answered sullenly. "I consider it a tribute—a graceful tribute."

Miss Fanhall arose and went forward to the edge of the cliff. She became absorbed in the falls. Far below her a bough of a hemlock drooped to the water, and each swirling, mad wave caught it and made it nod—nod—nod. Her back was half turned toward Hawker.

After a time Stanley, the dog, discovered some ants scurrying in the moss, and he at once began to watch them and wag his tail.

"Isn't it curious," observed Hawker, "how an animal as large as a dog will sometimes be so entertained by the very smallest things?"

190

Stanley pawed gently at the moss, and then thrust his head forward to see what the ants did under the circumstances.

"In the hunting season," continued Hawker, having waited a moment, "this dog knows nothing on earth but his master and the partridges. He is lost to all other sound and movement. He moves through the woods like a steel machine. And when he scents the bird—ah, it is beautiful! Shouldn't you like to see him then?"

Some of the ants had perhaps made war-like motions, and Stanley was pretending that this was a reason for excitement. He reared aback, and made grumbling noises in his throat.

After another pause Hawker went on: "And now see the precious old fool! He is deeply interested in the movements of the little ants, and as childish and ridiculous over them as if they were highly important.—There, you old blockhead, let them alone!"

Stanley could not be induced to end his investigations, and he told his master that the ants were the most thrilling and dramatic animals of his experience.

"Oh, by the way," said Hawker at last, as his glance caught upon the crags across the river, "did you ever hear the legend of those rocks yonder? Over there where I am pointing? Where I'm pointing? Did you ever hear it? What? Yes? No? Well, I shall tell it to you." He settled comfortably in the long grass.

CHAPTER VII.

"Once upon a time there was a beautiful Indian maiden, of course. And she was, of course, beloved by a youth from another tribe who was very handsome and stalwart and a mighty hunter, of course. But the maiden's father was, of course, a stern old chief, and when the question of his daughter's marriage came up, he, of course, declared that the maiden should be wedded only to a warrior of her tribe. And, of course, when the young man heard this he said that in such case he would, of course, fling himself headlong from that crag. The old chief was, of course, obdurate, and, of course, the youth did, of course, as he had said. And, of course, the maiden wept." After Hawker had waited for some time, he said with severity, "You seem to have no great appreciation of folklore."

The girl suddenly bent her head. "Listen," she said, "they're calling. Don't you hear Hollie's voice?"

They went to another place, and, looking down over the shimmering tree-tops, they saw Hollanden waving his arms. "It's luncheon," said Hawker. "Look how frantic he is!"

The path required that Hawker should assist the girl very often. His eyes shone at her whenever he held forth his hand to help her down a blessed steep place. She seemed rather pensive. The route to luncheon was very long. Suddenly he took a seat on an old tree, and said: "Oh, I don't know why it is, whenever I'm with you, I—I have no wits, nor good nature, nor anything. It's the worst luck!"

He had left her standing on a boulder, where she was provisionally helpless. "Hurry!" she said; "they're waiting for us."

Stanley, the setter, had been sliding down cautiously behind them. He now stood wagging his tail and waiting for the way to be cleared.

Hawker leaned his head on his hand and pondered dejectedly. "It's the worst luck!"

"Hurry!" she said; "they're waiting for us."

At luncheon the girl was for the most part silent. Hawker was superhumanly amiable. Somehow he gained the impression that they all quite fancied him, and it followed that being clever was very easy. Hollanden listened, and approved him with a benign countenance.

There was a little boat fastened to the willows at the edge of the black pool. After the spread, Hollanden navigated various parties around to where they could hear the great hollow roar of the falls beating against the sheer rocks. Stanley swam after sticks at the request of little Roger.

Once Hollanden succeeded in making the others so engrossed in being amused that Hawker and Miss Fanhall were left alone staring at the white bubbles that floated solemnly on the black water. After Hawker had stared at them a sufficient time, he said, "Well, you are an heiress, you know."

In return she chose to smile radiantly. Turning toward him, she said, "If you will be good now—always—perhaps I'll forgive you."

They drove home in the sombre shadows of the hills, with Stanley padding along under the wagon. The Worcester girls tried to induce Hollanden to sing, and in consequence there was quarrelling until the blinking lights of the inn appeared above them as if a great lantern hung there.

Hollanden conveyed his friend some distance on the way home from the inn to the farm. "Good time at the picnic?" said the writer.

"Yes."

"Picnics are mainly places where the jam gets on the dead leaves, and from thence to your trousers. But this was a good little picnic." He glanced at Hawker. "But you don't look as if you had such a swell time."

Hawker waved his hand tragically. "Yes—no—I don't know."

"What's wrong with you?" asked Hollanden.

"I tell you what it is, Hollie," said the painter darkly, "whenever I'm with that girl I'm such a blockhead. I'm not so stupid, Hollie. You know I'm not. But when I'm with her I can't be clever to save my life."

Hollanden pulled contentedly at his pipe. "Maybe she don't notice it."

"Notice it!" muttered Hawker, scornfully; "of course she notices it. In conversation with her, I tell you, I am as interesting as an iron dog." His voice changed as he cried, "I don't know why it is. I don't know why it is."

Blowing a huge cloud of smoke into the air, Hollanden studied it thoughtfully. "Hits some fellows that way," he said. "And, of course, it must be deuced annoying. Strange thing, but now, under those circumstances, I'm very glib. Very glib, I assure you."

"I don't care what you are," answered Hawker. "All those confounded affairs of yours—they were not——"

"No," said Hollanden, stolidly puffing, "of course not. I understand that. But, look here, Billie," he added, with sudden brightness, "maybe you are not a blockhead, after all. You are on the inside, you know, and you can't see from there. Besides, you can't tell what a woman will think. You can't tell what a woman will think."

"No," said Hawker, grimly, "and you suppose that is my only chance?"

"Oh, don't be such a chump!" said Hollanden, in a tone of vast exasperation.

They strode for some time in silence. The mystic pines swaying over the narrow road made talk sibilantly to the wind. Stanley, the setter, took it upon himself to discover some menacing presence in the woods. He walked on his toes and with his eyes glinting sideways. He swore half under his breath.

"And work, too," burst out Hawker, at last. "I came up here this season to work, and I haven't done a thing that ought not be shot at."

"Don't you find that your love sets fire to your genius?" asked Hollanden gravely.

"No, I'm hanged if I do."

Hollanden sighed then with an air of relief. "I was afraid that a popular impression was true," he said, "but it's all right. You would rather sit still and moon, wouldn't you?"

"Moon—blast you! I couldn't moon to save my life."

"Oh, well, I didn't mean moon exactly."

CHAPTER VIII.

The blue night of the lake was embroidered with black tree forms. Silver drops sprinkled from the lifted oars. Somewhere in the gloom of the shore there was a dog, who from time to time raised his sad voice to the stars.

"But still, the life of the studios——" began the girl.

Hawker scoffed. "There were six of us. Mainly we smoked. Sometimes we played hearts and at other times poker—on credit, you know—credit. And when we had the materials and got something to do, we worked. Did you ever see these beautiful red and green designs that surround the common tomato can?"

"Yes."

"Well," he said proudly, "I have made them. Whenever you come upon tomatoes, remember that they might once have been encompassed in my design. When first I came back from Paris I began to paint, but nobody wanted me to paint. Later, I got into green corn and asparagus——"

"Truly?"

"Yes, indeed. It is true."

"But still, the life of the studios——"

"There were six of us. Fate ordained that only one in the crowd could have money at one time. The other five lived off him and despised themselves. We despised ourselves five times as long as we had admiration."

"And was this just because you had no money?"

"It was because we had no money in New York," said Hawker.

"Well, after a while something happened——"

"Oh, no, it didn't. Something impended always, but it never happened."

"In a case like that one's own people must be such a blessing. The sympathy——"

"One's own people!" said Hawker.

"Yes," she said, "one's own people and more intimate friends. The appreciation——"

"'The appreciation!'" said Hawker. "Yes, indeed!"

He seemed so ill-tempered that she became silent. The boat floated through the shadows of the trees and out to where the water was like a blue crystal. The dog on the shore thrashed about in the reeds and waded in the shallows, mourning his unhappy state in an occasional cry. Hawker stood up and sternly shouted. Thereafter silence was among the reeds. The moon slipped sharply through the little clouds.

The girl said, "I liked that last picture of yours."

"What?"

"At the last exhibition, you know, you had that one with the cows—and things—in the snow—and—and a haystack."

"Yes," he said, "of course. Did you like it, really? I thought it about my best. And you really remembered it? Oh," he cried, "Hollanden perhaps recalled it to you."

"Why, no," she said. "I remembered it, of course."

"Well, what made you remember it?" he demanded, as if he had cause to be indignant.

"Why—I just remembered it because—I liked it, and because—well, the people with me said—said it was about the best thing in the exhibit, and they talked about it a good deal. And then I remember that Hollie had spoken of you, and then I—I——"

"Never mind," he said. After a moment, he added, "The confounded picture was no good, anyhow!"

The girl started. "What makes you speak so of it? It was good. Of course, I don't know—I can't talk about pictures, but," she said in distress, "everybody said it was fine."

"It wasn't any good," he persisted, with dogged shakes of the head.

From off in the darkness they heard the sound of Hollanden's oars splashing in the water. Sometimes there was squealing by the Worcester girls, and at other times loud arguments on points of navigation.

"Oh," said the girl suddenly, "Mr. Oglethorpe is coming to-morrow!"

"Mr. Oglethorpe?" said Hawker. "Is he?"

"Yes." She gazed off at the water.

"He's an old friend of ours. He is always so good, and Roger and little Helen simply adore him. He was my brother's chum in college, and they were quite inseparable until Herbert's death. He always brings me violets. But I know you will like him."

"I shall expect to," said Hawker.

"I'm so glad he is coming. What time does that morning stage get here?"

"About eleven," said Hawker.

"He wrote that he would come then. I hope he won't disappoint us."

"Undoubtedly he will be here," said Hawker.

The wind swept from the ridge top, where some great bare pines stood in the moonlight. A loon called in its strange, unearthly note from the lakeshore. As Hawker turned the boat toward the dock, the flashing rays from the boat fell upon the head of the girl in the rear seat, and he rowed very slowly.

The girl was looking away somewhere with a mystic, shining glance. She leaned her chin in her hand. Hawker, facing her, merely paddled subconsciously. He seemed greatly impressed and expectant.

At last she spoke very slowly. "I wish I knew Mr. Oglethorpe was not going to disappoint us."

Hawker said, "Why, no, I imagine not."

"Well, he is a trifle uncertain in matters of time. The children—and all of us—shall be anxious. I know you will like him."

CHAPTER IX.

"Eh?" said Hollanden. "Oglethorpe? Oglethorpe? Why, he's that friend of the Fanhalls! Yes, of course, I know him! Deuced good fellow, too! What about him?"

"Oh, nothing, only he's coming here to-morrow," answered Hawker. "What kind of a fellow did you say he was?"

"Deuced good fellow! What are you so—— Say, by the nine mad blacksmiths of Donawhiroo, he's your rival! Why, of course! Glory, but I must be thick-headed to-night!"

Hawker said, "Where's your tobacco?"

"Yonder, in that jar. Got a pipe?"

"Yes. How do you know he's my rival?"

"Know it? Why, hasn't he been—— Say, this is getting thrilling!" Hollanden sprang to his feet and, filling a pipe, flung himself into the chair and began to rock himself madly to and fro. He puffed clouds of smoke.

Hawker stood with his face in shadow. At last he said, in tones of deep weariness, "Well, I think I'd better be going home and turning in."

"Hold on!" Hollanden exclaimed, turning his eyes from a prolonged stare at the ceiling, "don't go yet! Why, man, this is just the time when—— Say, who would ever think of Jem Oglethorpe's turning up to harrie you! Just at this time, too!"

"Oh," cried Hawker suddenly, filled with rage, "you remind me of an accursed duffer! Why can't you tell me something about the man, instead of sitting there and gibbering those crazy things at the ceiling?"

"By the piper——"

"Oh, shut up! Tell me something about Oglethorpe, can't you? I want to hear about him. Quit all that other business!"

"Why, Jem Oglethorpe, he—why, say, he's one of the best fellows going. If he were only an ass! If he were only an ass, now, you could feel easy in your mind. But he isn't. No, indeed. Why, blast him, there isn't a man that knows him who doesn't like Jem Oglethorpe! Excepting the chumps!"

The window of the little room was open, and the voices of the pines could be heard as they sang of their long sorrow. Hawker pulled a chair close and stared out into the darkness. The people on the porch of the inn were frequently calling, "Good-night! Good-night!"

Hawker said, "And of course he's got train loads of money?"

"You bet he has! He can pave streets with it. Lordie, but this is a situation!"

A heavy scowl settled upon Hawker's brow, and he kicked at the dressing case. "Say, Hollie, look here! Sometimes I think you regard me as a bug and like to see me wriggle. But——"

"Oh, don't be a fool!" said Hollanden, glaring through the smoke. "Under the circumstances, you are privileged to rave and ramp around like a wounded lunatic, but for heaven's sake don't swoop down on me like that! Especially when I'm—when I'm doing all I can for you."

"Doing all you can for me! Nobody asked you to. You talk as if I were an infant."

"There! That's right! Blaze up like a fire balloon just because I said that, will you? A man in your condition—why, confound you, you are an infant!"

Hawker seemed again overwhelmed in a great dislike of himself. "Oh, well, of course, Hollie, it——" He waved his hand. "A man feels like—like——"

"Certainly he does," said Hollanden. "That's all right, old man."

"And look now, Hollie, here's this Oglethorpe——"

"May the devil fly away with him!"

"Well, here he is, coming along when I thought maybe—after a while, you know—I might stand some show. And you are acquainted with him, so give me a line on him."

"Well, I should advise you to——"

"Blow your advice! I want to hear about Oglethorpe."

"Well, in the first place, he is a rattling good fellow, as I told you before, and this is what makes it so——"

"Oh, hang what it makes it! Go on."

"He is a rattling good fellow and he has stacks of money. Of course, in this case his having money doesn't affect the situation much. Miss Fanhall——"

"Say, can you keep to the thread of the story, you infernal literary man!"

"Well, he's popular. He don't talk money—ever. And if he's wicked, he's not sufficiently proud of it to be perpetually describing his sins. And then he is not so hideously brilliant, either. That's great credit to a man in these days. And then he—well, take it altogether, I should say Jem Oglethorpe was a smashing good fellow."

"I wonder how long he is going to stay?" murmured Hawker.

During this conversation his pipe had often died out. It was out at this time. He lit another match. Hollanden had watched the fingers of his friend as the match was scratched. "You're nervous, Billie," he said.

Hawker straightened in his chair. "No, I'm not."

"I saw your fingers tremble when you lit that match."

"Oh, you lie!"

Hollanden mused again. "He's popular with women, too," he said ultimately; "and often a woman will like a man and hunt his scalp just because she knows other women like him and want his scalp."

"Yes, but not——"

"Hold on! You were going to say that she was not like other women, weren't you?"

"Not exactly that, but——"

"Well, we will have all that understood."

After a period of silence Hawker said, "I must be going."

As the painter walked toward the door Hollanden cried to him: "Heavens! Of all pictures of a weary pilgrim!" His voice was very compassionate.

Hawker wheeled, and an oath spun through the smoke clouds.

CHAPTER X.

"Where's Mr. Hawker this morning?" asked the younger Miss Worcester. "I thought he was coming up to play tennis?"

"I don't know. Confound him! I don't see why he didn't come," said Hollanden, looking across the shining valley. He frowned questioningly at the landscape. "I wonder where in the mischief he is?"

The Worcester girls began also to stare at the great gleaming stretch of green and gold. "Didn't he tell you he was coming?" they demanded.

"He didn't say a word about it," answered Hollanden. "I supposed, of course, he was coming. We will have to postpone the *mêlée*."

Later he met Miss Fanhall. "You look as if you were going for a walk?"

"I am," she said, swinging her parasol. "To meet the stage. Have you seen Mr. Hawker to-day?"

"No," he said. "He is not coming up this morning. He is in a great fret about that field of stubble, and I suppose he is down there sketching the life out of it. These artists—they take such a fiendish interest in their work. I dare say we won't see much of him until he has finished it. Where did you say you were going to walk?"

"To meet the stage."

"Oh, well, I won't have to play tennis for an hour, and if you insist——"

"Of course."

As they strolled slowly in the shade of the trees Hollanden began, "Isn't that Hawker an ill-bred old thing?"

"No, he is not." Then after a time she said, "Why?"

"Oh, he gets so absorbed in a beastly smudge of paint that I really suppose he cares nothing for anything else in the world. Men who are really artists—I don't believe they are capable of deep human affections. So much of them is occupied by art. There's not much left over, you see."

"I don't believe it at all," she exclaimed.

"You don't, eh?" cried Hollanden scornfully. "Well, let me tell you, young woman, there is a great deal of truth in it. Now, there's Hawker—as good a fellow as ever lived, too, in a way, and yet he's an artist. Why, look how he treats—look how he treats that poor setter dog!"

"Why, he's as kind to him as he can be," she declared.

"And I tell you he is not!" cried Hollanden.

"He is, Hollie. You—you are unspeakable when you get in these moods."

"There—that's just you in an argument. I'm not in a mood at all. Now, look—the dog loves him with simple, unquestioning devotion that fairly brings tears to one's eyes——"

"Yes," she said.

"And he—why, he's as cold and stern——"

"He isn't. He isn't, Holly. You are awf'ly unfair."

"No, I'm not. I am simply a liberal observer. And Hawker, with his people, too," he went on darkly; "you can't tell—you don't know anything about it—but I tell you that what I have seen proves my assertion that the artistic mind has no space left for the human affections. And as for the dog——"

"I thought you were his friend, Hollie?"

"Whose?"

"No, not the dog's. And yet you—really, Hollie, there is something unnatural in you. You are so stupidly keen in looking at people that you do not possess common loyalty to your friends. It is because you are a writer, I suppose. That has to explain so many things. Some of your traits are very disagreeable."

"There! there!" plaintively cried Hollanden. "This is only about the treatment of a dog, mind you. Goodness, what an oration!"

"It wasn't about the treatment of a dog. It was about your treatment of your friends."

"Well," he said sagely, "it only goes to show that there is nothing impersonal in the mind of a woman. I undertook to discuss broadly——

"Oh, Hollie!"

"At any rate, it was rather below you to do such scoffing at me."

"Well, I didn't mean—not all of it, Hollie."

"Well, I didn't mean what I said about the dog and all that, either."

"You didn't?" She turned toward him, large-eyed.

"No. Not a single word of it."

"Well, what did you say it for, then?" she demanded indignantly.

"I said it," answered Hollanden placidly, "just to tease you." He looked abstractedly up to the trees.

Presently she said slowly, "Just to tease me?"

At this time Hollanden wore an unmistakable air of having a desire to turn up his coat collar. "Oh, come now——" he began nervously.

"George Hollanden," said the voice at his shoulder, "you are not only disagreeable, but you are hopelessly ridiculous. I—I wish you would never speak to me again!"

"Oh, come now, Grace, don't—don't—— Look! There's the stage coming, isn't it?"

"No, the stage is not coming. I wish—I wish you were at the bottom of the sea, George Hollanden. And—and Mr. Hawker, too. There!"

"Oh, bless my soul! And all about an infernal dog," wailed Hollanden. "Look! Honest, now, there's the stage. See it? See it?"

"It isn't there at all," she said.

Gradually he seemed to recover his courage. "What made you so tremendously angry? I don't see why."

After consideration, she said decisively, "Well, because."

"That's why I teased you," he rejoined.

"Well, because—because——"

"Go on," he told her finally. "You are doing very well." He waited patiently.

"Well," she said, "it is dreadful to defend somebody so—so excitedly, and then have it turned out just a tease. I don't know what he would think."

"Who would think?"

"Why—he."

"What could he think? Now, what could he think? Why," said Hollanden, waxing eloquent, "he couldn't under any circumstances think—think anything at all. Now, could he?"

She made no reply.

"Could he?"

She was apparently reflecting.

"Under any circumstances," persisted Hollanden, "he couldn't think anything at all. Now, could he?"

"No," she said.

"Well, why are you angry at me, then?"

CHAPTER XI.

"John," said the old mother, from the profound mufflings of the pillow and quilts.

"What?" said the old man. He was tugging at his right boot, and his tone was very irascible.

"I think William's changed a good deal."

"Well, what if he has?" replied the father, in another burst of ill-temper. He was then tugging at his left boot.

"Yes, I'm afraid he's changed a good deal," said the muffled voice from the bed. "He's got a good many fine friends, now, John—folks what put on a good many airs; and he don't care for his home like he did."

"Oh, well, I don't guess he's changed very much," said the old man cheerfully. He was now free of both boots.

She raised herself on an elbow and looked out with a troubled face. "John, I think he likes that girl."

"What girl?" said he.

"What girl? Why, that awful handsome girl you see around—of course."

"Do you think he likes 'er?"

"I'm afraid so—I'm afraid so," murmured the mother mournfully.

"Oh, well," said the old man, without alarm, or grief, or pleasure in his tone.

He turned the lamp's wick very low and carried the lamp to the head of the stairs, where he perched it on the step. When he returned he said, "She's mighty good-look-in'!"

"Well, that ain't everything," she snapped. "How do we know she ain't proud, and selfish, and—everything?"

"How do you know she is?" returned the old man.

"And she may just be leading him on."

"Do him good, then," said he, with impregnable serenity. "Next time he'll know better."

"Well, I'm worried about it," she said, as she sank back on the pillow again. "I think William's changed a good deal. He don't seem to care about—us—like he did."

"Oh, go to sleep!" said the father drowsily.

She was silent for a time, and then she said, "John?"

"What?"

"Do you think I better speak to him about that girl?"

"No."

She grew silent again, but at last she demanded, "Why not?"

"'Cause it's none of your business. Go to sleep, will you?" And presently he did, but the old mother lay blinking wild-eyed into the darkness.

In the morning Hawker did not appear at the early breakfast, eaten when the blue glow of dawn shed its ghostly lights upon the valley. The old mother placed various dishes on the back part of the stove. At ten o'clock he came downstairs. His mother was sweeping busily in the parlour at the time, but she saw him and ran to the back part of the stove. She slid the various dishes on to the table. "Did you oversleep?" she asked.

"Yes. I don't feel very well this morning," he said. He pulled his chair close to the table and sat there staring.

She renewed her sweeping in the parlour. When she returned he sat still staring undeviatingly at nothing.

"Why don't you eat your breakfast?" she said anxiously.

"I tell you, mother, I don't feel very well this morning," he answered quite sharply.

"Well," she said meekly, "drink some coffee and you'll feel better."

Afterward he took his painting machinery and left the house. His younger sister was at the well. She looked at him with a little smile and a little sneer. "Going up to the inn this morning?" she said.

"I don't see how that concerns you, Mary?" he rejoined, with dignity.

"Oh, my!" she said airily.

"But since you are so interested, I don't mind telling you that I'm not going up to the inn this morning."

His sister fixed him with her eye. "She ain't mad at you, is she, Will?"

"I don't know what you mean, Mary." He glared hatefully at her and strode away.

Stanley saw him going through the fields and leaped a fence jubilantly in pursuit. In a wood the light sifted through the foliage and burned with a peculiar reddish lustre on the masses of dead leaves. He frowned at it for a while from different points. Presently he erected his easel and began to paint. After a time he threw down his brush and swore. Stanley, who had been solemnly staring at the scene as if he too was sketching it, looked up in surprise.

In wandering aimlessly through the fields and the forest Hawker once found himself near the road to Hemlock Inn. He shied away from it quickly as if it were a great snake.

While most of the family were at supper, Mary, the younger sister, came charging breathlessly into the kitchen. "Ma—sister," she cried, "I know why—why Will didn't go to the inn to-day. There's another fellow come. Another fellow."

"Who? Where? What do you mean?" exclaimed her mother and her sister.

"Why, another fellow up at the inn," she shouted, triumphant in her information. "Another fellow come up on the stage this morning. And she went out driving with him this afternoon."

"Well," exclaimed her mother and her sister.

"Yep. And he's an awful good-looking fellow, too. And she—oh, my—she looked as if she thought the world and all of him."

"Well," exclaimed her mother and her sister again.

"Sho!" said the old man. "You wimen leave William alone and quit your gabbling."

The three women made a combined assault upon him. "Well, we ain't a-hurting him, are we, pa? You needn't be so snifty. I guess we ain't a-hurting him much."

"Well," said the old man. And to this argument he added, "Sho!"

They kept him out of the subsequent consultations.

CHAPTER XII.

The next day, as little Roger was going toward the tennis court, a large orange and white setter ran effusively from around the corner of the inn and greeted him. Miss Fanhall, the Worcester girls, Hollanden, and Oglethorpe faced to the front like soldiers. Hollanden cried, "Why, Billie Hawker must be coming!" Hawker at that moment appeared, coming toward them with a smile which was not overconfident.

Little Roger went off to perform some festivities of his own on the brown carpet under a clump of pines. The dog, to join him, felt obliged to circle widely about the tennis court. He was much afraid of this tennis court, with its tiny round things that sometimes hit him. When near it he usually slunk along at a little sheep trot and with an eye of wariness upon it.

At her first opportunity the younger Worcester girl said, "You didn't come up yesterday, Mr. Hawker."

Hollanden seemed to think that Miss Fanhall turned her head as if she wished to hear the explanation of the painter's absence, so he engaged her in swift and fierce conversation.

"No," said Hawker. "I was resolved to finish a sketch of a stubble field which I began a good many days ago. You see, I was going to do such a great lot of work this summer, and I've done hardly a thing. I really ought to compel myself to do some, you know."

"There," said Hollanden, with a victorious nod, "just what I told you!"

"You didn't tell us anything of the kind," retorted the Worcester girls with one voice.

A middle-aged woman came upon the porch of the inn, and after scanning for a moment the group at the tennis court she hurriedly withdrew. Presently she appeared again, accompanied by five more middle-aged women. "You see," she said to the others, "it is as I said. He has come back."

The five surveyed the group at the tennis court, and then said: "So he has. I knew he would. Well, I declare! Did you ever?" Their voices were pitched at low keys and they moved with care, but their smiles were broad and full of a strange glee.

"I wonder how he feels," said one in subtle ecstasy.

Another laughed. "You know how you would feel, my dear, if you were him and saw yourself suddenly cut out by a man who was so hopelessly superior to you. Why, Oglethorpe's a thousand times better looking. And then think of his wealth and social position!"

One whispered dramatically, "They say he never came up here at all yesterday."

Another replied: "No more he did. That's what we've been talking about. Stayed down at the farm all day, poor fellow!"

"Do you really think she cares for Oglethorpe?"

"Care for him? Why, of course she does. Why, when they came up the path yesterday morning I never saw a girl's face so bright. I asked my husband how much of the Chambers Street Bank stock Oglethorpe owned, and he said that if Oglethorpe took his money out there wouldn't be enough left to buy a pie."

The youngest woman in the corps said: "Well, I don't care. I think it is too bad. I don't see anything so much in that Mr. Oglethorpe."

The others at once patronized her. "Oh, you don't, my dear? Well, let me tell you that bank stock waves in the air like a banner. You would see it if you were her."

"Well, she don't have to care for his money."

"Oh, no, of course she don't have to. But they are just the ones that do, my dear. They are just the ones that do."

"Well, it's a shame."

"Oh, of course it's a shame."

The woman who had assembled the corps said to one at her side: "Oh, the commonest kind of people, my dear, the commonest kind. The father is a regular farmer, you know. He drives oxen. Such language! You can really hear him miles away bellowing at those oxen. And the girls are shy, half-wild things—oh, you have no idea! I saw one of them yesterday when we were out driving. She dodged as we came along, for I suppose she was ashamed of her frock, poor child! And the mother—well, I wish you could see her! A little, old, dried-up thing. We saw her carrying a pail of water from the well, and, oh, she bent and staggered dreadfully, poor thing!"

"And the gate to their front yard, it has a broken hinge, you know. Of course, that's an awful bad sign. When people let their front gate hang on one hinge you know what that means."

After gazing again at the group at the court, the youngest member of the corps said, "Well, he's a good tennis player anyhow."

The others smiled indulgently. "Oh, yes, my dear, he's a good tennis player."

CHAPTER XIII.

One day Hollanden said, in greeting, to Hawker, "Well, he's gone."

"Who?" asked Hawker.

"Why, Oglethorpe, of course. Who did you think I meant?"

"How did I know?" said Hawker angrily.

"Well," retorted Hollanden, "your chief interest was in his movements, I thought."

"Why, of course not, hang you! Why should I be interested in his movements?"

"Well, you weren't, then. Does that suit you?"

After a period of silence Hawker asked, "What did he—what made him go?"

"Who?"

"Why—Oglethorpe."

"How was I to know you meant him? Well, he went because some important business affairs in New York demanded it, he said; but he is coming back again in a week. They had rather a late interview on the porch last evening."

"Indeed," said Hawker stiffly.

"Yes, and he went away this morning looking particularly elated. Aren't you glad?"

"I don't see how it concerns me," said Hawker, with still greater stiffness.

In a walk to the lake that afternoon Hawker and Miss Fanhall found themselves side by side and silent. The girl contemplated the distant purple hills as if Hawker were not at her side and silent. Hawker frowned at the roadway. Stanley, the setter, scouted the fields in a genial gallop.

At last the girl turned to him. "Seems to me," she said, "seems to me you are dreadfully quiet this afternoon."

"I am thinking about my wretched field of stubble," he answered, still frowning.

Her parasol swung about until the girl was looking up at his inscrutable profile. "Is it, then, so important that you haven't time to talk to me?" she asked with an air of what might have been timidity.

A smile swept the scowl from his face. "No, indeed," he said, instantly; "nothing is so important as that."

She seemed aggrieved then. "Hum—you didn't look so," she told him.

"Well, I didn't mean to look any other way," he said contritely. "You know what a bear I am sometimes. Hollanden says it is a fixed scowl from trying to see uproarious pinks, yellows, and blues."

A little brook, a brawling, ruffianly little brook, swaggered from side to side down the glade, swirling in white leaps over the great dark rocks and shouting challenge to the hillsides. Hollanden and the Worcester girls had halted in a place of ferns and wet moss. Their voices could be heard quarrelling above the clamour of the stream. Stanley, the setter, had soused himself in a pool and then gone and rolled in the dust of the road. He blissfully lolled there, with his coat now resembling an old door mat.

"Don't you think Jem is a wonderfully good fellow?" said the girl to the painter.

"Why, yes, of course," said Hawker.

"Well, he is," she retorted, suddenly defensive.

"Of course," he repeated loudly.

She said, "Well, I don't think you like him as well as I like him."

"Certainly not," said Hawker.

"You don't?" She looked at him in a kind of astonishment.

"Certainly not," said Hawker again, and very irritably. "How in the wide world do you expect me to like him as well as you like him?"

"I don't mean as well," she explained.

"Oh!" said Hawker.

"But I mean you don't like him the way I do at all—the way I expected you to like him. I thought men of a certain pattern always fancied their kind of men wherever they met them, don't you know? And I was so sure you and Jem would be friends."

"Oh!" cried Hawker. Presently he added, "But he isn't my kind of a man at all."

"He is. Jem is one of the best fellows in the world."

Again Hawker cried "Oh!"

They paused and looked down at the brook. Stanley sprawled panting in the dust and watched them. Hawker leaned against a hemlock. He sighed and frowned, and then finally coughed with great resolution. "I suppose, of course, that I am unjust to him. I care for you myself, you understand, and so it becomes——"

He paused for a moment because he heard a rustling of her skirts as if she had moved suddenly. Then he continued: "And so it becomes difficult for me to be fair to him. I am not able to see him with a true eye." He bitterly addressed the trees on the opposite side of the glen. "Oh, I care for you, of course. You might have expected it." He turned from the trees and strode toward the roadway. The uninformed and disreputable Stanley arose and wagged his tail.

As if the girl had cried out at a calamity, Hawker said again, "Well, you might have expected it."

CHAPTER XIV.

At the lake, Hollanden went pickerel fishing, lost his hook in a gaunt, gray stump, and earned much distinction by his skill in discovering words to express his emotion without resorting to the list ordinarily used in such cases. The younger Miss Worcester ruined a new pair of boots, and Stanley sat on the bank and howled the song of the forsaken. At the conclusion of the festivities Hollanden said, "Billie, you ought to take the boat back."

"Why had I? You borrowed it."

"Well, I borrowed it and it was a lot of trouble, and now you ought to take it back."

Ultimately Hawker said, "Oh, let's both go!"

On this journey Hawker made a long speech to his friend, and at the end of it he exclaimed: "And now do you think she cares so much for Oglethorpe? Why, she as good as told me that he was only a very great friend."

Hollanden wagged his head dubiously. "What a woman says doesn't amount to shucks. It's the way she says it—that's what counts. Besides," he cried in a brilliant afterthought, "she wouldn't tell you, anyhow, you fool!"

"You're an encouraging brute," said Hawker, with a rueful grin.

Later the Worcester girls seized upon Hollanden and piled him high with ferns and mosses. They dragged the long gray lichens from the chins of venerable pines, and ran with them to Hollanden, and dashed them into his arms. "Oh, hurry up, Hollie!" they cried, because with his great load he frequently fell behind them in the march. He once positively refused to carry these things another step. Some distance farther on the road he positively refused to carry this old truck another step. When almost to the inn he positively refused to carry this senseless rubbish another step. The Worcester girls had such vivid contempt for his expressed unwillingness that they neglected to tell him of any appreciation they might have had for his noble struggle.

As Hawker and Miss Fanhall proceeded slowly they heard a voice ringing through the foliage: "Whoa! Haw! Git-ap, blast you! Haw! Haw, drat your hides! Will you haw? Git-ap! Gee! Whoa!"

Hawker said, "The others are a good ways ahead. Hadn't we better hurry a little?"

The girl obediently mended her pace.

"Whoa! haw! git-ap!" shouted the voice in the distance. "Git over there, Red, git over! Gee! Git-ap!" And these cries pursued the man and the maid.

At last Hawker said, "That's my father."

"Where?" she asked, looking bewildered.

"Back there, driving those oxen."

The voice shouted: "Whoa! Git-ap! Gee! Red, git over there now, will you? I'll trim the shin off'n you in a minute. Whoa! Haw! Haw! Whoa! Git-ap!"

Hawker repeated, "Yes, that's my father."

"Oh, is it?" she said. "Let's wait for him."

"All right," said Hawker sullenly.

Presently a team of oxen waddled into view around the curve of the road. They swung their heads slowly from side to side, bent under the yoke, and looked out at the world with their great eyes, in which was a mystic note of their humble, submissive, toilsome lives. An old wagon creaked after them, and erect upon it was the tall and tattered figure of the farmer swinging his whip and yelling: "Whoa! Haw there! Git-ap!" The lash flicked and flew over the broad backs of the animals.

"Hello, father!" said Hawker.

"Whoa! Back! Whoa! Why, hello, William, what you doing here?"

"Oh, just taking a walk. Miss Fanhall, this is my father. Father——"

"How d' you do?" The old man balanced himself with care and then raised his straw hat from his head with a quick gesture and with what was perhaps a slightly apologetic air, as if he feared that he was rather over-doing the ceremonial part.

The girl later became very intent upon the oxen. "Aren't they nice old things?" she said, as she stood looking into the faces of the team. "But what makes their eyes so very sad?"

"I dunno," said the old man.

She was apparently unable to resist a desire to pat the nose of the nearest ox, and for that purpose she stretched forth a cautious hand. But the ox moved restlessly at the moment and the girl put her hand apprehensively behind herself and backed away. The old man on the wagon grinned. "They won't hurt you," he told her.

"They won't bite, will they?" she asked, casting a glance of inquiry at the old man and then turning her eyes again upon the fascinating animals.

"No," said the old man, still grinning, "just as gentle as kittens."

She approached them circuitously. "Sure?" she said.

"Sure," replied the old man. He climbed from the wagon and came to the heads of the oxen. With him as an ally, she finally succeeded in patting the nose of the nearest ox. "Aren't they solemn, kind old fellows? Don't you get to think a great deal of them?"

"Well, they're kind of aggravating beasts sometimes," he said. "But they're a good yoke—a good yoke. They can haul with anything in this region."

"It doesn't make them so terribly tired, does it?" she said hopefully. "They are such strong animals."

"No-o-o," he said. "I dunno. I never thought much about it."

With their heads close together they became so absorbed in their conversation that they seemed to forget the painter. He sat on a log and watched them.

Ultimately the girl said, "Won't you give us a ride?"

"Sure," said the old man. "Come on, and I'll help you up." He assisted her very painstakingly to the old board that usually served him as a seat, and he clambered to a place beside her. "Come on, William," he called. The painter climbed into the wagon and stood behind his father, putting his hand on the old man's shoulder to preserve his balance.

"Which is the near ox?" asked the girl with a serious frown.

"Git-ap! Haw! That one there," said the old man.

"And this one is the off ox?"

"Yep."

"Well, suppose you sat here where I do; would this one be the near ox and that one the off ox, then?"

"Nope. Be just same."

"Then the near ox isn't always the nearest one to a person, at all? That ox there is always the near ox?"

"Yep, always. 'Cause when you drive 'em a-foot you always walk on the left side."

"Well, I never knew that before."

After studying them in silence for a while, she said, "Do you think they are happy?"

"I dunno," said the old man. "I never thought." As the wagon creaked on they gravely discussed this problem, contemplating profoundly the backs of the animals. Hawker gazed in silence at the meditating two before him. Under the wagon Stanley, the setter, walked slowly, wagging his tail in placid contentment and ruminating upon his experiences.

At last the old man said cheerfully, "Shall I take you around by the inn?"

Hawker started and seemed to wince at the question. Perhaps he was about to interrupt, but the girl cried: "Oh, will you? Take us right to the door? Oh, that will be awfully good of you!"

"Why," began Hawker, "you don't want—you don't want to ride to the inn on an—on an ox wagon, do you?"

"Why, of course I do," she retorted, directing a withering glance at him.

"Well——" he protested.

"Let 'er be, William," interrupted the old man. "Let 'er do what she wants to. I guess everybody in th' world ain't even got an ox wagon to ride in. Have they?"

"No, indeed," she returned, while withering Hawker again.

"Gee! Gee! Whoa! Haw! Git-ap! Haw! Whoa! Back!"

After these two attacks Hawker became silent.

"Gee! Gee! Gee there, blast—s'cuse me. Gee! Whoa! Git-ap!"

All the boarders of the inn were upon its porches waiting for the dinner gong. There was a surge toward the railing as a middle-aged woman passed the word along her middle-aged friends that Miss Fanhall, accompanied by Mr. Hawker, had arrived on the ox cart of Mr. Hawker's father.

"Whoa! Ha! Git-ap!" said the old man in more subdued tones. "Whoa there, Red! Whoa, now! Wh-o-a!"

Hawker helped the girl to alight, and she paused for a moment conversing with the old man about the oxen. Then she ran smiling up the steps to meet the Worcester girls.

"Oh, such a lovely time! Those dear old oxen—you should have been with us!"

CHAPTER XV.

"Oh, Miss Fanhall!"

"What is it, Mrs. Truscot?"

"That was a great prank of yours last night, my dear. We all enjoyed the joke so much."

"Prank?"

"Yes, your riding on the ox cart with that old farmer and that young Mr. What's-his-name, you know. We all thought it delicious. Ah, my dear, after all—don't be offended—if we had your people's wealth and position we might do that sort of unconventional thing, too; but, ah, my dear, we can't, we can't! Isn't the young painter a charming man?"

Out on the porch Hollanden was haranguing his friends. He heard a step and glanced over his shoulder to see who was about to interrupt him. He suddenly ceased his oration, and said, "Hello! what's the matter with Grace?" The heads turned promptly.

As the girl came toward them it could be seen that her cheeks were very pink and her eyes were flashing general wrath and defiance.

The Worcester girls burst into eager interrogation. "Oh, nothing!" she replied at first, but later she added in an undertone, "That wretched Mrs. Truscot——"

"What did she say?" whispered the younger Worcester girl.

"Why, she said—oh, nothing!"

Both Hollanden and Hawker were industriously reflecting.

Later in the morning Hawker said privately to the girl, "I know what Mrs. Truscot talked to you about."

She turned upon him belligerently. "You do?"

"Yes," he answered with meekness. "It was undoubtedly some reference to your ride upon the ox wagon."

She hesitated a moment, and then said, "Well?"

With still greater meekness he said, "I am very sorry."

"Are you, indeed?" she inquired loftily. "Sorry for what? Sorry that I rode upon your father's ox wagon, or sorry that Mrs. Truscot was rude to me about it?"

"Well, in some ways it was my fault."

"Was it? I suppose you intend to apologize for your father's owning an ox wagon, don't you?"

"No, but——"

"Well, I am going to ride in the ox wagon whenever I choose. Your father, I know, will always be glad to have me. And if it so shocks you, there is not the slightest necessity of your coming with us."

They glowered at each other, and he said, "You have twisted the question with the usual ability of your sex."

She pondered as if seeking some particularly destructive retort. She ended by saying bluntly, "Did you know that we were going home next week?"

A flush came suddenly to his face. "No. Going home? Who? You?"

"Why, of course." And then with an indolent air she continued, "I meant to have told you before this, but somehow it quite escaped me."

He stammered, "Are—are you, honestly?"

She nodded. "Why, of course. Can't stay here forever, you know."

They were then silent for a long time.

At last Hawker said, "Do you remember what I told you yesterday?"

"No. What was it?"

He cried indignantly, "You know very well what I told you!"

"I do not."

"No," he sneered, "of course not! You never take the trouble to remember such things. Of course not! Of course not!"

"You are a very ridiculous person," she vouchsafed, after eying him coldly.

He arose abruptly. "I believe I am. By heavens, I believe I am!" he cried in a fury.

She laughed. "You are more ridiculous now than I have yet seen you."

After a pause he said magnificently, "Well, Miss Fanhall, you will doubtless find Mr. Hollanden's conversation to have a much greater interest than that of such a ridiculous person."

Hollanden approached them with the blithesome step of an untroubled man. "Hello, you two people, why don't you—oh—ahem! Hold on, Billie, where are you going?"

"I——" began Hawker.

"Oh, Hollie," cried the girl impetuously, "do tell me how to do that slam thing, you know. I've tried it so often, but I don't believe I hold my racket right. And you do it so beautifully."

"Oh, that," said Hollanden. "It's not so very difficult. I'll show it to you. You don't want to know this minute, do you?"

"Yes," she answered.

"Well, come over to the court, then. Come ahead, Billie!"

"No," said Hawker, without looking at his friend, "I can't this morning, Hollie. I've got to go to work. Good-bye!" He comprehended them both in a swift bow and stalked away.

Hollanden turned quickly to the girl. "What was the matter with Billie?

What was he grinding his teeth for? What was the matter with him?"

"Why, nothing—was there?" she asked in surprise.

"Why, he was grinding his teeth until he sounded like a stone crusher," said Hollanden in a severe tone. "What was the matter with him?"

"How should I know?" she retorted.

"You've been saying something to him."

"I! I didn't say a thing."

"Yes, you did."

"Hollie, don't be absurd."

Hollanden debated with himself for a time, and then observed, "Oh, well, I always said he was an ugly-tempered fellow——"

The girl flashed him a little glance.

"And now I am sure of it—as ugly-tempered a fellow as ever lived."

"I believe you," said the girl. Then she added: "All men are. I declare, I think you to be the most incomprehensible creatures. One never knows what to expect of you. And you explode and go into rages and make yourselves utterly detestable over the most trivial matters and at the most unexpected times. You are all mad, I think."

"I!" cried Hollanden wildly. "What in the mischief have I done?"

CHAPTER XVI.

"Look here," said Hollanden, at length, "I thought you were so wonderfully anxious to learn that stroke?"

"Well, I am," she said.

"Come on, then." As they walked toward the tennis court he seemed to be plunged into mournful thought. In his eyes was a singular expression, which perhaps denoted the woe of the optimist pushed suddenly from its height. He sighed. "Oh, well, I suppose all women, even the best of them, are that way."

"What way?" she said.

"My dear child," he answered, in a benevolent manner, "you have disappointed me, because I have discovered that you resemble the rest of your sex."

"Ah!" she remarked, maintaining a noncommittal attitude.

"Yes," continued Hollanden, with a sad but kindly smile, "even you, Grace, were not above fooling with the affections of a poor country swain, until he don't know his ear from the tooth he had pulled two years ago."

She laughed. "He would be furious if he heard you call him a country swain."

"Who would?" said Hollanden.

"Why, the country swain, of course," she rejoined.

Hollanden seemed plunged in mournful reflection again. "Well, it's a shame, Grace, anyhow," he observed, wagging his head dolefully. "It's a howling, wicked shame."

"Hollie, you have no brains at all," she said, "despite your opinion."

"No," he replied ironically, "not a bit."

"Well, you haven't, you know, Hollie."

"At any rate," he said in an angry voice, "I have some comprehension and sympathy for the feelings of others."

"Have you?" she asked. "How do you mean, Hollie? Do you mean you have feeling for them in their various sorrows? Or do you mean that you understand their minds?"

Hollanden ponderously began, "There have been people who have not questioned my ability to——"

"Oh, then, you mean that you both feel for them in their sorrows and comprehend the machinery of their minds. Well, let me tell you that in regard to the last thing you are wrong. You know nothing of anyone's mind. You know less about human nature than anybody I have met."

Hollanden looked at her in artless astonishment. He said, "Now, I wonder what made you say that?" This interrogation did not seem to be addressed to her, but was evidently a statement to himself of a problem. He meditated for some moments. Eventually he said, "I suppose you mean that I do not understand you?"

"Why do you suppose I mean that?"

"That's what a person usually means when he—or she—charges another with not understanding the entire world."

"Well, at any rate, it is not what I mean at all," she said. "I mean that you habitually blunder about other people's affairs, in the belief, I imagine, that you are a great philanthropist, when you are only making an extraordinary exhibition of yourself."

"The dev——" began Hollanden. Afterward he said, "Now, I wonder what in blue thunder you mean this time?"

"Mean this time? My meaning is very plain, Hollie. I supposed the words were clear enough."

"Yes," he said thoughtfully, "your words were clear enough, but then you were of course referring back to some event, or series of events, in which I had the singular ill fortune to displease you. Maybe you don't know yourself, and spoke only from the emotion generated by the event, or series of events, in which, as I have said, I had the singular ill fortune to displease you."

"How awf'ly clever!" she said.

"But I can't recall the event, or series of events, at all," he continued, musing with a scholarly air and disregarding her mockery. "I can't remember a thing about it. To be sure, it might have been that time when——"

"I think it very stupid of you to hunt for a meaning when I believe I made everything so perfectly clear," she said wrathfully.

"Well, you yourself might not be aware of what you really meant," he answered sagely. "Women often do that sort of thing, you know. Women often speak from motives which, if brought face to face with them, they wouldn't be able to distinguish from any other thing which they had never before seen."

"Hollie, if there is a disgusting person in the world it is he who pretends to know so much concerning a woman's mind."

"Well, that's because they who know, or pretend to know, so much about a woman's mind are invariably satirical, you understand," said Hollanden cheerfully.

A dog ran frantically across the lawn, his nose high in the air and his countenance expressing vast perturbation and alarm. "Why, Billie forgot to whistle for his dog when he started for home," said Hollanden. "Come here, old man! Well, 'e was a nice dog!" The girl also gave invitation, but the setter would not heed them. He spun wildly about the lawn until he seemed to strike his master's trail, and then, with his nose near to the ground, went down the road at an eager gallop. They stood and watched him.

"Stanley's a nice dog," said Hollanden.

"Indeed he is!" replied the girl fervently.

Presently Hollanden remarked: "Well, don't let's fight any more, particularly since we can't decide what we're fighting about. I can't discover the reason, and you don't know it, so——"

"I do know it. I told you very plainly."

"Well, all right. Now, this is the way to work that slam: You give the ball a sort of a lift—see!—underhanded and with your arm crooked and stiff. Here, you smash this other ball into the net. Hi! Look out! If you hit it that way you'll knock it over the hotel. Let the ball drop nearer to the ground. Oh, heavens, not on the ground! Well, it's hard to do it from the serve, anyhow. I'll go over to the other court and bat you some easy ones."

Afterward, when they were going toward the inn, the girl suddenly began to laugh.

"What are you giggling at?" said Hollanden.

"I was thinking how furious he would be if he heard you call him a country swain," she rejoined.

"Who?" asked Hollanden.

CHAPTER XVII.

Oglethorpe contended that the men who made the most money from books were the best authors. Hollanden contended that they were the worst. Oglethorpe said that such a question should be left to the people. Hollanden said that the people habitually made wrong decisions on questions that were left to them. "That is the most odiously aristocratic belief," said Oglethorpe.

"No," said Hollanden, "I like the people. But, considered generally, they are a collection of ingenious blockheads."

"But they read your books," said Oglethorpe, grinning.

"That is through a mistake," replied Hollanden.

As the discussion grew in size it incited the close attention of the Worcester girls, but Miss Fanhall did not seem to hear it. Hawker, too, was staring into the darkness with a gloomy and preoccupied air.

"Are you sorry that this is your last evening at Hemlock Inn?" said the painter at last, in a low tone.

"Why, yes—certainly," said the girl.

Under the sloping porch of the inn the vague orange light from the parlours drifted to the black wall of the night.

"I shall miss you," said the painter.

"Oh, I dare say," said the girl.

Hollanden was lecturing at length and wonderfully. In the mystic spaces of the night the pines could be heard in their weird monotone, as they softly smote branch and branch, as if moving in some solemn and sorrowful dance.

"This has been quite the most delightful summer of my experience," said the painter.

"I have found it very pleasant," said the girl.

From time to time Hawker glanced furtively at Oglethorpe, Hollanden, and the Worcester girl. This glance expressed no desire for their well-being.

"I shall miss you," he said to the girl again. His manner was rather desperate. She made no reply, and, after leaning toward her, he subsided with an air of defeat.

Eventually he remarked: "It will be very lonely here again. I dare say I shall return to New York myself in a few weeks."

"I hope you will call," she said.

"I shall be delighted," he answered stiffly, and with a dissatisfied look at her.

"Oh, Mr. Hawker," cried the younger Worcester girl, suddenly emerging from the cloud of argument which Hollanden and Oglethorpe kept in the air, "won't it be sad to lose Grace? Indeed, I don't know what we shall do. Sha'n't we miss her dreadfully?"

"Yes," said Hawker, "we shall of course miss her dreadfully."

"Yes, won't it be frightful?" said the elder Worcester girl. "I can't imagine what we will do without her. And Hollie is only going to spend ten more days. Oh, dear! mamma, I believe, will insist on staying the entire summer. It was papa's orders, you know, and I really think she is going to obey them. He said he wanted her to have one period of rest at any rate. She is such a busy woman in town, you know."

"Here," said Hollanden, wheeling to them suddenly, "you all look as if you were badgering Hawker, and he looks badgered. What are you saying to him?"

"Why," answered the younger Worcester girl, "we were only saying to him how lonely it would be without Grace."

"Oh!" said Hollanden.

As the evening grew old, the mother of the Worcester girls joined the group. This was a sign that the girls were not to long delay the vanishing time.

231

She sat almost upon the edge of her chair, as if she expected to be called upon at any moment to arise and bow "Good-night," and she repaid Hollanden's eloquent attention with the placid and absent-minded smiles of the chaperon who waits.

Once the younger Worcester girl shrugged her shoulders and turned to say, "Mamma, you make me nervous!" Her mother merely smiled in a still more placid and absent-minded manner.

Oglethorpe arose to drag his chair nearer to the railing, and when he stood the Worcester mother moved and looked around expectantly, but Oglethorpe took seat again. Hawker kept an anxious eye upon her.

Presently Miss Fanhall arose.

"Why, you are not going in already, are you?" said Hawker and Hollanden and Oglethorpe. The Worcester mother moved toward the door followed by her daughters, who were protesting in muffled tones. Hollanden pitched violently upon Oglethorpe. "Well, at any rate——" he said. He picked the thread of a past argument with great agility.

Hawker said to the girl, "I—I—I shall miss you dreadfully."

She turned to look at him and smiled. "Shall you?" she said in a low voice.

"Yes," he said. Thereafter he stood before her awkwardly and in silence. She scrutinized the boards of the floor. Suddenly she drew a violet from a cluster of them upon her gown and thrust it out to him as she turned toward the approaching Oglethorpe.

"Good-night, Mr. Hawker," said the latter. "I am very glad to have met you, I'm sure. Hope to see you in town. Good-night."

He stood near when the girl said to Hawker: "Good-bye. You have given us such a charming summer. We shall be delighted to see you in town. You must come some time when the children can see you, too. Good-bye."

"Good-bye," replied Hawker, eagerly and feverishly, trying to interpret the inscrutable feminine face before him. "I shall come at my first opportunity."

"Good-bye."

"Good-bye."

Down at the farmhouse, in the black quiet of the night, a dog lay curled on the door-mat. Of a sudden the tail of this dog began to thump, thump, on the boards. It began as a lazy movement, but it passed into a state of gentle enthusiasm, and then into one of curiously loud and joyful celebration. At last the gate clicked. The dog uncurled, and went to the edge of the steps to greet his master. He gave adoring, tremulous welcome with his clear eyes shining in the darkness. "Well, Stan, old boy," said Hawker, stooping to stroke the dog's head. After his master had entered the house the dog went forward and sniffed at something that lay on the top step. Apparently it did not interest him greatly, for he returned in a moment to the door-mat.

But he was again obliged to uncurl himself, for his master came out of the house with a lighted lamp and made search of the door-mat, the steps, and the walk, swearing meanwhile in an undertone. The dog wagged his tail and sleepily watched this ceremony. When his master had again entered the house the dog went forward and sniffed at the top step, but the thing that had lain there was gone.

CHAPTER XVIII.

It was evident at breakfast that Hawker's sisters had achieved information. "What's the matter with you this morning?" asked one. "You look as if you hadn't slep' well."

"There is nothing the matter with me," he rejoined, looking glumly at his plate.

"Well, you look kind of broke up."

"How I look is of no consequence. I tell you there is nothing the matter with me."

"Oh!" said his sister. She exchanged meaning glances with the other feminine members of the family. Presently the other sister observed, "I heard she was going home to-day."

"Who?" said Hawker, with a challenge in his tone.

"Why, that New York girl—Miss What's-her-name," replied the sister, with an undaunted smile.

"Did you, indeed? Well, perhaps she is."

"Oh, you don't know for sure, I s'pose."

Hawker arose from the table, and, taking his hat, went away.

"Mary!" said the mother, in the sepulchral tone of belated but conscientious reproof.

"Well, I don't care. He needn't be so grand. I didn't go to tease him. I don't care."

"Well, you ought to care," said the old man suddenly. "There's no sense in you wimen folks pestering the boy all the time. Let him alone with his own business, can't you?"

"Well, ain't we leaving him alone?"

"No, you ain't—'cept when he ain't here. I don't wonder the boy grabs his hat and skips out when you git to going."

"Well, what did we say to him now? Tell us what we said to him that was so dreadful."

"Aw, thunder an' lightnin'!" cried the old man with a sudden great snarl. They seemed to know by this ejaculation that he had emerged in an instant from that place where man endures, and they ended the discussion. The old man continued his breakfast.

During his walk that morning Hawker visited a certain cascade, a certain lake, and some roads, paths, groves, nooks. Later in the day he made a sketch, choosing an hour when the atmosphere was of a dark blue, like powder smoke in the shade of trees, and the western sky was burning in strips of red. He painted with a wild face, like a man who is killing.

After supper he and his father strolled under the apple boughs in the orchard and smoked. Once he gestured wearily. "Oh, I guess I'll go back to New York in a few days."

"Um," replied his father calmly. "All right, William."

Several days later Hawker accosted his father in the barnyard. "I suppose you think sometimes I don't care so much about you and the folks and the old place any more; but I do."

"Um," said the old man. "When you goin'?"

"Where?" asked Hawker, flushing.

"Back to New York."

"Why—I hadn't thought much about—— Oh, next week, I guess."

"Well, do as you like, William. You know how glad me an' mother and the girls are to have you come home with us whenever you can come. You know that. But you must do as you think best, and if you ought to go back to New York now, William, why—do as you think best."

"Well, my work——" said Hawker.

From time to time the mother made wondering speech to the sisters. "How much nicer William is now! He's just as good as he can be. There for a while he was so cross and out of sorts. I don't see what could have come over him. But now he's just as good as he can be."

Hollanden told him, "Come up to the inn more, you fool."

"I was up there yesterday."

"Yesterday! What of that? I've seen the time when the farm couldn't hold you for two hours during the day."

"Go to blazes!"

"Millicent got a letter from Grace Fanhall the other day."

"That so?"

"Yes, she did. Grace wrote—— Say, does that shadow look pure purple to you?"

"Certainly it does, or I wouldn't paint it so, duffer. What did she write?"

"Well, if that shadow is pure purple my eyes are liars. It looks a kind of slate colour to me. Lord! if what you fellows say in your pictures is true, the whole earth must be blazing and burning and glowing and——"

Hawker went into a rage. "Oh, you don't know anything about colour, Hollie. For heaven's sake, shut up, or I'll smash you with the easel."

"Well, I was going to tell you what Grace wrote in her letter. She said——"

"Go on."

"Gimme time, can't you? She said that town was stupid, and that she wished she was back at Hemlock Inn."

"Oh! Is that all?"

"Is that all? I wonder what you expected? Well, and she asked to be recalled to you."

"Yes? Thanks."

"And that's all. 'Gad, for such a devoted man as you were, your enthusiasm and interest is stupendous."

The father said to the mother, "Well, William's going back to New York next week."

"Is he? Why, he ain't said nothing to me about it."

"Well, he is, anyhow."

"I declare! What do you s'pose he's going back before September for, John?"

"How do I know?"

"Well, it's funny, John. I bet—I bet he's going back so's he can see that girl."

"He says it's his work."

CHAPTER XIX.

Wrinkles had been peering into the little dry-goods box that acted as a cupboard. "There are only two eggs and half a loaf of bread left," he announced brutally.

"Heavens!" said Warwickson from where he lay smoking on the bed. He spoke in a dismal voice. This tone, it is said, had earned him his popular name of Great Grief.

From different points of the compass Wrinkles looked at the little cupboard with a tremendous scowl, as if he intended thus to frighten the eggs into becoming more than two, and the bread into becoming a loaf. "Plague take it!" he exclaimed.

"Oh, shut up, Wrinkles!" said Grief from the bed.

Wrinkles sat down with an air austere and virtuous. "Well, what are we going to do?" he demanded of the others.

Grief, after swearing, said: "There, that's right! Now you're happy. The holy office of the inquisition! Blast your buttons, Wrinkles, you always try to keep us from starving peacefully! It is two hours before dinner, anyhow, and——"

"Well, but what are you going to do?" persisted Wrinkles.

Pennoyer, with his head afar down, had been busily scratching at a pen-and-ink drawing. He looked up from his board to utter a plaintive optimism. "The Monthly Amazement will pay me to-morrow. They ought to. I've waited over three months now. I'm going down there to-morrow, and perhaps I'll get it."

His friends listened with airs of tolerance. "Oh, no doubt, Penny, old man." But at last Wrinkles giggled pityingly. Over on the bed Grief croaked deep down in his throat. Nothing was said for a long time thereafter.

The crash of the New York streets came faintly to this room.

Occasionally one could hear the tramp of feet in the intricate corridors of the begrimed building which squatted, slumbering, and old, between two exalted commercial structures which would have had to bend afar down to perceive it. The northward march of the city's progress had happened not to overturn this aged structure, and it huddled there, lost and forgotten, while the cloud-veering towers strode on.

Meanwhile the first shadows of dusk came in at the blurred windows of the room. Pennoyer threw down his pen and tossed his drawing over on the wonderful heap of stuff that hid the table. "It's too dark to work." He lit a pipe and walked about, stretching his shoulders like a man whose labour was valuable.

When the dusk came fully the youths grew apparently sad. The solemnity of the gloom seemed to make them ponder. "Light the gas, Wrinkles," said Grief fretfully.

The flood of orange light showed clearly the dull walls lined with sketches, the tousled bed in one corner, the masses of boxes and trunks in another, a little dead stove, and the wonderful table. Moreover, there were wine-coloured draperies flung in some places, and on a shelf, high up, there were plaster casts, with dust in the creases. A long stove-pipe wandered off in the wrong direction and then turned impulsively toward a hole in the wall. There were some elaborate cobwebs on the ceiling.

"Well, let's eat," said Grief.

"Eat," said Wrinkles, with a jeer; "I told you there was only two eggs and a little bread left. How are we going to eat?"

Again brought face to face with this problem, and at the hour for dinner, Pennoyer and Grief thought profoundly. "Thunder and turf!" Grief finally announced as the result of his deliberations.

"Well, if Billie Hawker was only home——" began Pennoyer.

"But he isn't," objected Wrinkles, "and that settles that."

Grief and Pennoyer thought more. Ultimately Grief said, "Oh, well, let's eat what we've got." The others at once agreed to this suggestion, as if it had been in their minds.

Later there came a quick step in the passage and a confident little thunder upon the door. Wrinkles arranging the tin pail on the gas stove, Pennoyer engaged in slicing the bread, and Great Grief affixing the rubber tube to the gas stove, yelled, "Come in!"

The door opened, and Miss Florinda O'Connor, the model, dashed into the room like a gale of obstreperous autumn leaves.

"Why, hello, Splutter!" they cried.

"Oh, boys, I've come to dine with you."

It was like a squall striking a fleet of yachts.

Grief spoke first. "Yes, you have?" he said incredulously.

"Why, certainly I have. What's the matter?"

They grinned. "Well, old lady," responded Grief, "you've hit us at the wrong time. We are, in fact, all out of everything. No dinner, to mention, and, what's more, we haven't got a sou."

"What? Again?" cried Florinda.

"Yes, again. You'd better dine home to-night."

"But I'll—I'll stake you," said the girl eagerly. "Oh, you poor old idiots! It's a shame! Say, I'll stake you."

"Certainly not," said Pennoyer sternly.

"What are you talking about, Splutter?" demanded Wrinkles in an angry voice.

"No, that won't go down," said Grief, in a resolute yet wistful tone.

Florinda divested herself of her hat, jacket, and gloves, and put them where she pleased. "Got coffee, haven't you? Well, I'm not going to stir a step.

240

You're a fine lot of birds!" she added bitterly, "You've all pulled me out of a whole lot of scrape—oh, any number of times—and now you're broke, you go acting like a set of dudes."

Great Grief had fixed the coffee to boil on the gas stove, but he had to watch it closely, for the rubber tube was short, and a chair was balanced on a trunk, and two bundles of kindling was balanced on the chair, and the gas stove was balanced on the kindling. Coffee-making was here accounted a feat.

Pennoyer dropped a piece of bread to the floor. "There! I'll have to go shy one."

Wrinkles sat playing serenades on his guitar and staring with a frown at the table, as if he was applying some strange method of clearing it of its litter.

Florinda assaulted Great Grief. "Here, that's not the way to make coffee!"

"What ain't?"

"Why, the way you're making it. You want to take——" She explained some way to him which he couldn't understand.

"For heaven's sake, Wrinkles, tackle that table! Don't sit there like a music box," said Pennoyer, grappling the eggs and starting for the gas stove.

Later, as they sat around the board, Wrinkles said with satisfaction, "Well, the coffee's good, anyhow."

"'Tis good," said Florinda, "but it isn't made right. I'll show you how, Penny. You first——"

"Oh, dry up, Splutter," said Grief. "Here, take an egg."

"I don't like eggs," said Florinda.

"Take an egg," said the three hosts menacingly.

"I tell you I don't like eggs."

"Take—an—egg!" they said again.

"Oh, well," said Florinda, "I'll take one, then; but you needn't act like such a set of dudes—and, oh, maybe you didn't have much lunch. I had such a daisy lunch! Up at Pontiac's studio. He's got a lovely studio."

The three looked to be oppressed. Grief said sullenly, "I saw some of his things over in Stencil's gallery, and they're rotten."

"Yes—rotten," said Pennoyer.

"Rotten," said Grief.

"Oh, well," retorted Florinda, "if a man has a swell studio and dresses— oh, sort of like a Willie, you know, you fellows sit here like owls in a cave and say rotten—rotten—rotten. You're away off. Pontiac's landscapes——"

"Landscapes be blowed! Put any of his work alongside of Billie Hawker's and see how it looks."

"Oh, well, Billie Hawker's," said Florinda. "Oh, well."

At the mention of Hawker's name they had all turned to scan her face.

CHAPTER XX.

"He wrote that he was coming home this week," said Pennoyer.

"Did he?" asked Florinda indifferently.

"Yes. Aren't you glad?"

They were still watching her face.

"Yes, of course I'm glad. Why shouldn't I be glad?" cried the girl with defiance.

They grinned.

"Oh, certainly. Billie Hawker is a good fellow, Splutter. You have a particular right to be glad."

"You people make me tired," Florinda retorted. "Billie Hawker doesn't give a rap about me, and he never tried to make out that he did."

"No," said Grief. "But that isn't saying that you don't care a rap about Billie Hawker. Ah, Florinda!"

It seemed that the girl's throat suffered a slight contraction. "Well, and what if I do?" she demanded finally.

"Have a cigarette?" answered Grief.

Florinda took a cigarette, lit it, and, perching herself on a divan, which was secretly a coal box, she smoked fiercely.

"What if I do?" she again demanded. "It's better than liking one of you dubs, anyhow."

"Oh, Splutter, you poor little outspoken kid!" said Wrinkle in a sad voice.

Grief searched among the pipes until he found the best one. "Yes, Splutter, don't you know that when you are so frank you defy every law of your sex, and wild eyes will take your trail?"

"Oh, you talk through your hat," replied Florinda. "Billie don't care whether I like him or whether I don't. And if he should hear me now, he wouldn't be glad or give a hang, either way. I know that." The girl paused and looked at the row of plaster casts. "Still, you needn't be throwing it at me all the time."

"We didn't," said Wrinkles indignantly. "You threw it at yourself."

"Well," continued Florinda, "it's better than liking one of you dubs, anyhow. He makes money and——"

"There," said Grief, "now you've hit it! Bedad, you've reached a point in eulogy where if you move again you will have to go backward."

"Of course I don't care anything about a fellow's having money——"

"No, indeed you don't, Splutter," said Pennoyer.

"But then, you know what I mean. A fellow isn't a man and doesn't stand up straight unless he has some money. And Billie Hawker makes enough so that you feel that nobody could walk over him, don't you know? And there isn't anything jay about him, either. He's a thoroughbred, don't you know?"

After reflection, Pennoyer said, "It's pretty hard on the rest of us, Splutter."

"Well, of course I like him, but—but——"

"What?" said Pennoyer.

"I don't know," said Florinda.

Purple Sanderson lived in this room, but he usually dined out. At a certain time in his life, before he came to be a great artist, he had learned the gas-fitter's trade, and when his opinions were not identical with the opinions of the art managers of the greater number of New York publications he went to see a friend who was a plumber, and the opinions of this man he was thereafter said to respect. He frequented a very neat restaurant on Twenty-third Street. It was known that on Saturday nights Wrinkles, Grief, and Pennoyer frequently quarreled with him.

As Florinda ceased speaking Purple entered. "Hello, there, Splutter!" As he was neatly hanging up his coat, he said to the others, "Well, the rent will be due in four days."

"Will it?" asked Pennoyer, astounded.

"Certainly it will," responded Purple, with the air of a superior financial man.

"My soul!" said Wrinkles.

"Oh, shut up, Purple!" said Grief. "You make me weary, coming around here with your chin about rent. I was just getting happy."

"Well, how are we going to pay it? That's the point," said Sanderson.

Wrinkles sank deeper in his chair and played despondently on his guitar. Grief cast a look of rage at Sanderson, and then stared at the wall. Pennoyer said, "Well, we might borrow it from Billie Hawker."

Florinda laughed then.

"Oh," continued Pennoyer hastily, "if those Amazement people pay me when they said they would I'll have the money."

"So you will," said Grief. "You will have money to burn. Did the Amazement people ever pay you when they said they would? You are wonderfully important all of a sudden, it seems to me. You talk like an artist."

Wrinkles, too, smiled at Pennoyer. "The Eminent Magazine people wanted Penny to hire models and make a try for them, too. It would only cost him a stack of blues. By the time he has invested all his money he hasn't got, and the rent is three weeks overdue, he will be able to tell the landlord to wait seven months until the Monday morning after the day of publication. Go ahead, Penny."

After a period of silence, Sanderson, in an obstinate manner, said, "Well, what's to be done? The rent has got to be paid."

Wrinkles played more sad music. Grief frowned deeper. Pennoyer was evidently searching his mind for a plan.

Florinda took the cigarette from between her lips that she might grin with greater freedom.

"We might throw Purple out," said Grief, with an inspired air. "That would stop all this discussion."

"You!" said Sanderson furiously. "You can't keep serious a minute. If you didn't have us to take care of you, you wouldn't even know when they threw you out into the street."

"Wouldn't I?" said Grief.

"Well, look here," interposed Florinda, "I'm going home unless you can be more interesting. I am dead sorry about the rent, but I can't help it, and——"

"Here! Sit down! Hold on, Splutter!" they shouted. Grief turned to Sanderson: "Purple, you shut up!"

Florinda curled again on the divan and lit another cigarette. The talk waged about the names of other and more successful painters, whose work they usually pronounced "rotten."

CHAPTER XXI.

Pennoyer, coming home one morning with two gigantic cakes to accompany the coffee at the breakfast in the den, saw a young man bounce from a horse car. He gave a shout. "Hello, there, Billie! Hello!"

"Hello, Penny!" said Hawker. "What are you doing out so early?" It was somewhat after nine o'clock.

"Out to get breakfast," said Pennoyer, waving the cakes. "Have a good time, old man?"

"Great."

"Do much work?"

"No. Not so much. How are all the people?"

"Oh, pretty good. Come in and see us eat breakfast," said Pennoyer, throwing open the door of the den. Wrinkles, in his shirt, was making coffee. Grief sat in a chair trying to loosen the grasp of sleep. "Why, Billie Hawker, b'ginger!" they cried.

"How's the wolf, boys? At the door yet?"

"'At the door yet?' He's halfway up the back stairs, and coming fast. He and the landlord will be here to-morrow. 'Mr. Landlord, allow me to present Mr. F. Wolf, of Hunger, N. J. Mr. Wolf—Mr. Landlord.'"

"Bad as that?" said Hawker.

"You bet it is! Easy Street is somewhere in heaven, for all we know. Have some breakfast?—coffee and cake, I mean."

"No, thanks, boys. Had breakfast."

Wrinkles added to the shirt, Grief aroused himself, and Pennoyer brought the coffee. Cheerfully throwing some drawings from the table to the floor, they thus made room for the breakfast, and grouped themselves with beaming smiles at the board.

"Well, Billie, come back to the old gang again, eh? How did the country seem? Do much work?"

"Not very much. A few things. How's everybody?"

"Splutter was in last night. Looking out of sight. Seemed glad to hear that you were coming back soon."

"Did she? Penny, did anybody call wanting me to do a ten-thousand-dollar portrait for them?"

"No. That frame-maker, though, was here with a bill. I told him———"

Afterward Hawker crossed the corridor and threw open the door of his own large studio. The great skylight, far above his head, shed its clear rays upon a scene which appeared to indicate that some one had very recently ceased work here and started for the country. A distant closet door was open, and the interior showed the effects of a sudden pillage.

There was an unfinished "Girl in Apple Orchard" upon the tall Dutch easel, and sketches and studies were thick upon the floor. Hawker took a pipe and filled it from his friend the tan and gold jar. He cast himself into a chair and, taking an envelope from his pocket, emptied two violets from it to the palm of his hand and stared long at them. Upon the walls of the studio various labours of his life, in heavy gilt frames, contemplated him and the violets.

At last Pennoyer burst impetuously in upon him. "Hi, Billie! come over and—— What's the matter?"

Hawker had hastily placed the violets in the envelope and hurried it to his pocket. "Nothing," he answered.

"Why, I thought—" said Pennoyer, "I thought you looked rather rattled. Didn't you have—I thought I saw something in your hand."

"Nothing, I tell you!" cried Hawker.

"Er—oh, I beg your pardon," said Pennoyer. "Why, I was going to tell you that Splutter is over in our place, and she wants to see you."

"Wants to see me? What for?" demanded Hawker. "Why don't she come over here, then?"

"I'm sure I don't know," replied Pennoyer. "She sent me to call you."

"Well, do you think I'm going to—— Oh, well, I suppose she wants to be unpleasant, and knows she loses a certain mental position if she comes over here, but if she meets me in your place she can be as infernally disagreeable as she—— That's it, I'll bet."

When they entered the den Florinda was gazing from the window. Her back was toward the door.

At last she turned to them, holding herself very straight. "Well, Billie Hawker," she said grimly, "you don't seem very glad to see a fellow."

"Why, heavens, did you think I was going to turn somersaults in the air?"

"Well, you didn't come out when you heard me pass your door," said Florinda, with gloomy resentment.

Hawker appeared to be ruffled and vexed. "Oh, great Scott!" he said, making a gesture of despair.

Florinda returned to the window. In the ensuing conversation she took no part, save when there was an opportunity to harry some speech of Hawker's, which she did in short contemptuous sentences. Hawker made no reply save to glare in her direction. At last he said, "Well, I must go over and do some work." Florinda did not turn from the window. "Well, so-long, boys," said Hawker, "I'll see you later."

As the door slammed Pennoyer apologetically said, "Billie is a trifle off his feed this morning."

"What about?" asked Grief.

"I don't know; but when I went to call him he was sitting deep in his chair staring at some——" He looked at Florinda and became silent.

"Staring at what?" asked Florinda, turning then from the window.

Pennoyer seemed embarrassed. "Why, I don't know—nothing, I guess—I couldn't see very well. I was only fooling."

Florinda scanned his face suspiciously. "Staring at what?" she demanded imperatively.

"Nothing, I tell you!" shouted Pennoyer.

Florinda looked at him, and wavered and debated. Presently she said, softly: "Ah, go on, Penny. Tell me."

"It wasn't anything at all, I say!" cried Pennoyer stoutly. "I was only giving you a jolly. Sit down, Splutter, and hit a cigarette."

She obeyed, but she continued to cast the dubious eye at Pennoyer. Once she said to him privately: "Go on, Penny, tell me. I know it was something from the way you are acting."

"Oh, let up, Splutter, for heaven's sake!"

"Tell me," beseeched Florinda.

"No."

"Tell me."

"No."

"Pl-e-a-se tell me."

"No."

"Oh, go on."

"No."

"Ah, what makes you so mean, Penny? You know I'd tell you, if it was the other way about."

"But it's none of my business, Splutter. I can't tell you something which is Billie Hawker's private affair. If I did I would be a chump."

250

"But I'll never say you told me. Go on."

"No."

"Pl-e-a-se tell me."

"No."

CHAPTER XXII.

When Florinda had gone, Grief said, "Well, what was it?" Wrinkles looked curiously from his drawing-board.

Pennoyer lit his pipe and held it at the side of his mouth in the manner of a deliberate man. At last he said, "It was two violets."

"You don't say!" ejaculated Wrinkles.

"Well, I'm hanged!" cried Grief. "Holding them in his hand and moping over them, eh?"

"Yes," responded Pennoyer. "Rather that way."

"Well, I'm hanged!" said both Grief and Wrinkles. They grinned in a pleased, urchin-like manner. "Say, who do you suppose she is? Somebody he met this summer, no doubt. Would you ever think old Billie would get into that sort of a thing? Well, I'll be gol-durned!"

Ultimately Wrinkles said, "Well, it's his own business." This was spoken in a tone of duty.

"Of course it's his own business," retorted Grief. "But who would ever think——" Again they grinned.

When Hawker entered the den some minutes later he might have noticed something unusual in the general demeanour. "Say, Grief, will you loan me your—— What's up?" he asked.

For answer they grinned at each other, and then grinned at him.

"You look like a lot of Chessy cats," he told them.

They grinned on.

Apparently feeling unable to deal with these phenomena, he went at last to the door. "Well, this is a fine exhibition," he said, standing with his hand on the knob and regarding them. "Won election bets? Some good old auntie just died? Found something new to pawn? No? Well, I can't stand this. You resemble those fish they discover at deep sea. Good-bye!"

As he opened the door they cried out: "Hold on, Billie! Billie, look here! Say, who is she?"

"What?"

"Who is she?"

"Who is who?"

They laughed and nodded. "Why, you know. She. Don't you understand? She."

"You talk like a lot of crazy men," said Hawker. "I don't know what you mean."

"Oh, you don't, eh? You don't? Oh, no! How about those violets you were moping over this morning? Eh, old man! Oh, no, you don't know what we mean! Oh, no! How about those violets, eh? How about 'em?"

Hawker, with flushed and wrathful face, looked at Pennoyer. "Penny——" But Grief and Wrinkles roared an interruption. "Oh, ho, Mr. Hawker! so it's true, is it? It's true. You are a nice bird, you are. Well, you old rascal! Durn your picture!"

Hawker, menacing them once with his eyes, went away. They sat cackling.

At noon, when he met Wrinkles in the corridor, he said: "Hey, Wrinkles, come here for a minute, will you? Say, old man, I—I——"

"What?" said Wrinkles.

"Well, you know, I—I—of course, every man is likely to make an accursed idiot of himself once in a while, and I——"

"And you what?" asked Wrinkles.

"Well, we are a kind of a band of hoodlums, you know, and I'm just enough idiot to feel that I don't care to hear—don't care to hear—well, her name used, you know."

"Bless your heart," replied Wrinkles, "we haven't used her name. We don't know her name. How could we use it?"

"Well, I know," said Hawker. "But you understand what I mean, Wrinkles."

"Yes, I understand what you mean," said Wrinkles, with dignity. "I don't suppose you are any worse of a stuff than common. Still, I didn't know that we were such outlaws."

"Of course, I have overdone the thing," responded Hawker hastily. "But—you ought to understand how I mean it, Wrinkles."

After Wrinkles had thought for a time, he said: "Well, I guess I do. All right. That goes."

Upon entering the den, Wrinkles said, "You fellows have got to quit guying Billie, do you hear?"

"We?" cried Grief. "We've got to quit? What do you do?"

"Well, I quit too."

Pennoyer said: "Ah, ha! Billie has been jumping on you."

"No, he didn't," maintained Wrinkles; "but he let me know it was—well, rather a—rather a—sacred subject." Wrinkles blushed when the others snickered.

In the afternoon, as Hawker was going slowly down the stairs, he was almost impaled upon the feather of a hat which, upon the head of a lithe and rather slight girl, charged up at him through the gloom.

"Hello, Splutter!" he cried. "You are in a hurry."

"That you, Billie?" said the girl, peering, for the hallways of this old building remained always in a dungeonlike darkness.

254

"Yes, it is. Where are you going at such a headlong gait?"

"Up to see the boys. I've got a bottle of wine and some—some pickles, you know. I'm going to make them let me dine with them to-night. Coming back, Billie?"

"Why, no, I don't expect to."

He moved then accidentally in front of the light that sifted through the dull, gray panes of a little window.

"Oh, cracky!" cried the girl; "how fine you are, Billie! Going to a coronation?"

"No," said Hawker, looking seriously over his collar and down at his clothes. "Fact is—er—well, I've got to make a call."

"A call—bless us! And are you really going to wear those gray gloves you're holding there, Billie? Say, wait until you get around the corner. They won't stand 'em on this street."

"Oh, well," said Hawker, depreciating the gloves—"oh, well."

The girl looked up at him. "Who you going to call on?"

"Oh," said Hawker, "a friend."

"Must be somebody most extraordinary, you look so dreadfully correct. Come back, Billie, won't you? Come back and dine with us."

"Why, I—I don't believe I can."

"Oh, come on! It's fun when we all dine together. Won't you, Billie?"

"Well, I——"

"Oh, don't be so stupid!" The girl stamped her foot and flashed her eyes at him angrily.

"Well, I'll see—I will if I can—I can't tell——" He left her rather precipitately.

Hawker eventually appeared at a certain austere house where he rang the bell with quite nervous fingers.

But she was not at home. As he went down the steps his eyes were as those of a man whose fortunes have tumbled upon him. As he walked down the street he wore in some subtle way the air of a man who has been grievously wronged. When he rounded the corner, his lips were set strangely, as if he were a man seeking revenge.

CHAPTER XXIII.

"It's just right," said Grief.

"It isn't quite cool enough," said Wrinkles.

"Well, I guess I know the proper temperature for claret."

"Well, I guess you don't. If it was buttermilk, now, you would know, but you can't tell anything about claret."

Florinda ultimately decided the question. "It isn't quite cool enough," she said, laying her hand on the bottle. "Put it on the window ledge, Grief."

"Hum! Splutter, I thought you knew more than——"

"Oh, shut up!" interposed the busy Pennoyer from a remote corner. "Who is going after the potato salad? That's what I want to know. Who is going?"

"Wrinkles," said Grief.

"Grief," said Wrinkles.

"There," said Pennoyer, coming forward and scanning a late work with an eye of satisfaction. "There's the three glasses and the little tumbler; and then, Grief, you will have to drink out of a mug."

"I'll be double-dyed black if I will!" cried Grief. "I wouldn't drink claret out of a mug to save my soul from being pinched!"

"You duffer, you talk like a bloomin' British chump on whom the sun never sets! What do you want?"

"Well, there's enough without that—what's the matter with you? Three glasses and the little tumbler."

"Yes, but if Billie Hawker comes——"

"Well, let him drink out of the mug, then. He——"

"No, he won't," said Florinda suddenly. "I'll take the mug myself."

"All right, Splutter," rejoined Grief meekly. "I'll keep the mug. But, still, I don't see why Billie Hawker——"

"I shall take the mug," reiterated Florinda firmly.

"But I don't see why——"

"Let her alone, Grief," said Wrinkles. "She has decided that it is heroic. You can't move her now."

"Well, who is going for the potato salad?" cried Pennoyer again. "That's what I want to know."

"Wrinkles," said Grief.

"Grief," said Wrinkles.

"Do you know," remarked Florinda, raising her head from where she had been toiling over the *spaghetti*, "I don't care so much for Billie Hawker as I did once?" Her sleeves were rolled above the elbows of her wonderful arms, and she turned from the stove and poised a fork as if she had been smitten at her task with this inspiration.

There was a short silence, and then Wrinkles said politely, "No."

"No," continued Florinda, "I really don't believe I do." She suddenly started. "Listen! Isn't that him coming now?"

The dull trample of a step could be heard in some distant corridor, but it died slowly to silence.

"I thought that might be him," she said, turning to the *spaghetti* again.

"I hope the old Indian comes," said Pennoyer, "but I don't believe he will. Seems to me he must be going to see——"

"Who?" asked Florinda.

"Well, you know, Hollanden and he usually dine together when they are both in town."

Florinda looked at Pennoyer. "I know, Penny. You must have thought I was remarkably clever not to understand all your blundering. But I don't care so much. Really I don't."

"Of course not," assented Pennoyer.

"Really I don't."

"Of course not."

"Listen!" exclaimed Grief, who was near the door. "There he comes now." Somebody approached, whistling an air from "Traviata," which rang loud and clear, and low and muffled, as the whistler wound among the intricate hallways. This air was as much a part of Hawker as his coat. The *spaghetti* had arrived at a critical stage. Florinda gave it her complete attention.

When Hawker opened the door he ceased whistling and said gruffly, "Hello!"

"Just the man!" said Grief. "Go after the potato salad, will you, Billie? There's a good boy! Wrinkles has refused."

"He can't carry the salad with those gloves," interrupted Florinda, raising her eyes from her work and contemplating them with displeasure.

"Hang the gloves!" cried Hawker, dragging them from his hands and hurling them at the divan. "What's the matter with you, Splutter?"

Pennoyer said, "My, what a temper you are in, Billie!"

"I am," replied Hawker. "I feel like an Apache. Where do you get this accursed potato salad?"

"In Second Avenue. You know where. At the old place."

"No, I don't!" snapped Hawker.

"Why——"

"Here," said Florinda, "I'll go." She had already rolled down her sleeves and was arraying herself in her hat and jacket.

"No, you won't," said Hawker, filled with wrath. "I'll go myself."

"We can both go, Billie, if you are so bent," replied the girl in a conciliatory voice.

"Well, come on, then. What are you standing there for?"

When these two had departed, Wrinkles said: "Lordie! What's wrong with Billie?"

"He's been discussing art with some pot-boiler," said Grief, speaking as if this was the final condition of human misery.

"No, sir," said Pennoyer. "It's something connected with the now celebrated violets."

Out in the corridor Florinda said, "What—what makes you so ugly, Billie?"

"Why, I am not ugly, am I?"

"Yes, you are—ugly as anything."

Probably he saw a grievance in her eyes, for he said, "Well, I don't want to be ugly." His tone seemed tender. The halls were intensely dark, and the girl placed her hand on his arm. As they rounded a turn in the stairs a straying lock of her hair brushed against his temple. "Oh!" said Florinda, in a low voice.

"We'll get some more claret," observed Hawker musingly. "And some cognac for the coffee. And some cigarettes. Do you think of anything more, Splutter?"

As they came from the shop of the illustrious purveyors of potato salad in Second Avenue, Florinda cried anxiously, "Here, Billie, you let me carry that!"

"What infernal nonsense!" said Hawker, flushing. "Certainly not!"

"Well," protested Florinda, "it might soil your gloves somehow."

"In heaven's name, what if it does? Say, young woman, do you think I am one of these cholly boys?"

"No, Billie; but then, you know——"

"Well, if you don't take me for some kind of a Willie, give us peace on this blasted glove business!"

"I didn't mean——"

"Well, you've been intimating that I've got the only pair of gray gloves in the universe, but you are wrong. There are several pairs, and these need not be preserved as unique in history."

"They're not gray. They're——"

"They are gray! I suppose your distinguished ancestors in Ireland did not educate their families in the matter of gloves, and so you are not expected to——"

"Billie!"

"You are not expected to believe that people wear gloves only in cold weather, and then you expect to see mittens."

On the stairs, in the darkness, he suddenly exclaimed, "Here, look out, or you'll fall!" He reached for her arm, but she evaded him. Later he said again: "Look out, girl! What makes you stumble around so? Here, give me the bottle of wine. I can carry it all right. There—now can you manage?"

CHAPTER XXIV.

"Penny," said Grief, looking across the table at his friend, "if a man thinks a heap of two violets, how much would he think of a thousand violets?"

"Two into a thousand goes five hundred times, you fool!" said Pennoyer. "I would answer your question if it were not upon a forbidden subject."

In the distance Wrinkles and Florinda were making Welsh rarebits.

"Hold your tongues!" said Hawker. "Barbarians!"

"Grief," said Pennoyer, "if a man loves a woman better than the whole universe, how much does he love the whole universe?"

"Gawd knows," said Grief piously. "Although it ill befits me to answer your question."

Wrinkles and Florinda came with the Welsh rarebits, very triumphant. "There," said Florinda, "soon as these are finished I must go home. It is after eleven o'clock.—Pour the ale, Grief."

At a later time, Purple Sanderson entered from the world. He hung up his hat and cast a look of proper financial dissatisfaction at the remnants of the feast. "Who has been——"

"Before you breathe, Purple, you graceless scum, let me tell you that we will stand no reference to the two violets here," said Pennoyer.

"What the——"

"Oh, that's all right, Purple," said Grief, "but you were going to say something about the two violets, right then. Weren't you, now, you old bat?"

Sanderson grinned expectantly. "What's the row?" said he.

"No row at all," they told him. "Just an agreement to keep you from chattering obstinately about the two violets."

"What two violets?"

"Have a rarebit, Purple," advised Wrinkles, "and never mind those maniacs."

"Well, what is this business about two violets?"

"Oh, it's just some dream. They gibber at anything."

"I think I know," said Florinda, nodding. "It is something that concerns Billie Hawker."

Grief and Pennoyer scoffed, and Wrinkles said: "You know nothing about it, Splutter. It doesn't concern Billie Hawker at all."

"Well, then, what is he looking sideways for?" cried Florinda.

Wrinkles reached for his guitar, and played a serenade, "The silver moon is shining——"

"Dry up!" said Pennoyer.

Then Florinda cried again, "What does he look sideways for?"

Pennoyer and Grief giggled at the imperturbable Hawker, who destroyed rarebit in silence.

"It's you, is it, Billie?" said Sanderson. "You are in this two-violet business?"

"I don't know what they're talking about," replied Hawker.

"Don't you, honestly?" asked Florinda.

"Well, only a little."

"There!" said Florinda, nodding again. "I knew he was in it."

"He isn't in it at all," said Pennoyer and Grief.

Later, when the cigarettes had become exhausted, Hawker volunteered to go after a further supply, and as he arose, a question seemed to come to the edge of Florinda's lips and pend there. The moment that the door was closed upon him she demanded, "What is that about the two violets?"

"Nothing at all," answered Pennoyer, apparently much aggrieved. He sat back with an air of being a fortress of reticence.

"Oh, go on—tell me! Penny, I think you are very mean.—Grief, you tell me!"

"The silver moon is shining;

Oh, come, my love, to me!

My heart——"

"Be still, Wrinkles, will you?—What was it, Grief? Oh, go ahead and tell me!"

"What do you want to know for?" cried Grief, vastly exasperated. "You've got more blamed curiosity—— It isn't anything at all, I keep saying to you."

"Well, I know it is," said Florinda sullenly, "or you would tell me."

When Hawker brought the cigarettes, Florinda smoked one, and then announced, "Well, I must go now."

"Who is going to take you home, Splutter?"

"Oh, anyone," replied Florinda.

"I tell you what," said Grief, "we'll throw some poker hands, and the one who wins will have the distingu

ished honour of conveying Miss Splutter to her home and mother."

Pennoyer and Wrinkles speedily routed the dishes to one end of the table. Grief's fingers spun the halves of a pack of cards together with the pleased eagerness of a good player. The faces grew solemn with the gambling solemnity. "Now, you Indians," said Grief, dealing, "a draw, you understand, and then a show-down."

Florinda leaned forward in her chair until it was poised on two legs. The cards of Purple Sanderson and of Hawker were faced toward her. Sanderson was gravely regarding two pair—aces and queens. Hawker scanned a little pair of sevens. "They draw, don't they?" she said to Grief.

"Certainly," said Grief. "How many, Wrink?"

"Four," replied Wrinkles, plaintively.

"Gimme three," said Pennoyer.

"Gimme one," said Sanderson.

"Gimme three," said Hawker. When he picked up his hand again Florinda's chair was tilted perilously. She saw another seven added to the little pair. Sanderson's draw had not assisted him.

"Same to the dealer," said Grief. "What you got, Wrink?"

"Nothing," said Wrinkles, exhibiting it face upward on the table. "Good-bye, Florinda."

"Well, I've got two small pair," ventured Pennoyer hopefully. "Beat 'em?"

"No good," said Sanderson. "Two pair—aces up."

"No good," said Hawker. "Three sevens."

"Beats me," said Grief. "Billie, you are the fortunate man. Heaven guide you in Third Avenue!"

Florinda had gone to the window. "Who won?" she asked, wheeling about carelessly.

"Billie Hawker."

"What! Did he?" she said in surprise.

"Never mind, Splutter. I'll win sometime," said Pennoyer. "Me too," cried Grief. "Good night, old girl!" said Wrinkles. They crowded in the doorway. "Hold on to Billie. Remember the two steps going up," Pennoyer called intelligently into the Stygian blackness. "Can you see all right?"

Florinda lived in a flat with fire-escapes written all over the front of it. The street in front was being repaired. It had been said by imbecile residents of the vicinity that the paving was never allowed to remain down for a sufficient time to be invalided by the tramping millions, but that it was kept perpetually stacked in little mountains through the unceasing vigilance of a virtuous and heroic city government, which insisted that everything should be repaired. The alderman for the district had sometimes asked indignantly of his fellow-members why this street had not been repaired, and they, aroused, had at once ordered it to be repaired. Moreover, shopkeepers, whose stables were adjacent, placed trucks and other vehicles strategically in the darkness. Into this tangled midnight Hawker conducted Florinda. The great avenue behind them was no more than a level stream of yellow light, and the distant merry bells might have been boats floating down it. Grim loneliness hung over the uncouth shapes in the street which was being repaired.

"Billie," said the girl suddenly, "what makes you so mean to me?"

A peaceful citizen emerged from behind a pile of *débris*, but he might not have been a peaceful citizen, so the girl clung to Hawker.

"Why, I'm not mean to you, am I?"

"Yes," she answered. As they stood on the steps of the flat of innumerable fire-escapes she slowly turned and looked up at him. Her face was of a strange pallour in this darkness, and her eyes were as when the moon shines in a lake of the hills.

He returned her glance. "Florinda!" he cried, as if enlightened, and gulping suddenly at something in his throat. The girl studied the steps and moved from side to side, as do the guilty ones in country schoolhouses. Then she went slowly into the flat.

There was a little red lamp hanging on a pile of stones to warn people that the street was being repaired.

CHAPTER XXV.

"I'll get my check from the Gamin on Saturday," said Grief. "They bought that string of comics."

"Well, then, we'll arrange the present funds to last until Saturday noon," said Wrinkles. "That gives us quite a lot. We can have a *table d'hôte* on Friday night."

However, the cashier of the Gamin office looked under his respectable brass wiring and said: "Very sorry, Mr.—er—Warwickson, but our pay-day is Monday. Come around any time after ten."

"Oh, it doesn't matter," said Grief.

When he plunged into the den his visage flamed with rage. "Don't get my check until Monday morning, any time after ten!" he yelled, and flung a portfolio of mottled green into the danger zone of the casts.

"Thunder!" said Pennoyer, sinking at once into a profound despair

"Monday morning, any time after ten," murmured Wrinkles, in astonishment and sorrow.

While Grief marched to and fro threatening the furniture, Pennoyer and Wrinkles allowed their under jaws to fall, and remained as men smitten between the eyes by the god of calamity.

"Singular thing!" muttered Pennoyer at last. "You get so frightfully hungry as soon as you learn that there are no more meals coming."

"Oh, well——" said Wrinkles. He took up his guitar.

Oh, some folks say dat a niggah won' steal,

'Way down yondeh in d' cohn'-fiel';

But Ah caught two in my cohn'-fiel',

Way down yondeh in d' cohn'-fiel'.

"Oh, let up!" said Grief, as if unwilling to be moved from his despair.

"Oh, let up!" said Pennoyer, as if he disliked the voice and the ballad.

In his studio, Hawker sat braced nervously forward on a little stool before his tall Dutch easel. Three sketches lay on the floor near him, and he glared at them constantly while painting at the large canvas on the easel.

He seemed engaged in some kind of a duel. His hair dishevelled, his eyes gleaming, he was in a deadly scuffle. In the sketches was the landscape of heavy blue, as if seen through powder-smoke, and all the skies burned red. There was in these notes a sinister quality of hopelessness, eloquent of a defeat, as if the scene represented the last hour on a field of disastrous battle. Hawker seemed attacking with this picture something fair and beautiful of his own life, a possession of his mind, and he did it fiercely, mercilessly, formidably. His arm moved with the energy of a strange wrath. He might have been thrusting with a sword.

There was a knock at the door. "Come in." Pennoyer entered sheepishly. "Well?" cried Hawker, with an echo of savagery in his voice. He turned from the canvas precisely as one might emerge from a fight. "Oh!" he said, perceiving Pennoyer. The glow in his eyes slowly changed. "What is it, Penny?"

"Billie," said Pennoyer, "Grief was to get his check to-day, but they put him off until Monday, and so, you know—er—well——"

"Oh!" said Hawker again.

When Pennoyer had gone Hawker sat motionless before his work. He stared at the canvas in a meditation so profound that it was probably unconscious of itself.

The light from above his head slanted more and more toward the east.

Once he arose and lighted a pipe. He returned to the easel and stood staring with his hands in his pockets. He moved like one in a sleep. Suddenly the gleam shot into his eyes again. He dropped to the stool and grabbed a brush. At the end of a certain long, tumultuous period he clinched his pipe more firmly in his teeth and puffed strongly. The thought might have occurred to him that it was not alight, for he looked at it with a vague, questioning glance. There came another knock at the door. "Go to the devil!" he shouted, without turning his head.

Hollanden crossed the corridor then to the den.

"Hi, there, Hollie! Hello, boy! Just the fellow we want to see. Come in—sit down—hit a pipe. Say, who was the girl Billie Hawker went mad over this summer?"

"Blazes!" said Hollanden, recovering slowly from this onslaught. "Who—what—how did you Indians find it out?"

"Oh, we tumbled!" they cried in delight, "we tumbled."

"There!" said Hollanden, reproaching himself. "And I thought you were such a lot of blockheads."

"Oh, we tumbled!" they cried again in their ecstasy. "But who is she? That's the point."

"Well, she was a girl."

"Yes, go on."

"A New York girl."

"Yes."

"A perfectly stunning New York girl."

"Yes. Go ahead."

"A perfectly stunning New York girl of a very wealthy and rather old-fashioned family."

"Well, I'll be shot! You don't mean it! She is practically seated on top of the Matterhorn. Poor old Billie!"

"Not at all," said Hollanden composedly.

It was a common habit of Purple Sanderson to call attention at night to the resemblance of the den to some little ward in a hospital. Upon this night, when Sanderson and Grief were buried in slumber, Pennoyer moved restlessly. "Wrink!" he called softly into the darkness in the direction of the divan which was secretly a coal-box.

"What?" said Wrinkles in a surly voice. His mind had evidently been caught at the threshold of sleep.

"Do you think Florinda cares much for Billie Hawker?"

Wrinkles fretted through some oaths. "How in thunder do I know?" The divan creaked as he turned his face to the wall.

"Well——" muttered Pennoyer.

CHAPTER XXVI.

The harmony of summer sunlight on leaf and blade of green was not known to the two windows, which looked forth at an obviously endless building of brownstone about which there was the poetry of a prison. Inside, great folds of lace swept down in orderly cascades, as water trained to fall mathematically. The colossal chandelier, gleaming like a Siamese headdress, caught the subtle flashes from unknown places.

Hawker heard a step and the soft swishing of a woman's dress. He turned toward the door swiftly, with a certain dramatic impulsiveness. But when she entered the room he said, "How delighted I am to see you again!"

She had said, "Why, Mr. Hawker, it was so charming in you to come!"

It did not appear that Hawker's tongue could wag to his purpose. The girl seemed in her mind to be frantically shuffling her pack of social receipts and finding none of them made to meet this situation. Finally, Hawker said that he thought Hearts at War was a very good play.

"Did you?" she said in surprise. "I thought it much like the others."

"Well, so did I," he cried hastily—"the same figures moving around in the mud of modern confusion. I really didn't intend to say that I liked it. Fact is, meeting you rather moved me out of my mental track."

"Mental track?" she said. "I didn't know clever people had mental tracks. I thought it was a privilege of the theologians."

"Who told you I was clever?" he demanded.

"Why," she said, opening her eyes wider, "nobody."

Hawker smiled and looked upon her with gratitude. "Of course, nobody. There couldn't be such an idiot. I am sure you should be astonished to learn that I believed such an imbecile existed. But——"

"Oh!" she said.

"But I think you might have spoken less bluntly."

"Well," she said, after wavering for a time, "you are clever, aren't you?"

"Certainly," he answered reassuringly.

"Well, then?" she retorted, with triumph in her tone. And this interrogation was apparently to her the final victorious argument.

At his discomfiture Hawker grinned.

"You haven't asked news of Stanley," he said. "Why don't you ask news of Stanley?"

"Oh! and how was he?"

"The last I saw of him he stood down at the end of the pasture—the pasture, you know—wagging his tail in blissful anticipation of an invitation to come with me, and when it finally dawned upon him that he was not to receive it, he turned and went back toward the house 'like a man suddenly stricken with age,' as the story-tellers eloquently say. Poor old dog!"

"And you left him?" she said reproachfully. Then she asked, "Do you remember how he amused you playing with the ants at the falls?"

"No."

"Why, he did. He pawed at the moss, and you sat there laughing. I remember it distinctly."

"You remember distinctly? Why, I thought—well, your back was turned, you know. Your gaze was fixed upon something before you, and you were utterly lost to the rest of the world. You could not have known if Stanley pawed the moss and I laughed. So, you see, you are mistaken. As a matter of fact, I utterly deny that Stanley pawed the moss or that I laughed, or that any ants appeared at the falls at all."

"I have always said that you should have been a Chinese soldier of fortune," she observed musingly. "Your daring and ingenuity would be prized by the Chinese."

"There are innumerable tobacco jars in China," he said, measuring the advantages. "Moreover, there is no perspective. You don't have to walk two miles to see a friend. No. He is always there near you, so that you can't move a chair without hitting your distant friend. You——"

"Did Hollie remain as attentive as ever to the Worcester girls?"

"Yes, of course, as attentive as ever. He dragged me into all manner of tennis games——"

"Why, I thought you loved to play tennis?"

"Oh, well," said Hawker, "I did until you left."

"My sister has gone to the park with the children. I know she will be vexed when she finds that you have called."

Ultimately Hawker said, "Do you remember our ride behind my father's oxen?"

"No," she answered; "I had forgotten it completely. Did we ride behind your father's oxen?"

After a moment he said: "That remark would be prized by the Chinese. We did. And you most graciously professed to enjoy it, which earned my deep gratitude and admiration. For no one knows better than I," he added meekly, "that it is no great comfort or pleasure to ride behind my father's oxen."

She smiled retrospectively. "Do you remember how the people on the porch hurried to the railing?"

CHAPTER XXVII.

Near the door the stout proprietress sat intrenched behind the cash-box in a Parisian manner. She looked with practical amiability at her guests, who dined noisily and with great fire, discussing momentous problems furiously, making wide, maniacal gestures through the cigarette smoke. Meanwhile the little handful of waiters ran to and fro wildly. Imperious and importunate cries rang at them from all directions. "Gustave! Adolphe!" Their faces expressed a settled despair. They answered calls, commands, oaths in a semi-distraction, fleeting among the tables as if pursued by some dodging animal. Their breaths came in gasps. If they had been convict labourers they could not have surveyed their positions with countenances of more unspeakable injury. Withal, they carried incredible masses of dishes and threaded their ways with skill. They served people with such speed and violence that it often resembled a personal assault. They struck two blows at a table and left there a knife and fork. Then came the viands in a volley. The clatter of this business was loud and bewilderingly rapid, like the gallop of a thousand horses.

In a remote corner a band of mandolins and guitars played the long, sweeping, mad melody of a Spanish waltz. It seemed to go tingling to the hearts of many of the diners. Their eyes glittered with enthusiasm, with abandon, with deviltry. They swung their heads from side to side in rhythmic movement. High in air curled the smoke from the innumerable cigarettes. The long, black claret bottles were in clusters upon the tables. At an end of the hall two men with maudlin grins sang the waltz uproariously, but always a trifle belated.

An unsteady person, leaning back in his chair to murmur swift compliments to a woman at another table, suddenly sprawled out upon the floor. He scrambled to his feet, and, turning to the escort of the woman, heatedly blamed him for the accident. They exchanged a series of tense, bitter insults, which spatted back and forth between them like pellets. People arose from their chairs and stretched their necks. The musicians stood in a body, their faces turned with expressions of keen excitement toward this quarrel, but their fingers still twinkling over their instruments, sending into the middle of this turmoil the passionate, mad, Spanish music. The proprietor of the place came in agitation and plunged headlong into the argument, where he thereafter appeared as a frantic creature harried to the point of insanity, for they buried him at once in long, vociferous threats, explanations, charges, every form of declamation known to their voices. The music, the noise of the galloping horses, the voices of the brawlers, gave the whole thing the quality of war.

There were two men in the *café* who seemed to be tranquil. Hollanden carefully stacked one lump of sugar upon another in the middle of his saucer and poured cognac over them. He touched a match to the cognac and the blue and yellow flames eddied in the saucer. "I wonder what those two fools are bellowing at?" he said, turning about irritably.

"Hanged if I know!" muttered Hawker in reply. "This place makes me weary, anyhow. Hear the blooming din!"

"What's the matter?" said Hollanden. "You used to say this was the one natural, the one truly Bohemian, resort in the city. You swore by it."

"Well, I don't like it so much any more."

"Ho!" cried Hollanden, "you're getting correct—that's it exactly. You will become one of these intensely—— Look, Billie, the little one is going to punch him!"

"No, he isn't. They never do," said Hawker morosely. "Why did you bring me here to-night, Hollie?"

"I? I bring you? Good heavens, I came as a concession to you! What are you talking about?—Hi! the little one is going to punch him, sure!"

He gave the scene his undivided attention for a moment; then he turned again: "You will become correct. I know you will. I have been watching. You are about to achieve a respectability that will make a stone saint blush for himself. What's the matter with you? You act as if you thought falling in love with a girl was a most extraordinary circumstance.—I wish they would put those people out.—Of course I know that you—— There! The little one has swiped at him at last!"

After a time he resumed his oration. "Of course, I know that you are not reformed in the matter of this uproar and this remarkable consumption of bad wine. It is not that. It is a fact that there are indications that some other citizen was fortunate enough to possess your napkin before you; and, moreover, you are sure that you would hate to be caught by your correct friends with any such *consommé* in front of you as we had to-night. You have got an eye suddenly for all kinds of gilt. You are in the way of becoming a most unbearable person.—Oh, look! the little one and the proprietor are having it now.—You are in the way of becoming a most unbearable person. Presently many of your friends will not be fine enough.—In heaven's name, why don't they throw him out? Are you going to howl and gesticulate there all night?"

"Well," said Hawker, "a man would be a fool if he did like this dinner."

"Certainly. But what an immaterial part in the glory of this joint is the dinner! Who cares about dinner? No one comes here to eat; that's what you always claimed.—Well, there, at last they are throwing him out. I hope he lands on his head.—Really, you know, Billie, it is such a fine thing being in love that one is sure to be detestable to the rest of the world, and that is the reason they created a proverb to the other effect. You want to look out."

"You talk like a blasted old granny!" said Hawker. "Haven't changed at all. This place is all right, only——"

"You are gone," interrupted Hollanden in a sad voice. "It is very plain— you are gone."

276

CHAPTER XXVIII.

The proprietor of the place, having pushed to the street the little man, who may have been the most vehement, came again and resumed the discussion with the remainder of the men of war. Many of these had volunteered, and they were very enduring.

"Yes, you are gone," said Hollanden, with the sobriety of graves in his voice. "You are gone.—Hi!" he cried, "there is Lucian Pontiac.—Hi, Pontiac! Sit down here."

A man with a tangle of hair, and with that about his mouth which showed that he had spent many years in manufacturing a proper modesty with which to bear his greatness, came toward them, smiling.

"Hello, Pontiac!" said Hollanden. "Here's another great painter. Do you know Mr. Hawker?—Mr. William Hawker—Mr. Pontiac."

"Mr. Hawker—delighted," said Pontiac. "Although I have not known you personally, I can assure you that I have long been a great admirer of your abilities."

The proprietor of the place and the men of war had at length agreed to come to an amicable understanding. They drank liquors, while each firmly, but now silently, upheld his dignity.

"Charming place," said Pontiac. "So thoroughly Parisian in spirit. And from time to time, Mr. Hawker, I use one of your models. Must say she has the best arm and wrist in the universe. Stunning figure—stunning!"

"You mean Florinda?" said Hawker.

"Yes, that's the name. Very fine girl. Lunches with me from time to time and chatters so volubly. That's how I learned you posed her occasionally. If the models didn't gossip we would never know what painters were addicted to profanity. Now that old Thorndike—he told me you swore like a drill-sergeant if the model winked a finger at the critical time. Very fine girl, Florinda.

And honest, too—honest as the devil. Very curious thing. Of course honesty among the girl models is very common, very common—quite universal thing, you know—but then it always strikes me as being very curious, very curious. I've been much attracted by your girl Florinda."

"My girl?" said Hawker.

"Well, she always speaks of you in a proprietary way, you know. And then she considers that she owes you some kind of obedience and allegiance and devotion. I remember last week I said to her: 'You can go now. Come again Friday.' But she said: 'I don't think I can come on Friday. Billie Hawker is home now, and he may want me then.' Said I: 'The devil take Billie Hawker! He hasn't engaged you for Friday, has he? Well, then, I engage you now.' But she shook her head. No, she couldn't come on Friday. Billie Hawker was home, and he might want her any day. 'Well, then,' said I, 'you have my permission to do as you please, since you are resolved upon it anyway. Go to your Billie Hawker.' Did you need her on Friday?"

"No," said Hawker.

"Well, then, the minx, I shall scold her. Stunning figure—stunning! It was only last week that old Charley Master said to me mournfully: 'There are no more good models. Great Scott! not a one.' 'You're 'way off, my boy,' I said; 'there is one good model,' and then I named your girl. I mean the girl who claims to be yours."

"Poor little beggar!" said Hollanden.

"Who?" said Pontiac.

"Florinda," answered Hollanden. "I suppose——"

Pontiac interrupted. "Oh, of course, it is too bad. Everything is too bad. My dear sir, nothing is so much to be regretted as the universe. But this Florinda is such a sturdy young soul! The world is against her, but, bless your heart, she is equal to the battle. She is strong in the manner of a little child. Why, you don't know her. She——"

"I know her very well."

"Well, perhaps you do, but for my part I think you don't appreciate her formidable character and stunning figure—stunning!"

"Damn it!" said Hawker to his coffee cup, which he had accidentally overturned.

"Well," resumed Pontiac, "she is a stunning model, and I think, Mr. Hawker, you are to be envied."

"Eh?" said Hawker.

"I wish I could inspire my models with such obedience and devotion. Then I would not be obliged to rail at them for being late, and have to badger them for not showing up at all. She has a beautiful figure—beautiful."

CHAPTER XXIX.

When Hawker went again to the house of the great window he looked first at the colossal chandelier, and, perceiving that it had not moved, he smiled in a certain friendly and familiar way.

"It must be a fine thing," said the girl dreamily. "I always feel envious of that sort of life."

"What sort of life?"

"Why—I don't know exactly; but there must be a great deal of freedom about it. I went to a studio tea once, and——"

"A studio tea! Merciful heavens—— Go on."

"Yes, a studio tea. Don't you like them? To be sure, we didn't know whether the man could paint very well, and I suppose you think it is an imposition for anyone who is not a great painter to give a tea."

"Go on."

"Well, he had the dearest little Japanese servants, and some of the cups came from Algiers, and some from Turkey, and some from—— What's the matter?"

"Go on. I'm not interrupting you."

"Well, that's all; excepting that everything was charming in colour, and I thought what a lazy, beautiful life the man must lead, lounging in such a studio, smoking monogrammed cigarettes, and remarking how badly all the other men painted."

"Very fascinating. But——"

"Oh! you are going to ask if he could draw. I'm sure I don't know, but the tea that he gave was charming."

"I was on the verge of telling you something about artist life, but if you have seen a lot of draperies and drunk from a cup of Algiers, you know all about it."

"You, then, were going to make it something very terrible, and tell how young painters struggled, and all that."

"No, not exactly. But listen: I suppose there is an aristocracy who, whether they paint well or paint ill, certainly do give charming teas, as you say, and all other kinds of charming affairs too; but when I hear people talk as if that was the whole life, it makes my hair rise, you know, because I am sure that as they get to know me better and better they will see how I fall short of that kind of an existence, and I shall probably take a great tumble in their estimation. They might even conclude that I can not paint, which would be very unfair, because I can paint, you know."

"Well, proceed to arrange my point of view, so that you sha'n't tumble in my estimation when I discover that you don't lounge in a studio, smoke monogrammed cigarettes, and remark how badly the other men paint."

"That's it. That's precisely what I wish to do."

"Begin."

"Well, in the first place——"

"In the first place—what?"

"Well, I started to study when I was very poor, you understand. Look here! I'm telling you these things because I want you to know, somehow. It isn't that I'm not ashamed of it. Well, I began very poor, and I—as a matter of fact—I—well, I earned myself over half the money for my studying, and the other half I bullied and badgered and beat out of my poor old dad. I worked pretty hard in Paris, and I returned here expecting to become a great painter at once. I didn't, though. In fact, I had my worst moments then. It lasted for some years. Of course, the faith and endurance of my father were by this time worn to a shadow—this time, when I needed him the most. However, things got a little better and a little better, until I found that by working quite hard I could make what was to me a fair income. That's where I am now, too."

"Why are you so ashamed of this story?"

"The poverty."

"Poverty isn't anything to be ashamed of."

"Great heavens! Have you the temerity to get off that old nonsensical remark? Poverty is everything to be ashamed of. Did you ever see a person not ashamed of his poverty? Certainly not. Of course, when a man gets very rich he will brag so loudly of the poverty of his youth that one would never suppose that he was once ashamed of it. But he was."

"Well, anyhow, you shouldn't be ashamed of the story you have just told me."

"Why not? Do you refuse to allow me the great right of being like other men?"

"I think it was—brave, you know."

"Brave? Nonsense! Those things are not brave. Impression to that effect created by the men who have been through the mill for the greater glory of the men who have been through the mill."

"I don't like to hear you talk that way. It sounds wicked, you know."

"Well, it certainly wasn't heroic. I can remember distinctly that there was not one heroic moment."

"No, but it was—it was——"

"It was what?"

"Well, somehow I like it, you know."

CHAPTER XXX.

"There's three of them," said Grief in a hoarse whisper.

"Four, I tell you!" said Wrinkles in a low, excited tone.

"Four," breathed Pennoyer with decision.

They held fierce pantomimic argument. From the corridor came sounds of rustling dresses and rapid feminine conversation.

Grief had kept his ear to the panel of the door. His hand was stretched back, warning the others to silence. Presently he turned his head and whispered, "Three."

"Four," whispered Pennoyer and Wrinkles.

"Hollie is there, too," whispered Grief. "Billie is unlocking the door. Now they're going in. Hear them cry out, 'Oh, isn't it lovely!' Jinks!" He began a noiseless dance about the room. "Jinks! Don't I wish I had a big studio and a little reputation! Wouldn't I have my swell friends come to see me, and wouldn't I entertain 'em!" He adopted a descriptive manner, and with his forefinger indicated various spaces of the wall. "Here is a little thing I did in Brittany. Peasant woman in sabots. This brown spot here is the peasant woman, and those two white things are the sabots. Peasant woman in sabots, don't you see? Women in Brittany, of course, all wear sabots, you understand. Convenience of the painters. I see you are looking at that little thing I did in Morocco. Ah, you admire it? Well, not so bad—not so bad. Arab smoking pipe, squatting in doorway. This long streak here is the pipe. Clever, you say? Oh, thanks! You are too kind. Well, all Arabs do that, you know. Sole occupation. Convenience of the painters. Now, this little thing here I did in Venice. Grand Canal, you know. Gondolier leaning on his oar. Convenience of the painters. Oh, yes, American subjects are well enough, but hard to find, you know—hard to find. Morocco, Venice, Brittany, Holland—all oblige with colour, you know—quaint form—all that. We are so hideously modern over here; and, besides, nobody has painted us much. How the devil can I paint America when nobody has done it before me? My dear sir, are you aware that that would be originality? Good heavens! we are not æsthetic, you understand. Oh, yes, some good mind comes along and understands a thing and does it, and after that it is æsthetic. Yes, of course, but then—well——Now, here is a little Holland thing of mine; it——"

The others had evidently not been heeding him. "Shut up!" said Wrinkles suddenly. "Listen!" Grief paused his harangue and they sat in silence, their lips apart, their eyes from time to time exchanging eloquent messages. A dulled melodious babble came from Hawker's studio.

At length Pennoyer murmured wistfully, "I would like to see her."

Wrinkles started noiselessly to his feet. "Well, I tell you she's a peach. I was going up the steps, you know, with a loaf of bread under my arm, when I chanced to look up the street and saw Billie and Hollanden coming with four of them."

"Three," said Grief.

"Four; and I tell you I scattered. One of the two with Billie was a peach—a peach."

"O, Lord!" groaned the others enviously. "Billie's in luck."

"How do you know?" said Wrinkles. "Billie is a blamed good fellow, but that doesn't say she will care for him—more likely that she won't."

They sat again in silence, grinning, and listening to the murmur of voices.

There came the sound of a step in the hallway. It ceased at a point opposite the door of Hawker's studio. Presently it was heard again. Florinda entered the den. "Hello!" she cried, "who is over in Billie's place? I was just going to knock——"

They motioned at her violently. "Sh!" they whispered. Their countenances were very impressive.

"What's the matter with you fellows?" asked Florinda in her ordinary tone; whereupon they made gestures of still greater wildness. "S-s-sh!"

Florinda lowered her voice properly. "Who is over there?"

"Some swells," they whispered.

Florinda bent her head. Presently she gave a little start. "Who is over there?" Her voice became a tone of deep awe. "She?"

Wrinkles and Grief exchanged a swift glance. Pennoyer said gruffly, "Who do you mean?"

"Why," said Florinda, "you know. She. The—the girl that Billie likes."

Pennoyer hesitated for a moment and then said wrathfully: "Of course she is! Who do you suppose?"

"Oh!" said Florinda. She took a seat upon the divan, which was privately a coal-box, and unbuttoned her jacket at the throat. "Is she—is she—very handsome, Wrink?"

Wrinkles replied stoutly, "No."

Grief said: "Let's make a sneak down the hall to the little unoccupied room at the front of the building and look from the window there. When they go out we can pipe 'em off."

"Come on!" they exclaimed, accepting this plan with glee.

Wrinkles opened the door and seemed about to glide away, when he suddenly turned and shook his head. "It's dead wrong," he said, ashamed.

"Oh, go on!" eagerly whispered the others. Presently they stole pattering down the corridor, grinning, exclaiming, and cautioning each other.

At the window Pennoyer said: "Now, for heaven's sake, don't let them see you!—Be careful, Grief, you'll tumble.—Don't lean on me that way, Wrink; think I'm a barn door? Here they come. Keep back. Don't let them see you."

"O-o-oh!" said Grief. "Talk about a peach! Well, I should say so."

Florinda's fingers tore at Wrinkle's coat sleeve. "Wrink, Wrink, is that her? Is that her? On the left of Billie? Is that her, Wrink?"

"What? Yes. Stop punching me! Yes, I tell you! That's her. Are you deaf?"

285

CHAPTER XXXI.

In the evening Pennoyer conducted Florinda to the flat of many fire-escapes. After a period of silent tramping through the great golden avenue and the street that was being repaired, she said, "Penny, you are very good to me."

"Why?" said Pennoyer.

"Oh, because you are. You—you are very good to me, Penny."

"Well, I guess I'm not killing myself."

"There isn't many fellows like you."

"No?"

"No. There isn't many fellows like you, Penny. I tell you 'most everything, and you just listen, and don't argue with me and tell me I'm a fool, because you know that it—because you know that it can't be helped, anyhow."

"Oh, nonsense, you kid! Almost anybody would be glad to——"

"Penny, do you think she is very beautiful?" Florinda's voice had a singular quality of awe in it.

"Well," replied Pennoyer, "I don't know."

"Yes, you do, Penny. Go ahead and tell me."

"Well——"

"Go ahead."

"Well, she is rather handsome, you know."

"Yes," said Florinda, dejectedly, "I suppose she is." After a time she cleared her throat and remarked indifferently, "I suppose Billie cares a lot for her?"

"Oh, I imagine that he does—in a way."

"Why, of course he does," insisted Florinda. "What do you mean by 'in a way'? You know very well that Billie thinks his eyes of her."

"No, I don't."

"Yes, you do. You know you do. You are talking in that way just to brace me up. You know you are."

"No, I'm not."

"Penny," said Florinda thankfully, "what makes you so good to me?"

"Oh, I guess I'm not so astonishingly good to you. Don't be silly."

"But you are good to me, Penny. You don't make fun of me the way—the way the other boys would. You are just as good as you can be.—But you do think she is beautiful, don't you?"

"They wouldn't make fun of you," said Pennoyer.

"But do you think she is beautiful?"

"Look here, Splutter, let up on that, will you? You keep harping on one string all the time. Don't bother me!"

"But, honest now, Penny, you do think she is beautiful?"

"Well, then, confound it—no! no! no!"

"Oh, yes, you do, Penny. Go ahead now. Don't deny it just because you are talking to me. Own up, now, Penny. You do think she is beautiful?"

"Well," said Pennoyer, in a dull roar of irritation, "do you?"

Florinda walked in silence, her eyes upon the yellow flashes which lights sent to the pavement. In the end she said, "Yes."

"Yes, what?" asked Pennoyer sharply.

"Yes, she—yes, she is—beautiful."

"Well, then?" cried Pennoyer, abruptly closing the discussion.

Florinda announced something as a fact. "Billie thinks his eyes of her."

"How do you know he does?"

"Don't scold at me, Penny. You—you———"

"I'm not scolding at you. There! What a goose you are, Splutter! Don't, for heaven's sake, go to whimpering on the street! I didn't say anything to make you feel that way. Come, pull yourself together."

"I'm not whimpering."

"No, of course not; but then you look as if you were on the edge of it. What a little idiot!"

CHAPTER XXXII.

When the snow fell upon the clashing life of the city, the exiled stones, beaten by myriad strange feet, were told of the dark, silent forests where the flakes swept through the hemlocks and swished softly against the boulders.

In his studio Hawker smoked a pipe, clasping his knee with thoughtful, interlocked fingers. He was gazing sourly at his finished picture. Once he started to his feet with a cry of vexation. Looking back over his shoulder, he swore an insult into the face of the picture. He paced to and fro, smoking belligerently and from time to time eying it. The helpless thing remained upon the easel, facing him.

Hollanden entered and stopped abruptly at sight of the great scowl. "What's wrong now?" he said.

Hawker gestured at the picture. "That dunce of a thing. It makes me tired. It isn't worth a hang. Blame it!"

"What?" Hollanden strode forward and stood before the painting with legs apart, in a properly critical manner. "What? Why, you said it was your best thing."

"Aw!" said Hawker, waving his arms, "it's no good! I abominate it! I didn't get what I wanted, I tell you. I didn't get what I wanted. That?" he shouted, pointing thrust-way at it—"that? It's vile! Aw! it makes me weary."

"You're in a nice state," said Hollanden, turning to take a critical view of the painter. "What has got into you now? I swear, you are more kinds of a chump!"

Hawker crooned dismally: "I can't paint! I can't paint for a damn! I'm no good. What in thunder was I invented for, anyhow, Hollie?"

"You're a fool," said Hollanden. "I hope to die if I ever saw such a complete idiot! You give me a pain. Just because she don't——"

"It isn't that. She has nothing to do with it, although I know well enough—I know well enough——"

"What?"

"I know well enough she doesn't care a hang for me. It isn't that. It is because—it is because I can't paint. Look at that thing over there! Remember the thought and energy I—— Damn the thing!"

"Why, did you have a row with her?" asked Hollanden, perplexed. "I didn't know——"

"No, of course you didn't know," cried Hawker, sneering; "because I had no row. It isn't that, I tell you. But I know well enough"—he shook his fist vaguely—"that she don't care an old tomato can for me. Why should she?" he demanded with a curious defiance. "In the name of Heaven, why should she?"

"I don't know," said Hollanden; "I don't know, I'm sure. But, then, women have no social logic. This is the great blessing of the world. There is only one thing which is superior to the multiplicity of social forms, and that is a woman's mind—a young woman's mind. Oh, of course, sometimes they are logical, but let a woman be so once, and she will repent of it to the end of her days. The safety of the world's balance lies in woman's illogical mind. I think——"

"Go to blazes!" said Hawker. "I don't care what you think. I am sure of one thing, and that is that she doesn't care a hang for me!"

"I think," Hollanden continued, "that society is doing very well in its work of bravely lawing away at Nature; but there is one immovable thing—a woman's illogical mind. That is our safety. Thank Heaven, it——"

"Go to blazes!" said Hawker again.

CHAPTER XXXIII.

As Hawker again entered the room of the great windows he glanced in sidelong bitterness at the chandelier. When he was seated he looked at it in open defiance and hatred.

Men in the street were shovelling at the snow. The noise of their instruments scraping on the stones came plainly to Hawker's ears in a harsh chorus, and this sound at this time was perhaps to him a *miserere*.

"I came to tell you," he began, "I came to tell you that perhaps I am going away."

"Going away!" she cried. "Where?"

"Well, I don't know—quite. You see, I am rather indefinite as yet. I thought of going for the winter somewhere in the Southern States. I am decided merely this much, you know—I am going somewhere. But I don't know where. 'Way off, anyhow."

"We shall be very sorry to lose you," she remarked. "We——"

"And I thought," he continued, "that I would come and say 'adios' now for fear that I might leave very suddenly. I do that sometimes. I'm afraid you will forget me very soon, but I want to tell you that——"

"Why," said the girl in some surprise, "you speak as if you were going away for all time. You surely do not mean to utterly desert New York?"

"I think you misunderstand me," he said. "I give this important air to my farewell to you because to me it is a very important event. Perhaps you recollect that once I told you that I cared for you. Well, I still care for you, and so I can only go away somewhere—some place 'way off—where—where—— See?"

"New York is a very large place," she observed.

"Yes, New York is a very large—— How good of you to remind me! But then you don't understand. You can't understand. I know I can find no place where I will cease to remember you, but then I can find some place where I can cease to remember in a way that I am myself. I shall never try to forget you. Those two violets, you know—one I found near the tennis court and the other you gave me, you remember—I shall take them with me."

"Here," said the girl, tugging at her gown for a moment—"Here! Here's a third one." She thrust a violet toward him.

"If you were not so serenely insolent," said Hawker, "I would think that you felt sorry for me. I don't wish you to feel sorry for me. And I don't wish to be melodramatic. I know it is all commonplace enough, and I didn't mean to act like a tenor. Please don't pity me."

"I don't," she replied. She gave the violet a little fling.

Hawker lifted his head suddenly and glowered at her. "No, you don't," he at last said slowly, "you don't. Moreover, there is no reason why you should take the trouble. But——"

He paused when the girl leaned and peered over the arm of her chair precisely in the manner of a child at the brink of a fountain. "There's my violet on the floor," she said. "You treated it quite contemptuously, didn't you?"

"Yes."

Together they stared at the violet. Finally he stooped and took it in his fingers. "I feel as if this third one was pelted at me, but I shall keep it. You are rather a cruel person, but, Heaven guard us! that only fastens a man's love the more upon a woman."

She laughed. "That is not a very good thing to tell a woman."

"No," he said gravely, "it is not, but then I fancy that somebody may have told you previously."

She stared at him, and then said, "I think you are revenged for my serene insolence."

"Great heavens, what an armour!" he cried. "I suppose, after all, I did feel a trifle like a tenor when I first came here, but you have chilled it all out of me. Let's talk upon indifferent topics." But he started abruptly to his feet. "No," he said, "let us not talk upon indifferent topics. I am not brave, I assure you, and it—it might be too much for me." He held out his hand. "Good-bye."

"You are going?"

"Yes, I am going. Really I didn't think how it would bore you for me to come around here and croak in this fashion."

"And you are not coming back for a long, long time?"

"Not for a long, long time." He mimicked her tone. "I have the three violets now, you know, and you must remember that I took the third one even when you flung it at my head. That will remind you how submissive I was in my devotion. When you recall the two others it will remind you of what a fool I was. Dare say you won't miss three violets."

"No," she said.

"Particularly the one you flung at my head. That violet was certainly freely—given."

"I didn't fling it at your head." She pondered for a time with her eyes upon the floor. Then she murmured, "No more freely—given than the one I gave you that night—that night at the inn."

"So very good of you to tell me so!"

Her eyes were still upon the floor.

"Do you know," said Hawker, "it is very hard to go away and leave an impression in your mind that I am a fool? That is very hard. Now, you do think I am a fool, don't you?"

She remained silent. Once she lifted her eyes and gave him a swift look with much indignation in it.

"Now you are enraged. Well, what have I done?"

It seemed that some tumult was in her mind, for she cried out to him at last in sudden tearfulness: "Oh, do go! Go! Please! I want you to go!"

Under this swift change Hawker appeared as a man struck from the sky. He sprang to his feet, took two steps forward, and spoke a word which was an explosion of delight and amazement. He said, "What?"

With heroic effort she slowly raised her eyes until, alight with anger, defiance, unhappiness, they met his eyes.

Later, she told him that he was perfectly ridiculous.

About Author

Stephen Crane (November 1, 1871 – June 5, 1900) was an American poet, novelist, and short story writer. Prolific throughout his short life, he wrote notable works in the Realist tradition as well as early examples of American Naturalism and Impressionism. He is recognized by modern critics as one of the most innovative writers of his generation.

The ninth surviving child of Methodist parents, Crane began writing at the age of four and had published several articles by the age of 16. Having little interest in university studies though he was active in a fraternity, he left Syracuse University in 1891 to work as a reporter and writer. Crane's first novel was the 1893 Bowery tale Maggie: A Girl of the Streets, generally considered by critics to be the first work of American literary Naturalism. He won international acclaim in 1895 for his Civil War novel The Red Badge of Courage, which he wrote without having any battle experience.

In 1896, Crane endured a highly publicized scandal after appearing as a witness in the trial of a suspected prostitute, an acquaintance named Dora Clark. Late that year he accepted an offer to travel to Cuba as a war correspondent. As he waited in Jacksonville, Florida for passage, he met Cora Taylor, with whom he began a lasting relationship. En route to Cuba, Crane's vessel the SS Commodore sank off the coast of Florida, leaving him and others adrift for 30 hours in a dinghy. Crane described the ordeal in "The Open Boat". During the final years of his life, he covered conflicts in Greece (accompanied by Cora, recognized as the first woman war correspondent) and later lived in England with her. He was befriended by writers such as Joseph Conrad and H. G. Wells. Plagued by financial difficulties and ill health, Crane died of tuberculosis in a Black Forest sanatorium in Germany at the age of 28.

At the time of his death, Crane was considered an important figure in American literature. After he was nearly forgotten for two decades, critics revived interest in his life and work. Crane's writing is characterized by vivid intensity, distinctive dialects, and irony. Common themes involve fear, spiritual crises and social isolation. Although recognized primarily for The Red Badge of Courage, which has become an American classic, Crane is also known for his poetry, journalism, and short stories such as "The Open Boat", "The Blue Hotel", "The Bride Comes to Yellow Sky", and The Monster. His writing made a deep impression on 20th-century writers, most prominent among them Ernest Hemingway, and is thought to have inspired the Modernists and the Imagists.

Biography

Early years

Stephen Crane was born on November 1, 1871, in Newark, New Jersey, to Jonathan Townley Crane, a minister in the Methodist Episcopal church, and Mary Helen Peck Crane, daughter of a clergyman, George Peck. He was the fourteenth and last child born to the couple. At 45, Helen Crane had suffered the early deaths of her previous four children, each of whom died within one year of birth. Nicknamed "Stevie" by the family, he joined eight surviving brothers and sisters—Mary Helen, George Peck, Jonathan Townley, William Howe, Agnes Elizabeth, Edmund Byran, Wilbur Fiske, and Luther.

The Cranes were descended from Jaspar Crane, a founder of New Haven Colony, who had migrated there from England in 1639. Stephen was named for a putative founder of Elizabethtown, New Jersey, who had, according to family tradition, come from England or Wales in 1665, as well as his great-great-grandfather Stephen Crane (1709–1780), a Revolutionary War patriot who served as New Jersey delegate to the First Continental Congress in Philadelphia. Crane later wrote that his father, Dr. Crane, "was a great, fine, simple mind," who had written numerous tracts on theology. Although his mother was a popular spokeswoman for the Woman's Christian Temperance Union and a highly religious woman, Crane wrote that he did not believe "she was as narrow as most of her friends or family." The young Stephen was raised primarily by his sister Agnes, who was 15 years his senior. The family moved to Port Jervis, New York, in 1876, where Dr. Crane became the pastor of Drew Methodist Church, a position that he retained until his death.

As a child, Stephen was often sickly and afflicted by constant colds.

When the boy was almost two, his father wrote in his diary that his youngest son became "so sick that we are anxious about him." Despite his fragile nature, Crane was an intelligent child who taught himself to read before the age of four. His first known inquiry, recorded by his father, dealt with writing; at the age of three, while imitating his brother Townley's writing, he asked his mother, "how do you spell O?" In December 1879, Crane wrote a poem about wanting a dog for Christmas. Entitled "I'd Rather Have –", it is his first surviving poem. Stephen was not regularly enrolled in school until January 1880, but he had no difficulty in completing two grades in six weeks. Recalling this feat, he wrote that it "sounds like the lie of a fond mother at a teaparty, but I do remember that I got ahead very fast and that father was very pleased with me."

Dr. Crane died on February 16, 1880, at the age of 60; Stephen was eight years old. Some 1,400 people mourned Dr. Crane at his funeral, more than double the size of his congregation. After her husband's death, Mrs. Crane moved to Roseville, near Newark, leaving Stephen in the care of his older brother Edmund, with whom the young boy lived with cousins in Sussex County. He next lived with his brother William, a lawyer, in Port Jervis for several years.

His older sister Helen took him to Asbury Park to be with their brother Townley and his wife, Fannie. Townley was a professional journalist; he headed the Long Branch department of both the New-York Tribune and the Associated Press, and also served as editor of the Asbury Park Shore Press. Agnes, another Crane sister, joined the siblings in New Jersey. She took a position at Asbury Park's intermediate school and moved in with Helen to care for the young Stephen.

Within a couple of years, the Crane family suffered more losses. First, Townley and his wife lost their two young children. His wife Fannie died of Bright's disease in November 1883. Agnes Crane became ill and died on June 10, 1884, of meningitis at the age of 28.

Schooling

Crane wrote his first known story, "Uncle Jake and the Bell Handle", when he was 14. In late 1885, he enrolled at Pennington Seminary, a ministry-focused coeducational boarding school 7 miles (11 km) north of Trenton. His father had been principal there from 1849 to 1858. Soon after her youngest son left for school, Mrs. Crane began suffering what the Asbury Park Shore Press reported as "a temporary aberration of the mind." She had apparently recovered by early 1886, but later that year, her son, 23-year-old Luther Crane, died after falling in front of an oncoming train while working as a flagman for the Erie Railroad. It was the fourth death in six years among Stephen's immediate family.

After two years, Crane left Pennington for Claverack College, a quasi-military school. He later looked back on his time at Claverack as "the happiest period of my life although I was not aware of it." A classmate remembered him as a highly literate but erratic student, lucky to pass examinations in math and science, and yet "far in advance of his fellow students in his knowledge of History and Literature", his favorite subjects. While he held an impressive record on the drill field and baseball diamond, Crane generally did not excel in the classroom. Not having a middle name, as was customary among other students, he took to signing his name "Stephen T. Crane" in order "to win recognition as a regular fellow". Crane was seen as friendly, but also moody and rebellious. He sometimes skipped class in order to play baseball, a game in which he starred as catcher. He was also greatly interested in the school's military training program. He rose rapidly in the ranks of the student battalion. One classmate described him as "indeed physically attractive without being handsome", but he was aloof, reserved and not generally popular at Claverack. Although academically weak, Crane gained experience at Claverack that provided background (and likely some anecdotes from the Civil War veterans on the staff) that proved useful when he came to write The Red Badge of Courage.

In mid-1888, Crane became his brother Townley's assistant at a New Jersey shore news bureau, working there every summer until 1892. Crane's first publication under his byline was an article on the explorer Henry M. Stanley's famous quest to find the Scottish missionary David Livingstone in Africa. It appeared in the February 1890 Claverack College Vidette. Within a few months, Crane was persuaded by his family to forgo a military career and transfer to Lafayette College in Easton, Pennsylvania, in order to pursue a mining engineering degree. He registered at Lafayette on September 12, and promptly became involved in extracurricular activities; he took up baseball again and joined the largest fraternity, Delta Upsilon. He also joined both rival literary societies, named for (George) Washington and (Benjamin) Franklin. Crane infrequently attended classes and ended the semester with grades for four of the seven courses he had taken.

After one semester, Crane transferred to Syracuse University, where he enrolled as a non-degree candidate in the College of Liberal Arts. He roomed in the Delta Upsilon fraternity house and joined the baseball team. Attending just one class (English Literature) during the middle trimester, he remained in residence while taking no courses in the third semester.

Concentrating on his writing, Crane began to experiment with tone and style while trying out different subjects. He published his fictional story, "Great Bugs of Onondaga," simultaneously in the Syracuse Daily Standard and the New York Tribune. Declaring college "a waste of time", Crane decided to become a full-time writer and reporter. He attended a Delta Upsilon chapter meeting on June 12, 1891, but shortly afterward left college for good.

Full-time writer

In the summer of 1891, Crane often camped with friends in the nearby area of Sullivan County, New York, where his brother Edmund occupied a house obtained as part of their brother William's Hartwood Club (Association) land dealings. He used this area as the geographic setting for several short stories, which were posthumously published in a collection under the title Stephen Crane: Sullivan County Tales and Sketches. Crane showed two of these works to Tribune editor Willis Fletcher Johnson, a friend of the family, who accepted them for the publication. "Hunting Wild Dogs" and "The Last of the Mohicans" were the first of fourteen unsigned Sullivan County sketches and tales that were published in the Tribune between February and July 1892. Crane also showed Johnson an early draft of his first novel, Maggie: A Girl of the Streets.

Later that summer, Crane met and befriended author Hamlin Garland, who had been lecturing locally on American literature and the expressive arts; on August 17 he gave a talk on novelist William Dean Howells, which Crane wrote up for the Tribune. Garland became a mentor for and champion of the young writer, whose intellectual honesty impressed him. Their relationship suffered in later years, however, because Garland disapproved of Crane's alleged immorality, related to his living with a woman married to another man.

Stephen moved into his brother Edmund's house in Lakeview, a suburb of Paterson, New Jersey, in the fall of 1891. From here he made frequent trips into New York City, writing and reporting particularly on its impoverished tenement districts. Crane focused particularly on The Bowery, a small and once prosperous neighborhood in the southern part of Manhattan. After the Civil War, Bowery shops and mansions had given way to saloons, dance halls, brothels and flophouses, all of which Crane frequented. He later said he did so for research. He was attracted to the human nature found in the slums, considering it "open and plain, with nothing hidden". Believing nothing honest and unsentimental had been written about the Bowery, Crane became determined to do so himself; this was the setting of his first novel. On December 7, 1891, Crane's mother died at the age of 64, and the 20-year-old appointed Edmund as his guardian.

Despite being frail, undernourished and suffering from a hacking cough, which did not prevent him from smoking cigarettes, in the spring of 1892 Crane began a romance with Lily Brandon Munroe, a married woman who was estranged from her husband. Although Munroe later said Crane "was not a handsome man", she admired his "remarkable almond-shaped gray eyes." He begged her to elope with him, but her family opposed the match because Crane lacked money and prospects, and she declined. Their last meeting likely occurred in April 1898, when he again asked her to run away with him and she again refused.

Between July 2 and September 11, 1892, Crane published at least ten news reports on Asbury Park affairs. Although a Tribune colleague stated that Crane "was not highly distinguished above any other boy of twenty who had gained a reputation for saying and writing bright things," that summer his reporting took on a more skeptical, hypocrisy-deflating tone. A storm of controversy erupted over a report he wrote on the Junior Order of United American Mechanics' American Day Parade, entitled "Parades and Entertainments". Published on August 21, the report juxtaposes the "bronzed, slope-shouldered, uncouth" marching men "begrimed with dust" and the spectators dressed in "summer gowns, lace parasols, tennis trousers, straw hats and indifferent smiles". Believing they were being ridiculed, some JOUAM marchers were outraged and wrote to the editor. The owner of the Tribune, Whitelaw Reid, was that year's Republican vice-presidential candidate, and this likely increased the sensitivity of the paper's management to the issue. Although Townley wrote a piece for the Asbury Park Daily Press in his brother's defense, the Tribune quickly apologized to its readers, calling Stephen Crane's piece "a bit of random correspondence, passed inadvertently by the copy editor". Hamlin Garland and biographer John Barry attested that Crane told them he had been dismissed by the Tribune, although Willis Fletcher Johnson later denied this. The paper did not publish any of Crane's work after 1892.

> Such an assemblage of the spraddle-legged men of the middle class, whose hands were bent and shoulders stooped from delving and constructing, had never appeared to an Asbury Park summer crowd, and the latter was vaguely amused.

> — Stephen Crane, account of the JOUAM parade as it appeared in the Tribune.

Life in New York

Crane struggled to make a living as a free-lance writer, contributing sketches and feature articles to various New York newspapers. In October 1892, he moved into a rooming house in Manhattan whose boarders were a group of medical students. During this time, he expanded or entirely reworked Maggie: A Girl of the Streets, which is about a girl who "blossoms in a mud-puddle" and becomes a pitiful victim of circumstance. In the winter of 1893, Crane took the manuscript of Maggie to Richard Watson Gilder, who rejected it for publication in The Century Magazine.

Crane decided to publish it privately, with money he had inherited from his mother. The novel was published in late February or early March 1893 by a small printing shop that usually printed medical books and religious tracts. The typewritten title page for the Library of Congress copyright application read simply: "A Girl of the Streets, / A Story of New York. / —By—/Stephen Crane." The name "Maggie" was added to the title later. Crane used the pseudonym "Johnston Smith" for the novel's initial publication, later telling friend and artist Corwin Knapp Linson that the nom de plume was the "commonest name I could think of. I had an editor friend named Johnson, and put in the "t", and no one could find me in the mob of Smiths." Hamlin Garland reviewed the work in the June 1893 issue of The Arena, calling it "the most truthful and unhackneyed study of the slums I have yet read, fragment though it is." Despite this early praise, Crane became depressed and destitute from having spent $869 for 1,100 copies of a novel that did not sell; he ended up giving a hundred copies away. He would later remember "how I looked forward to publication and pictured the sensation I thought it would make. It fell flat. Nobody seemed to notice it or care for it... Poor Maggie! She was one of my first loves."

In March 1893, Crane spent hours lounging in Linson's studio while having his portrait painted. He became fascinated with issues of the Century that were largely devoted to famous battles and military leaders from the Civil War. Frustrated with the dryly written stories, Crane stated, "I wonder that some of those fellows don't tell how they felt in those scraps. They spout enough of what they did, but they're as emotionless as rocks." Crane returned to these magazines during subsequent visits to Linson's studio, and eventually the idea of writing a war novel overtook him. He would later state that he "had been unconsciously working the detail of the story out through most of his boyhood" and had imagined "war stories ever since he was out of knickerbockers." This novel would ultimately become The Red Badge of Courage.

> A river, amber-tinted in the shadow of its banks, purled at the army's feet; and at night, when the stream had become of a sorrowful blackness, one could see across it the red, eyelike gleam of hostile camp-fires set in the low brows of distant hills.

— Stephen Crane, The Red Badge of Courage

From the beginning, Crane wished to show how it felt to be in a war by writing "a psychological portrayal of fear." Conceiving his story from the point of view of a young private who is at first filled with boyish dreams of the glory of war and then quickly becomes disillusioned by war's reality, Crane borrowed the private's surname, "Fleming", from his sister-in-law's maiden name. He later said that the first paragraphs came to him with "every word in place, every comma, every period fixed." Working mostly nights, he wrote from around midnight until four or five in the morning. Because he could not afford a typewriter, he wrote carefully in ink on legal-sized paper, seldom crossing through or interlining a word. If he did change something, he would rewrite the whole page.

While working on his second novel, Crane remained prolific, concentrating on publishing stories to stave off poverty; "An Experiment in Misery", based on Crane's experiences in the Bowery, was printed by the New York Press. He also wrote five or six poems a day. In early 1894, he showed some of his poems or "lines" as he called them, to Hamlin Garland, who said he read "some thirty in all" with "growing wonder." Although Garland and William Dean Howells encouraged him to submit his poetry for publication, Crane's free verse was too unconventional for most. After brief wrangling between poet and publisher, Copeland & Day accepted Crane's first book of poems, The Black Riders and Other Lines, although it would not be published until after The Red Badge of Courage. He received a 10 percent royalty and the publisher assured him that the book would be in a form "more severely classic than any book ever yet issued in America."

In the spring of 1894, Crane offered the finished manuscript of The Red Badge of Courage to McClure's Magazine, which had become the foremost magazine for Civil War literature. While McClure's delayed giving him an answer on his novel, they offered him an assignment writing about the Pennsylvania coal mines. "In the Depths of a Coal Mine", a story with pictures by Linson, was syndicated by McClure's in a number of newspapers, heavily edited. Crane was reportedly disgusted by the cuts, asking Linson:

"Why the hell did they send me up there then? Do they want the public to think the coal mines gilded ball-rooms with the miners eating ice-cream in boiled shirt-fronts?"

Sources report that following an encounter with a male prostitute that spring, Crane began a novel on the subject entitled Flowers of Asphalt, which he later abandoned. The manuscript has never been recovered.

After discovering that McClure's could not afford to pay him, Crane took his war novel to Irving Bacheller of the Bacheller-Johnson Newspaper Syndicate, which agreed to publish The Red Badge of Courage in serial form. Between the third and the ninth of December 1894, The Red Badge of Courage was published in some half-dozen newspapers in the United States. Although it was greatly cut for syndication, Bacheller attested to its causing a stir, saying "its quality [was] immediately felt and recognized." The lead editorial in the Philadelphia Press of December 7 said that Crane "is a new name now and unknown, but everybody will be talking about him if he goes on as he has begun".

Travels and fame

At the end of January 1895, Crane left on what he called "a very long and circuitous newspaper trip" to the west. While writing feature articles for the Bacheller syndicate, he traveled to Saint Louis, Missouri, Nebraska, New Orleans, Galveston, Texas and then Mexico City. Irving Bacheller would later state that he "sent Crane to Mexico for new color", which the author found in the form of Mexican slum life. Whereas he found the lower class in New York pitiful, he was impressed by the "superiority" of the Mexican peasants' contentment and "even refuse[d] to pity them."

Returning to New York five months later, Crane joined the Lantern (alternately spelled "Lanthom" or "Lanthorne") Club organized by a group of young writers and journalists. The Club, located on the roof of an old house on William Street near the Brooklyn Bridge, served as a drinking establishment of sorts and was decorated to look like a ship's cabin. There Crane ate one good meal a day, although friends were troubled by his "constant smoking, too much coffee, lack of food and poor teeth", as Nelson Greene put it. Living in near-poverty and greatly anticipating the publication of his books, Crane began work on two more novels: The Third Violet and George's Mother.

The Black Riders was published by Copeland & Day shortly before his return to New York in May, but it received mostly criticism, if not abuse, for the poems' unconventional style and use of free verse. A piece in the Bookman called Crane "the Aubrey Beardsley of poetry," and a commentator from the Chicago Daily Inter-Ocean stated that "there is not a line of poetry from the opening to the closing page. Whitman's Leaves of Grass were luminous in comparison. Poetic lunacy would be a better name for the book." In June, the New York Tribune dismissed the book as "so much trash." Crane was pleased that the book was "making some stir".

In contrast to the reception for Crane's poetry, The Red Badge of Courage was welcomed with acclaim after its publication by Appleton in September 1895. For the next four months, the book was in the top six on various bestseller lists around the country. It arrived on the literary scene "like a flash of lightning out of a clear winter sky", according to H. L. Mencken, who was about 15 at the time. The novel also became popular in Britain; Joseph Conrad, a future friend of Crane, wrote that the novel "detonated... with the impact and force of a twelve-inch shell charged with a very high explosive." Appleton published two, possibly three, printings in 1895 and as many as eleven more in 1896. Although some critics considered the work overly graphic and profane, it was widely heralded for its realistic portrayal of war and unique writing style. The Detroit Free Press declared that The Red Badge would give readers "so vivid a picture of the emotions and the horrors of the battlefield that you will pray your eyes may never look upon the reality."

Wanting to capitalize on the success of The Red Badge, McClure Syndicate offered Crane a contract to write a series on Civil War battlefields. Because it was a wish of his to "visit the battlefield—which I was to describe— at the time of year when it was fought", Crane agreed to take the assignment. Visiting battlefields in Northern Virginia, including Fredericksburg, he would later produce five more Civil War tales: "Three Miraculous Soldiers", "The Veteran", "An Indiana Campaign", "An Episode of War" and The Little Regiment.

Scandal

At the age of 24, Crane, who was reveling in his success, became involved in a highly publicized case involving a suspected prostitute named Dora Clark. At 2 a.m. on September 16, 1896, he escorted two chorus girls and Clark from New York City's Broadway Garden, a popular "resort" where he had interviewed the women for a series he was writing. As Crane saw one woman safely to a streetcar, a plainclothes policeman named Charles Becker arrested the other two for solicitation; Crane was threatened with arrest when he tried to interfere. One of the women was released after Crane confirmed her erroneous claim that she was his wife, but Clark was charged and taken to the precinct. Against the advice of the arresting sergeant, Crane made a statement confirming Dora Clark's innocence, stating that "I only know that while with me she acted respectably, and that the policeman's charge was false." On the basis of Crane's testimony, Clark was discharged. The media seized upon the story; news spread to Philadelphia, Boston and beyond, with papers focusing on Crane's courage. The Stephen Crane story, as it became known, soon became a source for ridicule; the Chicago Dispatch in particular quipped that "Stephen Crane is respectfully informed that association with women in scarlet is not necessarily a 'Red Badge of Courage' ".

A couple of weeks after her trial, Clark pressed charges of false arrest against the officer who had arrested her. The next day, the officer physically attacked Clark in the presence of witnesses for having brought charges against him. Crane, who initially went briefly to Philadelphia to escape the pressure of publicity, returned to New York to give testimony at Becker's trial despite advice given to him from Theodore Roosevelt, who was Police Commissioner at the time and a new acquaintance of Crane. The defense targeted Crane: police raided his apartment and interviewed people who knew him, trying to find incriminating evidence in order to lessen the effect of his testimony. A vigorous cross-examination took place that sought to portray Crane as a man of dubious morals; while the prosecution proved that he frequented brothels, Crane claimed this was merely for research purposes. After the trial ended on October 16, the arresting officer was exonerated, and Crane's reputation was ruined.

Cora Taylor and the Commodore shipwreck

None of them knew the color of the sky. Their eyes glanced level and were fastened upon the waves that swept toward them. These waves were of the hue of slate, save for the tops, which were of foaming white, and all of the men knew the colors of the sea.

— Stephen Crane, "The Open Boat"

Given $700 in Spanish gold by the Bacheller-Johnson syndicate to work as a war correspondent in Cuba as the Spanish–American War was pending, the 25-year-old Crane left New York on November 27, 1896, on a train bound for Jacksonville, Florida. Upon arrival in Jacksonville, he registered at the St. James Hotel under the alias of Samuel Carleton to maintain anonymity while seeking passage to Cuba. While waiting for a boat, he toured the city and visited the local brothels. Within days he met 31-year-old Cora Taylor, proprietor of the downtown bawdy house Hotel de Dream. Born into a respectable Boston family, Taylor (whose legal name was Cora Ethel Stewart) had already had two brief marriages; her first husband, Vinton Murphy, divorced her on grounds of adultery. In 1889, she had married British Captain Donald William Stewart. She left him in 1892 for another man, but was still legally married. By the time Crane arrived, Taylor had been in Jacksonville for two years. She lived a bohemian lifestyle, owned a hotel of assignation, and was a well-known and respected local figure. The two spent much time together while Crane awaited his departure. He was finally cleared to leave for the Cuban port of Cienfuegos on New Year's Eve aboard the SS Commodore.

The ship sailed from Jacksonville with 27 or 28 men and a cargo of supplies and ammunition for the Cuban rebels. On the St. Johns River and less than 2 miles (3.2 km) from Jacksonville, Commodore struck a sandbar in a dense fog and damaged its hull. Although towed off the sandbar the following day, it was beached again in Mayport and again damaged. A leak began in the boiler room that evening and, as a result of malfunctioning water pumps, the ship came to a standstill about 16 miles (26 km) from Mosquito Inlet. As the ship took on more water, Crane described the engine room as resembling "a scene at this time taken from the middle kitchen of hades." Commodore's lifeboats were lowered in the early hours of the morning on

January 2, 1897 and the ship ultimately sank at 7 a.m. Crane was one of the last to leave the ship in a 10-foot (3.0 m) dinghy. In an ordeal that he recounted in the short story "The Open Boat", Crane and three other men (including the ship's Captain) foundered off the coast of Florida for a day and a half before trying to land the dinghy at Daytona Beach. The small boat overturned in the surf, forcing the exhausted men to swim to shore; one of them died. Having lost the gold given to him for his journey, Crane wired Cora Taylor for help. She traveled to Daytona and returned to Jacksonville with Crane the next day, only four days after he had left on the Commodore.

The disaster was reported on the front pages of newspapers across the country. Rumors that the ship had been sabotaged were widely circulated but never substantiated. Portrayed favorably and heroically by the press, Crane emerged from the ordeal with his reputation enhanced, if not restored, after the battering he had received in the Dora Clark affair. Meanwhile, Crane's affair with Taylor blossomed.

Three seasons of archaeological investigation were conducted in 2002-04 to examine and document the exposed remains of a wreck near Ponce Inlet, FL conjectured to be that of the SS Commodore. The collected data, and other accumulated evidence, finally substantiated the identification of the Commodore beyond a reasonable doubt.

Greco-Turkish War

Despite contentment in Jacksonville and the need for rest after his ordeal, Crane became restless. He left Jacksonville on January 11 for New York City, where he applied for a passport to Cuba, Mexico and the West Indies. Spending three weeks in New York, he completed "The Open Boat" and periodically visited Port Jervis to see family. By this time, however, blockades had formed along the Florida coast as tensions rose with Spain, and Crane concluded that he would never be able to travel to Cuba. He sold "The Open Boat" to Scribner's for $300 in early March. Determined to work as a war correspondent, Crane signed on with William Randolph Hearst's New York Journal to cover the impending Greco-Turkish conflict. He brought along Taylor, who had sold the Hotel de Dream in order to follow him.

On March 20, they sailed first to England, where Crane was warmly received. They arrived in Athens in early April; between April 17 (when Turkey declared war on Greece) and April 22, Crane wrote his first published report of the war, "An Impression of the 'Concert' ". When he left for Epirus in the northwest, Taylor remained in Athens, where she became the Greek war's first woman war correspondent. She wrote under the pseudonym "Imogene Carter" for the New York Journal, a job that Crane had secured for her. They wrote frequently, traveling throughout the country separately and together. The first large battle that Crane witnessed was the Turks' assault on General Constantine Smolenski's Greek forces at Velestino. Crane wrote, "It is a great thing to survey the army of the enemy. Just where and how it takes hold upon the heart is difficult of description." During this battle, Crane encountered "a fat waddling puppy" that he immediately claimed, dubbing it "Velestino, the Journal dog". Greece and Turkey signed an armistice on May 20, ending the 30-day war; Crane and Taylor left Greece for England, taking two Greek brothers as servants and Velestino the dog with them.

Spanish–American War

After staying in Limpsfield, Surrey, for a few days, Crane and Taylor settled in Ravensbrook, a plain brick villa in Oxted. Referring to themselves as Mr. and Mrs. Crane, the couple lived openly in England, but Crane concealed the relationship from his friends and family in the United States. Admired in England, Crane thought himself attacked back home: "There seem so many of them in America who want to kill, bury and forget me purely out of unkindness and envy and—my unworthiness, if you choose", he wrote. Velestino the dog sickened and died soon after their arrival in England, on August 1. Crane, who had a great love for dogs, wrote an emotional letter to a friend an hour after the dog's death, stating that "for eleven days we fought death for him, thinking nothing of anything but his life." The Limpsfield-Oxted area was home to members of the socialist Fabian Society and a magnet for writers such as Edmund Gosse, Ford Madox Ford and Edward Garnett. Crane also met the Polish-born novelist Joseph Conrad in October 1897, with whom he would have what Crane called a "warm and endless friendship".

Although Crane was confident among peers, strong negative reviews of the recently published The Third Violet were causing his literary reputation to dwindle. Reviewers were also highly critical of Crane's war letters, deeming them self-centered. Although The Red Badge of Courage had by this time gone through fourteen printings in the United States and six in England, Crane was running out of money. To survive financially, he worked at a feverish pitch, writing prolifically for both the English and the American markets. He wrote in quick succession stories such as The Monster, "The Bride Comes to Yellow Sky", "Death and the Child" and "The Blue Hotel". Crane began to attach price tags to his new works of fiction, hoping that "The Bride", for example, would fetch $175.

As 1897 ended, Crane's money crisis worsened. Amy Leslie, a reporter from Chicago and a former lover, sued him for $550. The New York Times reported that Leslie gave him $800 in November 1896 but that he'd repaid only a quarter of the sum. In February he was summoned to answer Leslie's claim. The claim was apparently settled out of court, because no record of adjudication exists. Meanwhile, Crane felt "heavy with troubles" and "chased to the wall" by expenses. He confided to his agent that he was $2,000 in debt but that he would "beat it" with more literary output.

Soon after the USS Maine exploded in Havana Harbor on February 15, 1898, under suspicious circumstances, Crane was offered a £60 advance by Blackwood's Magazine for articles "from the seat of war in the event of a war breaking out" between the United States and Spain. His health was failing, and it is believed that signs of his pulmonary tuberculosis, which he may have contracted in childhood, became apparent. With almost no money coming in from his finished stories, Crane accepted the assignment and left Oxted for New York. Taylor and the rest of the household stayed behind to fend off local creditors. Crane applied for a passport and left New York for Key West two days before Congress declared war. While the war idled, he interviewed people and produced occasional copy.

In early June, he observed the establishment of an American base in Cuba when Marines seized Guantánamo Bay. He went ashore with the Marines, planning "to gather impressions and write them as the spirit moved." Although he wrote honestly about his fear in battle, others observed his calmness and composure. He would later recall "this prolonged tragedy of the night" in the war tale "Marines Signaling Under Fire at Guantanamo". After showing a willingness to serve during fighting at Cuzco, Cuba, by carrying messages to company commanders, Crane was officially cited for his "material aid during the action".

He continued to report upon various battles and the worsening military conditions and praised Theodore Roosevelt's Rough Riders, despite past tensions with the Commissioner. In early July, Crane was sent to the United States for medical treatment for a high fever. He was diagnosed with yellow fever, then malaria. Upon arrival in Old Point Comfort, Virginia, he spent a few weeks resting in a hotel. Although Crane had filed more than twenty dispatches in the three months he had covered the war, the World's business manager believed that the paper had not received its money's worth and fired him. In retaliation, Crane signed with Hearst's New York Journal with the wish to return to Cuba. He traveled first to Puerto Rico and then to Havana. In September, rumors began to spread that Crane, who was working anonymously, had either been killed or disappeared. He sporadically sent out dispatches and stories; he wrote about the mood in Havana, the crowded city sidewalks, and other topics, but he was soon desperate for money again. Taylor, left alone in England, was also penniless. She became frantic with worry over her lover's whereabouts; they were not in direct communication until the end of the year. Crane left Havana and arrived in England on January 11, 1899.

Death

Rent on Ravensbrook had not been paid for a year. Upon returning to England, Crane secured a solicitor to act as guarantor for their debts, after which Crane and Taylor relocated to Brede Place. This manor in Sussex, which dated to the 14th century and had neither electricity nor indoor plumbing, was offered to them by friends at a modest rent. The relocation appeared to give hope to Crane, but his money problems continued. Deciding that he could no longer afford to write for American publications, he concentrated on publishing in English magazines.

Crane pushed himself to write feverishly during the first months at Brede; he told his publisher that he was "doing more work now than I have at any other period in my life". His health worsened, and by late 1899 he was asking friends about health resorts. The Monster and Other Stories was in production and War Is Kind, his second collection of poems, was published in the United States in May. None of his books after The Red Badge of Courage had sold well, and he bought a typewriter to spur output. Active Service, a novella based on Crane's correspondence experience, was published in October. The New York Times reviewer questioned "whether the author of 'Active Service' himself really sees anything remarkable in his newspapery hero."

In December, the couple held an elaborate Christmas party at Brede, attended by Conrad, Henry James, H. G. Wells and other friends; it lasted several days. On December 29 Crane suffered a severe pulmonary hemorrhage. In January 1900 he'd recovered sufficiently to work on a new novel, The O'Ruddy, completing 25 of the 33 chapters. Plans were made for him to travel as a correspondent to Gibraltar to write sketches from Saint Helena, the site of a Boer prison, but at the end of March and in early April he suffered two more hemorrhages. Taylor took over most of Crane's correspondence while he was ill, writing to friends for monetary aid. The couple planned to travel on the continent, but Conrad, upon visiting Crane for the last time, remarked that his friend's "wasted face was enough to tell me that it was the most forlorn of all hopes."

On May 28, the couple arrived at Badenweiler, Germany, a health spa on the edge of the Black Forest. Despite his weakened condition, Crane continued to dictate fragmentary episodes for the completion of The O'Ruddy. He died on June 5, 1900, at the age of 28. In his will he left everything to Taylor, who took his body to New Jersey for burial. Crane was interred in Evergreen Cemetery in what is now Hillside, New Jersey.

Fiction and poetry

Style and technique

Stephen Crane's fiction is typically categorized as representative of

Naturalism, American realism, Impressionism or a mixture of the three. Critic Sergio Perosa, for example, wrote in his essay, "Stephen Crane fra naturalismo e impressionismo," that the work presents a "symbiosis" of Naturalistic ideals and Impressionistic methods. When asked whether or not he would write an autobiography in 1896, Crane responded that he "dare not say that I am honest. I merely say that I am as nearly honest as a weak mental machinery will allow." Similarities between the stylistic techniques in Crane's writing and Impressionist painting—including the use of color and chiaroscuro—are often cited to support the theory that Crane was not only an Impressionist but also influenced by the movement. H. G. Wells remarked upon "the great influence of the studio" on Crane's work, quoting a passage from The Red Badge of Courage as an example: "At nightfall the column broke into regimental pieces, and the fragments went into the fields to camp. Tents sprang up like strange plants. Camp fires, like red, peculiar blossoms, dotted the night.... From this little distance the many fires, with the black forms of men passing to and fro before the crimson rays, made weird and satanic effects." Although no direct evidence exists that Crane formulated a precise theory of his craft, he vehemently rejected sentimentality, asserting that "a story should be logical in its action and faithful to character. Truth to life itself was the only test, the greatest artists were the simplest, and simple because they were true."

Poet and biographer John Berryman suggested that there were three basic variations, or "norms", of Crane's narrative style. The first, being "flexible, swift, abrupt and nervous", is best exemplified in The Red Badge of Courage, while the second ("supple majesty") is believed to relate to "The Open Boat", and the third ("much more closed, circumstantial and 'normal' in feeling and syntax") to later works such as The Monster. Crane's work, however, cannot be determined by style solely on chronology. Not only does his fiction not take place in any particular region with similar characters, but it varies from serious in tone to reportorial writing and light fiction. Crane's writing, both fiction and nonfiction, is consistently driven by immediacy and is at once concentrated, vivid and intense. The novels and short stories contain poetic characteristics such as shorthand prose, suggestibility, shifts in perspective

315

and ellipses between and within sentences. Similarly, omission plays a large part in Crane's work; the names of his protagonists are not commonly used and sometimes they are not named at all.

Crane was often criticized by early reviewers for his frequent incorporation of everyday speech into dialogue, mimicking the regional accents of his characters with colloquial stylization. This is apparent in his first novel, in which Crane ignored the romantic, sentimental approach of slum fiction; he instead concentrated on the cruelty and sordid aspects of poverty, expressed by the brashness of the Bowery's crude dialect and profanity, which he used lavishly. The distinct dialect of his Bowery characters is apparent at the beginning of the text; the title character admonishes her brother saying: "Yeh knows it puts mudder out when yes comes home half dead, an' it's like we'll all get a poundin'."

Major themes

Crane's work is often thematically driven by Naturalistic and Realistic concerns, including ideals versus realities, spiritual crises and fear. These themes are particularly evident in Crane's first three novels, Maggie: A Girl of the Streets, The Red Badge of Courage and George's Mother. The three main characters search for a way to make their dreams come true, but ultimately suffer from crises of identity. Crane was fascinated by war and death, as well as fire, disfigurement, fear and courage, all of which inspired him to write many works based on these concepts. In The Red Badge of Courage, the main character both longs for the heroics of battle but ultimately fears it, demonstrating the dichotomy of courage and cowardice. He experiences the threat of death, misery and a loss of self.

Extreme isolation from society and community is also apparent in Crane's work. During the most intense battle scenes in The Red Badge of Courage, for example, the story's focus is mainly "on the inner responses of a self unaware of others". In "The Open Boat", "An Experiment in Misery" and other stories, Crane uses light, motion and color to express degrees of epistemological uncertainty. Similar to other Naturalistic writers, Crane scrutinizes the position of man, who has been isolated not only from society, but also from God and nature. "The Open Boat", for example, distances itself from Romantic optimism and affirmation of man's place in the world by concentrating on the characters' isolation.

While he lived, Stephen Crane was denominated by critical readers a realist, a naturalist, an impressionist, symbolist, Symboliste, expressionist and ironist; his posthumous life was enriched by critics who read him as nihilistic, existentialist, a neo-Romantic, a sentimentalist, protomodernist, pointilliste, visionist, imagist and, by his most recent biographer, a "bleak naturalist." At midcentury he was a "predisciple of the New Criticism"; by its end he was "a proto-deconstructionist anti-artist hero" who had "leapfrogged modernism, landing on postmodernist ground." Or, as Sergio Perosa wrote in 1964, "The critic wanders in a labyrinth of possibilities, which every new turn taken by Crane's fiction seems to explode or deny."

One undeniable fact about Crane's work, as Anthony Splendora noted in 2015, is that Death haunts it; like a threatening eclipse it overshadows his best efforts, each of which features the signal demise of a main character. Allegorically, "The Blue Hotel," at the pinnacle of the short story form, may even be an autothanatography, the author's intentional exteriorization or objectification, in this case for the purpose of purgation, of his own impending death. Crane's "Swede" in that story can be taken, following current psychoanalytical theory, as a surrogative, sacrificial victim, ritually to be purged.

Transcending this "dark circumstance of composition," Crane had a particular telos and impetus for his creation: beyond the tautologies that all art is alterity and to some formal extent mimesis, Crane sought and obviously found "a form of catharsis" in writing. This view accounts for his uniqueness, especially as operative through his notorious "disgust" with his family's religion, their "vacuous, futile psalm-singing". His favorite book, for example, was Mark Twain's Life on the Mississippi, in which God is mentioned only twice—once as irony and once as "a swindle." Not only did Crane call out God specifically with the lines "Well then I hate thee / righteous image" in "The Black Riders" (1895), but even his most hopeful tropes, such as the "comradeship" of his "Open Boat" survivors, make no mention of deity, specifying only "indifferent nature." His antitheism is most evident in his characterization of the human race as "lice clinging to a space-lost bulb," a climax-nearing speech in "The Blue Hotel," Ch. VI. It is possible that Crane utilized religion's formal psychic space, now suddenly available resulting from the recent "Death of God", as a milieu for his compensative art.

Novels

Beginning with the publication of Maggie: A Girl of the Streets in 1893, Crane was recognized by critics mainly as a novelist. Maggie was initially rejected by numerous publishers because of its atypical and true-to-life depictions of class warfare, which clashed with the sentimental tales of that time. Rather than focusing on the very rich or middle class, the novel's characters are lower-class denizens of New York's Bowery. The main character, Maggie, descends into prostitution after being led astray by her lover. Although the novel's plot is simple, its dramatic mood, quick pace and portrayal of Bowery life have made it memorable. Maggie is not merely an account of slum life, but also represents eternal symbols. In his first draft, Crane did not give his characters proper names. Instead, they were identified by epithets: Maggie, for example, was the girl who "blossomed in a mud-puddle" and Pete, her seducer, was a "knight". The novel is dominated by bitter irony and anger, as well as destructive morality and treacherous sentiment. Critics would later call the novel "the first dark flower of American Naturalism" for its distinctive elements of naturalistic fiction.

Written thirty years after the end of the Civil War and before Crane had any experience of battle, The Red Badge of Courage was innovative stylistically as well as psychologically. Often described as a war novel, it focuses less on battle and more on the main character's psyche and his reactions and responses in war. It is believed that Crane based the fictional battle in the novel on that of Chancellorsville; he may also have interviewed veterans of the 124th New York Volunteer Infantry Regiment, commonly known as the Orange Blossoms, in Port Jervis, New York. Told in a third-person limited point of view, it reflects the private experience of Henry Fleming, a young soldier who flees from combat. The Red Badge of Courage is notable in its vivid descriptions and well-cadenced prose, both of which help create suspense within the story. Similarly, by substituting epithets for characters' names ("the youth", "the tattered soldier"), Crane injects an allegorical quality into his work, making his characters point to a specific characteristic of man. Like Crane's first novel, The Red Badge of Courage has a deeply ironic tone which increases in severity as the novel progresses. The title of the work is ironic; Henry wishes "that he, too, had a wound, a red badge of courage", echoing a wish to have been wounded in battle. The wound he does receive (from the rifle butt of a fleeing Union soldier) is not a badge of courage but a badge of shame.

The novel expresses a strong connection between humankind and nature, a frequent and prominent concern in Crane's fiction and poetry throughout his career. Whereas contemporary writers (Ralph Waldo Emerson, Nathaniel Hawthorne, Henry David Thoreau) focused on a sympathetic bond on the two elements, Crane wrote from the perspective that human consciousness distanced humans from nature. In The Red Badge of Courage, this distance is paired with a great number of references to animals, and men with animalistic characteristics: people "howl", "squawk", "growl", or "snarl".

Since the resurgence of Crane's popularity in the 1920s, The Red Badge of Courage has been deemed a major American text. The novel has been anthologized numerous times, including in the 1942 collection Men at War: The Best War Stories of All Time, edited by Ernest Hemingway. In the introduction, Hemingway wrote that the novel "is one of the finest books of our literature, and I include it entire because it is all as much of a piece as a great poem is."

Crane's later novels have not received as much critical praise. After the success of The Red Badge of Courage, Crane wrote another tale set in the Bowery. George's Mother is less allegorical and more personal than his two previous novels, and it focuses on the conflict between a church-going, temperance-adhering woman (thought to be based on Crane's mother) and her single remaining offspring, who is a naive dreamer. Critical response to the novel was mixed. The Third Violet, a romance that he wrote quickly after publishing The Red Badge of Courage, is typically considered as Crane's attempt to appeal to popular audiences. Crane considered it a "quiet little story." Although it contained autobiographical details, the characters have been deemed inauthentic and stereotypical. Crane's second to last novel, Active Service, revolves around the Greco-Turkish War of 1897, with which the author was familiar. Although noted for its satirical take on the melodramatic and highly passionate works that were popular of the nineteenth century, the novel was not successful. It is generally accepted by critics that Crane's work suffered at this point due to the speed which he wrote in order to meet his high expenses. His last novel, a suspenseful and picaresque work entitled The O'Ruddy, was finished posthumously by Robert Barr and published in 1903.

Short fiction

Crane wrote many different types of fictional pieces while indiscriminately applying to them terms such as "story", "tale" and "sketch". For this reason, critics have found clear-cut classification of Crane's work problematic. While "The Open Boat" and "The Bride Comes to Yellow Sky" are often considered short stories, others are variously identified.

In an 1896 interview with Herbert P. Williams, a reporter for the Boston Herald, Crane said that he did "not find that short stories are utterly different in character from other fiction. It seems to me that short stories are the easiest things we write." During his brief literary career, he wrote more than a hundred short stories and fictional sketches. Crane's early fiction was based in camping expeditions in his teen years; these stories eventually became known as The Sullivan County Tales and Sketches. He considered these "sketches", which are mostly humorous and not of the same caliber of work as his later fiction, to be "articles of many kinds," in that they are part fiction and part journalism.

The subject matter for his stories varied extensively. His early New York City sketches and Bowery tales accurately described the results of industrialization, immigration and the growth of cities and their slums. His collection of six short stories, The Little Regiment, covered familiar ground with the American Civil War, a subject for which he became famous with The Red Badge of Courage. Although similar to Crane's noted novel, The Little Regiment was believed to lack vigor and originality. Realizing the limitations of these tales, Crane wrote: "I have invented the sum of my invention with regard to war and this story keeps me in internal despair."

The Open Boat and Other Tales of Adventure (1898) contains thirteen short stories that deal with three periods in Crane's life: his Asbury Park boyhood, his trip to the West and Mexico in 1895, and his Cuban adventure in 1897. This collection was well received and included several of his most critically successful works. His 1899 collection, The Monster and Other Stories, was similarly well received.

Two posthumously published collections were not as successful. In August 1900 The Whilomville Stories were published, a collection of thirteen stories that Crane wrote during the last year of his life. The work deals almost exclusively with boyhood, and the stories are drawn from events occurring in Port Jervis, where Crane lived from the age of six to eleven.Focusing on small-town America, the stories tend toward sentimentality, but remain perceptive of the lives of children. Wounds in the Rain, published in September 1900, contains fictional tales based on Crane's reports for the World and the Journal during the Spanish–American War. These stories, which Crane wrote while desperately ill, include "The Price of the Harness" and "The Lone Charge of William B. Perkins" and are dramatic, ironic and sometimes humorous.

Despite Crane's prolific output, only four stories--"The Open Boat", "The Blue Hotel", "The Bride Comes to Yellow Sky", and The Monster— have received extensive attention from scholars. H. G. Wells considered "The Open Boat" to be "beyond all question, the crown of all his work", and it is one of the most frequently discussed of Crane's works.

Poetry

> Many red devils ran from my heart
>
> And out upon the page.
>
> They were so tiny
>
> The pen could mash them.
>
> And many struggled in the ink.

It was strange

To write in this red muck

Of things from my heart.

— Stephen Crane

Crane's poems, which he preferred to call "lines", are typically not given as much scholarly attention as his fiction; no anthology contained Crane's verse until 1926. Although it is not certain when Crane began to write poetry seriously, he once said that his overall poetic aim was "to give my ideas of life as a whole, so far as I know it". The poetic style used in both of his books of poetry, The Black Riders and Other Lines and War is Kind, was unconventional for the time in that it was written in free verse without rhyme, meter, or even titles for individual works. They are typically short in length; although several poems, such as "Do not weep, maiden, for war is kind", use stanzas and refrains, most do not. Crane also differed from his peers and poets of later generations in that his work contains allegory, dialectic and narrative situations.

Critic Ruth Miller claimed that Crane wrote "an intellectual poetry rather than a poetry that evokes feeling, a poetry that stimulates the mind rather than arouses the heart". In the most complexly organized poems, the significance of the states of mind or feelings is ambiguous, but Crane's poems tend to affirm certain elemental attitudes, beliefs, opinions and stances toward God, man and the universe. The Black Riders in particular is essentially a dramatic concept and the poems provide continuity within the dramatic structure. There is also a dramatic interplay in which there is frequently a major voice reporting an incident seen ("In the desert / I saw a creature, naked, bestial") or experienced ("A learned man came to me once"). The second voice or additional voices represent a point of view which is revealed to be inferior; when these clash, a dominant attitude emerges.

Legacy

In four years, Crane published five novels, two volumes of poetry, three short story collections, two books of war stories, and numerous works of short fiction and reporting. Today he is mainly remembered for The Red Badge of Courage, which is regarded as an American classic. The novel has been adapted several times for the screen, including John Huston's 1951 version. By the time of his death, Crane had become one of the best known writers of his generation. His eccentric lifestyle, frequent newspaper reporting, association with other famous authors, and expatriate status made him somewhat of an international celebrity. Although most stories about his life tended toward the romantic, rumors about his alleged drug use and alcoholism persisted long after his death.

By the early 1920s, Crane and his work were nearly forgotten. It was not until Thomas Beer published his biography in 1923, which was followed by editor Wilson Follett's The Work of Stephen Crane (1925–1927), that Crane's writing came to the attention of a scholarly audience. Crane's reputation was then enhanced by faithful support from writer friends such as Joseph Conrad, H. G. Wells and Ford Madox Ford, all of whom either published recollections or commented upon their time with Crane. John Berryman's 1950 biography of Crane further established him as an important American author. Since 1951 there has been a steady outpouring of articles, monographs and reprints in Crane scholarship.

Today, Crane is considered one of the most innovative writers of the 1890s. His peers, including Conrad and James, as well as later writers such as Robert Frost, Ezra Pound and Willa Cather, hailed Crane as one of the finest creative spirits of his time. His work was described by Wells as "the first expression of the opening mind of a new period, or, at least, the early emphatic phase of a new initiative." Wells said that "beyond dispute", Crane was "the best writer of our generation, and his untimely death was an irreparable loss to our literature." Conrad wrote that Crane was an "artist" and "a seer with a gift for rendering the significant on the surface of things and with an incomparable insight into primitive emotions". Crane's work has proved inspirational for future writers; not only have scholars drawn similarities between Hemingway's A Farewell to Arms and The Red Badge of Courage, but Crane's fiction is thought to have been an important inspiration for Hemingway and his fellow Modernists. In 1936, Hemingway wrote in The Green Hills of Africa that "The good writers are Henry James, Stephen Crane, and Mark Twain. That's not the order they're good in. There is no order for good writers." Crane's poetry is thought to have been a precursor to the Imagist movement, and his short fiction has also influenced American literature. "The Open Boat", "The Blue Hotel", The Monster and "The Bride Comes to Yellow Sky" are generally considered by critics to be examples of Crane's best work.

Several institutions and places have endeavored to keep Crane's legacy alive. Badenweiler and the house where he died became something of a tourist attraction for its fleeting association with the American author; Alexander Woollcott attested to the fact that, long after Crane's death, tourists would be directed to the room where he died. Columbia University Rare Book and Manuscript Library has a collection of Crane and Taylor's personal correspondence dating from 1895 to 1908. Near his brother Edmund's Sullivan County home in New York, where Crane stayed for a short time, a pond is named after him. The Stephen Crane House in Asbury Park, New Jersey, where the author lived with his siblings for nine years, is operated as a museum dedicated to his life and work. Syracuse University has an annual Stephen Crane Lecture Series which is sponsored by the Dikaia Foundation.

Columbia University purchased much of the Stephen Crane materials held by Cora Crane at her death. The Crane Collection is one of the largest in the nation of his materials. Columbia University had an exhibit: 'The Tall Swift Shadow of a Ship at Night': Stephen and Cora Crane, November 2, 1995 through February 16, 1996, about the lives of the couple, featuring letters and other documents and memorabilia. (Source : Wikipedia)

NOTABLE WORKS

NOVELS

Maggie: A Girl of the Streets, 1893.

The Red Badge of Courage, 1895.

George's Mother, 1896.

The Third Violet, 1897.

Active Service, 1899.

Crane, Stephen and Robert Barr. The O'Ruddy, 1903.

The Black Riders and Other Lines, 1895.

The Open Boat and Other Tales of Adventure, 1898

War is Kind, 1899

The Monster and Other Stories, 1899

Wounds in the Rain, 1900

Great Battles of the World, 1901

The O'Ruddy, 1903

SHORT STORY COLLECTIONS

The Little Regiment and Other Episodes from the American Civil War, 1896.

The Open Boat and Other Tales of Adventure, 1898.

The Monster and Other Stories, 1899.

Whilomville Stories, 1900.

Wounds in the Rain: War Stories, 1900.

Great Battles of the World, 1901.

The Monster,1901.

Last Words, 1902.

POETRY COLLECTIONS

The Black Riders and Other Lines, 1895.

War is Kind, 1899.

UNFINISHED WORKS

Sources report that following an encounter with a male prostitute in the spring of 1894, Crane began a novel on the subject entitled Flowers of Asphalt. He reportedly abandoned the project and the manuscript has never been recovered.